Praise for The

MW00883694

A sexy, supernatural thriller that creeps up on you until your mind is spinning, and your heart is pumping. Brilliant Concept!
~New York Times Bestselling Author, Cherry Adair

Hornsby has written a fascinating and engaging paranormal romance, skillfully presenting both Tina's mourning and a vivid picture of Hawaiian culture. The relationship between Jamey and Tina and Tina's love for Hank are believable and richly portrayed. ~ **Publisher's Weekly**

A mysterious murder and vivid, strange dreams are the perfect recipe for an engaging story. Readers who enjoy a good adrenaline rush will find this a brilliant romantic thriller.
~ **Chanticleer Book Reviews**

Romance, a bizarre mystery and a gorgeous setting brought to a magical life in a debut novel. The surprises at the end are worth the wait! ~**Christine M. Fairchild, author of *An Eye for Danger***

A mysterious skill that straddles the line between paranormal and possible, a woman mourning her husband lost at sea, and the sunny embrace of Maui all come together in an evocative narrative that quickly becomes a real page-turner.
~ **Lisa Costantino, Award-Winning Author of *Maiden's Veil***

The author blew my senses with mystery, romance and secrets deep, dark and dangerous

A compelling and magical read!
~ **Desere Steenberg, Romance Book Haven**

One of a kind characters, numerous plot twists and even authentic bonus recipes ensure this story to be a favorite among many! ~**InD'Tale Magazine**

LOVED this book. It's little wonder The Dream Jumper's Promise was nominated for Best Indie First Book. I got hooked like a mahimahi. The story cracks along at a taut pace, and it has everything: mystery, suspense, and a romance with deep emotional content.
~**ParaYourNormal Reviews**

THE DREAM JUMPER'S PROMISE

KIM HORNSBY

10 TOP PRESS

Seattle~Maui

Jennifer !

Sweet Dreams !

Kim Hornsby

Paperback ISBN-13: 978-1500177096

Dream Jumper Series

The Dream Jumper's Promise
The Dream Jumper's Secret
The Dream Jumper's Pursuit
Dream Come True
Girl of his Dream

Dedication

To Laurie, Christine, Lisa and Geri, my safety net in this kooky writer's world. Without their encouragement and expertise, I'd still be writing paragraphs with two POV's, three tenses, and no storyline. Thank you for making me feel like an author

.

"Dreams are the royal road to the unconscious."

Sigmund Freud, the Interpretation of Dreams

the front window of Tina and
r opened, the overhead bell
ered the store. The uniform, gun
st eyes were all familiar sights.
a had seen more than she wanted

t the body," everyone said.
ced Hank was dead. Not yet, even
been abandoned after only one
ight hours—ten thousand and eighty
g minutes of hoping.
, Obi, trotted over to the policeman, as if the
t seconds away from pounding another nail in
s empty coffin. "We found your husband's wallet."

The leather in the cop's outstretched hand was a small
but powerful reminder of Hank. Memories meteored
towards her—his gypsy-black hair and twinkling eyes. At
the beach, driving his truck, smiling from their bed. She
cupped the wallet in her hand and closed her fingers around
its edges. For all that remained of a dynamic man, it was
surprisingly light.

"Where?" She tucked a wayward strand of hair behind
her ear.

"Off the path, above Honolua."

No one takes a wallet surfing. "Thanks." It would hold
his credit cards, medical insurance card, driver's license,
dive instructor card—all part of Hank's life on Maui. A life
he'd cherished. Married only sixteen months, would a man
simply abandon his wife and a charmed life in Hawaii
without a word?

The faint chugging of the air compressor in the shop's back alley broke through her thoughts. Katie, her shop girl, was in the back-alley filling scuba tanks. Tina looked around to see the policeman had gone. She pulled the driver's license from its slot and grains of sand fell, sand that Hank might have touched before he went into the water that day.

"Did I hear you talking to someone?" Katie popped in from the back room, her blond hair swinging.

"Police." Tina held up the wallet. "Hank's." Katie froze.

Someone barely of drinking age would know little of consoling a thirty-four-year-old widow. "Katie, can you do the coffee run now? I'll finish filling the tanks if you'll get me a double." Tina needed something, and she hoped it was just coffee.

She walked through to the back alley and lowered herself to sit on an overturned milk crate, waiting for the group of submerged scuba tanks in a metal trough to fill to 3000 psi. Leaning against the wall, her gaze drifted towards the sky. The gray clouds held in the humidity like a wool blanket and sweat trickled down the small of her back into the waistband of her board shorts.

This new turn of events didn't completely eliminate the possibility that Hank might have faked his own death. He was smart enough to know credit cards were useless to someone who wanted to disappear. Still. The wallet felt cool in her hand. She'd have to tell Noble it had turned up. Open that bag of snakes. Poor Noble.

She extracted a picture tucked into a fold of the wallet and a stab of loneliness shot through her. In the photo, she and Hank were smiling from a sun-drenched, black-sand beach in Hana. She'd fit perfectly into the curve of his long, lean body. Like phantom pain in an amputated leg, the memory of how it felt to tuck in under his shoulder lingered.

They'd driven to the sleepy town of Hana, that day,

with their best friend Noble and a girlfriend, hoping to take a break from the craziness of the Lahaina scene. Back when she knew he loved her, beyond any doubt.

But now there was doubt. He'd disappeared. Either dead or gone. Days before his death, he'd said, "No matter what, always remember how much I love you." She'd thought he was worried about how their relationship would change when she got pregnant, a plan they were working on with feverish diligence. "Silly man," she'd said, kissing him.

Tina tucked the photo back in the wallet. Memories would drive her crazy if she didn't get a grip soon. A deep breath revealed the scent of plumeria flowers from the tree across the laneway at Mr. Takeshimi's house.

Watching the elderly neighbor sweeping the porch of his pristine cottage, his broom swishing a gentle rhythm, she called out. "Hey, Mr. T." He was a fighter, still holding onto his real estate despite million-dollar offers. Hank's plan had been to buy Mr. T's house when he was ready to sell and open an art gallery. But now she was in debt and that plan was long forgotten. Someone would come along eventually and make it a tacky T-shirt shop. Or a competing dive shop.

When Mr. T straightened, Tina increased her volume in case he hadn't heard her. "Big storm coming in."

He nodded. "Doesn't scare me."

No, it wouldn't. He'd endured World War II as a Japanese American in Hawaii. Sixty-one years after the Pearl Harbor attack, he was sweeping his porch. He stared at her, his face a question in waiting.

"Me neither." She tried to believe in her own words.

Mr. Takeshimi nodded, as if this explained something. "Fall seven times and stand up eight, Tina." Japanese proverbs lived on the tip of his tongue. He'd once said, "Good things come to those who wait," and then Hank came into her life.

She stood. "I'm up. Thanks, Mr. T." She smiled his

way, knowing he'd worry without it.

Back in the shop, Tina met the gaze of a fist-sized octopus in one of the aquariums. Staring directly into the cephalopod's eyes, she tried to convey an apology. Five days in an aquarium was too long for an intelligent creature. "I'll see you get released today."

It was eight a.m. Time to open the store for the day. Flipping the wall switch, she illuminated all six fish tanks to create the underwater look to her Lahaina Towne shop. Over two years before, Hank had installed the wall of sixty-gallon aquariums to stylize the store and lure customers in. Even during the recent shutdown, the tanks had been maintained and viewed through the windows, still colorful, the fish vibrant, even though Hank was probably dead.

Passing a fish tank, she noticed the octopus watching her. Its scrutiny made her feel like she was not only being watched but judged. A ridiculous thought. She tilted her head and contemplated what it must be thinking. "Being caged sucks," she said, not necessarily to the octopus.

Her dog, a pit mix named Obi Wan, bared his teeth in a smile, his usual reaction to any word ending in 'uck.' "It's okay. Mommy's having a good day." She scratched behind her dog's ears, his favorite spot, and then moved to the back room. Tucking the wallet in the top drawer of her messy desk, her palm lingered on the metal front in silent apology to Hank for shutting him away.

"Here you go, Boss." Katie entered the back room and then set the double espresso with extra sugar on the desk. Ever since Katie's boyfriend, Ned confessed that her constant talking drove him crazy, she'd been trying to use fewer words. She now hovered over Tina, her smile hinting at all the unspoken sentences rattling around inside her mouth.

Tina arched her brows in question. "Just say it Katie. I won't tell Ned."

"My Uncle Jamey's coming today." The words shot

4

from Katie's lips like dice thrown on a table.

"From Seattle?"

She nodded.

"My offer stands. Tell him he can dive free on slow days." A soldier on leave from Afghanistan could dive on her nickel any day there was space. "He might have to wait until this Kona storm blows through." Bad conditions would put a halt on diving for the next few days. Katie beamed and skipped into the next room, a sunny influence to have around.

Tina took a sip of the steaming coffee and wondered which problem to tackle first. The desk was littered with bills and phone messages from creditors. Before she could open another letter from the bank, Katie's scream made her fly out of her chair and run into the next room. She rounded the doorway to see a man grab Katie roughly and lift her off her feet. The scream turned to a squeal that ended in a giggle. This was not Ned, who was lean and scruffy and always looked like he just woke up. This was an adult, a manly looking man--tall, with sandy-colored hair on the long side of a crew cut and muscular arms. His crisp white T-shirt that read *Maui Parasail* stretched across a broad back.

"I can't believe you're here." Katie pulled away from the hug. "I miss everyone. You know? How is everybody? I mean really. How's Dad and Grandpops?" She stopped to take a breath as her resolve to use fewer words went flying out the window.

"Everyone's good," he said.

Katie did a little happy dance, her smile stretching from ear to ear. "I hoped you'd call this morning. I was just telling my boss that you'd come today. The diving isn't looking good. I'm sorry about the storm coming in and Tina said it's not likely he'll dive tomorrow but the weather here can change in a few hours, just like Seattle."

Tina stepped forward, knowing an interruption would be necessary. "You're Katie's uncle, I presume." She

5

extended her hand.

As the man turned to face her, Tina froze. It had been a while, but she knew this person well enough to know that when he slept on his back, he snored. And that he had a small birthmark shaped like South America below his belly button. Far below. She'd once pointed to Tierra del Fuego, and then inched southward, with her tongue.

His slightly lopsided smile was achingly familiar and once so dear to her that her breath caught in her throat and produced a tiny warble she hoped was inaudible. He must recognize her too. As their palms made contact, Tina felt a powerful surge pass between them, like an electric shock. She tried to pull her hand away as a curtain of darkness clouded her vision and blackness took over.

"Kristina?" The familiar timbre of James' voice sounded far away, muffled, as she fought for consciousness. Sinking to the floor, the last thing she felt was his arm moving behind her back.

***

"Katie, get some water." Jamey sensed Kristina was going to black out before her eyes took on that blank expression of nothingness. He grabbed her small frame in a loose hug and lowered her to the carpeted floor. *Shit, what's going on?* He'd sensed something horribly melancholy about her when he turned around. Tragedy, sadness. *Damn this clairvoyance.* Pinching the inside of her thigh made her flinch and those gorgeous chocolate-colored eyes fluttered open. "Kristina?" She smelled like gardenia flowers. He couldn't help notice, this close.

"What?" Her voice was paper thin. She reached for the dog that had moved in to lick her face. "How long?"

"Ten seconds." Jamey watched her scan the room. Her carotid pulse was strong.

"I felt something weird." She turned her head to look at him and he leaned back to put a few more inches between them. "Faint or hungry or…overjoyed to see me?" He attempted a smile but she didn't notice. Already she was struggling to sit up.

"Just lay there for a bit."

"I'm okay now."

He remembered how stubborn she was and helped her up, his arm under her elbow. Unsteadily, she reached for the counter. Her face had more color but hell, she still looked terrible. Deathly. Katie ran into the room with a bottle of water. "Oh, my God, Tina. What happened? Should I phone 911?" She stopped short of hugging her boss.

Kristina grabbed the counter's edge for support while he took the water bottle from Katie. "Thanks, sweetie," Jamey said, "but I think she has low blood sugar. Can you find fruit or a carb?"

"We have juice in the back fridge."

"That'll do." Jamey nodded, not taking his eyes from Kristina. He cracked the water bottle's seal and handed it over.

Tina took a swig and set it down on the glass counter.

"Deep breaths," he advised.

She exhaled and then looked into his face. "James Dunn." It was a statement.

He remembered when they couldn't keep their hands off each other. "Kristina Greene." Her cap logo said 'Tina and Hank's Dive Shop.' Ah yes, the husband.

"I go by Tina now."

She backed away and he didn't blame her. The way he'd left things, he deserved a slap. Or a punch. "I'm surprised you're still on the island." She'd said she wouldn't last long on Maui if her parents didn't get off her back.

They shared a smile. Hers looked forced. His felt the same way. She stepped behind the counter, putting distance between them. "I thought I'd seen the last of you."

"That's not why you fainted?" He needed her to say it

wasn't his fault.

"Here's POG." Katie rounded the corner, balancing an overfilled Dixie cup. She stood and watched Tina gulp the sugary pink juice.

"That did the trick. Thanks, Katie."

Her eyes had lost the foggy look. "Maybe you need food," Jamey said. He'd take her for breakfast if she'd let him.

"No thanks." She pulled her hat further down her forehead.

His heart still raced at the sight of her again, his palms still clammy. Kristina. Wow. Definitely recognizable as the spunky dive instructor he'd fallen for ten years ago, she still had that turned-up nose, big brown eyes and a face that said 'naughty girl next door.' He realized that he was staring at her like she was a textbook and he had a test coming up. "You should see a doctor, just in case," he said.

A smile didn't accompany her chuckle. "Believe me, I will. Excuse me." She turned and disappeared into the back room with the striped dog on her heels.

***

Tina's sheets were a tangle of soft cotton when she slipped out of bed before dawn and walked to the dresser, where the wallet sat. Picking it up, she pressed it to her cheek. The leather was cool against her flushed face. She hoped it would smell like him, but nothing of Hank lingered in the leather's scent. Every new discovery took him further away.

Opening the sliding glass door, she stepped onto the front deck of her house. The air was thick with the incoming storm. An ionic sizzle hung in the darkness. Soon the sky would lighten and the wind would replace the stillness. Yesterday the humidity had been oppressive, with no hint of a trade wind. Scuba diving would be canceled all over Maui when the storm came.

Damn.

Her business had already suffered terribly, and she needed to maintain the momentum of making money and paying bills. Grieving had been expensive and, although she had equity in real estate, risking her beloved house was out of the question. Built and paid for, it was the one thing to verify she was not a colossal screw-up. With no husband, no baby, and a failing business, she was almost back at the beginning of her life plan. Back to when she'd arrived on Maui eleven years ago, armed with an MBA and inheritance money from her grandmother.

She climbed back into the bed she still thought of as hers and Hank's, and slithered into the nest of sheets. "It's hot, isn't it, Obi?" Her toes swirled around the dog's silky fur. She'd always talked to Obi but more so these days, when flimsy strings of words were the only conversation that filled the solitary hours.

Looking at the dark timbers of her bedroom's ceiling, she began the relaxation exercises recently suggested by the grief counselor at Maui Memorial Hospital.

Breathe in, and out. Imagine a lovely, safe place. The ocean. Scuba diving. The carefree days, when Hank was alive. When diving was her joy. When she could still dive.

Empty your mind of everything but the thought of that beautiful place. She pictured the aqua water and colorful fish with perfect clarity, and soon a feeling of familiarity hugged her.

Breathe in and out. Feel yourself arrive.

As she fell deeper from the surface of consciousness, light pressure surrounded her body. She drifted down, falling…slowly. She felt lovely, safe.

Light crept into the corners of her vision, fuzzy, then brighter, as it fanned across her view. Slanted sunshine indicated late afternoon. A sandy surface waited below her feet. The water felt neither cool, nor warm. Just pleasant. Her nightgown swirled around her body in the twinkling, sun-washed water.

When her feet touched the sand and planted firmly on the ocean floor, she glanced up. Thirty feet to the surface. The ocean's visibility was beyond anything she'd experienced in ten years as a scuba instructor on Maui. Clarity of two hundred feet was expected in air but an impossible phenomenon for Hawaiian waters, even on a quiet summer day.

In front of her was a massive rock wall, like a never-ending pointillistic mural, covered in pink corals and purple anemones and sea urchins. Tropical fish darted in and out of the cracks to feed and hide. The intensity of color showed prolific growth of coral and oceanic plants, with no sign of the pesticide damage from the Maui pineapple crop runoff. Tina hadn't seen such a dive site in Hawaii. It was a joy to be diving again. A somersault later, she kicked herself forward to explore the wall. It had been too long since she'd been in the ocean like this. She felt light, carefree. The moment belonged to abandonment. And to her.

Kicking along the wall, she explored nooks and cracks in search of a moray eel or an octopus. Fish parted as she swam through their groupings. A large shadow tucked into the curved wall ahead and Tina stopped. This shallow, it would be a barracuda or a reef shark, nothing more. Dangerous sharks were in deep water and, even then, wouldn't approach a diver unless there was blood involved. Lots of blood. She continued along the wall. At the corner, she saw the creature.

A shark.

Not the docile kind.

This was a ten-foot tiger shark, one of the most aggressive deep-water sharks in Hawaii. And it was looking straight at her. She backed into the wall.

Tiger sharks wouldn't attack unprovoked, but poor eyesight might encourage it to advance out of curiosity. The shark's size was not extraordinary for its kind, but still the length of a car. She concentrated on willing it gone and waited. It didn't move.

Why did she not have control over her own fantasy? Tina tried to open her eyes, end the relaxation exercise. She couldn't. She felt the water; tasted the salt on her lips. Pinching her arm did nothing to release her from the dream.

The shark veered from the wall, as though returning to the depths, then swerved and headed straight for her. She tried yelling to jar herself awake, but no sound emerged.

It was only forty feet away, then thirty. It would be sizing her up as an adversary.

Heading into the open, she extended her arms to appear larger than her petite stature. The shark continued.

Twenty feet away. If it got close enough, she'd have to stick her fingers in its eyes or punch it in the gills. Hitting the nose in defense was only a myth.

Her heart beat wildly. This was the closest she'd ever been to a tiger shark. As she locked eyes with the beast, it passed inches from her left shoulder. She'd forgotten to hook the eyes. Next, it would bump her before taking a bite to draw blood. Typical behavior. Tina hoped to poke its eyes before that happened.

With arms stretched in a ready position, she prepared. Adrenaline pumped through her like a high-speed train. The tiger shark circled again and came straight for her. This time she focused on its eyes, ready to jab straight in. But five feet before making contact, it turned abruptly, its tail whacking her chest hard enough to leave her momentarily stunned. This was the bump and bite. She knew what came next. Struggling to regain her wits, she watched the shark head out and turn around.

Then, the beast stopped, as though agitated by its tail. Making tight circles, it spun around quickly. She could try to make an escape to the surface while it was distracted but, knowing sharks were attracted to surface thrashing, she stayed put.

Its circling became tornadic until the shark was only a

mesmerizing blur. She backed against the wall, unable to look away. When the movement finally slowed, in the shark's place stood a man. He turned and faced her.

Hank's black hair swirled around his shoulders in the afternoon sunshine. He wore the swim shorts and wetsuit jacket from the day he'd disappeared. Something caught in her throat and she stifled a cry.

As she closed the space between them, he turned and swam away, eventually curving in towards the wall.

Wait!

She was determined not to lose him again, but he stayed beyond her reach. They continued this way until the rock wall angled in to shallow water and the surface got closer. The churning of the surf overhead was a frothy mix of ocean and air, the turbulence expressing its force on the rocks above. She could feel the push and pull of the ocean's swell. Tina stopped. It was risky to continue to shallow water. Hank would know this. They could get caught in the powerful churn and be thrown onto the jagged lava rocks.

Hank stopped and turned to her. His expression of concern was a heartbreaking reminder of the man who always put her first. Tina motioned that they should turn around, but Hank pointed to something ahead.

The intensifying pull on her body out to open ocean indicated that a big swell was coming. She barely had enough time to find something to grab on to. With this much force, she'd soon be plastered against the wall with an equal reaction. She held a handful of coral affixed to rock with both hands and hoped that Hank was safe.

There was a moment's reprieve after the sucking, and then the water gradually changed direction to push her against the wall. The force built and pinned her body against the points of igneous rock. Tina twisted her head to glance at the expanse of sand behind her. Then ahead. Hank was gone. She would let go after this and get pulled out to where she'd sink to the sand. She'd dig in with her hands, try to stay put before the assault returned.

But the pushing did not let up. It continued to hold her to the wall. No wave or ocean swell could do that. Looking up, she saw that the surface had disappeared. She was in very deep water. The sunlight was far away, the water dark. Her first thought was that a tsunami or rogue wave had come in. She hadn't needed to equalize the pressure in her ears; the dive was not real, even with the taste of salt on her tongue.

Still, her legs and arms screamed with the pain of being pressed against the jagged coral. A rumbling noise like a subway's approach gained volume, her vision went black, and she was freed from the swell's force as she was sucked backwards through blackness at an unreal speed.

Gradually, her vision cleared and the ceiling of her bedroom stared down at her, the room dimly lit by dawn's light. Gasps filled the room. They were hers, like she'd been holding her breath.

Hank had not been real. It was a dream. Her gasp turned to a sob. Obi looked up from his place at the bottom of the bed, familiar with the sound of misery. Realizing that her fingers were clenched around something hard and cold, Tina lifted her right hand from under the sheet and squinted to see what it was.

A chunk of wet, jagged coral.

CHAPTER 2

Tina flung the coral across the room and sprang from the bed, leaving a drenched spot in the center of the sheets. Drops slid down her legs and arms to pool on the hardwood floor. She turned to the open closet door and stared into the mirror to see her flimsy nightgown flattened against her body. Lifting the gown revealed a mess of scrapes and coral cuts. She licked her hand. Salty. Her fingernails dug into her arms as she backed up against the wall, expecting to hear maniacal laughter at her expense.

She reached for her robe and wrapped it around her wet shoulders, trying to squelch the shivers that had very little to do with being cold. *What the hell just happened?* There was no sign of water anywhere beyond her recent steps, no puddles by the door. She put her hand on Obi's back. Dry.

The screen door to the deck was still locked. The palm of her hand stung. Absently, she blotted the blood on her robe. She'd worry about the stain when there was a logical explanation for what just transpired.

A wind whispered through her room, snaking around her wet legs and rustling the diaphanous curtains. Tina glanced back at Obi, her consistent barometer of change. Her dog was going back to sleep. Stepping closer to the cluster of coral, she bent to examine what she'd recently held in her bloodied palm. It was similar to the souvenirs sold in Lahaina shops, except for one difference. It wasn't bleached or painted but alive, the microscopic animals still fighting for life in the atmosphere. This cluster hadn't been out of the ocean for more than a few minutes.

Beyond the window, everything looked normal. Her

driveway was lined with coconut palm trees, two trucks were parked in their usual spots and a light glimmered at the neighbors' house.

Wriggling out of the wet gown, Tina let it drop to the floor in a pile of cerulean silk. She'd bought it for her honeymoon to Lanai, less than two years before. *Wait.* She hadn't worn that gown to bed.

Hours earlier, Tina had put on one of Hank's T-shirts that read 'Pink Floyd' across the front. The shirt was now folded and sitting on the dresser, beside his wallet.

The hairs on the back of her neck prickled and she jumped away from the gown, knocking into the bedside table and tipping over the clock. As she righted it, she saw that it was after six. Either the alarm hadn't rung at its usual time or she'd forgotten to set it. The alarm's malfunction was only one small bloom in a whole bouquet of uncertainty.

As much as she wanted to put a name to what had happened, there was business she had to take care of first. Having overslept, she was now late in calling off the morning dive charter. Customers needed to be contacted. Making a wide circle around the nightgown, she left the bedroom.

The wind gained momentum and forced its way through the screened windows like an unwanted, angry visitor. A Chinese screen in the dining room crashed to the hardwood floor. Rain drops pelted the roof, at first sporadically and then more insistently. As she scrambled to slam the kitchen windows, the sound of the rain became deafening, sending Obi running to the bedroom's safety.

The Kona storm had arrived.

Rain drove through the open windows with the bravado of a toreador. Sliding the last one shut, she noticed a wet patch too late and slipped. Her hand reached to grab the dining room table and a vase of flowers crashed to the floor as she went down. The vase shattered across the hardwood, spraying glass, water and flowers across the floor. Her knee throbbed. *Come on, Tina. Fall seven, up eight.*

Pulling herself to stand, she limped to her desk and surveyed the front yard through the window. Palm fronds crackled and twisted with the sudden wind. Rain drove sideways, and, several miles across the ocean, the looming island of Molokai was barely visible in dawn's light. Crazy gusts of wind painted the ocean's surface white with froth and foam. Tina had to believe that all Hawaiian boat charters would be canceled.

Then the lights went out. Power outage. She stood at her desk, her knee throbbing. There'd be no house phone. The CB radio at her desk ran on a battery. Before looking for her cell phone in the dark bedroom, she'd try the CB radio.

Her dive instructor, Dave Shade, answered. "Howdy, Tina." His voice was always husky, any time of day. "It's gnarly out there. I canceled. I just tried to call your cell phone but you didn't answer."

"I'm coming in." Canceling, especially with humpback whale watching season over and two slow months ahead, was worrisome but he was right.

Next, she called her shrink. Frequent flyers had special privileges, like a doctor's cell phone number. "I need to see you. Something is going on with my dreams."

"Medication very often brings on extremely vivid dreams."

"I doubt it's the Lexapro or the Xanax." Tina told her about the coral. She worried the doctor might think her problem was pathological lying, at the very least. "I swear to God that I woke up drenched in salt water. My hair is still wet." The inside of Tina's cheek was raw from chewing on it.

"I'm concerned that you're sleepwalking," Doctor Chan said. "Let's start by taking you off the Xanax, maybe find something else for anxiety, and if the hallucinations persist, we'll switch antidepressants."

Changing medications this late in the process would be tricky, as well as scary for Tina. It had taken months to find the right combination of drugs to battle her problems.

"Come in this morning and I'll take a look at your prescriptions," the doctor advised.

Tina pulled on a pair of long white cargo pants. Being overdressed and sweaty was better than explaining how she'd banged up her legs and arms. If she could hide behind denial for just another few hours, maybe she and Doc Chan would uncover an explanation.

***

At nine-thirty that night, Tina locked up the dive shop and put Obi in the truck cab. Noble's nightly performance in "Drums of the Pacific" was finished at the Hyatt Hotel, and soon his old red truck would motor down the driveway. For the last ten months, he'd been the one she ran to when circumstances pulled her below the level of tolerability.

Tonight, she wouldn't worry him with the strange dream, especially because she still hadn't figured out how she'd woken up wet and with coral in her hand. Doc Chan had chalked it up to medication, but something didn't fit. Noble had enough on his plate without guilt taking up more than its share. She wouldn't tell him.

Tina turned in to the grocery store exit to get a six-pack of beer. If she was going to cut back on the Xanax, she sure as hell was going to have a beer if she wanted one.

In the Honokawai Superette parking lot, she saw James Dunn cross the pavement, heading for a group of cars in the far corner. His gait suggested he didn't have a care in the world.

In ten years, he hadn't changed much, just a few gray hairs creeping into his hair along the temples and the hint of smile lines. He'd be forty now. Still easy on the eyes, with that clean-cut cop look. He opened the door to a bright yellow jeep and disappeared inside. Spying on Jamey seemed beneath her, especially with everything she had on her mind. But as she crossed the lot, the jeep swung up beside her. The driver's window rolled down and Tina noticed a woman leaning forward from the passenger seat.

"Tina." Jamey said her name like he was practicing. A six-pack of Corona sat between him and the girlfriend, a stunning beauty who looked more like a martini drinker.

"Carrie, this is Tina, the instructor who taught me how to dive. Remember I told you about her?" He'd just minimized all they'd had in one sentence. The woman nodded and flashed her perfect smile Tina's way. "This is my wife, Carrie." At least he didn't make eye contact when he said that. Tina nodded, trying to smile. Ten years of wondering what she looked like, and there she was like some goddamned movie star. Carrie had been the old girlfriend when she'd first met Jamey. Then Tina was the girlfriend, then not. They'd replaced each other briefly, but any way you looked at it, Jamey ended up with Carrie.

As if in answer to a prayer, the clouds grew heavy and a downpour forced Tina to say her goodbyes. Thank God for weather.

With a to-go tub of chicken teriyaki in hand, she grabbed a six-pack of Corona and a lime and headed for the checkout. She remembered that Jamey liked his beer ice cold, almost frozen. She'd once trickled a few drops playfully on his flat abdomen and licked it off. He'd called her a beer temptress.

Now he had a wife. A beautiful wife who looked to be everything Tina wasn't. Glamorous, tall, blond—strangely similar to Hank's fiancée when Tina first met him.

Tina's truck tires crunched the lava pebbles of the driveway. As she swung into her parking spot, the headlights illuminated Noble's burly form standing in the yard. His long black hair blew in the night wind and he looked like a wild Hawaiian god. Except for the T-shirt and jeans that stretched against muscular thighs, Tina might have believed that Noble was Kane, the Hawaiian god of procreation, a part he relished playing in his nightly hula show. She grabbed the grocery bag and the six-pack of beer and hopped out with Obi.

"I worried about you today." Noble took the beer from her and shut the truck door.

His possessiveness was comforting and her arm linked with his. "I'm sorry." They climbed the outside stairs to the second-floor deck. She nodded to the front yard, where the palm trees were battling the wind. "I've been running all day trying to keep from losing money over this bad weather." She kissed his arm, as high as she could reach.

He slid open the patio door. "If I'd known you were on your way home, I would have saved you some dried tako." He smirked. "You know I don't eat octopus." Tina cringed, remembering the creature still back at the shop. In the kitchen, she opened a beer and took a swig from the frosty bottle. "Scale of one to ten." They'd done this on a daily basis ever since Hank's death.

"Maybe a two," he offered. "What about you?"

"Three." Seeing Jamey's wife had set her back one notch.

"I'm not going to watch the news tonight." Noble moved to the inside back stairs like he was heading to bed before ten o'clock.

Tina stopped to stare at him. "Now I'm a two. Stay. I'll brush your hair if you like." She'd often brushed Hank's long hair while they watched TV and had started brushing Noble's recently. His had more of a wave and was longer, stretching halfway down his back.

"I'm tired," he said apologetically. He disappeared down the stairs to his cottage out back.

Tina settled on the couch with her Styrofoam container of teriyaki and an ice-cold beer. She stopped the fork in mid-air. *What if Noble was sick?* Her breath caught in her throat. *Oh, God. What would she do if Noble died?*

Her heart pounded in her chest. She had to calm herself. The man who just bounded down the back stairs was not ill. He couldn't be. Her gaze rested on the overturned Chinese screen that had crashed in the morning's wind. It was one of Hank's favorite pieces, and she wasn't ready to check the damage.

At the second commercial, Noble returned. "I see they found Hank's wallet." He sat down beside her. "You have to give up hoping, Tina."

"I'm not sure why I can't just give up."

"This is going to drive you crazy." His face looked twisted, his eyes distant. "Don't let it take you under."

"I'm trying," she whispered as he moved in to hug her. "Maybe he's still out there somewhere."

CHAPTER 3

Tina watched tufts of whitecaps slowly materialize in the channel between Maui and Molokai as the sky lightened. The rain had stopped. When the French roast dripped enough for a first cup of coffee, she poured in a finger of milk and emptied five packets of sugar into her oversized mug.

Red sky in morning, sailor's warning. Dive conditions were improving, but... She picked up the remote to switch on the news just as her cell phone rang.

"Hey, Boss Lady. I think Molokini might work. I'm willing to try if you are." Dave sounded confident about taking out the boat, and Tina knew his motivation. If a dive instructor didn't dive, he didn't get paid.

"Hmmm. I hate to cancel two days in a row."

Dave paused. "We didn't cancel yesterday. We went to Lanai."

"Dave? We canceled Molokini yesterday."

"Dude. What are you smoking?" He sounded serious. "We went to Lanai yesterday—the Cathedrals, then Turtle Reef. Remember when I came back, we talked about you fainting?"

"Yesterday we canceled Molokini." Tina stared at the phone, and then brought it back to her ear. The pause on the other end made her wonder if Dave was checking a calendar. "Today is Wednesday." He sounded sober enough.

"I'll call you right back." Glancing at the TV news, she saw that today was indeed Wednesday, March twenty second. She froze. Dave hadn't lost a day. She had.

She sank to the floor and covered her mouth with her

hand. What happened to the day she knew as yesterday? The one where she'd woken from the dream with coral in her hand and gone to see Dr. Chan? She looked to the aquarium, where she'd put the coral from her dream. It wasn't there.

The phone rang. Without saying hello, Dave asked if he should take out the charter.

In a fog of confusion, she whispered that she'd leave the decision to him and hung up. Trying to remember details of yesterday that would confirm she wasn't going crazy, she looked down to see her legs perfectly clear, free from coral cuts.

The broken vase sat exactly where it had been two days before, whole and beautiful, with the bouquet of flowers her friend Pepper had brought on Sunday. The Chinese screen was upright. Undamaged.

She crossed to the kitchen to confirm the existence of last night's beer and teriyaki, but the fridge was empty, with only condiments on the shelves and a fuzzy papaya rotting in the crisper. She held onto the refrigerator handle until she knew she wasn't going to drop to the floor like the faint in the dive shop two days ago. No— yesterday. Had she not woken with coral in her hand, soaking wet, with scrapes on her body?

Maybe she was dreaming right now and Dave's call was a part of the dream. A pinch on her forearm was painful. Obi's look of concern mirrored hers. "Am I losing my mind?" Saying it out loud gave the idea life and a shiver sped up Tina's spine.

The Xanax bottle was on the bathroom counter in the same position as when she'd gone to bed two nights before. She hadn't put the prescription away after Doc Chan told her to stop taking it, because Emily Chan had never told her to stop.

Sitting on the edge of her bed, Tina tried to process the fact that she hadn't woken with coral in her hand, gone to see Dr. Chan, been taken off Xanax. Nor had she watched TV with Noble and then drifted off into a sleep without dreams. She hadn't even seen Jamey with his wife at the grocery store. As far as she knew, Jamey didn't have a wife. She'd dreamed so vividly, it had been impossible to tell dreamscape from reality.

Running her fingers through her layered brown hair, Tina attempted to erase one day from her life. It seemed inconceivable that it was only eight hours since she'd slipped into bed on Tuesday night, the day the police gave her Hank's wallet. Shortly after that, she'd seen James Dunn in the dive shop. Or had she? Tina had to think for a minute to sort out if that had been a dream too. No. She'd fainted and woke up looking at James. Jamey.

Hurrying to the bedroom, she noticed the wallet on the corner of her antique French dresser, right where she'd left it. And she was wearing the Pink Floyd T-shirt from Tuesday night. The cerulean nightgown was neatly folded in a drawer, wrapped in tissue paper.

A gust of wind forced its way through her yard and the slant of the palms momentarily distracted her. The sky was quickly lightening to gray. Today would be a stormy one, the first day of the Kona storm, not the second. The rain hadn't arrived yet.

She called Dave. He'd cancelled the charter. "You feeling okay today?" he asked. She could almost hear him holding his breath.

"I was groggy from a sleeping pill, but I'm fine now."

Dave sounded convinced that she could be that confused. After all, it wasn't so long ago that Dave's girlfriend, Sally, had rescued him from the bars of Maui and introduced him to the Lahaina Alano Club and AA. Dave was not quick to judge another person's confusion. Especially someone who'd recently spent months in bed mourning the disappearance of her husband.

On the good side, Tina had not canceled a day of diving. And now she must continue the day as if the strange dream hadn't picked up her life and shaken it upside down like a snow globe, dislodging everything that wasn't glued down.

A real visit to Doc Chan would now be at the top of her list.

Tina's non-appointment the day before had been full of the fear of waking with coral in her wet hand. Today her concerns were entirely different. She'd have to admit to her shrink that she'd experienced a whole day that did not exist.

***

Lahaina's downtown was traffic-free as Tina drove the stretch that attracted tourists from all over the world. Lahaina had everything visitors wanted in a quaint Hawaiian town—picturesque sea wall, statues of salty whalers and one-eyed fishermen, colorful buildings trimmed in sea-foam white, restaurants boasting Jimmy Buffet-type entertainment. All this, and dependably good weather. The Hawaiian word *lahaina* meant 'merciless sun,' appropriately so, because the town was protected from bad weather by the towering mountains on the east side. Not today, though. This bad weather came from the south.

Tina didn't notice any of this as she raced to the medical building to get as much time with her shrink as possible, before the other crazies—the scheduled ones—arrived.

"I'm concerned that your dreams are confusing you." Emily Chan's foot tapped the edge of her desk as she suggested the problem might be the Xanax. Doctor Chan was the only psychiatrist on Maui's west side. Fresh from Loma Linda medical school, she was familiar with new treatments and drugs. Being current was immensely appreciated by Tina. "The drug could be producing lifelike dreams," she said. "I'm going to suggest you use it only for emergencies."

Tina's eyes widened. "That's basically what you said in my dream." Another thought came to mind. "Do you know of any way to wake up during a dream? If this happens again, I'm going to need to know if it's real life." At the very least, the consequences might be embarrassing if she thought she was in a dream state, only to find out it was reality. "And how could a dream span twenty-four hours?"

The doctor didn't seem as worried that the dream lasted a full twenty-four hours. "Dreams can appear to span long periods of time, when in fact, they really only take a few minutes of sleep." Pages from the German psychoanalyst, Carl Jaspers, lay across Dr. Chan's desk. "You had what is called W.I.L.D. a Wake-Initiated Lucid Dream, meaning you didn't fall asleep knowingly but entered a dream state straight from consciousness. Then you experienced what is referred to as a false awakening. In this case it was what Dr. Celia Green categorized as type two. Listen to this: 'The subject appears to wake up in a realistic manner, but to an atmosphere of suspense. His surroundings may at first appear normal, and he may gradually become aware of something uncanny in the atmosphere, and perhaps of unwonted sounds and movements. Or he may 'awake' immediately to a 'stressed' and 'stormy' atmosphere. In either case, the end result would appear to be characterized by feelings of suspense, excitement or apprehension."

The doctor looked up. "Shouting sometimes works to wake up. Concentrate on opening your mouth, taking a breath and yelling. If that doesn't work, try closing your eyes in the dream and opening them again. Sometimes that causes the dreamer to actually open their eyes. Or kick hard. Concentrate on feeling the kick and hope to wake from the jolt." Doc Chan nodded at her patient. "Have a routine when you think you are awake to confirm your state of consciousness, like splashing cold water on your face or counting to one hundred. In dreams, you would not stop long enough to count."

The more Tina recounted the day that didn't exist, the more pockets of dead time she found. She hadn't actually experienced a whole day. She'd skipped from her doctor visit to the grocery store to being home with Noble. She'd had a W.I.L.D. and a false awakening, type 2. Fine. Identifying the problem was only the first step.

Stepping out of Dr. Chan's pristine office, the real problem hit her smack in the gut. Would these dreams continue, and if they did, how could she control them before she did something regrettable?

***

Tina ran up the stairs to her darkened house, dodging the streaming waterfalls pouring off the roof. Her hair hung in wet clumps and her pink stretch dress was drenched.

From the deck, she could see Noble was standing in the kitchen, the stove light illuminating his form. A wave of relief engulfed her. She hadn't wanted to be alone. Was he going to make dinner for her? These days, Noble ate at work and Tina brought home takeout. He hadn't cooked in a long time, and it looked like tonight was her lucky night.

He turned when she slid the screen door aside, and the look on his face reassured her that if she was going crazy, Noble was her sanity. This man kept Tina grounded when she started to float away. With Noble's smiling face in front of her, moving on seemed possible.

"Are you cooking?" She took a sniff but there was no scent of food simmering on the stove.

"No." He looked mournful, like he wished he had made dinner for them. "But I'm a four today." He said this hopefully.

"I'm three. But let's order pizza and I'll be a four."

She tromped off to her bedroom to change into dry clothes.

When she emerged in an old T-shirt of Hank's and a pair of Capri pants, Noble was gone. She seated herself in front of the TV. But when an hour had passed and he still hadn't returned with a pizza, she went to bed, confused. When he disappeared to his cottage out back, it was usually because he didn't want to impose his mood on her. But he'd said he was a four. Tina couldn't help wondering if she was dreaming again and she was still asleep.

***

Tina flew through the shop's back door, left her backpack on the counter and greeted her paying customers. "Good morning, everyone. Don't worry. It's still a good day for diving. Rain on the water's surface makes no difference to scuba divers unless the water is turbid from soil runoff. That will not be the case at Molokini, it being an isolated rock with little dirt on it, miles off Maui." Several of them smiled at her. "It's windy, but I've been out in much worse," she said just as Jamey walked in. *Oh yeah, he was on the roster to dive.*

His hair was just long enough to look wet, like he'd showered before a dive charter. The other customers looked like they'd barely rolled out of bed and would be using the dive to wake up. She smiled, remembering that Jamey was a neat freak. Once he'd told her that his neatness came from a need to keep his life organized and orderly, and she'd laughed at the seriousness of his expression. Now that he was in the army, she imagined he got to be as fastidious as he wanted. It wouldn't hurt to have an extra hand that morning, especially as Dave looked hung-over, with droopy, red-rimmed eyes and matted white-blond hair that suggested he'd lost his comb days ago. She hoped to hell he wasn't drinking after six months of sobriety.

Jamey smiled at the other customers and glanced at Tina like the last ten years never happened. Looking down at his hand, Tina noticed the absence of a wedding ring.

"Let's fit everyone for wetsuits." Tina touched Dave's arm on her way to the rack of neoprene jackets. "Please free the octopus today."

He pulled his cell phone away from his ear and clicked it shut. "Sally's sick. She can't work the boat."

Tina's shoulders slumped. Goddammit. They didn't have time to phone around for another dive instructor. They needed to get out on the water before the wind got worse. Or, before the customers chickened out. Tina would have to take Sally's place. No question. "I'll drive, you dive." The words were in the air before she gave them much thought.

Coast Guard law stipulated that someone with a captain's license was needed to stay on the boat at all times. Tina had a license. She couldn't get in the water anymore but sitting on the boat might be possible. It had been months since she'd tried. Her heart twisted. Her face was hot. She had to do it. On her way out the door, she checked for her emergency supply of Xanax in the side pocket of her backpack.

***

The Maalaea harbor was the closest boat launch to Molokini, one of Hawaii's most talked-about dive sites. Molokini Crater was a sunken volcanic top, miles off the coast of Maui, but still shallow enough to dive the center.

Tina drove her boat, *Maui Dream,* past the jetty. As the wind forced itself against them, she angled the craft to absorb as little of the wave crashing as possible. In anticipation of heavy seas, the customers were already in wetsuits, their dive masks at the ready. There was no way to get everyone to Molokini without getting jostled and soaked to the core. Tina stood behind a Plexiglas shield at the center console and slung her mask over the throttle, hoping to duck behind the shield when the crashing waves marred her vision. "Hang on," she yelled. Easing the throttle forward, she found a suitable speed for the ordeal and settled in at the wheel, feet planted firmly apart.

The boat pounded the ocean's surface for the entire thirty-minute crossing. Finally, Tina steered into the center of the crater and tucked in to the calmest water available. The usual first dive at the tip of the crescent, Reef's End, was too exposed to the wind today. They'd dive inside the crater. She dropped anchor carefully in the sand.

After donning gear, the divers jumped off the boat and descended with Dave. Jamey had helped others launch and would bring up the back of the group. "You still comfortable in the water?" Tina asked.

"Yup." He jumped off the swim step and plunged into the turquoise water. "Aloha," he said, just before putting the regulator in his mouth. She watched him drop below the surface without the fussy preamble of a beginner diver. Because she'd trained him beyond basic certification, she allowed herself to feel proud and partially responsible, even though it had been a decade.

Earlier, she'd overheard him tell someone that he'd done a lot of diving. *Had he been on Maui, and with whom?* She just assumed he never came back to the islands after they broke up. Her interest in him was both surprising and disappointing.

Looking over the side of the boat, she located a blurry blob of wavy colors, the customers waiting below. The visibility looked awesome and everyone would be happy they'd been talked into this dive, especially because there were no other boats brave enough to dive in the crater that morning. They'd feel like heroes for taking on the crossing and, as the story gained momentum over a sunset Mai Tai that night, they'd become daring adventurers, modern-day pirates.

After months of being landlocked, it was good to be back on the boat. Nine months was a long time for her to not be in the water. Or near the water. Last time she was on the boat was at Hank's memorial. She never suspected then she'd be landlocked so long.

That day she'd insisted on driving *Maui Dream*, despite her friends' protests. "Let Noble drive," Pepper had suggested. But Tina wanted to captain her own boat. She hoped to draw strength from the familiarity. Pepper worried that reality hadn't hit Tina yet. It hadn't.

More than twenty boats comprised the flotilla that motored their way up the Maui coast to the northern bay. Even the *Lin Wa* and the *Trilogy,* both busy sunset charter boats, cancelled customers and joined the procession. Making money that night had been secondary.

It was a lovely tribute to her husband's popularity in town.

Tina had worried about not looking enough like a grieving widow, but a corner of her heart still hoped he'd simply left the island, run away. How could she look distraught when there was no body? She hadn't accepted his death with one hundred percent finality. Glancing at the cliffs, she half-expected to see Hank waving to them. *Look, everyone, he's not dead and he didn't desert me. He had amnesia.*

That day they'd followed Hawaiian tradition by throwing flower leis into the water and watched the blossoms bob on the pink sunset waves. As the mourners said prayers and goodbyes, Tina was thankful her parents hadn't come to Maui for the memorial. Only months after 9/11, her mother was terrified of flying.

When they pulled out of the bay where Hank presumably surfed the last day of his life, Tina looked back to see a small humpback whale emerge near the floating leis. It blew a spray of water, sending a fountain of flowers into the air. "Look!" she'd cried. They cut the motors and watched the whale jump among the leis, cutting the surface in sprays of frothy waves and blooms. For weeks afterwards, that moment was referred to with reverence. Some said it was Hank, showing he lived on in the ocean, but Tina hadn't been convinced.

Now she watched sea birds tuck into Molokini's pocked rock face to return to their sheltered nests, waiting for her customers to return to the boat. Soon bubbles would appear at the stern, indicating the first divers were back. The deepest dive was always first and took less time than a shallow one because of the need for more air at depth. They'd go eighty feet on the first dive and thirty on the second, a thought that left her panicked.

Tina stared at the water and waited. *How in hell would she ever get back in the ocean*? All her talk of ear infections and rashes was a thin veil of an excuse. Already, conversations had started around town about her selling the shop. If the dive community on Maui knew why she was beached, she could kiss her business goodbye. The other scuba shops in Lahaina would circle hers like sharks waiting to feed on a dying seal. Pacific Dive and Surf from Honolulu, had been waiting on the periphery for months, having asked for first consideration if she decided to sell.

Months ago, her dive shop had acquired an envied reputation and notoriety when a photo of Tina with Hollywood's hottest couple had found its way into a recent edition of *People* magazine. Hank had set up the outing in a marketing strategy just before he died but never got to see the published photo. It was that burst of publicity that finally got Tina out of bed to reopen the dive shop. And now, all that free advertising might be short-lived for a widow who had a crippling aversion to the water. How could she promote the safety of diving when she couldn't even get in the ocean?

The customers returned from their deep dive. Gear was sorted and tanks changed for the second dive. Waiting on the surface, they breathed off accumulated nitrogen and chatted amicably. Tina caught the odd sentence and smiled when anyone looked her way. Jamey's ease of sociability was familiar. When he and an older gentleman struck up a conversation, her interest piqued. "Where're you from, Jamey?" the man asked.

"Seattle area, but I'm posted in Afghanistan right now," Jamey said.

"My son is over there." The man cleared his throat. "He's a doctor and is bored with all the waiting around."

Jamey nodded. "Better that than watching U.S. soldiers die on his operating table." Jamey smiled sympathetically as the man agreed. "I'm on leave from the base in Kandahar."

The two continued a subdued conversation about the military in Afghanistan while Tina hooked buoyancy control jackets and regulators to tanks. The other customers laughed loudly in the bow, their gaiety in direct contrast to the low voices at the stern. From what she could hear, Jamey skirted questions like a press secretary.

"Sounds like you're on a covert mission." The older man had noticed too.

Jamey chuckled. "Nothing like that," he said.

But Tina knew Jamey's laugh well enough to know he hadn't found humor in the comment.

CHAPTER 4

The Maui rain fell against Jamey's jeep top, creating a sense of safety inside the vehicle. Many nights in Afghanistan he'd driven in vehicles feeling worse than unsafe. One time, when the Hummer was pelted with enemy fire, Jamey ducked below the dashboard in a ball of compressed bones, muscle and skin, praying he'd live to see his daughters again, watch them blossom into teenagers and beyond. The United States military had originally assured him that he wouldn't see combat. "No immediate danger," the higher powers had promised.

He'd hoped they could deliver. They hadn't.

Pulling onto West Maui's main road, Jamey saw Tina's baseball cap on the seat beside him. *Tina and Hank's Dive Shop.* She'd worn it backwards to keep her hair from blowing in her face on the ride to Molokini, her hair just long enough to whip at her eyes and mouth. Years ago, it had been long enough to spread across the pillows. At the harbor, Jamey had grabbed the hat off Tina's head and put it on backwards, trying to engage her with his best Tina impersonation. "I'm Tina, your captain. This is only going to be a three-hour tour, a three-hour tour." He sang the tune from *Gilligan's Island* menacingly, an inside joke in the charter business about everyone ending up shipwrecked.

Although her lips curled into a half-smile, the sadness in her eyes was almost intolerable. Where was that spark in her personality that had defined her years ago? He'd expected her to grab the hat and hit him with it. Instead she looked like his father when the Yankees lost the World Series. "You can have that hat," she said. "I had to order more with the new logo."

"What? No sea turtle?"

"No Hank," she muttered, and threw him a bag of gear to stow in the truck.

He didn't need to be a genius to figure out the source of her sadness. Tina was a widow. Jamey tried to recall what Katie said about Hank and Tina. "Great couple, so in love, tragic surfing accident." Jamey doubted that Tina ever thought about the days when he was the man in her life. At least, he hoped she didn't. She had enough to worry about without rehashing his hasty departure. Pulling onto Honoapiilani Road, he slowed the jeep to a snail's pace, enjoying the view. The lower road dead-ended just past his father's place, resulting in very little traffic. Most tourists chose the upper highway long before they got to *The Ridge* property. It was faster and, although tourists came to Maui to relax, it seemed like everyone was in a hurry to get somewhere.

Pulling into his dad's parking spot, Jamey did a quick scan of the property. He wasn't totally in the clear yet, but he doubted after all this time that anyone was following him. Every day that he wasn't abducted was another step towards security. If the enemy really wanted him and knew who and where he was, he had to believe they'd have grabbed him weeks ago when he was still in Afghanistan or jumping between airports on the trip home.

He noted the cars in the parking lot. Nothing unusual. The view always stopped him. Overlooking Molokai, Pops' place sat on the northern cliffs off Ironwood Beach. The majestic Molokai, the Garden Isle loomed in the distance, its mountains towering to meet the low clouds. The condo had been a pricey purchase even in 1988, but Pops rented it out, saving two or three months in the calendar year for family vacations. It had been a brilliant investment. And a godsend for Jamey.

"As much as you love us," Pops had said only a week earlier, "you need to get away, Son. Take a month on

Maui. Just like your superiors said. Think about the Armed Forces while you're over there walking the beach, and whether you even want to go back to the war zone. That is, if you still have what they want."

If he did regain his ability... Even though Jamey hadn't given Sixth Force his answer, how could he not go back? What else was he going to do? Years ago he'd given up his right to daily doses of his children by agreeing to divorce their mother.

Settling into the deck chair with an icy beer in hand, Jamey thought of Tina, and the day he'd left her. Stepping onto that plane bound for Seattle, he doubted anything would ever be the same. Not after the dream he'd experienced the night before. At the age of thirty-five, he'd never had a precognitive dream. Not that he knew. Now he knew the colors were dull, the edges fuzzy. He'd promised Uncle Don that if he ever had one, he'd do everything in his power to not alter the future.

Letting Tina go was one of the hardest things he'd ever done, especially knowing something was headed her way. That part hadn't been as clear in the dream, but the message was still obvious. She'd marry another man. He had to let her go, pretend to lose interest. The double whammy hit when his future took an unexpected turn, taking him down a matrimonial path he hadn't anticipated.

Jamey entered the condo and ducked into the master bathroom. The morning's divers were meeting for sunset cocktails at Leilani's in an hour and he'd asked one of the single ladies to save him a seat. He had nothing else to do. Katie was out with her boyfriend, and walking a rainy beach was kind of lonely.

The water pressure in the shower was lacking but sufficient. Soaping his body, Jamey thought of Tina. She was thinner but still filled out a bikini like a goddamned Sports Illustrated swimsuit model. He recalled what it felt like to roll around in bed with her, skin on skin, all hands, lips, legs. Back then, they'd been like dogs in heat. He soaped himself and let the water pelt his back as he remembered what he and Tina liked to do to each other. Damn. He should be fantasizing about the gal who just phoned to make sure he would be at Leilani's. He was pretty sure they could have some fun between the sheets later. But, as he brought himself to a climax, his thoughts were only about Tina.

***

The wind died down just after sunset, and by the time Tina got ready for bed, there was a definite improvement in the weather. The rain had returned, but it wasn't being driven sideways. The palm trees in her yard did not look angry anymore, only busy. If the sun appeared tomorrow, the flooded lower roads would dry up much faster. A thick layer of brown murky water that was runoff from the pineapple fields would linger offshore for a week, canceling all beach activities. No one wanted to swim in latte-colored ocean. But it was a favorite with sharks.

Tina had just settled into bed when Noble peeked in the bedroom door, his look tender. "You look like a little girl sitting in bed, waiting for her parents to come say goodnight."

Her parents had never come into her bedroom to say goodnight or good morning, for that matter. She was brought to them, by the nanny, for goodnights. "Do I?" She considered patting the side of the bed for Noble but held off, instead pulling Hank's big T-shirt down to cover her thighs.

Noble filled most of the doorway. "Scale of one to ten. I'm a five."

"Me too." Five was good for them. She looked to where the rain had been popping off the windows earlier and told Noble that the six pack dive boat went out with only four customers that day. She didn't mention that

Katie's uncle was the fourth, or that they'd once been lovers. It would feel disrespectful to Hank to even mention Jamey to Noble. And she withheld the fact she'd been on the boat. Even though she was proud of her accomplishment, Tina harbored it like a tiny present hiding in her pocket. When she was diving again, she'd announce her breakthrough.

"I miss you now you're back at work," he said.

Their eyes met and they shared a smile. When she'd been too frightened to sleep alone, Noble had been there. Off and on, but for many months. Tina almost always woke up with him still beside her, on top of the sheets, fully clothed, sleep having claimed him before he could find his own bed.

"G'night, everyone." Noble walked over. He kissed her forehead, his lips lingering. Obi issued a low growl.

"Obi, stop." Tina smiled to think her dog might have opinions on who came into her bedroom. He'd recently taken an aversion to Noble's presence.

Rising from the bed to close her door behind Noble, she then inserted a dollar-size piece of paper in the crack. If the door opened, the paper would fall. She did the same to the patio door, and as an extra measure, she locked both. Before getting back into the bed, she opened her eyes wide and closed them several times. Satisfied she wasn't dreaming, Tina fell back against the cluster of pillows. Her current suspense novel was heavy in her hands and she rested it in the V of her bent body, realizing that the luxury of losing herself in someone else's problems was freeing, especially when her problems seemed insurmountable. But thoughts of Hank plagued her and she eventually gave in to the memories.

The day Hank went missing had been a stormy one. All night Tina and Hank had listened to the huge waves crashing into the rocks two blocks away. Hank was restless knowing that when light appeared in the sky he would leave to surf the waves. They'd had sex in the middle of the night, trying to "make a baby," and when he rolled out of bed at six, Tina teased him to come back and make twins.

"Can't," he smirked. "But I'll be back later. You just lie there and think baby." He kissed her on the forehead. "Girl or boy, I don't care." And then he left to wake Noble.

"Going to ride the big one," he'd called on his way out the door, leaving his wife hugging her pillow, smiling lazily.

And now he was gone. She fell asleep thinking of Hank and that last moment with him. Then shortly after four-thirty, woke. Obi was not with her but she wasn't concerned. It seemed perfectly possible that he might have left the house.

As she stepped out of bed, water surrounded her bed, creeping up around her nightgown. She continued walking into the black ocean. Her skin welcomed the water's cool touch after the humidity of the storm. The ocean's surface was flat calm. The salt water encased her shoulders, and then claimed her neck and head. Swimming underwater, her destination was clear. A pinprick of light waited in the distance and she knew she had to get to him.

For the second time in three days, Tina woke from a diving dream as though she'd been holding her breath. She turned on the lamp, illuminating the room with a deceptively calm, peachy glow. At first glance, nothing looked out of the ordinary. Obi was lying at the bottom of the bed, his blocky head raised, staring at her. Slipping out of the bed, she inspected her legs and arms, felt her face and looked in the closet mirror. Not wet. She pinched herself. Pain. Obi whined.

"What is it, boy?"

The clock read 4:32—only two minutes past the time when she'd risen from bed and found herself in the ocean. No, that hadn't been real. The clock never actually read 4:30 because it was only a dream.

Unlike days before, this dream took place at night and

without a current or swell, she'd been perfectly capable of following Hank into the cave. But it never happened. She'd woken just as she started for the black opening, never seeing either the interior of the cave or the surface.

Like the last one, this dream seemed incredibly real to her. The water had been refreshingly cool when she first entered it, her nightgown billowing up around her like a jellyfish refusing to submerge. Now she wore the green T-shirt she'd worn to bed hours before. Hank's shirt. Hank. Seeing her husband like this, even if it was just in dreams, was setting her back, the benefits of therapy quickly dissolving.

A gecko ran across her ceiling, its ability to hang onto the plastered surface impressive. Everyone was impressive these days except her, who couldn't even tell reality from dream life. Maybe now that she was easing back on the meds, the dreams were emerging. Or they'd always been there but she couldn't remember them before. Regardless, she felt close to Hank as a result of them. Enjoying a joint love of the ocean had been the glue in their relationship. She didn't surf like him and couldn't tell a beautiful work of art from a crappy reproduction, so diving had been their thing. Walking to the bathroom, she flipped on the light and screamed.

Something lay on the floor.

It looked like a small dead animal. Backing up as if she'd seen a face at a darkened window, she hit the door frame. A wet lump of cloth sat in a puddle in the center of the tile. Her back pressed against the wood of the doorway, offering stability as she slid down to sit on the floor. The small piece of paper she'd inserted into the door crack was lying on the hall floor. She'd forgotten about it when she left the bedroom.

Staring at the lump, an idea came to mind. It resembled a thrift shop costume she'd worn at the Front Street festivities on Halloween, Hank as Frankenstein and Tina, his bride. She stared at the wet muslin, wondering how on earth…

Reaching forward, her fingers found the edge and brushed the gown briefly. Drawing back her hand, she touched her lips. Salt. She thought of splashing her face with cold water, as suggested. Across the bathroom, the hair dryer was plugged in. She stood and crossed to reach for it. Warm. Her cropped hair style would only take a few tousles to dry. The hair dryer hadn't been used in years. Tina licked her arm.

No salt.

The sight of droplets clinging to the shower tiles made her take a step back. She flattened her body against the wall. Someone had just taken a shower and used the hair dryer. Was it her? Her inclination was to get out of the house as quickly as she could. But something held her to that wall and she couldn't move. Her eyes darted around the room for anything to verify that she wasn't losing her mind. The lump of muslin, the hair dryer, the wet shower… Everything pointed to sleepwalking at the very best and insanity at the very worst.

She flung herself off the wall and took off down the back stairs and into the backyard. A light shone through the window of Noble's cottage. Jazz music was barely audible. Noble moved in front of the window and Tina watched him pull someone into his arms. She sank to the ground, using the cover of a ginger bush to hide her from view. Noble slow-danced in full view with a man. Blood rushed to her face and her heart beat fast. *What the hell?*

Muffled words wafted from the cottage, then the music died and the light inside the cottage was extinguished, turning the backyard into a dark expanse.

The noise of a Harley Davidson on the road behind the backyard crashed through the silence as it roared southward. Now was a perfect time for Tina to make a run for it. Turning towards her house, she caught the edge of her foot on the path's flagstone rock and fell, face first, onto the hard surface.

When she jolted awake, Obi jumped off the disheveled bed and barked. Her bedroom was hot and dark, the door was closed. Tina reached over and turned on the light.

Swinging her legs over the side, she took several calming breaths but wasn't sure what to hope for. Had she just run through her backyard or not? Her arm felt the pinch. The pile of M&M's she'd been eating before sleep was still on her bedside table. She stood. Kicking her mattress to jolt herself, she stubbed her toe on the metal ridge. "Fuck, fuck, fuck." She sank to the floor to grab her foot. This degree of pain might be a good sign. Obi slinked into the closet, his thin tail between his legs. If she'd had another false awakening, it would be good news. Explaining the wet costume on the bathroom floor would be a nonissue if it was never there. Summoning courage, Tina checked the paper she'd inserted before she went to bed. The small rectangle peeked out above the doorknob, a folded corner on top, just as she'd left it. Good news, so far.

She flicked on the bathroom's overhead light and was instantly relieved to see nothing unusual on the bathroom floor, or anywhere in the room—no water droplets on the walls of the shower, and no hair dryer on the counter. Her reflection in the mirror showed that she still wore the green T-shirt, but her face looked almost unfamiliar in its paleness. Haunted eyes stared back.

Padding through the house to a back window, Tina wasn't sure what Noble's house might reveal, but she heaved a sigh of relief when she saw the cottage was dark, no light, no music. She had to assume he hadn't been slow dancing with a man only moments before. Why in hell would she dream something like that?

Obi wagged his tail and sat down in front of her, waiting for his next cue. After giving him a treat from the jar on the counter simply because he was normal, Tina returned to the bathroom and, as suggested by Doc Chan, splashed cold water on her face. She'd pinched herself in the dream and registered pain, which now suggested that pinching was unreliable. Maybe kicking the bed frame and splashing cold water on her frightened face were better indicators.

She took a ribbon out of her nightstand drawer and tied it around Obi's collar. She was willing to try anything that would help her identify reality from this weird dream life that appeared to be stalking her. After the ribbon was fixed on Obi's leather collar, she lowered her head cautiously to the pillows. The bed did not feel like her sanctuary anymore. Her place of solace had turned against her.

***

Jamey sat up in bed. Something was wrong. He'd been dreaming—just something frivolous about running around with the twins at the top of the Seattle Space Needle. This heaviness had nothing to do with a silly dream of his daughters. It was as if the premonition interrupted his dream with a singular thought, a sense of danger, nothing more tangible. Still, he had to make sure his daughters, his only responsibility in the whole world, were safe.

Pops picked up on the second ring. "Hey, kid, it's 4:30, your time, and besides, isn't it kind of early to be phoning a retiree?" His dad's voice had a measure of concern mixed with curiosity.

"I know you need all the beauty sleep you can get, Pops, but I just woke with a funny feeling, like dread."

"Nothing happened here, son." The gravelly words on the other end reassured Jamey that all was well in Carnation, Washington.

Jamey didn't want to disturb Carrie and the kids so early when all he had was a feeling. Carrie had had enough of his "crazy feelings" for a lifetime of worry. He scratched his face, his morning beard bristly. "Did Uncle Don ever feel like this?" Jamey needed to hear it was normal, or as normal as possible for someone like him.

"Donny didn't have the full gift you have. I don't recall him specifically talking about this, but he didn't tell me everything. Remember, everyone wakes with bad feelings from time to time, son." Pops always knew what to say and how to say it. Talk about gifts.

"I've had it before, coming out of a bad dream jump. Only this time, I wasn't jumping." Jamey opened the patio door and stared at the dark beach below him. The wind had died to leave an after-storm gentleness, a reprieve.

"If you think it has meaning, stay sharp." Pops had good reason to worry. Don's tragic death, years before, had left him anxious about his son, especially now that he was using crazy abilities against war criminals. He'd told Jamey this many times.

"Can you check on the girls for me?"

"I'd be happy for an excuse to go over. I'll let Carrie make me coffee. Don't forget, you're supposed to be enjoying Maui, so don't go getting all analytical about stuff while you're on vacation, y'hear?"

Too many times in the last few months Jamey wished he knew someone like him who jumped into dreams. Having someone to share these anomalies would be invaluable. But as far as he knew, no one had the ability. Not even Uncle Don had everything he had. His paternal grandmother was rumored to be a dream reader, but only her husband was privy to the secret before she passed on, and now they were both gone. At the time, Jamey joined Sixth Force to dream jump for his country, the army was desperate to have him on their team, knowing of no one else who entered dreams. They'd claimed that what Jamey could do and see in a dream was exceptional to anything they already had on the Force. Not only could he read emotions from across a room but he had the mysterious ability to insert himself into a subject's dreams and participate. Having always felt like a freak, Jamey was seduced by the army's need for his talent. With words like "brilliant", "amazing" and "hero" he got used to being a celebrity within the Force even if he never had contact with the other members--only the support team and doctors knew who he was, and they referred to him as Freud.

Lying back in bed, Jamey was lonely for the first time in a long while. Not for love. He was used to that. But lonely for someone who understood the bizarre twist in his existence—someone who could understand and accept him as he was.

CHAPTER 5

When Tina came around the corner of the dive shop, she looked like shit. Her eyes were puffy and her face was drawn in an expression Jamey didn't recognize. He and Dave were hoisting tanks into the truck for the morning charter. The roster was not full and Jamey'd been asked to join the Molokini run. He had a new underwater Nikonos camera and got some amazing shots of an eagle ray on the dive yesterday. Already he had plans to make posters for the twins' ocean-themed bedroom. If he didn't go back to Afghanistan, he'd bring the girls to Maui for a few weeks in the summer, snorkel the calm bays, buy them puka shell necklaces, and make sandcastles...

"Good morning, everyone," Tina addressed the four customers. "It's windy out there but no worse than yesterday, and we had a fantastic dive inside Molokini Crater. Underwater, it is nice and calm." She nodded at Jamey. "Just bumpy on the crossing." She clapped her hands together. "Let's go diving."

Tina sounded like a camp counselor Jamey would gladly follow anywhere. But behind the façade, he could tell she was sick, tired, or hung over. Her skin had a strange tinge of grayness and her smile was forced.

"You coming?" he whispered privately.

Tina nodded without looking at him and his feeling of dread intensified. Did his premonition have something to do with Tina? If so, he wanted to be on that boat. He'd claim sea-sickness to stay with her topside. It wasn't worth diving if something was about to happen to Tina.

***

On Tina's last scuba dive before the anxiety overshadowed her passion, she'd led a group of four beginners in Kapalua Bay. After motioning for everyone to surface, she'd lied that something stung her and they needed to get out of the water. But it was the vision of Hank's decomposing body that made her shoot to the surface that day, his flesh rotting off the bone, his sunken eyes, and his black hair covered in a brown film.

Only later, when she couldn't forget the gory apparition, did she wonder if her subconscious was trying to tell her that all hope of Hank's desertion was foolish. He was dead. Gone.

And now she was about as good with a group of divers as a first timer. Worse—beginners didn't see dead bodies and then have crippling anxiety attacks in the ocean.

Over the last months, both Dave and Sally had attempted beach dives with her, but when she sank below the surface, things always went wrong. Each time, Tina would feel an overwhelming urge to shoot to the top, desperate to get out of the water. And the risk of surfacing too quickly became the problem. If Tina didn't remember to exhale the whole way up, she was flirting with a fatal air embolism. "Second rule of diving, remember?" Sally had warned repeatedly. "As slow as your bubbles," Dave yelled at her.

"It's easy for you. You don't see a decomposing body. And when I do, I don't remember the rules of diving." Funny thing was that even on the surface, with her regulator out of her mouth, she still couldn't get enough air.

***

Distraction and worry shadowed Tina as she backed the boat trailer into the water at Maalaea. Sally was still out sick and Dave wasn't looking much better. If Dave was drinking again, she'd be pissed. That kind of self-inflicted illness was worrisome, but she really needed her dive instructor right now. She had hundreds of dollars in front of her and a reputation to maintain. The dive must go now that the wind had lost some power. Molokini was one of the only dive sites with any worthwhile visibility, so it was that or nothing. She parked the truck and trailer and met Jamey at the dock. "Dave's not feeling well," she told him, "so we might need to pick up the slack."

"You driving the boat?" he asked.

"Yup."

"Don't you dive anymore?"

"I do, but not today." Should she feign sickness to avoid questions? He was staring at her in analytical silence. It always annoyed her when he did that. He didn't have that right anymore.

"I'm too tired to dive today."

He continued staring at her.

"Bad dreams." Did he know she was a widow? Or that the body was unrecovered? Tina reminded herself to avoid looking into Jamey's face when she said stuff like this. He'd always been able to read her moods too well.

Jamey extended his hand to help the single nurses from Chicago onto the boat and Tina wondered if twenty-five-year-old nurses were attractive to forty-year-old Jamey. Of course they would be. Look at him. Jamey was a great flirt. His charm went a long way. She'd been a victim of it herself, long ago.

It was almost embarrassing to watch the nurses doing the conversational courtship dance around Jamey. Giggling. Jamey was a very funny guy.

Dave untied the boat from the dock while Jamey joked about wearing his dive mask for the boat ride. Feeling envious of their frivolous mood, she tried to concentrate on something else like how much money she'd put towards her debt from this week's profit.

"Here we go and hang on, everyone." Easing the throttle forward, they set out in the direction of Molokini. All eyes were on the small, crescent-shaped crater as they zoomed across the wavy plain to the dive site.

Once they were anchored and the customers got geared up, Jamey said he'd hang back on the boat, but she gave him an incredulous look that hopefully cut him to the quick. Again, he was the last to suit up, watching while the others fell overboard and descended into the blue expanse.

"Try to get in a nap while we're gone," he said before he popped his regulator in his mouth and disappeared over the side.

What? Did he think they were all suffering because she was tired? Tina's brow wrinkled in annoyance. After switching on the CB radio, she asked Katie if Doc Chan had returned her call.

"Not yet."

It was only 8:20. "Is that octopus still in the aquarium?" Dave was supposed to bring it today and release it. She'd asked him several times. Or had she only dreamed that?

"The octopus is looking at me right now and I'll tell you what, it's kinda freaky because his eyes follow you all over the room and you feel like he's alive. Well, he's alive, but you know? It feels like he knows what I'm doing and is watching me. Freaky." Katie was losing the battle against unnecessary conversation.

When Dave's head broke through the surface five minutes later, Tina was puzzled. He'd left the customers on the bottom-- a big no no. "What's up?" she called.

Dave spit out his regulator and ripped off his mask. "I'm going to blow chunks."

Tina could see the wavy colors of paying customers twenty feet below with no licensed instructor. If Dave couldn't dive, they were screwed. Jamey couldn't legally lead the dive. She had to get her butt in that water. Fast.

Dave yelled, "I might be able to follow them on top,

but I can't dive like this." He turned his head and vomited on the ocean's surface. Fish immediately raced in to feed.

This was the moment Tina had been dreading for months—the one where she had to dive, regardless of how terrified she was. "Keep your eye on them, Dave." She slid into a set of gear. *Gotta do it.* She grabbed an eight-pound weight belt, a mask and fins and jumped in up-current from the floating bits of vomit and the feeding frenzy it had created. If she couldn't do this dive, she'd either die trying, kill her customers, or both.

Tina popped the regulator in her mouth and as she dropped below the surface, she swung the weight belt around her hips and fastened the buckle. A speedy descent was necessary, especially because the nurses were newly certified beginners. Clearing her mask of water, she then equalized the pressure in her ears. Alternately buckling her BCD jacket and clearing her ears, she looked to the group below her feet. The sight of Jamey provided momentary relief from her nervousness as she approached the ocean floor. So far so good, but then descending had never been her problem. Staying under was the challenge.

Landing on the sandy bottom, she made the hand signal to say she would lead and everyone else would follow. Under normal conditions it felt glorious to be wet and underwater, especially after a long hiatus, but Tina knew what came next. If she couldn't keep her panic under control, she wouldn't be able to pull this off. She gave them the wave for 'let's go,' and the group followed. Stopping at a nearby coral head filled with moray eel hiding spots, she turned to swim backwards, verified everyone was following, and saw Jamey's gaze fixed on her. There was a familiarity in being underwater with Jamey, and as they gathered around the rock, she tried to concentrate on that instead of waiting for Hank's decomposing body to present itself.

Jamey was a good diver. He kicked in a perfect horizontal position, the nurses directly in front of him.

Years ago, Jamey had told her that he was a butt man. "Kristina, it's worth the price of admission to dive behind that cute little behind of yours," he'd said.

No eels lurked in the coral head. She'd have to find something else to make the dive worth the money. Especially before she freaked out and ruined the day. The group continued on, her swimming backwards to watch the group, and once again she tried to concentrate on Jamey.

He had a perfect kick with those extra-large fins. Only divers with extremely strong, muscular legs could pull that much water. She recalled those very legs wrapped around her during their most intimate moments. Once, with Hank, when she'd lain in bed after adequate sex, she'd thought about Jamey's sexual finesse and quickly chastised herself for mentally rating her lovers. It wasn't fair to Hank who'd chosen to stay with her, marry her. Jamey hadn't. His love had come with a price. Desertion. Still, it was hard to forget that James Dunn made love like every second could be his last, getting the absolute most out of each moment, kissing deeply, touching like he was blindly trying to memorize her every curve. Jamey had cherished her body every time they made love like it was his first time.

The memories were a good distraction. Katie had sold the morning activity to these customers with the promise they'd get to the center of the crater at eighty feet and she was determined to make that happen. Divers liked to brag about going deep, even though the most interesting dives were usually in the first forty feet. Feeling her heart rate increase, she concentrated on breathing slowly, calmly, and glanced ahead to deeper water.

First, she'd show them the garden eels at seventy feet, and then she'd see if the eagle ray was hanging around like the day before. If they saw a ray, she might get away with only seventy feet and then would take everyone back to the boat by way of the most direct route.

Doc Chan had told Tina to sing a song when panic threatened— something light and familiar. She began to hum through the regulator even before settling on a specific tune.

The garden eels were below her, waving in the current like a field of giant fingers planted in the sand. If they got too close, the elusive creatures would disappear into their holes. Tina pointed to them and simulated applause to the divers, signifying that this was good stuff. Jamey moved in beside her, almost proprietarily, she thought.

Tina estimated the time it would take to navigate the amount of water between her and the surface at a safe clip. Feeling the enormity of the water's weight on her, her breathing rate increased, and she wondered if anyone could tell she was on the verge of losing it. When the nurses signaled to Jamey that they were okay, Tina remembered that this was their first real dive after certification and knew that she had to pull it together. Deep breaths. She asked everyone to check their pressure gauges to make sure no one was at 1,000 psi, which would indicate a heavy breather and make it time to turn around and head back under the boat. Everyone had plenty of air. Damn it.

She kicked herself horizontal and aimed down, like a missile headed to the center of the volcanic crater, her heart pounding inside her wetsuit, her fists clenched. Jamey moved in beside her, and Tina saw the man with the next most experience fall back to bring up the sweep.

She continued into darker water. The surface would be getting farther away. Suddenly fear engulfed her like a cloud of cyanide gas. Bubbles raced by her ears on their way to the surface and she wanted to go with them, or to jump inside one and let it carry her to safety. The noise of her own heartbeat reminded her that she was seconds away from full-scale panic. It escalated, racing past logical reasoning towards out-of-control craziness. Jamey looked at her and signaled to ask if she was okay. Was it obvious to him, or anyone, that she wasn't?

Without waiting for an answer, he grabbed her arm. She gave the signal for 'okay' and shrugged him off.

They'd reached seventy-five feet. Good enough. She swung the group around to head back to shallow water.

A truck-size boulder was just ahead. She set her sights on that landmark. Thoughts of exploring that rock in happier days calmed her temporarily. She'd bought herself time. The real trick would be to hang onto the tenuous control she clung to. Her fingernails dug into the palms of her hands. Humming frantically, she made a circle of the rock, looking for eels. She hadn't consciously chosen a song, but what came to her was an old classic of Frank Sinatra's. *And through it all, I did something... and did it my way.*

The rock usually housed a small, white-tipped reef shark nicknamed 'Bruce' by the dive community. Tina concentrated on finding him. Seeing any sort of shark in the wild was always a crowd-pleaser, and Bruce usually cooperated. Realizing that her humming was building to a feverish crescendo, Tina abandoned the tune in favor of a happy one. *You are my sunshine...*

Jamey stopped to adjust one of the nurses' jacket buckles while the others followed Tina around to the back side of the rock. Even though Bruce always tucked under the same ledge, Tina was startled when he swerved in front of her.

She motioned that the shark was harmless and glanced up to see the surface forty-five feet away. The customers kept a safe distance from Bruce, and as Tina turned to see their reactions, she was hit with the vision of Hank swimming without scuba gear just behind the group.

He'd arrived, whole and perfect—not the dead or decomposing vision she'd been seeing on dives. His black hair snaked around his head, his red wetsuit vivid in the blueness of the underwater tapestry. This was her Hank, the man she'd married.

You are my sunshine, my only sunshine. Tina resisted the urge to kick herself over to him. He smiled and her heart calmed, her breathing slowed. *Please don't take my sunshine away.*

If anyone turned around, Tina guessed they'd see nothing but water. No apparition of Hank. The customers were facing a different direction, focused on the reef shark circling behind her. And Hank existed only in her imagination.

Slowly letting water into her mask, she cleared it, hoping that visual clarity would bring logic. But no. Hank smiled sweetly, like he'd wait until she was ready.

In the last months, she'd missed his smile; the one he used to convince her to close the shop early and come home with him. Just as she smiled back through her regulator, Jamey and the nurse who'd needed help came around the corner of the rock. Tina held her breath, but neither diver slowed and swam through Hank, oblivious to what she saw. Then Jamey stopped and made a full circle, looking for something where Hank stood.

You are my sunshine; my only sunshine… Tina looked at the customers. By now Bruce was gone, but she noticed a crown of thorns starfish on the sandy bottom, offering a distraction. The venomous and highly dangerous reef killer could not be touched without painful repercussions, and Tina weighed the danger of picking it up with shooting to the surface. Both could be fatal. As the group circled the starfish, Tina hoped she'd do neither. The diving signal for danger was a fist in front and after making the signal, she glanced back to see that Hank was now standing just behind the nurses. She whimpered into her regulator and her hand flew to her heart.

Mimicking her, Hank's broad hand went to his heart. *You'll never know dear, how much I love you.* He blew her a kiss with his free hand and as he turned to go, the left side of his head became exposed to reveal Hank's skull gaping open and brain matter trailing into the water.

Tina screamed into her regulator. Someone grabbed her arm and spun her around. Jamey stared hard into her eyes. She gave him the signal to indicate she was going to the surface, and he took his extra regulator and handed it over.

No, she wasn't out of air. The surface was needed for other reasons. Looking back, she saw that instead of Hank, the space was now occupied by a small school of goatfish, lazily hovering in the water behind the nurses.

Jamey signaled 'danger' and pointed to the goatfish. Had she seen danger?

She shook her head. What she saw was only a hallucination. Goatfish weren't dangerous and beyond that nothing threatened— not anyone else, at least. Tina tried to keep the regulator in her mouth, biting the grip with her teeth.

How could she explain through hand signals that she'd just seen her dead husband's body? She clutched Jamey's arm and stared into his face in an effort to slow her breathing.

Jamey glanced at the group, and then back to Tina.

Oh God, this was bad. If she went for the surface, the emergency would include abandoning customers on a dive. Not anything like Dave needing to abandon the dive. This was more serious, because they were now in deep water, nowhere near the boat. If the divers surfaced safely and found their way back to the boat without her, it would be all over town that the instructor left them to fend for themselves on the ocean floor.

Jamey gripped Tina's hand and locked eyes with her. She felt herself calming. Her heart wasn't pounding on her chest anymore. Waving for the others to follow, she and Jamey took off hand in hand.

When I awoke dear, I was mistaken and I hung my head and I cried. Kicking rhythmically, she concentrated on finding the boat's underside and listening to the bubbles racing past her ears. Kicking and breathing. Still tethered to Jamey, she glanced at the other divers. Bubbles gurgled by her ears.

Finally, the sight of the white hull in the distance gave

her hope that disaster had been avoided and she let go of Jamey's hand. She'd give herself to the count of fifty before heading up. One, two, three...

At forty-five, Tina pointed to the boat and signaled they could stay under the boat in pairs until they reached 500 psi on their gauges. At that point, they'd have only five minutes of air at thirty feet under. Then they had to ascend slowly. This had always been the plan, but now they were on the honor system, without her. Jamey indicated he would stay with the group. *Good. He was better than no one.*

In a more controlled ascent than she thought was possible, she headed up, aiming for the boat's swim step, no faster than her smallest bubbles. Breaking through the surface, she saw that Dave waited, watching for her. She swung her weight belt into his waiting hand.

"Everyone's just under the boat," she said, ripping off her mask and throwing it into the vessel. "Jamey's with them but you'd better watch." She rolled out of her scuba unit, pushed it over to the swim step, and then hoisted herself out, gasping for air.

"See Hank down there?" Dave asked.

"If you can call that Hank," she said.

CHAPTER 6

Something was seriously wrong with Tina, and Jamey didn't need to be a fricking psychic to realize that. She panicked on dives. A fat lot of good it did him to have this heightened intuition if he couldn't help her.

She'd shrugged off ascending early as a cramp and the customers seemed to believe that's why Jamey had to hold her hand. But later, when he told Katie that Tina dove, she was surprised.

"You're kidding? Tina went in the water?"

"Why is that surprising?"

"No reason. She just hasn't been diving lately."

Katie said something about a skin condition, but he knew his niece was lying. Besides, a rash wouldn't spur a panic attack. What he'd seen and felt had been terror. Tina freaked out down there, and whatever set her off hadn't been life-threatening for the others. Just her.

They'd unloaded the gear from the truck to the back room of the shop when Jamey requested ten minutes alone with Tina. She stopped what she was doing and stared straight ahead, presumably considering his request. "I'll find you after I check the tank hookups," she said. He'd been told why Tina monitored Katie when she did the scuba tanks. Four years earlier, Tina had lost track of time, overfilled a tank and when the tank exploded, she was lucky to escape with only the one laceration. She'd ended up with twenty-six stitches on her chin and two surgeries in Honolulu. So much had changed since he'd last seen the Kristina he'd once known and the thought of her life going on without him tugged at his heart.

The rock wall across the street was low enough to sit on. Jamey plunked down on the sun-warmed surface to wait. He watched a young man with a goofy hat, a macaw and a Polaroid camera take pictures of tourists with the parrot on their shoulder for a twenty. While he thought about if the bird liked his job, Tina emerged from the shop, smiled at the guy and sauntered across the street.

Wearing only a pink bikini and flip flops, she looked as comfortable as if she was wearing a business suit on Wall Street. Hell, this getup was her business suit.

"It's sunny!" She held out her arms and offered her face to the sky. "Feels good."

"Finally," he said.

"You picked the wrong time to come to Maui, with this storm blowing through." She sat beside him on the wall, four feet away, and closed her eyes, her face tilted towards the sky. "Are you just here for the week?"

He swung his sunglasses on top of his head. "Probably two or three weeks, but it depends."

"On the weather?"

"Not really."

"Should improve now and get back to normal." She paused.

"We've been reduced to talking about the weather."

The heaviness between them was gone for the moment, and he chuckled. "It's a safe subject for you and me." She smiled, still not making eye contact.

"You finally smiled." His heart felt light.

"I do that a lot." She sounded defensive.

"I haven't seen it." He paused, thinking how to proceed. "Is it hard having me around? I can dive with another place if I remind you of what a shit I was."

"No, it's fine. Don't worry."

Was this a good segue? "I enjoyed this morning's dive..." He felt her gates close. He almost heard the click.

"Those garden eels were something else."

"Glad you came along."

He rubbed his chin, took a different tactic. "I wanted to talk about how I left things ten years ago." Jamey stared at her profile, hoping she'd turn to look at him, open the gate.

She watched an approaching truck turn onto the street. He wanted to smooth things over even if he couldn't reveal everything. "I wasn't free, as it turned out, to take on…you. To offer anything to you, in those days." He swallowed the more truthful words. "I got home and realized my future involved Carrie." Now he was stumbling all over himself and she hadn't said a word. "I didn't know when I met you that anything was still left in that relationship..." A gathering of noisy myna birds screeched from the trees behind them.

Tina cleared her throat and locked eyes with him. "I get it." She stood. "I should see if Katie needs help."

He knew she didn't trust him. "Wait." How could he get her to talk to him without trust?

She stopped. "It's okay, Jamey. It's in the past now. We're done. But I did want to tell you that it helped to have you on the dive today." She folded her arms across her chest.

Jamey knew what was coming.

"I'm sure you heard that my husband is either missing or dead. It's been tough. Time heals everything, they say." Tina looked like if she'd had a hat on, she would've pulled it low to hide the pain in her eyes. Instead, she looked over his shoulder at the plumeria trees on the Baldwin museum property. "Did you ever get married?" Her voice was high, strained.

What answer wouldn't hurt her feelings? He shrugged. "I'm divorced."

Tina flinched but there was nothing he could do about that. "Kids?" She looked as though she was more interested in the stone building behind him, but he knew better.

"Twins." He tried to hold back the smile that always accompanied thoughts of his children, thinking it might look like bragging. "Both girls."

Tina nodded. "Did you know I was a twin?"

He was surprised to hear it. "No." At one point in their relationship she'd told him all about her domineering parents in Seattle, and how living in Hawaii was just far enough from them. Her father was a corporate attorney, very hard on her, never satisfied with anything she accomplished. Extremely disappointed to see his daughter waste her MBA in Hawaii, the father was a pain in the ass. The mother was rigid, from what he remembered.

"My twin brother died when I was four. Fell into our swimming pool," she said in a far-off voice, as though she was remembering. "I still feel like a twin, even though he's gone." She looked back at the dive shop and cleared her throat. "I should go." She started across the street, and then turned around. "It's nice diving with you again."

"Yeah. You too." How did they start with the weather and end with her feelings of abandonment from a dead twin, with only a few sentences in between? A strange feeling invaded his gut from the bits and pieces of conversation they'd had. Tina was hiding something but also reaching out, like she was a prisoner in her own mind, unable to find an escape route. He'd stay close for the next few days to see if an opportunity arose to finish what she started to tell him.

$* * *$

Tina entered the dive shop, her face hot. Bile rose in her throat at the thought that Jamey and his wife had twins.

This piece of information was heartbreaking. After all she'd gone through to replace James, he'd gone off and not only married, but had babies. Two of them. At once. The realization made him seem selfish. Even if she wasn't resentful of anyone with a baby these days, this was more than that. He'd gone home and made twins while she'd tried to pick up the pieces of her broken heart for years afterwards. A heart he broke. Selfish prick. Her feelings of wanting a baby so much it hurt, usually lived farther in her sub-conscious. Damn.

Staring at the octopus in the aquarium, she locked eyes with the creature. "You're still here?" Dave needed to let him go. The octopus had to be miserable in captivity. What if he was a she, pregnant and worrying about giving birth in captivity?

Deep breath. She swallowed and willed herself to breath slowly. Jamey had two babies. She had none. But, every person's baby was not the one she could have had. Maybe she'd waited too long for motherhood. Her plan to build the business first seemed perfect when she still thought she had years ahead with Hank. But Hank was gone. She had been left childless. If he was alive somewhere living an alternate life, she would hate him forever for doing this to her.

He'd gone out one morning to surf, either got himself killed or left for God knows what reason, and now here she was, expected to continue on. When would she accept there might never be a body to prove that Hank had loved her and simply died?

Glancing out the window, she saw Jamey still sitting on the wall, staring at the chaos of Front Street. Something still hurt in her heart when she saw him. Maybe he'd go home soon.

Katie walked by with an armload of rental gear. "Uncle Jamey said you did one of the dives this morning. I didn't know your rash was better."

"He's a big help on the dives." With Katie's penchant

for conversation, Tina wanted to keep her diving problems under wraps. Maybe she should have told Jamey to keep the disaster to himself. She doubted he'd have told Katie about their previous relationship. "Your uncle's a good guy."

Katie nodded. "Isn't he? My family just loves him to bits. Everyone loves him, especially because of all he does for his country and everything. He's one of the nicest guys I know. Everyone says so. Especially anyone who knows about…" Katie looked horrified. "About how great he is!" Her voice reached an unnatural high at the end of the sentence, confirming that she was the worst liar ever.

"Knows about what?" Tina stared hard at her.

"Oh, serving in the forces and stuff."

Tina continued to stare. "What stuff?"

"Nothing, really. He's on a special team or something. I don't know because it's secret, but once I overheard something. It's not like a SWAT team or anything. Besides, I've said too much according to my new goal and I'm not supposed to talk about it." It rolled off her tongue so easily, poor kid.

"He's on leave from Afghanistan, right?"

Katie nodded.

"And before that, he worked as a police officer?"

Katie nodded again, biting down on her sealed lips.

"It must be difficult with twin girls." Tina followed Katie's line of vision out the front window to a group of ladies gathered around Jamey, who looked like he was giving directions.

"The twins, I can talk about." Katie and Tina tackled a pile of snorkel gear and fit fins into cubbyholes. "Seems like they were just born. And now they're ten. Jade and Jasmine." Katie sat on the floor and paired the lefts with rights. "They're sweet. I love 'em to bits. I personally do not like his ex-wife, Carrie, because she left him. Even though Dad said Uncle Jamey was better off without…a wife, it hurt him to lose his girls. But now everything seems to be fine, and Jamey is still really good friends with Carrie. It's weird."

Tina unloaded a bunch of masks onto the counter. "They're ten, huh?"

"What? Oh yeah, the twins. He's good friends with her new husband, too. Uncle Jamey goes over there for dinner when he's home. They all go to the fair together; they invite him for holiday dinners. It's nice for him. Carrie and her new husband have a son, Wyatt, and they just had a baby, who they named Mango, which I think is a strange name for a baby, but I really don't care because Jade and Jasmine are my cousins really, not Wyatt or Mango." She looked over at Tina. "I'm nice to Wyatt and of course Mango because she's just a baby but I know the twins better. I got to see Mango before I moved here, and she's got Carrie's auburn hair, just like a little mango. But the twins look like Jamey. Exactly. It's so weird."

Tina stopped in her tracks. If Jamey's children were ten years old, how did his wife's pregnancy with the twins figure into the relationship she'd had with Jamey ten years ago? She wandered into the back room, calculating numbers and sat at her desk.

She'd met Jamey in September of 1992—nine years and seven months ago. Was Jamey married at that time with newborn twins? A wave of nausea swept through her and she sank to a chair. Was that the reason James Dunn dumped her?

All these years she'd treasured her memories with James. The romance itself had been thrilling, like the first time at Disneyland. But his departure was heartbreaking. Confused about what happened to make him dump her, she went through a strange time that began one night when she cut off her long hair. Shortly after that, she asked people to shorten her name to Tina. Then she planned the dive shop and poured herself into making it happen, even though it would take years. James was later replaced by an Australian dive instructor who was a jerk, and then numerous tourist flings. Three years later she was finally able to trust again and had her first long-term relationship with a restaurant owner from Los Angeles. The distance thing was too much after a year of going back and forth, and they agreed to call it quits.

Had Jamey been married with twins when he was on Maui with her? A sob burst from her throat and Obi put his head in her lap. He knew the routine. This time though, she wouldn't cry. Not over James Dunn.

This day was getting worse by the hour, and Tina wasn't sure she could wait for her two o'clock appointment with Doc Chan to feel better. Blowing her nose into a tissue, she reached for the phone and a hand's weight rested on her shoulder. "I'm okay, Katie." The hand remained, solid, heavy. It gently squeezed, exactly like Hank. A chill shot through her body. "Hank?" she whispered and spun her chair around.

The shock of seeing Jamey's face confused her. *Of course it wasn't Hank*.

"It's me." He knelt in front of her, his head now level with hers, his worried eyes looking into her teary ones. His hand moved to her knee, the gesture familiar.

"I'm so sorry, Tina." Had he mistaken her crying for grief over Hank?

She shrugged off his hand and stood. "Thanks." She wouldn't correct his assumption.

He persisted. "Diving today… You saw something, didn't you?" When she didn't reply, he continued. "You're having anxiety attacks, hallucinations?"

"I have a shrink, thanks."

"What does your shrink say about your dreams?"

"How do you know about my dreams?" Tina spun around to search his face.

"You told me, remember? And you cry at your desk in the middle of the day." Jamey's forehead was creased, his face looked pained. His questions felt invasive coming from a man who was fucking her when he had a wife and newborn twins back home.

She grabbed the logo T-shirt from the back of her chair and pulled it over her head to cover her bikini-clad body. It fell to her knees. "As a matter of fact, I'm going to be late for my shrink appointment." She pretended to check her watch as she headed out the back door, Obi following. "Katie. I'll be back in an hour," she called, leaving Jamey standing next to her cluttered desk.

CHAPTER 7

James Dunn had been Tina's first romantic fling with a dive student. For a year, she'd watched male dive instructors charm tourists into bed. As one of the only women scuba instructors on Maui, Tina was above that kind of behavior. Not only that, but she'd graduated with honors from Stanford, for crying out loud. Her fling was with the island of Maui itself, seeing that her parents vehemently objected to anyone wasting this caliber of education in the islands.

Then James walked into Lahaina Scuba one sunny morning and asked if anyone could certify him as a deep diver. Tina was captaining the boat the next day and planning a deep dive on the backside of Molokini Crater. She agreed to take the job. An extra hundred would come in handy for rent that month.

Almost immediately, her handsome new student was flirting with her. "You are my fantasy woman, Kristina." They unloaded gear from the truck after the morning boat dive. "You can lift two tanks at once, drive a truck…I bet you even drink beer," he'd joked.

She ignored his attempt to flirt, even though she didn't have a boyfriend. "Stop jabbering and do your share of the work." After another hour of this, Tina's resolve started disintegrating. James, the Seattle cop, was funny. No doubt about it. He wasn't her type physically, but definitely not hard to look at, even if he was too handsome for her. And seeing they were spending a few days together, she allowed herself to look.

They went to the Pioneer Inn for a beer and to review the lesson on the dive tables. The old hotel was one of

Maui's historic sites situated at Lahaina's picturesque harbor. It had seen many a sailor and whaler in its day. At late-afternoon the bar was packed and buzzing, but James found a little table in the hall and pulled it into the room, and then got two chairs and told her to sit while he ordered Coronas at the bar. She admired his resourcefulness.

When her lesson on decompression sickness ended, they ordered another beer and stayed to listen to the band that had set up for the sunset crowd. They danced, had another drink, and then Tina told him the bad news. He wasn't her type. She tried to look convincing.

"I like the surfer boy look. You're too big and too…too…"

"Manly?" He grinned.

She rolled her eyes. "I don't know. I just know you're not my type. You look like someone my parents would put in front of me."

He took her hands in his and stared sweetly into her face. "Please reconsider."

"You're too…perfect."

He laughed like that was the most absurd thing he'd ever heard and showed her a scar under his hairline from a baseball injury when he was fourteen. Then, jokingly, he told her he had six toes on his left foot. "I'm a freak," he whispered in her ear.

She left him at his parked rental car on Front Street that night, but on the second day of lessons, her feelings changed when James chivalrously offered to help with her heavy dive gear.

"I already feel emasculated and unwanted after your rejection last night. At least let me lift something for you with my big manly muscles."

"I can do it, thank you." For years, she'd done the lifting herself.

"Humor me, okay? My dad taught me to do this kind of thing, and besides…you're what? All of ninety pounds?"

"One hundred and fifteen." She reached for the gear, but before her hands made contact, he lifted her up into his arms.

"One fourteen and a quarter, I'd say." He looked at her reproachfully. "Did someone forget to have a good breakfast?"

She'd laughed. "Okay, Hulk, put me down." There was a pause as they stared at each other. At that precise moment, her defense against his charm became a wisp of smoke carried away by the Hawaiian trade winds.

James must have felt his opening too, because after he set her on the ground he began to woo her like his life depended on it. And truthfully, after the laid-back style of Maui guys, and the business-minded tightasses of college, Tina was intrigued. Older by seven years, James was an adult, and there was something wildly exciting about that fact. Especially after dating guys who called you 'dude.'

When the training dive ended, they found themselves in the truck kissing, and then in the hotel elevator groping, and finally in James' hotel room, messing up the perfectly made Hyatt bed. Eventually, they woke up at dawn with limbs wrapped around each other, Tina's long hair tousled, her lips overworked and sore.

The next morning, she dragged him out of the bed early and took him on a black coral dive in the channel between Maui and Lanai. Teaching him how to do a decompression stop, they waited out their time fifteen feet below the surface, finger tips teasing each other's bodies, grins through the regulator mouthpiece.

Back on board, James took her in his arms and kissed her long and deep. When they came up for air, he pecked the tip of her nose. "I'm enjoying this romance diving class. The lessons are invaluable."

"It's a long course," Tina said. "I may not be able to certify you for months."

With no boats in sight, they finished what they'd started right there under the Maui sky.

All book lessons after that were conducted at the Hyatt pool on lounge chairs, interrupted by kisses under the pool's waterfall and groping in the darkness of the pool's grotto. Kissing became "tongue diving certification," and James joked that he'd secured his ticket in night groping and instructor ravaging.

Two weeks turned to three, and although Kristina was teaching other classes in the mornings, James monopolized the rest of her schedule. From deep diving, they moved to the night diving course. For five straight nights they dove off Maui beaches with underwater flashlights, after which they'd find themselves back in the Hyatt bed. With two more weeks of accumulated vacation time, James' father's condo became available and they moved from the Hyatt to The Ridge.

Talk involved his returning to Maui in a few months, maybe even to live there forever. He told her that being a Maui cop looked extremely appealing.

But on the morning of his flight back to Seattle, Tina woke to find him troubled and distracted, and she couldn't seem to penetrate the wall he'd built around himself. Something was wrong and she was too young to know enough to ask him about it. Soon her fears became a reality.

After putting him on the plane, she worried on the drive back to the Lahaina side. The next day, he finally picked up his phone. "I'm really sorry, but things changed when I got home. I got back with my girlfriend." He sounded only mildly disappointed, while her heart pooled at her feet. "I feel badly that this happened." She was dumbfounded, unable to respond.

"You need to forget me." This man did not sound like her James at all.

The embarrassment of being told to forget him threw her into a back paddle, like what they had was disposable. How the hell had James turned from someone she could love forever to a snake in one flight?

"I will do just that and be glad I did, I'm sure. It's just that two days ago you planned on coming back. I'm surprised I was such a rotten judge of character."

When he didn't reply, she continued. "You know what?" Tina tried to salvage her dignity. "You're absolutely right. It was just a fling with a tourist. You aren't my type."

She hung up, only to cry into her hands.

***

Pulling in to her parking spot behind the dive shop, Tina remembered what Dr. Chan told her in the morning's appointment. "You're doing well, Tina. Next time we need to talk about Noble and what to do about him."

But all the good work done at Tina's morning appointment with Dr. Chan was undone by a phone call two hours later.

"This is Officer Sakamoto with Maui Police Department. A large piece of surfboard was recovered up north today and we'd like you to come by to take a look." Months earlier, they'd found one small chunk of a surfboard, but it wasn't big enough to be identifiable.

She was in the middle of teaching the classroom portion of a night diving course in the shop's back room and when she hung up the phone, the students stared at her. "Read chapter four, do the questions at the end and I'll be right back." She grabbed her backpack and whistled for Obi to follow.

Dave and Jamey were filling tanks for the night dive in the back alley, laughing about something.

"I need you to take over the class, Dave."

"Sure. What's up?"

"I have to run to the police station. A piece of surfboard turned up." She opened her truck door and let Obi jump in.

"I'll go with you." Jamey rounded the front and hopped into the passenger seat.

Backing out of her parking spot, she turned just in time to see a bicycle flying down the back lane directly in her path. She slammed on the brakes barely in time to avoid hitting it.

Mr. Takeshimi, who stood on the front stoop of his house with a real estate agent, stared at her, obviously distracted by the cursing bicyclist. Fall seven, up eight. What if you break your legs on impact?

"How 'bout I drive?" Jamey got out to switch places and she willingly moved to the passenger seat.

They took off for the police station, down Dickenson Street. "My husband is presumed dead from a surfing accident. There is no body." Saying it out loud, she sounded more detached than she felt.

"If it's his board, will it be good news?"

"I don't know." Her voice was tiny, distant. Dead.

Tina's flip flops clapped noisily at her heels as she walked up to the Maui Police Station's front counter. Jamey shadowed her like a bodyguard silently waiting to be called to action. She knew, as she laid her arms on the cold Formica counter, that everyone in the office was looking at her. Or at least trying not to. Just like the day she came in to identify the first piece. The pity in their eyes that day had been more than she could bear. Today was a bit easier. Was she becoming used to other people's pity?

"Tina Greene, for Officer Sakamoto?" Everything seemed to be a question these days. Jamey moved in beside her, their shoulders touching. He'd been a cop and his presence was reassuring. She resisted the urge to grab his hand only because she knew everyone would judge. It was such a small island for gossip.

What was left of Hank's surfboard was propped against the far wall of the back room, by an exit door. Her hand flew to cover her mouth. The questioning look in the policeman's eyes eventually spurred Tina to nod in recognition. The board had a distinctive shark graphic and an emblem on the tip. It was as familiar as Hank's wallet. More so, in some ways. He'd loved to surf. He might have been happy at the thought of dying while surfing.

Jamey put his arm around her shoulders and pulled her in to him.

"Where did it come in?" Her voice sounded forced.

"Someone found it on the rocks, the other side of Kahakuloa." The policeman looked uncomfortable. "You can have it if you want, or…" Sakamoto had been one of the nicest on the case, very patient and understanding.

She nodded, unsure of whether she'd treasure it as one of the last objects to exist alongside Hank, or drive straight to a garbage bin big enough to contain the piece of surfboard that had let him down in his time of greatest need.

Jamey crossed the room and tucked the broken board under his arm.

On the walk to her truck, she tried to figure out how Hank might have faked his death by throwing his surfboard off a cliff, leaving his wallet intentionally, and remaining alive somewhere in the world. Oh shit. He was dead, wasn't he? How much longer could this undying hope continue? Was it optimism or blind hope? What if they never found a body? Could she live a normal life if she couldn't accept his death?

When Jamey pulled onto Dickenson Street, Dave and his friend, Allan, an electrician, stood outside the shop's front door. The neon sign that read 'Tina and Hank's Dive Shop' lay at their feet, and the old sign hung in its place, the one that said 'Tina's Dive Shop.'

"What's going on here?" she asked.

Like someone caught cheating on a test, Dave looked sheepish. "Pepper asked us to do this."

Jamey jumped out and surveyed their work. "Need help?"

Tina had recently told Pepper she should change the

sign, but she didn't foresee that her friend would actually arrange it. Or the emotions it would stir in her. This was the reminder that she'd gone from a neon life to one of simple painted wood. One name, old sign. She jumped into the driver's seat. Getting out of town seemed necessary.

At the Pizza Hut stoplight, she looked in the rear-view mirror and saw the board. Panic was rising in her and she might have to pull over. Hank hadn't had air as he floated face down in the surf, unconscious. She might never know exactly how he died, how long it took, or if he suffered.

She drove north thinking if she couldn't get her anxiety under control she'd find Noble. He wouldn't be at the Hyatt just yet, too early for Drums of the Pacific. She'd seen all the luau shows over the years, and Drums was her favorite. Not just because Noble's dancing was a pleasure to watch, but the costumes, the lighting, the fire juggler and the sexual connotations of the Tahitian dancing made it more primal, more feverish than the others. Noble's dancing made the show what it was. He looked close to Hawaiian with his black hair and dark skin, but Tina knew he was part Mexican.

She knew this because Hank had told her. Hank had been raised by a single mother who died when he was seventeen, and being Mexican had always been a source of pride for him. "Noble says he's Hawaiian because of the show," Hank had explained. When Tina questioned this, Hank defended him. "When we lived in Vegas, he danced in an Elvis show and he isn't Elvis."

Pulling into her driveway, she saw Noble standing on the deck. Taking the outside stairs in several bounds, he met her as she got out of the truck and wrapped his arms around her. "You okay?" Noble smelled like Hank, like home. "The board?" he asked.

He'd seen it. "They found it past Kahakuloa." Tears wouldn't come. They stayed that way for over a minute, until Noble broke the silence. "The police didn't want to keep it or anything?"

"No."

"What did they say about the investigation?"

"Nothing." Her cheek rested against his warm chest.

Noble pulled back. "I have to leave for work soon. Are you going to be alright?"

She nodded, smiled at her dear friend and climbed the stairs to her house, leaving the surf board to deal with later.

Inside she grabbed a beer from the fridge and planted herself at the lanai railing, watching people on their twilight walks down the street. Everyone had somewhere to go, someone to share memories with. Two men bicycled side by side, talking. Four teens ran by with several dogs of various sizes on leashes and two women in fashionable running clothes power-walked past her driveway.

"That's where Tina lives," one of them said. "You know, the one whose husband disappeared surfing last year."

She looked at Obi, whose gaze suggested complete devotion. "Did Hank disappear or did he die?" she asked the dog. "And if he left me, then why?"

Obi sat down on the warm deck floor and cocked his head.

"Do you think Hank might have bumped his head, gotten amnesia and is living up north with some hermits?" She heaved a sigh to think of it. "Or did he leave me for another woman?" Obi barked.

"That would never happen. Let's get you some dinner."

She overfilled Obi's dish and kibble spilled to the floor. Obi moved in to clean up the bits of food. For two years, the brindled dog had followed Tina everywhere—from room to room, in and out of the truck, the house, the dive shop. When she and Hank first found him scavenging around Launiopoko Park, flea and tick bites freckled every inch of his skinny body. That day she'd told her brand new husband, "If we can save this dog's life, we'll make great parents." They'd grinned at each other like they'd have plenty of time to fulfill that dream.

She leaned against the kitchen counter and watched Obi eat carefully, like he'd been a dog that never had to scrounge at the side of the road. The memory of Hank's surfboard in her truck made her think of Noble and how he hadn't surfed since Hank's death. Would he ever get back to his favorite sport? The 'what-ifs' after Hank's disappearance had driven Noble crazy, poor guy. He'd once confessed that guilt over not being with Hank when he died was eating him up inside.

"You need to get help," she'd said.

When Noble mentioned leaving Maui, maybe only for a few months to get his head straight, she'd begged him to stay. "We can do this together," she'd said.

"I'm not sure." Noble wasn't sleeping, not eating and had called in too sick to dance for more nights than they would allow. His job was at stake early on. Then everything seemed fine again, thank god.

Tina went back out on deck and contemplated what to do with the reminder of Hank's disappearance. Now that Noble's guilt seemed to be dissipating, she couldn't resurrect it or feed it by keeping the board in full view. She pulled it out of the truck's back end and slid the board behind some beach chairs in the garage.

Hours later, she slipped into a sleep shirt and was sitting on the bed when Noble walked through the patio door to the bedroom. "Ti?" He was still in his scanty costume from the show, a haku lei of ti leaves, a sarong hugging his hips.

"I had this feeling you needed me."

His concern touched Tina's heart. "I'm better. I'm a six and rising," she lied.

He sat on the side of the bed and removed the lei around his head, tossing it to the dresser. "I've been thinking about you all night. Wondering how you are." His gaze lingered where the flimsy cotton lay against her small breasts. "Want some company?"

"Okay." She did want a friend, another body to share her first night of knowing the board had been recovered.

"Move over, Obi." Noble said, sliding in beside her.

He hadn't had a girlfriend since Hank's death. She'd probably ruined his chances by needing him so much. Noble stretched the length of the bed on his side facing her. The familiarity of having him close was different tonight. For one thing, he was under the covers, something he rarely did.

Obi growled at her bed partner. "Obi, stop," Tina said. Had the dog noticed Noble was under the covers? "I feel weird about them finding the board."

"I do too." He reached over and laid a hand on her arm.

Cool air breezed past her and she pulled the covers around her shoulders. Had she made the right decision to ask him to stay, after months of sleeping without him? "I'm sorry I've needed you so much this year, Noble."

He moved his hand under the blanket. "S'alright, Ti. I needed you too." He was so close that his warm breath moved strands of her hair. He shifted closer. The fabric of his sarong rubbed against her hip.

"You're still wearing your costume."

"I don't wear much underneath this."

She'd never noticed what he wore to bed before because she was always such a wreck, drugged on sleeping pills, crying, and he was on top of the covers, probably in a T-shirt and shorts. Tonight they weren't waiting for Tina's sleeping pill to take effect. She was suddenly disturbed at such physical closeness. Her face became hot, and her heart raced. She wanted to ask him to leave. But after all he'd done, she didn't want to sound ungracious.

"Noble…I…" She shifted away from him. Something more than compassion flashed in his eyes. His intent was like a Polaroid picture developing in front of her. A look of sexuality had crept into his face and when his eyes drifted to her mouth, Tina found herself swallowing hard. "I think

I misunderstood. Did you just want to talk?"

Noble stared at her. Still, the look.

"I think it would be a mistake, Noble. Wrong."

He stroked her cheek lovingly. "I think it's the only thing that's right, Ti. But I don't want to hurry you." Noble was Hank's best friend. She didn't think of him sexually. What if it was the only thing that *was* right? What if her salvation was right in front of her and she'd been too distracted to see it? Tina freed her hand from under the covers and touched Noble's lips. As her finger trailed the outline of his mouth, Noble closed his eyes and took a deep breath.

"We're not hurting anybody," she said, needing reassurance.

"No one." Noble leaned in and his soft lips were on hers. Just a feathery touch. "No, we're not hurting anybody," he said against her mouth. "Maybe even helping ourselves."

She pulled back, took a deep breath and looked into his eyes. Noble. Her Noble. His warmth was familiar. His hand cupped one side of her face. This time Tina allowed the kiss, once, twice, then deeper.

"Is this okay?" His lips brushed lightly against hers.

"Hmmm." It was.

He kissed her cheeks, nuzzled her neck and then back to her lips. Gently, he locked his upper leg over her hips and pressed himself into her, making it clear what he wanted.

Feeling his readiness, she was momentarily startled and pulled back. But Noble kissed her again, until she gave in to the need that had taken over her good sense.

It was such a welcome relief, this letting go that she surrendered completely. They kissed passionately. He tasted salty. When Obi jumped off the bed barking, the momentum of the moment ground to a halt. Good sense now had time to present its case.

What the hell was she doing?

This would change everything. There would be no going back. This was Noble, for God's sake. Not Hank. Tina sat up in bed, pulling her oversized T-shirt down over her body. "No, wait, oh God…" She ran her hand through her hair. The dog across the street barked and Obi went to the window to part the curtain with his nose. Tina held her breath, waiting for something. "I can't, Noble. I'm sorry."

If disappointment set in, his words denied it. "I understand. It's alright, Ti."

Moments passed. The feeling was like cheating on a test.

Noble kissed her forehead and smiled at her lovingly. "I took advantage. I'm sorry."

"Oh, my God, Noble. We almost ruined everything." Tina fell back on the pillows, her hand going to cover her mouth. She waited for him to agree.

"I'll leave if you're all right now." Grabbing his sarong from under the sheets, Noble slipped out of bed and swung the fabric around his hips.

She looked away but not before seeing his erection. "Aside from embarrassment about almost, almost... I'm alright." She gulped.

Noble nodded and left, pulling the door closed behind him. Tina jumped off the bed and locked the door. Not against Noble, she told herself, but in case she dreamed. The curtains rustled with the evening's breeze and an icy shiver domino'ed down her torso all the way to her toes. What the hell just happened, and why had she let it get that far with Noble?

CHAPTER 8

Jamey parked himself in Pops' deck lounger with an ice-cold beer and stared out at the lavender pink sunset. Soon the beach would be dark below. It was his favorite time of day to walk along the surf line. Good thinking time. And he had a lot to think about. For one thing, he needed to decide what he would do if he couldn't dream jump anymore. Back in Kandahar they'd asked him to lay off any jumping while on leave, but that was a ridiculous suggestion. He needed to know if he was done with it forever and the only way to know that was to jump.

The day he left for Ramstein in Germany, his superior officer, Sergeant Milton, had taken him to the plane. "Take a break, Private." He put the jeep in park. "And no dream jumping."

Jamey had nodded, not sure if he'd comply, and grabbed his duffel out of the back. He boarded the plane with the two burly bodyguards who would accompany him from Afghanistan to Ramstein Air Base in Germany, then on to America. Once on U.S. soil, the guards would return to Sixth Force in Afghanistan.

Known only as 'Freud' in Sixth Force, Jamey took every precaution imaginable to ensure he wasn't followed or recognized after he left Kandahar. His long, shaggy hair came off before the plane ride to Germany, along with all facial hair and the fake glasses. Luckily he'd never gotten a tattoo and had no easily identifiable marks on his body. Not that anyone else could see. Several days and many flights later, under several names and passports, he finally made it home to Seattle.

The last jump for the army had almost done him in.

He almost bit the dust. He'd been revived and rushed to the base hospital when his heart stopped. That was bad enough but, not only had he been seen by the dreamer, but the army killed the man because of the slip. Freud vehemently protested the extermination of the enemy soldier. "You're nothing but murderers!" he'd shouted at his superior officers. "You didn't need to do that. He was just a kid. You're fucking, God-damned killers."

"Private, we understand you're upset, but he had an allergic reaction to our drugs, something we couldn't have predicted. He woke up early, saw you, and our protocol in a situation like this..."

"There is no protocol for something like this. I'm the only fucking dream jumper, and if I'm willing to risk it..." After that, he'd spent hours in the psychiatrist's chair, trying to justify what happened, figuring out his part in the thing. Trouble was, the dreamer died and all contact with him was lost—unless you counted Jamey's recurring dream that he sliced the young man's head off with a sword. That doozy came every night for a month, and then tapered off to every so often.

Sixth Force gave Freud three months' leave, knowing he might be finished jumping forever. All attempts to jump before he left Afghanistan had been met with failure, as though he'd never be able to slip into dreams again.

"Get your skills back," they'd said, like it was as easy as that. Jamey didn't know if he was done forever but was glad for some time off, time away from the desert of Afghanistan, the constant worry of being shot or bombed, the army food, the boredom. He hadn't been home in almost ten months, and his arms were aching to hold his daughters.

With the physical transformation complete, Jamey took commercial flights from Atlanta to Chicago to Dallas, where he ran to make a flight to Mexico City. Then he headed north to Houston, and then Seattle. He'd changed disguises and passports five times, holed up in an airport hotel, snuck out, and when he was sure he wasn't being followed, he called Pops and asked him to meet him at SeaTac Airport. When they connected on the curb outside baggage claim he thought his father would never let go. "I missed you, Jamey." The tears in his father's eyes had him feeling guilty for how he spent his life these days.

"Let's go home, Pops."

They jumped in the truck and drove north to Seattle and then east to his hometown of Carnation. Forty minutes later, Jamey was comparing the mountains beyond Kandahar with the Cascade Mountain Range. They crossed the Tolt River and on to Pops' house. This was farming country—the epitome of small-town rural life. Jamey couldn't wait to sleep in his old bed again.

Pops' place, a ramshackle two-story structure, sat at the end of a long lane overlooking the river. As they bumped down the driveway, Jamey laughed. "Some things never change."

Pops chuckled with him. "Saved these potholes for you to plug in the next few weeks. Didn't want you getting all squishy on leave."

After dropping his duffel at the front door, Jamey glanced at photos on the hall table—he and his brothers fishing the Tolt; helping Uncle Don bring in the hay one year; Jamey and his baby sister, Jenny, at the father/daughter Valentine's dance the year Pops had the flu. Far enough from the big city, Carnation was a perfect place to spread teenage wings—especially if you were a little wild, with a big wingspan. And, didn't have a mother.

One night the twins stayed overnight with him at their grandfather's house. Jamey sat on the side of Jade's bed, scratching her little nine-year-old back. She fought to stay awake, talking in slurrish half-sentences to her dad. When her dream journey began, he considered jumping in. Over the years he'd shared countless dreams with his daughters. If he was going to try jumping again, an innocent child wouldn't hold much risk. Hoping to avoid the life altering headache that had left him hooked up to drug drips and machinery, this seemed like a perfect opportunity. He matched Jade's breathing, took her little hand in his and attempted to slide into another dimension.

Nothing happened. He tried again with no result. Frustrated, he moved to Jasmine's bed and waited until she fell into a dream. Still, the ability eluded him. Knowing he might never again be able to share a dream with someone, the emptiness of it made him feel both relieved and wistful and he went downstairs to join Pops for a game of euchre.

After two weeks of playing Barbie dolls, kicking soccer balls, and hanging around both Carrie's and Pops' houses, Maui called to him. When Pop's condo had a cancellation, it seemed like a sign and Jamey bought a ticket.

"I'll be home for your birthday in a few weeks," he promised the girls. "And I'll bring you a special surprise."

"A dolphin!" Jade said.

"Or a whale!" Jasmine giggled.

"How about a shark?" he teased, tickling them.

Turned out Maui was quiet enough for his thoughts to drive him ten types of crazy. The notion that he messed with lives by dream jumping into another dimension haunted him. The dream of him cutting off the young soldier's head resurfaced. Among others. Once again, jumping dreams played with his sense of decency and left him waking in a cold sweat. He tried to stop over-thinking. He was on Maui to exhale, not hold his breath.

A week after he arrived on the island, he awoke disturbed by a different type of dream. This one was lovely and emotionally draining in a very good way. He and Tina were slow dancing on a white dance floor that extended infinitely. The depth of feelings he had for her was immeasurable, almost intolerable, like nothing Jamey had ever experienced in real life.

Then they were diving, about seventy feet down. His

emotions were foreign, like they didn't belong to him. Whoever they belonged to had a big secret. Whose mind was this? It was not completely unheard of for a psychic to feel someone's emotions, but it was still unnerving with this degree of intensity. If Tina knew the secret this man harbored, she'd be heartbroken. His first thought was Hank. A feeling of validation settled over him, proving he was correct. Tina's presence in Hank's life was the best thing that ever happened to him. His wall of resolve had to hold up to protect the woman he loved. Guarding the secret was the most important thing in Hank's life, even if it meant betraying Tina. But what the hell was Hank's secret?

Kicking through schools of fish, they continued through the coral gardens. Tina smiled at him and Jamey smiled back. When he looked down, he didn't recognize his hand—elegant fingers, a wedding ring, and differently shaped nails. Tina was his savior, rescuing his soul from the black pit where he'd been headed. Where Hank had been headed. Maybe now his life would be salvageable, have meaning beyond his years of regrets. He didn't deserve her.

But still, he vowed to spend the rest of his life making up for that fact. The rest of Hank's life, not Jamey's.

Tina turned and waved at him, beckoning him around a corner with a curve of her finger. In two kicks, she disappeared from sight. Jamey rounded the edge of the rock and saw her standing on the sandy ocean floor. But instead of the expected smile, she was horrified to see him. He stopped and descended to a standing position but didn't reach the bottom when he should have. Jamey looked down to see that he had no feet, no legs. What the fuck? Was he invisible?

Tina backed up against the rock. He tried to reach down but found he had no arms. He bumped on the sandy bottom and, twisting his torso, was able to ascend a few feet. Tina's eyes were big and frightened. A quick look assured Jamey there was no blood in the water, but when he caught a shadow of something behind him, he turned to see a tail. A large gray shark tail twisted with him.

He'd become a shark.

When he glanced back, Tina was gone. Not above him, not ahead of him. Jamey did a full circle and saw nothing but his own tail.

He called out to her, but when he opened his eyes, he was in the queen-size bed in Pops' condo with only the final trace of a moan in the room. Reaching for his watch on the bedside table, he noticed it was just after three a.m., still worth trying to get back to sleep. He lay back with his hands behind his head, thankful to have hands. In the dream he'd had such depth of feeling for Tina. Shit. Thinking about her led to memories, which led to a hard-on. His feelings for Tina would have to stay buried if he was going to spend the morning with her on a small dive boat.

Jamey lay in bed listening to the surf break on the rocks below at Ironwood Beach and wondered if the dream had an actual connection to Hank's psyche, or if he'd simply made up the dream.

At seven a.m., Lahaina Town was just waking up. The streets were still clear of traffic, and as Jamey pulled into a prime parking spot on Dickenson Street, he felt lucky to be alive; especially after all he'd been through in Afghanistan. This life was a gift, and he was going to enjoy the day like no other, to love life as deeply as Hank had loved Tina in the dream.

"Good morning, First Mate." Tina called, loading scuba tanks into the truck.

"Here, let me help you." Jamey set down his coffee cup and grabbed two aluminum cylinders. Then two more. "I'll never understand how that little body of yours can sling these heavy tanks."

"Are you still underestimating me?" Tina smirked.

"Only when loading tanks, sweetheart." She blushed

at that one and he chuckled under his breath.

By the time they hooked up the boat's trailer to the truck, Jamey was sweating. It would feel good to get in the ocean. Today was a wreck dive on the south coast and he was looking forward to diving on a sunken wreck.

As they closed the back end of the truck, Tina brushed up against him accidentally, and with that physical contact, Jamey got something from her. He sensed she was excited by a romantic relationship in her life. Excited and confused. It wasn't an unreasonable idea, Tina having feelings for someone, but it threw him off his game, especially after his emotional dream about her. He had no right to feel jealousy. He'd have to work on getting rid of the leftover emotion he harbored for Tina. It wasn't his to claim. The morning's dive was his first priority and he had to focus on helping her. After all, he'd been diving free of charge and he owed her one.

Pulling away from the boat ramp, the *Maui Dream* raced south along the coast of Kihei, a town known for its calm beaches below the lava fields from Haleakala's last eruption. Breaking through the clear morning air, they zipped across the water to their destination— a sunken World War II tank and landing craft. The group was made of five return customers. The year before, they'd gone out on the boat with both Hank and Tina. "He was such a great guy," they whispered, when Tina wasn't listening. Jamey had nodded, like he knew him well and agreed.

During World War II, the military had used south Maui beaches to practice invasion tactics with landing crafts. Tina knew a lot about the history of Maui. "It's thought that a barge got tossed by the waves and dropped a perfectly good tank into the ocean. After which the landing craft slid off, providing Maui with two small wrecks to dive," Tina explained.

The sun climbed slowly into the sky, and everyone was ready to dive by the time Tina slowed the boat and took lineup measurements from the land. How she knew exactly where to anchor was baffling to Jamey. Nothing of the wreck was visible until the boat swung directly above to reveal a faint darkness below them.

"On your way between the two sights, look for sea biscuits and cone shells, but remember not to touch the pointy ends of the shells. They're poisonous," Tina said, ever the cautious dive instructor. Jamey was used to briefings and carrying out orders. "Will do."

"It's a cool site. Just don't try to go inside the tank. It's too tight." She shook her finger at the customers. "If I hear you entered the tank, I'll leave you here to swim to shore."

Everyone laughed, but Jamey knew Tina well enough to believe her. When he'd taken his specialty diving courses, she'd been a stickler for details and very strict, especially for someone who was making love with him several times a night. In those days he'd called her 'hard-ass' for more than one reason.

Before Jamey jumped off the boat, Tina touched his arm. "Make sure everyone follows me to the second site when I move the boat."

"Roger that," he'd mumbled through the regulator. Did she know he'd follow her just about anywhere?

***

Tina sipped a Coke while the customers explored the wreck below and thought about last night. Embarrassment didn't begin to explain Tina's residual feelings at almost giving in to Noble. Why had she pretended she was free to kiss him? Did she need reassurance of her ability to attract a man? Finding out that Jamey had a pregnant wife when she'd shared his bed had spurred feelings in her that obviously couldn't be buried. But she didn't think she was using Noble to feel wanted. She certainly didn't see Noble as a replacement for Hank, or even as a potential boyfriend.

Flirting with him was wrong, or encouraging him or whatever it was called when a woman kissed a man in her bed and then told him to leave. Giving in to her need to be touched had been a moment of weakness.

Tina stared at the divers' bubbles that surrounded the boat. She did not need more heartache in her life. Aside from the obvious, Noble had as many problems as she did, and it was unfair of her to take advantage of him this way. They needed to talk. Shame over leading Noble on was a feeling she didn't want to host for long. She counted the groupings of bubbles on the ocean's surface. There were six distinctive clusters for six divers. Good. She honked the horn and, put the boat in gear, pointing the bow towards the landing craft site. The year before, this same group of wealthy software designers dived the island of Kahoolawe with Hank, when the government opened the forbidden island for one weekend to dive groups. They'd partied for days with Hank after that, and Tina had teased that one of the women had the hots for him. This year she'd been unable to get away from work and was the only one in the group who hadn't come.

After circling the landing craft, Tina lowered the anchor to a sandy patch near the site. The trade winds had come up, and the boat swung around to position itself over the divers. Satisfied with her efforts, she sat on the bow to watch the bubbles. So far, so good. No grotesque hallucinations surfaced in front of her.

Thirty minutes later, when the divers broke through the surface, she grabbed their gear, weight belts first.

"Thanks Jamey for finding all that cool stuff to look at," someone said.

"Sounds like Jamey's wasting his time in the army," Tina said, as she lifted the gear into the boat. Jamey's grin made her look away quickly, her face hot. How could he still have this effect on her?

Between dives, Jamey swam off the boat with the customers, cracking jokes. He was a sociable guy.

When he splashed her and said, "Get in the water!" she thought about what Mr. Takeshimi had told her recently. "The day you decide to do, it is your lucky day."

Stepping up onto the bow, she dove into the turquoise ocean. She laughed when she popped up to the surface. "Feels good!" Her heart raced, but the feeling was glorious as she swam around the boat.

Tina had always been a swimmer; ever since her brother died in the family pool. Tina was driven to swim even if neither parent went near water after that. They wouldn't even attend her swim meets in college.

Lingering near the swim step, she tread water as she observed the others in the ocean. When Jamey dove under the boat and came up in front of her, she had a weird flash of recognition. His smile sparked a feeling in her that wasn't residual attraction from years ago but something new, something born recently, maybe even as early as yesterday.

The feeling presented itself again after the charter, when they unloaded tanks in the back alley. Jamey turned to her, his face was very close, illuminated by the midday sunshine. They'd been here before. Was it déjà vu? She and Jamey had been face to face recently, but she'd been afraid of him. Very frightened. Then she remembered that he'd been a shark. They'd been diving in one of her dreams, and he'd turned into Hank, then transformed into a dangerous shark. She'd dreamed about him.

In her life, both Jamey and Hank had left her. Thoughts of abandonment forced panic to threaten. She wasn't sure what the strange shark dream meant, and taking a few deep calming breaths, at her desk, she made a mental note to talk to Doc Chan about this.

* * *

The sun dipped behind the island of Lanai as Tina

pulled into her driveway and drove to her parking spot. It had been an emotionally charged day. They all seemed to be humdingers these days. She grabbed her backpack and headed up the stairs with Obi. It was Noble's day off and the truck sat in its parking spot. All day she'd been thinking about what to say to Noble, how to come to an agreement about no intimacy. Everything she thought to say sounded rude and trite.

She pulled the screen door open. The patio door was always unlocked at her house, the screen only closed to keep out bugs. Locking the house seemed silly in her neighborhood. Anything of value that she owned was at the dive shop or locked away in containers hidden in her bedroom closet. And her grandmother's paintings were valuable only to her for sentimental reasons. They were worth a thousand, if that, Hank had told her. He knew art.

Noble sat on the couch, a throw pillow on his lap, watching TV. "Hi, you." She threw her backpack on the floor, slipped out of her flip flops and sat beside him, not touching.

Noble hit the 'off' button and made a show of looking at the distance between them. "Is this weird now?" He pulled her over, causing her to fall against his shoulder.

"We can get past it." She was almost on his lap, their bodies pressed up against each other. His hand rested on her knee, something new. Tina leaned away slightly from the man who'd intimately kissed her only hours before.

"Do we want to?" he asked. He must've known what was coming next.

"We need to talk about all that," she said. The unspoken words hovered between them like bees ready to sting, and she shifted to put distance between them. Would Noble be relieved or disappointed? "I can't offer you anything, Noble," she said.

Noble raised his hand to silence her. "I know what we are to each other." He took her hand again and lifted it to kiss her knuckles. "And we don't need to put a name on it.

I know what it was last night and you do, too."

She did. They were going to be fine. Noble understood. Tina exhaled the breath she'd been holding. "You are my rock, Noble. I thank you from the bottom of my heart for understanding."

"And that's why I want to say something," he continued.

She tilted her head, totally unprepared for what came next.

"I want to suggest we have a baby together." He looked serious.

Tina's mouth fell open.

He continued. "I know you want a baby and I think we would make an amazing child." His smile couldn't be contained.

When Tina closed her mouth, then opened it to speak, he touched her lips with his finger.

"Just think about it, Ti. You want a baby. I'm offering."

Tina's protestations lingered at the edge of her tongue as she pictured a baby from her and Noble, already feeling the warmth and weight in her arms, a thought that both terrified and excited her.

CHAPTER 9

Dream jumping was both a curse and a gift, no doubt about it. Ever since he was ten, Jamey had been trying to deny his ability. He'd hidden what he knew for years. As a teen, it was inconvenient and annoying to know what other people thought about him. When he figured out how to use the talent to his teenage advantage, he decided to embrace it.

At first his skills helped him sneak out of the house, and then they helped boost his dating prospects. When plans backfired, and revealed more than he wanted to know, Jamey saw the ugly side of his intuition.

In his early twenties, he tried to lead a normal life, and dream jumping became like a bonus skill that he was too scared to use. Various jobs never worked out when mind reading got in the way. Knowing the thoughts of his bosses and coworkers was too much for an inexperienced young man to handle. He had yet to learn to block other people's emotions.

Jamey had some rough years, and then was accepted into the police academy at the age of twenty-six, same as his Uncle Don, who was the only other person he knew with abilities like his. Donald Dunn was a detective with the Seattle Police Force. He secretly used his extra sense for the greater good, and he'd been trying for years to convince Jamey it was the right thing to do.

Keeping his cards close to his chest in the police academy, Jamey didn't reveal his secret, agreeing with Uncle Don that it was best for everyone. When Jamey became a decorated policeman, guilt robbed him of any joy. He didn't deserve the commendation; it was his ability. Standing in front of a group of deserving police officers, he felt like an imposter. Still, he kept the secret. Jamey was an expert at keeping secrets.

Years later, Don died from a heart attack while dream jumping with a serial killer and Jamey quit the police force. Carrie divorced him and he went through a dark period of drinking heavily. Don was the only other jumper he'd known and the gift had killed him. Eventually Pops convinced Jamey that he was dishonoring his uncle by falling apart. Shortly after that speech, Jamey took a new approach to dream jumping.

It was during this transition that the armed forces found James Dunn. He never knew how they discovered him. The day they found him coming out of Pops' house, they told him they wanted to talk to him privately. Jamey looked around the deserted yard. "This is good enough." After showing him their credentials, they said they wanted to test his ability. They had others in a special force who had sixth senses. Jamey was desperate to know someone else who could dream jump and agreed to the testing. It was too good to be true.

After months of tests and enough interviews to make his head spin, Sixth Force was desperate to have James Dunn. They offered him a position with the team in Afghanistan and made him swear an oath to keep his dream jumping ability a secret. Later, he'd learn that an undisclosed member of the force had ferreted him out through his ability. And, he was told that he'd never meet the other members of Sixth Force. Not the ones with abilities, anyhow.

***

Tina's boat hummed along, riding the sunny-day swells as they motored across the channel between Maui and Lanai, the pineapple island. Today's destination was the Cathedral Caverns; a dive site Jamey knew well from Tina's diving class years ago.

Unable to read her mood, Jamey was miffed that his ability eluded him. He recalled that she'd always been a tough read but never this difficult. How was he going to keep a watch on her if he couldn't tune in?

With her hat pulled over her forehead and her Maui Jim sunglasses hiding her eyes, Tina stood like a statue, her hands on the wheel. She said nothing on the thirty-minute crossing to the house sized boulder known as Sweetheart Rock.

"Have you done this dive before?" a customer asked Jamey when they slowed to approach the site. He recalled the day he and Tina tried to make love in the underwater cavern, only to be amused by the difficulty of having sex underwater.

"Yes, it's a beauty." Catching Tina's suppressed smile, he knew she remembered.

"Jamey, can you get the anchor for me?" Tina eased back on the throttle and guided the boat to the exact place on the water where an anchor could be safely dropped in the sand.

Letting out the line, he knew Tina was staring at him from under her hat, watching him for reasons beyond the anchor's placement. He smiled to himself. What usually eluded him with her was now crystal clear, if only for a brief moment. Tina still had some leftover feelings for him. The joy from that knowledge was only slightly overshadowed by the immediate task of anchoring. Feeling the pronged edge catch in the sand, he was satisfied. "All done, Captain.

Perfect parking job, as always," he said.

Tina smiled, her veil of sadness temporarily lifted. "Thank you, James."

A newlywed couple stood by Tina. "Are you diving with us?" the husband asked.

"Not today, but Dave'll take good care of you," she

said. "I'm trying to dry out for a few days." Everyone chuckled. "Use the flashlights inside the cavern. You'll be amazed at the colors." She pulled out five underwater flashlights and attached them to the BCD jackets. They talked about not touching the coral, or the sea life, and then everyone got into gear.

Once again, Jamey was the last to jump off the boat. Descending slowly, he kept an eye on the others heading down the anchor line. The visibility was not ideal—only thirty feet of clarity. Dave would want to keep them all close because of this fact. If someone drifted more than fifty feet away, they would be impossible to see.

Appropriately named, the main cathedral resembled the inside of a small church, with shafts of sunlight piercing through multiple ceiling holes like stained-glass windows. Front and back door openings provided perfect access to the lava-rock structure, making the dive safer than a cave with limited escape routes and total darkness. This cavern was a rare gift to Hawaiian divers, formed long ago when gases were trapped inside cooling lava.

Jamey drifted through the arched opening at the end of the line of divers who'd already stirred up the silt. The sunlight coming through the cathedral windows bounced off the particles in the water to make the murk more exciting for him. Jamey recalled a dive with Tina in this particular grotto, trying to get her to remove her bathing suit top. She'd kicked him away, and eventually they'd had to surface from laughing. They'd descended again and tried to do the nasty deed but found it was pretty much impossible, if not uncomfortable.

When he got through the cavern door into the sunshine, Dave counted bodies. Jamey did the same. Four. Where was the fifth?

Dave signaled them to stay and hurried back inside the cavern. When Dave came out alone, he signaled for Jamey to ascend, take a look. Jamey started up slowly, turning as he went. When a diver goes missing the meeting point is always on the surface, where it's much easier to locate someone in the clarity of air.

Breaking the surface, Jamey noticed Tina on the swim step, hands on hips. "What's going on?"

"Seen anyone up here? We only have four."

"What? No."

Jamey put his regulator back in his mouth and descended slowly, turning in a circle all the way down, checking. When he reached the group, he shook his head at Dave and then noticed the fifth had shown up. Dave signaled all was okay and they took off to explore the reef.

But ten minutes later, when they finished the dive and surfaced, he sensed Tina's panic. One look from her told him that she'd been frantically waiting. Jamey put his hand on her shoulder and whispered. "Didn't you assume we found him?"

"Well, I hoped." Her words came out too fast, too clipped to involve any confidence, and when she shot Dave a look of anger, it didn't go unnoticed by Jamey. Or Dave. The worry of a missing diver had taken its toll on Tina, and now she was barely able to answer questions about Lanai with the customers. Her hands were shaking. Had she ever lost a diver? Hadn't her twin brother drowned? Shit! He should have surfaced to tell her they found the diver. "Sorry I didn't come up to fill you in," he said.

For the second dive of the day, the boat motored around the coast of Lanai to a turtle reef in front of a tourist attraction called Club Lanai. Fingers of coral-encrusted lava rock fanned out from the island, hiding green sea turtles under their rocky ledges. The customers had been instructed to stay away from the giant turtles. They were an endangered species, and the days of grabbing them to ride were long gone. Even touching them was illegal.

When Jamey ascended early from the second dive, he found Tina sitting cross-legged on the swim step. "Anything wrong?" Tina's face was filled with tension.

"No." He pulled off his mask and put his weight belt

on the swim step beside her. "I just wanted to come up early." Did she actually flinch, or did he just feel her tension?

She stood to hoist his tank into the boat and he climbed the ladder. "Why?" Tina didn't meet his eyes.

"I wanted to ask you something."

She froze. "Please don't."

"Don't worry. I just wanted to ask if you'd do my cavern certification. It's the only specialty course I have left, and I'd like to make this vacation count for something besides drinking Corona." Jamey reached around to pull off his wetsuit, but before he could, Tina grabbed the shoulder part and yanked one side off his shoulder.

"Thanks."

"You did ice diving?" She took a towel from the pile and threw it at him.

He nodded. "In Minnesota."

"That's brave." Tina looked into his face. "I can't do your dives, only the academics, but Dave or Sally will dive with you."

Jamey stared, daring her to look away. "Why can't you?" This is what he'd been waiting for.

The pause that overtook her end of the conversation told him she was trying to think of a better excuse than a rash. Jamey was ready to call her bluff, but then a wave of surrender passed between them.

"I don't dive…because…I see my dead husband's body underwater." Tina stared hard into Jamey's face. "I'm having hallucinations that lead to panic attacks." She gulped. "Obviously, I don't want this to be common knowledge." He nodded.

"It's inconvenient, at the very least." She continued disassembling Jamey's dive gear. "We haven't found Hank's body and..." Tina stopped short.

He wanted to console her, but she'd probably be uncomfortable if he did that and there was little else he could offer.

Tina's life sucked these days. Grieving widow, not sleeping, bad dreams, business in jeopardy, can't dive…more than the average person could handle without falling off the deep end. She probably had friends who were keeping an eye on her. Still, he had more resources than the average person, including an intimate past with Kristina Greene. It didn't go unnoticed by Jamey that maybe fate had delivered him to Maui for a reason. He believed in fate.

At the port side of the boat, air bubbled to the surface and heads popped through. The conversation was over for now.

***

The ribbon Tina had been tying to Obi's collar each night was always still there when she woke, a cautiously good sign. But she'd been awake every hour to check if she'd dreamed or gotten out of bed. By morning, she was exhausted.

There was no logical explanation for the strange dreams. The only way to move on was to hope it had been something to do with the medication. Doc Chan didn't have any ideas except to ease off on the Xanax. Her doctor's lack of knowledge and imagination concerned Tina. More than once Tina considered a quick trip to the mainland to see someone who knew more about this type of thing, but, truth was, after 9/11, flying didn't hold much appeal and she'd rather wait to see if changing meds helped.

She and the Doc had shuffled around different doses of this and that for months until they found the best amounts of the medications that would allow her to function like a normal person. And now she was trying to give up her beloved Xanax. Some days it was the only thing that kept her from curling into a ball and giving up.

As the sky lightened, bird calls broke through the silence of the Maui morning. Doves cooed from the trees in her front yard and the bird next door began its morning ritual. The dreamless night gave Tina a glimmer of hope and, for once, she felt lighthearted, free enough to move on to other problems.

Noble.

That problem was like a battle lost. One minute they were talking like always, and the next she was falling down that slippery slope to something more than friendship. And now he'd suggested himself as her baby's father. It was tempting to imagine Noble as a wonderful father, but she suspected he wanted sex to be a starting point for something more, even if he denied it.

Obi watched the street, his head jutting out between the deck rails. She knew her dog well enough to know he was contemplating his morning wander through the yard. Surveying the neighborhood, Tina stretched and watched Obi pad down the stairs to the enticing smells below. Yellow papayas hung from three of her trees, ready for picking, as did a cluster of lemons from the tree at the south end of the property. "Small wonders," Hank had said about their growth of fruit and vegetables. He'd loved the domestic life. And would've been a wonderful father. It was Hank she'd wanted to father her child. Still, Noble...Children were drawn to him like puppies to the food bowl.

In the distance, the ocean's surface was calm, finally. Farther out, closer to Molokai, a humpback whale jumped. By now the leviathans had mostly left the warm waters of Hawaii in a parade like exodus to the Arctic, and she wondered if this jumping whale had been left behind. She knew the feeling.

Thoughts of being pregnant, then holding a baby in her arms wouldn't be buried as Obi sniffed the periphery of his territory in the vast yard.

Noble rounded the house. "Hey there."

"Noble." His sudden presence surprised her.

"Howzit?" His voice held none of the sexy intonations from two nights before, and Tina was relieved to think that normalcy might exist between them.

"Nice day today," she gestured.

He crossed his arms across his massive chest and smiled up at her. "Yes, yes it is."

They stared at each other, grinning. *What was he thinking with that smile?* Obi broke through the trees, stopped short when he saw Noble and barked like he didn't recognize him.

"Obi, stop. It's Noble." She looked at Noble. "Where are you going so early?" she asked.

"Nowhere. Wanna come?" he joked.

Everything had sexual connotations. She hated this.

***

The Barefoot Bar was still buzzing from the sunset crowd when Jamey found two seats at the counter. The funky bar was in the heart of the Kaanapali strip of mega-hotels and a great place for a drink before deciding where to eat a meal of mahimahi or kalua pork. Jamey scanned the group of tourists who were seated in clusters in a wide U around the stage. Happy groups drank and ate while their toes dug into the loose sand under their tables. A child of about five crouched at his mother's feet playing with a digger truck, running the toy up and down little sand hills he'd made.

Jamey ordered a beer at the bar and waited for Tina to arrive. He was pretty sure she wouldn't stand him up even though when he asked her to meet him, she'd been hesitant. Wary.

His beer arrived and he took a swig from the dewy bottle. Glancing up, he noticed that beyond the stage, Tina walked up from the beach, like she'd just gotten off a boat.

Her flip flops swung from her right hand and she waved to him with her left. No smile. Still dressed in her bikini top, a stretch of fabric hugging her hips like a last-minute addition to satisfy some dress code. He chuckled.

Didn't she own clothes? He stood as she approached. "Do you mind sitting here at the bar?"

"Not at all." Tina swung her backpack under the tall bar stool and hopped up. When she ordered a Corona with lime, he laughed about how some things never change. "Still Corona?" The question was meant to be an icebreaker but Tina didn't smile. Instead she nodded and scanned the bar.

"Tina, we used to be friends, more than friends, and like it or not, that gives us a familiarity that won't go away." She took a deep breath.

"I see you every day trying to balance your business and your life."

She stared at him.

"I know things have been tough." He took a deep breath and proceeded. "I wonder if I can do anything to make life easier."

"I'm surprised you even ask." The musicians played the opening bars to "Honolulu City Lights" and Tina's face softened. "This is a favorite song," she said. The beer came and she took a long drink from the bottle.

Okay, the conversation is still alive. She hadn't blown out the spark by changing the subject. Not really. "You have dark circles under your eyes, I couldn't help notice."

"Thanks for reminding me."

"Is it the dreams?" Color rose in her cheeks and Jamey continued. "I know you don't owe me an explanation, but I'd like to think the closeness we shared counts for something." He leaned forward and stared her down like he had a right to.

Tina pursed her mouth and looked sideways, as if to collect her anger. The same resentment he'd felt for days was plastered all over her face. "It's interesting you say that, Jamey. But, I think before you start claiming that we were friends, you need to ask yourself why we were sleeping together in the first place."

"What do you mean?" Jamey shifted in his seat, feeling her anger like a snake about to strike.

"Why did you feel free enough to carry on with me when it was only temporary?"

Shit. Jamey rubbed his two-day growth. "Tina, I'm sorry that things turned out the way they did between us. I am. I didn't know it would be temporary." He looked her in the eyes and shook his head. If he couldn't tell her about his ability to jump, he sure as hell couldn't explain that he'd jumped her dream and found out more than he wanted to know about Kristina Greene's future. "It wasn't meant to be." That had to be good enough.

"Why?" Her look bored right through his heart, as if challenging him to give her the piece of information that was the final puzzle piece she needed to forgive him.

He could say that when he got home, he found out that his ex-girlfriend was three months pregnant with his child, only to find out a month later they were having twins. Did he want to? When he left Tina that day, Carrie's pregnancy had nothing to do with why he abandoned Tina.

Tina chugged her beer like she couldn't wait to see the bottom of it. Like they were done.

"Look, Tina. Can't we move on? I just wish you'd forgive me." Ukulele music wafted through the warm Maui night as the Hawaiian duo on stage sang a song about unrequited love. Waitresses scooted through the sand with trays of Mai Tai's and beers. A bead of sweat trickled down his chest under his T-shirt.

"I gotta go," she said, setting her empty beer bottle on the bar.

"Wait." He laid his hand on her forearm. "One more thing before you go. Would you be willing to try diving with me sometime? I'm not an instructor, but we've done a bunch of dives together and maybe you wouldn't see Hank if you were with me." He wanted to take her hand but didn't.

"It wouldn't make a difference."

"How do you know?"

"I tried diving, and it's a disaster." She looked at the table top and drew a circle in the droplets of water from her beer. "Fear overtakes me, even if I don't hallucinate."

"But we dove the other day and you stayed down for almost the whole dive. Over twenty minutes."

"I'm not sure how that happened, but I know that it took every ounce of strength I had to not rush to the surface."

"See? Maybe you can dive with me." She shook her head.

"Well, then, how did you stay under with me the other day?"

She thought for a moment. "You did that thing with your eyes."

He paused. "What thing?"

"That staring thing. It helped me continue." Tina gave the waitress her empty, nodded at the offer of another and sat back down.

Jamey held up two fingers.

"If you hadn't been holding my hand...I can't lead dives. End of story."

"We could try. What does your therapist say?"

Tina looked incredulous that he'd even asked. He'd overstepped his boundaries, something he did on a regular basis when he knew someone's thoughts.

The beers arrived and Tina smiled warmly at the waitress. How was it she could offer kindness to someone who only brought her a beer but couldn't even talk to him? Jamey waited. Whoever speaks first loses. Finally, he couldn't stand it. "Have you tried anything like self-talk or visualization?" He would start slow, offer benign ideas, feel her out. He'd have to approach this situation so carefully she wouldn't see it coming. Then he'd ease into detonating the bomb he was about to drop on Tina's life to crack it wide open.

"Kind of. My therapist is in over her head with this one." She squinted at him. "I'm having strange dreams. Things I can't explain." She shook her head as if to clear her thoughts. "And on that dive at Molokini, I saw Hank floating in front of me." She looked into Jamey's face. "It's terrifying, even though realistically, I know he's not there." Her hands were clenched in her lap. "He looks so real." Her voice rose in intensity and lowered in volume. "He's injured. His head is split open, his body is decomposing." She covered her mouth with her hand.

Jamey moved in closer. His heart felt like someone had stomped on it. "I might be able to help." He had to offer what he could. This was not a conversation for the Barefoot Bar.

"Help me dive? Or help me forget my husband, James?"

Ah, she called him James. That might be headway. The musical duo started in on a sing-along Beatles medley, making the bar too noisy for a conversation.

Jamey leaned in to be heard. "Let's go for a walk. I want to tell you something." He had to tell her. Now.

CHAPTER 10

The way Jamey looked at her left Tina wondering if he still held some tenderness for her. Or if someone who'd dumped her so easily had felt much to begin with. If he tried anything romantic on the walk, she'd deck him. As much as any petite woman could deck an over six-foot tall trained cop and soldier. "Okay, let's walk," she said.

They paid the bill, crossed the boardwalk and when Jamey saw a woman trying to get her husband back in his wheelchair from the beach, he stopped.

"Here, let me help," he said. Jamey was a nice guy; that much she knew. "No problem," he nodded when the couple thanked him, and joined Tina. With footwear off, they continued to the water's edge.

The cold sand felt good on Tina's tired feet. She'd been running around all day with meetings with the bank, her accountant, and others she owed money. She squished the sand through her toes. The surf was so slight that barely enough water to be called a wave lapped gently against the beach. Ripples. "Great night for a dive." She used to love diving at night like it was a forbidden PJ party activity, like sneaking out after midnight.

"Water looks clear." Jamey took a deep breath, only feet away from her. "I mentioned visualization because it's a proven method used by a lot of counselors and psychiatrists, and it works. I don't know where you stand on this sort of thing, or if you'd be open to trying."

Tina turned north towards the infamous Black Rock, where long ago Hawaiians made human sacrifices to their god. "Visualization doesn't work for me. I tried it and other stuff. My grief counselor has me doing these relaxation exercises that make me fall asleep and have bizarre dreams."

He picked up a piece of coral and threw it into the ocean. "So you're saying you're having hallucinations while diving and strange dreams at night?"

She nodded.

"Dreaming while asleep is extremely complex and entirely different from hallucinating." Jamey sounded like he was lecturing to a stranger. All of a sudden, this guy didn't seem like Jamey. "Seeing your husband's form while diving could be a recollection from a dream." He paused and looked at her." Do you believe in intuition?"

"Yes." Of course, she did. She had great gut feelings on things.

"I do too." He looked so intense.

"And you have a feeling you can get me diving again. I get it, but I'm a widow with an unrecovered body for a dead husband. Not being able to dive is only the tip of the iceberg. I'm on all kinds of meds, I can't sleep. I'm angry. I feel like that empty shell you just threw back in the ocean." She looked into Jamey's face. "My problems are really big."

"Remember that staring thing I did with you on the Molokini dive?"

"Yes."

Jamey's face was lit by the tiki torches wedged into the massive rock at the end of the beach.

"Tina." He looked up as if he'd find the answer in the sky and took a deep breath. "Something you don't know about me is that I have a type of intuition that most people don't have. It's stronger, more reliable."

"Okay..." *What the hell?*

"I'm unbelievably accurate in what I get from my intuition."

If he was bullshitting her, she'd leave and drive home very fast with all the windows down to clear her head.

He picked up a piece of dead coral and tossed it in his

hand. "I use my intuition to help people."

She shot him a sideways look. "This is a bit much, Jamey."

"It's true." He turned her to face him. "For instance, I know right now that this piece of coral makes you uneasy for some reason. It reminds you of something disturbing."

It looked like the chunk she'd brought back from the dream. "Why would coral make me feel uneasy?" *Could he tell?*

Jamey shrugged. "You tell me."

What was he saying? That he was psychic? "Let's suppose you have great intuition. How does that help me?"

"I might be able to help you figure out what's going on with your dreams."

"Are you trying to tell me that you read minds?" He'd better not be leading her on about all this, giving her false hope. "So you just go around reading everyone's mind and knowing more than the rest of us?" She chuckled and dug her toes into the cool sand, her hands on her hips. *What a crock.*

He opened his arms wide, looking apologetic. "I don't usually tell people this because it makes them uneasy. And it sounds cuckoo." Jamey looked so convincing that a shiver shot through her. "In certain situations, I can delve deeper into my intuition than most people." They stared at each other. "I know things I don't necessarily want to know. Sometimes it's like people have a sign on them that feeds me information and I can't look away before I see it. Sometimes it's subtler."

Then she saw it for what it was. He was trying to tell her to stop grieving for Hank. The psychic angle was new, though. "Jamey, stop. I know what you're doing."

He interrupted. "I know, for instance, that there's something going on with you and a man. Romantically." He shrugged.

"You're wrong there." She continued walking.

"And that he is very protective of you. Something

happened. Thursday night, to be exact."

"There's no one. So there." Her arms hugged her chest tighter.

"And I know you're worried about Obi, but you can't bring yourself to take him to the vet, because you don't want him to die on you too."

Tina spun around to face him. "Shut up. There is nothing wrong with my dog." *Lumps come and go all the time.* Taking a deep breath, she let her arrow fly. "If what you say about intuition is true, then you must know that I don't like you, Jamey, and that I only agreed to meet with you tonight so Katie wouldn't feel bad." Katie had been trying to fix them up with about as much subtlety as an orangutan. "And if you can read my mind, then shame on you because that is a gross invasion of privacy."

"Let me help you, Tina."

Jamey was too close and she shoved him as hard as she could. "You don't get it!" Her voice rose to a level she hadn't used in years. "I don't like you and I don't trust you." She waited for that to sink in. "Obi's lump is nothing. You hear me? So, stop talking about it." He must've seen Obi's underside, but how did he know she couldn't take her dog to the vet?

"I'm not talking about his lump. I'm just telling you something I feel about you. You're the one who won't take him to the vet."

"Shut up!" She poked him again. And again. "You are sticking your nose where it doesn't belong."

Jamey grabbed her shoulders, pulled her in and hugged her. "I can take him to the doctor, if you like. Please, let me do something for you."

Tina pulled back to see concern flash in his eyes. Genuine. They stood staring at each other, and when he leaned down and kissed her lips, it felt like something left over from years ago—tender, beautifully familiar. Dammit.

And it lasted only long enough for Tina to realize it was her second stab at physical intimacy in forty-eight hours. Breaking away, she stepped back. She was pitiful, letting men all over Maui kiss her. "I need to go home," she said, disgust trailing her words.

Jamey moved in front to block a getaway. "Wait. Hear me out. I read dreams. I want you to know that before this chance is lost." She swerved to go around him.

He caught up to her. "That's how I think I might be able to help you the most, Tina. Not diving."

They were now standing between a noisy mashup of two different songs coming from two hotels. Her head was full.

He took several steps towards her and lowered his voice. "I read dreams."

She stopped. "Oh come on, Jamey. First you say you read minds, now dreams. Which is it?" Tina stared hard into his face, trying to determine the truth from lies. As much as she wanted to walk away, the word "dreams" had her attention.

"I am an expert on dreams. I swear." He looked like he believed what he was saying.

Her shoulders slumped. "I'm not saying I believe you but if you're not telling the truth, I will never speak to you again."

"I'm telling the truth. I swear on my life, Tina. I read dreams."

Revealing her dreams to this man would feel like letting him watch her undress. If he was a philandering adulterer when she met him, why would he be telling the truth now?

"You have nothing to lose but the privacy of the dream, and I promise I can keep a secret."

"Oh, I know you can keep secrets." She didn't intend to sound accusatory.

"This is what I do with my life now," he added.

Wasn't he a soldier in Afghanistan? "In the army?"

"Yes." He seemed to be measuring his words. "For the military in Afghanistan."

Jamey interpreted dreams for the army? Was she supposed to believe that?

"I know this is a lot to take in, especially because you once knew me, but I am a dream expert."

What the hell? "Did you know how to do all this when…we knew each other…before?"

He nodded. "But it's developed."

Tina considered how well she knew him before. If she pretended to trust him, she could withhold personal information and hope his intuition wasn't as good as he said. Just because she was angry with him didn't mean he might not be able to help her. The only lights on the beach were those from the massive hotels of Kaanapali behind them and she lowered herself to sit on a mound of sand, the remains of a fallen castle from someone's day at the beach. "It's a long story."

He sat down beside her and waited. Recounting the dreams about the cave, the shark and diving without scuba equipment was like opening a wound she'd bandaged poorly. All the work in denying the dreams was now undone as she slowly, methodically, described how she'd dived with Hank to a cave.

"Hank turns into a tiger shark and disappears inside a cave?"

"Yes, and sometimes he's just himself."

"And you think you wake up but it's still the dream?" Jamey's voice had reached a pitch she'd never heard before. He sounded like he had heightened interest, not just heightened intuition. "Your first dream about Hank might be what the experts call "WILD," a wake induced lucid dream. Relaxation exercises took you into the dream. It's called the holy grail of lucid dreaming because you took yourself to a dream state from fully awake."

Her mistrust dissolved. Slightly. He knew what he was talking about.

After asking about Hank, her usual dreaming patterns, and what she saw during the dive, Jamey was silent.

Resting her chin on her knee, Tina watched a group of night divers exit the water at Black Rock. Not Dave and his class. They'd gone to Airport Beach.

"Here's what I think: you suspect his body is in an underwater cave and that you might subconsciously know the location. Is it possible that your mind is hiding a known location?"

"I've never done this dive before, I'm sure of that."

He continued. "Did Hank ever mention a dive like this? Is it possible he dove on the morning he disappeared, not surfed?" She shook her head.

"I'm wondering if this cave exists. As for the continuation of your dreams when you think you're awake, that's not uncommon, but you're dreaming so vividly that it's confusing you. Tying the ribbon to Obi's collar was a stroke of genius." He twirled a stick in the sand. "And Hank turning into a shark is your worry that sharks have taken the body from you and essentially Hank has become part of a shark."

She wasn't sure what to say next. Jamey seemed to be miles away. The silence hung over them until Tina was embarrassed. She'd opened her heart for so little in return. "I better get back to Obi in the car." Tina had to wonder what she'd expected. She'd opened the wound and he didn't have a good enough first-aid kit. Maybe she'd wanted the reassurance that Hank was alive and hiding on another continent.

"This isn't over. For me to help, I need you to keep a journal of your dreams for the next few nights." Jamey looked serious enough for Tina to nod.

"I don't dream every night."

"I want to know when you do and at what time. Even the dreams you already told me about from the past week. The dates and content. Everything. Put it all in there." He seemed excited at the prospect of studying her dreams.

"Alright." She would. But now she had to get back to her truck. Obi would be asleep in the passenger seat, waiting. "I need to go." She didn't like leaving her dog this long. Especially now. Jamey stood and reached out to help her to stand.

Tina stood and shook the sand from her skirt. "Can you read my thoughts now?" She was thinking that Jamey had always had such gentlemanly manners. "Can you?" If this new revelation was true, it would be unnerving.

"Not really. Just that you appreciate me helping you, which is obvious."

Tina's brow wrinkled. "That's enough."

Walking through the bar and restaurant, they crossed a wooden bridge over a koi pond into the Whaler's Village Shopping Center. The kiosks were closed up for the evening. "If you notice the obvious, what's obvious right now?" Tina asked.

"You want to get back to Obi and you're embarrassed about the kiss. You're sorry you told me so much because you think I wasn't much help."

Oh, my God. He was right. She wanted to get away from Jamey and re-think everything she'd ever said to him. Obi must've caught her scent because when they got close he sat up in the seat and stuck his head out the window. Someone had left a note on her truck windshield saying that she shouldn't leave a pit bull in a truck with the windows down.

She opened the truck door and let Obi jump out. Jamey leaned against the car, his arms folded across his chest. "He's a great dog."

"Can you tell if he's sick?"

He waited for Obi to return from the bushes and then put his hand on the dog's underside. Obi licked his face. "I don't feel anything threatening."

Tina stared at him petting her dog. "It's an unbelievable claim, that you read minds."

"That's exactly why I don't tell anyone. Why I never told you before. Even if you don't believe me yet, please keep my secret. Katie doesn't know, for obvious reasons."

He almost smiled.

She thought about telling him more, like her hope that Hank was still alive, but the trust wasn't there. "Did your wife know?"

He nodded. "I used it during her pregnancy to see how the fetuses were growing." He looked at Tina long and hard. "It's not always amazingly accurate. I know you are very mad at me, but I can't get a handle on what I did to make you this upset."

She jumped into the truck cab and put the key in the ignition.

"I think it has to do with me leaving you, marrying, having kids, but there's something more to it."

"Well then, you're not that good, are you?" She backed out of the parking spot, leaving Jamey staring after her.

Noble was at the deck railing when she got out of her truck.

"I've been waiting for you." He looked agitated.

"I see that." Tina took a deep breath and steeled herself. "Do you have a boyfriend or something?" He followed her into the house.

Tina stopped in her tracks. "Did you see me with Jamey?"

Noble folded his arms across his chest. "Who's Jamey?"

She stared at him. Jealousy didn't suit Noble. It wasn't his loyalty to Hank that brought this on, and she had only herself to blame.

He waited for her answer.

"Why are you doing this? If you are here waiting for me because you're upset that I met up with an old friend, this proves it was wrong...what we almost did the other night."

"No." He moved in and hugged her. Feeling trapped, she eased away.

"It's okay," he added. "We'll figure it out. I know

111

you're not ready."

Something had changed between them, like they'd almost headed down a glass-strewn path in their bare feet and turned around. She couldn't have a baby with Noble. He had feelings for her she couldn't reciprocate.

"We'll get back on track." He nodded.

"Noble..." Tina couldn't find the right words. Anything she thought to say would sound patronizing. "You mean so much to me."

His expression was concerning.

"We *will* get back on track, but now I have to go to bed or I'm going to drop on the spot," she said.

They hugged and she walked into her bedroom as Noble descended the back stairs. Was there any hope of regaining their friendship, or had everything already changed too much? At least all this drama was distracting her from the worry that she might be going crazy.

She switched her bikini top and pareo for an old T-shirt of Hanks. What had Jamey told her tonight? He was psychic...hyper intuitive, he said, with the ability to read dreams. Maybe he was a weirdo.

Ten years ago, she'd only known him a few weeks, but he definitely did not seem crazy then. But now, as a soldier on leave, she had to wonder if he had Post Traumatic Stress Disorder. She'd overheard him say that he wasn't involved in combat. He was on some type of leave, though, and she had to wonder what had happened to give him three months off. She'd seen him in swim trunks for the last two weeks, with no sign of recent wounds.

Rubbing Obi's tummy, she picked off two ticks from her dog's exposed underside. Her hand lingered on the lump. Jamey could have noticed the lump while petting him. Considering that she'd once been prepared to give Jamey her heart, it was surprising to think that now she wasn't even comfortable telling him the whole truth about her dreams. Burrowing into the covers, she adjusted her pillows, closed her heavy eyes and finally fell into a deep sleep.

Tina found herself floating, sinking in the cool water. She remained motionless, happy to let the current carry her. In front was the coral-encrusted wall. As usual in her dream, the water was incredibly clear. She drifted towards the cave. The shark hadn't appeared. Tina remained alert, with the wall on her right, like scenery passing from a car window, thinking she must remember to tell Jamey about this lucid dream.

And then, there it was. The shark. Flooded in sunlight. Its body was gray and sleek. Its eyes were cold, exactly as she remembered from before. Just a shark. Tina grabbed the wall and stopped her momentum, her pink nightgown continuing to drift forward.

What if the shark wasn't Hank and attacked her? Tiger sharks were unpredictable like that. Wasn't this a dream? How painful would an attack be in a dream? Then the shark turned and began to spin in a circle, faster and faster. Tina held onto a knob of rock and watched the transformation from shark to man.

When it stopped, Hank stood before her. The whole Hank she'd known and loved. Not the ghostly apparition of a battered body. She was only a few kicks from her husband. This Hank had laugh lines and kind eyes that beckoned her to follow him, just like before. Tina's heart was heavy with the repetition of the dream's purpose. As much as she wanted to go to Hank, she needed to ascend and identify a landmark above ground, just in case the dream was telling her something. Instead, when he waved her to him, she accepted the invitation to follow.

Hank led her to the cave's black opening and, before disappearing inside, turned and blew her a kiss. Typical Hank. Tina always pretended the kiss landed on her breast and would give him a look like he'd been a naughty boy to plant it there. But this time when she looked up reproachfully, he was gone, the cave opening a gaping, toothless mouth, black and still, with no sign of a recent visitor.

Looking to the surface, Tina weighed the options. She kicked her way up thirty feet, turning in a slow circle to keep her eyes on approaching dangers. As her head cut through to air, the last thing she saw was a stony beach in the distance, with large rock formations leading into the ocean. Then she fell into blackness and was quickly sucked backwards at a preposterous rate.

***

An hour into the paperwork that had piled up on her desk, Tina was interrupted by her friend, Pepper, walking through the shop to the back room. "What are you doing up so early, Pepper? It's only 7:30." Pepper usually worked until midnight and never woke before noon.

"I'm still up from last night." Pepper hugged Tina tightly, as was her custom, and hung on long after Tina would've let go. Her small group of good friends had protectively surrounded her after Hank's accident. But after ten months of helping her through the doldrums, the friends had thinned out, most had backed off. Pepper, however, continued to check in every day.

"I had exciting news last night." Pepper looked exhilarated, not exhausted.

Tina needed good news, even if it was someone else's. "What is it?"

"Goldy and Burn were at the Ritz last night, and she offered me a job singing backup on her next tour." Pepper's eyes widened. "They leave in a month and one of her singers just backed out!" Pepper gave a little scream.

"Oh, my God!" Tina's hands flew to her heart. This was exciting news for her friend. Going on tour with Goldy, the international rock star, would be an amazing opportunity. "Are you kidding?"

"No, I'm leaving for Los Angeles in two weeks to

start rehearsals."

Pepper divulged the particulars of Goldy wandering into the Ritz lounge specifically to hear Maui's beloved singer. The rock star had just lost one of her backup singers. Goldy and her husband, Burn, sat at the back of the room in the shadows, with their drummer Tzolt, a man who Pepper had a huge crush on with good reason. They'd hooked up months ago, or almost. Flirting and kissing counted as far as she was concerned. Soon Pepper would leave soon for almost one year on a tour that included the hunky drummer. Tina was happy for her friend. Maybe good news rubbed off on people and she was next. "We must celebrate." The words felt strange coming out of Tina's mouth, considering all that was going on.

"We will. On my next night off." Pepper nodded out the door. "Is Mr. T selling his house?"

"Yes. Isn't that sad?"

Pepper searched Tina's face. "Kind of, but he's old and probably tired of keeping up the house."

"You're right. It's probably a good thing." Why did Tina think of it as defeat?

"Do you hate me for having the guys take the shop sign down? I made an executive decision."

"Another good idea. Thanks." Tina tried to smile.

Pepper made an apologetic face just as Jamey walked through the alleyway door with two to-go coffees in sleeves.

Tina made introductions.

"Hello," Pepper crooned, like she wasn't already interested in Goldy's drummer. Pepper extended her hand flirtatiously with no idea that Jamey and Tina had once been lovers.

Familiar with Pepper's moves, Tina was almost amused to watch Jamey squirm.

"I'm sorry I didn't bring enough coffees," Jamey said. "If you like drip with milk, you're welcome to this one." He held out a cup and handed Tina the other one. "Or maybe Tina will give you hers with ten sugars." He made a face.

"Four," Tina corrected.

"No thanks, I'm going home to sleep," Pepper said. "And I couldn't possibly maintain this body if I drank coffee with sugar." Pepper's flirt factor had ramped up to high. "But you owe me a beverage. You can buy me a drink tonight at the Ritz. I sing in the lobby bar from nine to midnight." She batted her eyelashes at Jamey and he laughed.

A pang of jealousy invaded Tina's heart, thinking of Jamey and Pepper at the lobby bar, getting to know each other. She sipped her sweet coffee to keep from saying anything. "I'm diving tonight," Jamey said. "Sorry. Maybe Tina and I can come see you another time."

"I'm there all weekend." Pepper stood and slung her purse over her shoulder. "Home to get my beauty sleep."

Before Jamey could say something cheesy like Pepper was already beautiful enough, Tina jumped in. "I'll call you later."

Jamey's eyes did not follow Pepper out of the room, which Tina found interesting, seeing her friend was wearing a tight mini dress and looked what she and her friends called "Pepperlicious." Most men—single, married, or gay—couldn't resist watching that backside leave a room. It was sizeable and showcased perfectly. Next to Pepper's curves, Tina often felt boyish.

Jamey merely sat down in the chair that had been occupied by Pepper and asked if Tina had dreamed the night before.

She nodded. "It was similar to the usual, but this time there was no current or swell and I was able to surface before I woke. I only had a quick look before I was awake." Her eyes widened. "Is it possible that this place exists?"

"Yes. It's possible, but let's keep that idea between us, just like we talked about last night. What did you see?"

Jamey asked.

The more she fought to remember that flash of scenery, the more the visual seemed to fade, like a photograph exposed too long to sunlight. But, she managed to give a simple description of the beach and Jamey looked like he was listening to every word. "I didn't recognize anything."

"You need to take the boat out and check the coastline," he said.

Tina had to agree, as strange as it sounded to be looking for a landform from a dream. "When the charter comes back, I can go up north and take a look." This small scrap of an idea was someplace to start. Jamey's involvement gave Tina new hope. Choosing to confide in him had been the right move. "Can you come with me?"

"If you want, sure." He dunked his empty coffee cup into the trash can across the room. "Don't tell anyone why we're taking the boat out, though. Say we're looking for a new dive site or something. Here's a different topic. When you saw Hank at Molokini, did I swim right through him, near that rock?"

She nodded.

"That wasn't a thermocline then," he said to himself.

"Did you see him?" She wanted the answer to be yes.

Jamey looked like he had an idea brewing. "No, I only felt his sadness. And the water was abnormally cold."

CHAPTER 11

Jamey watched Tina ease the boat down the ramp at Mala Wharf. Although she barely glanced in the rear-view mirror, the rig ended up perfectly placed alongside the dock. He shook his head. Tina was good at this. She was definitely at home here in the dive business of Maui. Being near the ocean gave her joy. He could feel it emanating from her. The underlying feeling of fear of the ocean was only temporary. When they found Hank, she'd be able to dive again. A decomposing body, ten months in the ocean would be a gruesome sight, even if you hadn't once loved that person.

Jamey grabbed the boat lines and pulled the floating craft off the submerged trailer and tied it to the dock. Tina drove the empty trailer up to the parking lot and he stood thinking about their upcoming afternoon. If she recognized the dive site today, they'd hopefully be that much closer to finding the body.

Somewhere deep in her heart, Tina said she still believed Hank might be out there, alive, but Jamey had his own reasons to believe otherwise.

He jumped on board, turned the key and started the engine. Hearing the motor rev up, Obi raced ahead of Tina and jumped from the dock to the boat, settling in at the bow. The usual Maala Wharf drifters, known locally as "wharf rats," sat at a dilapidated card table in the shade of a stand of trees, drinking beer. He could hear their hooting over the sound of *Maui Dream*'s purring motor. They were a motley group of lean, leather-skinned men whose stars had extinguished long before ending up on Maui.

Tina waved to them as she passed by and trotted down the ramp to the dock. Jamey imagined they enjoyed watching her bikini-clad body run by.

"Friends of yours?" he asked when she pushed the boat away from the dock and jumped on.

She shrugged. "They're here every day. Some have nowhere else to go but here, sleeping on someone's couch at night. I give them the leftover charter food sometimes. Rumor is that most of them are felons wanted stateside." Jamey backed away from the dock. "The islands attract people who are running away from something."

That was too true for Jamey. Over the last six weeks, he'd become more used to the idea that Al Qaeda might not know who the dream jumper was. If that were true, his choices included not only returning to Afghanistan if his ability was intact, but living in Carnation or even Maui if it wasn't. "What about you? What are you running away from?"

"That's one of the easiest questions you've ever asked me." She looked directly into his eyes as though it was the only time she'd say this and he'd better remember. "My parents." Tina motioned to the wheel. "Go ahead and take her out."

"Alright Captain." It had been a long time since he'd driven a boat. He remembered leaving from this ramp ten years before with Tina. They were doing deep dives in the channel between Maui and Lanai. One afternoon she'd taught Jamey how to back out of Maala Wharf and turn quickly to get around the jetty without running into the rocks. They'd laughed over the story of the wharf's concrete being made with salt water, causing it to fall apart years later.

Tina pointed to the decrepit wharf. "This would be a nice dive if the water was deeper. I've done it, but not with customers because of the liability of falling chunks of concrete. They gated off the wharf, but the fishermen still find their way in." She pointed to a group of men clustered at the end of the wharf with poles in the water. "That's the beauty of Maui."

Jamey loved this place with its laid-back style. Lawsuits did not dictate normal behavior. "Let's shoot up past Honolua." He pushed the throttle down and they took off.

The wind blew Tina's sun-streaked hair from her face. "I know this part of the coastline inside and out, until we get past the lighthouse," she called over the noise of the motor. "And even then, I don't ever remember seeing a beach like the one in the dream." She looked hopeful in spite of her words, and Jamey remembered the girl he'd met years before—such a free spirit.

When he'd first met Tina and they'd gotten hot and heavy quickly, he'd considered divulging the long tale of him and Carrie. She deserved the information, but he just couldn't bring that part of his life into the mix. Not yet. Not when their relationship was so new and moving full steam ahead. He thought the path was clear for both of them. Then he'd betrayed her without warning. She must have hated him. But for many reasons, Tina was better off without him in those days.

The turmoil created by his life as an empath was enough to drive anyone from his affections. True, Tina never knew that part of him and never got the chance to choose, but that was how it had to play out. Besides, being with someone who could read your mind, see remembrances through dreams, see the future randomly, and jump into your dreams, had to be the biggest relationship deterrent Jamey could think of.

And now here they were, looking for her husband's decomposing body. Jamey set a course for the northern end of Maui and silently prayed he could help Tina move on. For his sake as well as hers. He needed to know he wasn't on Maui uselessly chasing the hope of helping Tina while men died in Afghanistan because of his absence.

It had been hours since leaving Mala Wharf and Jamey knew that disappointment and relief were jostling for top spot in Tina's mind. Steering the boat around a rocky point, she slowed and lifted her sunglasses to stare at the water. "Maybe this is something." She pulled in as close as was safe, cutting the engine. "Hank used to come here with Noble, looking for lobster." Her brow wrinkled. "I feel like I dove here recently, but I didn't."

"Let's take a look." Jamey laid an open palm on her shoulder.

As Tina lowered the anchor, she started to shake. A reassuring look from Jamey did little to keep her terror at bay.

"At the very least, let's jump in and cool off," he said.

Tina shook her head. "I can't. I'll stay with Obi on the boat."

"Being scared could be a good sign. I'll take a look first." Already Jamey had his snorkel and mask in his hands.

"Tell me if it looks like this?" Tina drew a quick sketch on her dive slate. The swim step bobbed up and down, slapping the water's surface in the afternoon waves. "I know I should go in, but I can't." She shook her head vehemently, shivering in the Maui sunshine. "Wear your fins in case there's a current."

With one last glance, he slipped into the dark blue water and took off across the surface.

The picture Tina had drawn on her slate looked familiar but more like the topography in the dream when he became Hank and turned into a shark. A dream that still puzzled him. When she'd mentioned that dream, Jamey wondered how he'd been a part of it without intentionally dream jumping. Unanswered questions rattled around in his head. Too many to be comfortable about what was happening.

Twenty-five feet below him were clusters of boulders dotting the ocean floor, but not a wall, like in the recurring dream. The underwater rock formations looked like the dream where he was Hank and then became a shark.

When he returned to the boat, Tina was still at the center console, staring at the floor. Shivering. He hoisted himself out of the water and stood on the swim step.

"No cave. Not the dream site," he said. The wind had come up, and after being in the eighty-six-degree water for thirty minutes, he was cold. The towel draped over the back bench had been warmed by the sun and felt good against his back. "No rock wall down there, just piles of boulders." She let go of the console. Obi licked the salty water off Jamey's legs, wagging his tail.

How could Jamey ask Tina about the shark dream without revealing he'd accidentally been in it? He decided to try. "Did you have a dream with me in it? I turned into Hank and then he turned into a shark?"

Tina's face drained of color.

"It wasn't the cave site, right? This was about a week ago?" She nodded. "It looked like this." Jamey drew on the slate.

"How do you know that?" Tina sat on the stern's cushioned bench seat.

"I got a glimpse just now." Jamey hoped she'd believe this. "You motioned Hank around a corner and when he got there, he'd become the shark and you were terrified."

Tina nodded again, her eyes wide, as if she now realized Jamey did have a crazy ability.

"I don't know if the two sites have a connection, but I think that dream was separate. This area seemed familiar to you because it was the site of another dream."

"How would I dream about it and know the underwater topography? I haven't ever dived here." Tina pulled away, looking flustered.

"Didn't you say Hank used to go here for octopus or lobster or something? Maybe he described it." Hell, this was getting more confusing with every new discovery. "Let's go back to Lahaina. You're tired and cold." He wrapped a towel around her back and kissed the top of her head. She smelled like flowers, and although he wanted to hold her, reassure her, he resisted. "Tomorrow we can try South Maui." They both knew South Maui was a long shot. The body would never have drifted all the way down there, even if sharks hadn't eaten it.

Jamey persevered. "Let's get some food when we get back. We can make a plan."

Tina shriveled into herself with every minute. "No thanks. I'm working the store tonight." She pulled away from him and started the boat motor.

***

The only road through Kaanapali to the north part of the island was busier than the Hollywood Freeway, and Jamey made a mental note to avoid this time of day from now on. Sitting in traffic, he had a thought. Tina wasn't interested in searching the southern coastline. She'd told him firmly it wasn't a possibility. So, when he got through the rat's nest of traffic, he would drive around the north end to see if he could get a feeling for anything. With a personal item of Hank's, something might come through. How difficult would it be to get something that belonged to Hank?

Jamey pulled off at the Honolua Store to get a plate of kalua pork. While he ate at a picnic table on the porch outside, he phoned Tina. "I know it sounds strange, but it might help if I took a watch or wallet—something personal."

"Sure." Her tone suggested he could knock himself out. Whatever. "His wallet is in my bedroom on the dresser."

Tina's house was built in the old-time plantation style, situated at the end of a long, palm-lined driveway, making only the roof visible from the street. This place was definitely an improvement from years ago when she'd lived in a small apartment with two other girls.

The patio door was unlocked and Jamey let himself into the expansive great room. Making a mental note that Tina's security was lacking for a woman living alone, he considered mentioning that fact to her.

As he passed through the bedroom door, Jamey was hit with a sense of something powerful. He stood in the center of the bedroom and closed his eyes. The air was all but bursting with the presence of someone and it wasn't Tina. It was something else. Someone else. Hank, he guessed.

He looked in the open closet. Then he checked under the bed in case a live body was hiding there. Exhausting that possibility, he went back to the notion of Hank's spiritual presence. There was such a profound sense of sadness and desperation that Jamey found himself caught up in the emotion.

"Hank?" Jamey listened and waited. "I want to help you." He chose his words carefully. "I'm a friend of Tina's." He left himself wide open. Nothing. Only the sense of waiting. He wasn't sure if it was his own waiting.

The wallet sat on the dresser. "If you are unable to cross over, Hank, I might be able to help." Jamey closed his eyes and firmly gripped the wallet. "Tina and I are trying to find your body." A thought popped into his mind. If Hank was lingering, was he feeding Tina the location of his dead body? He'd never heard of any of this shit before.

"The dreams are helping, but we can't find the site." Had he just imagined the shift of air that laced through the room? Jamey opened his eyes. "Hank?" He turned around slowly, searching the smallest parts of the room in case something, even if it was barely perceptible, changed. Curtains remained still, a pencil on the dresser didn't move, there was no indentation on the bed. Something might move just a hair. Jamey's eyes scanned the room. Nothing.

This wasn't his area of expertise—ghosts—and he happened to know from Sixth Force training that it was almost impossible for spirits to move something on demand. He hoped for a sign, regardless.

The feeling of Hank's presence was strong, but no obvious communication resulted and eventually he gave up. At the bedroom doorway, Jamey held up the wallet. "I'm borrowing this. I'll bring it back."

As he headed out the driveway, he glanced in the rear-view mirror to see a large man with long black hair, standing on Tina's deck. He jammed on the brakes. This guy was bigger than Hank, more muscular. When Jamey turned around, no one remained. Who the hell was in Tina's house? He backed the car to the stairs, ran up to the deck and shouted into the house. "Hey, hi. I'm Tina's friend." Nothing. He walked through her house but found no one lingering. Did she have a roommate?

Driving north, he soon became lost in thought. How he could do an intentional dream jump without telling Tina about his ability? That is, assuming Jamey was able to dream jump purposely and without repercussions. He'd jumped into Tina's dream with Hank, but how he'd done that was a mystery.

His team in Afghanistan had cautioned him against trying again for a while. They'd discussed that he might have taken his last jump.

His brain-wave activity had changed drastically on the last jump. But the immediate problem was that he had an overpowering desire to help Tina, something he found impossible to ignore, like he'd somehow become a part of the mystery. A conduit.

He drove along the twisting north road towards Kahakuloa. Passing cow pastures and turnoffs to beaches, strange wisps of images presented themselves, like scents in the air, but he didn't know what most of them meant. The man on Tina's deck had been Hank's friend. He now knew that from the images that were coming to him.

Hank's physique was similar to Noble's, with black hair and dark skin, but Hank had been slim, his personality more jovial, less intense.

What Jamey got from the wallet was conflicting and confusing, but normal for a well-used wallet. Happiness and sadness, confusion and clarity. What he really wanted was a flash of where the body might be, not character traits. He didn't need to know Hank, the man who'd ultimately married her.

As he drove farther away, the connection became weaker. He put the wallet aside and drove past the Maui Airport and along the coast. Passing Paia, the island's windsurfing hangout, Jamey stopped at a pullout near Hookipa and watched the wave jumpers. Lines of white surf were dotted with neon-colored sails jumping the waves, speckling the turquoise water.

Back in the jeep, he doubled back towards Kahului, passing the sign to Mama's Fish House, one of the best restaurants on Maui.

Years before, on their only vacation without the twins, he and Carrie had eaten there. Pops had given them the condo for a week, hoping to save their marriage. But it turned out that the marriage was over, as well as the romance. Without the twins, Jamey and Carrie had dead space between them that couldn't be filled, and when they returned to the mainland, talk of divorce showed its worrisome head.

Reaching over to turn up the radio, Jamey sang along to a Pink Floyd song. He knew every word, every beat. Thing was, he'd never been a fan. Didn't realize he knew the song. Where had that come from? Jamey moved the wallet from his pocket to the passenger seat beside him and knew that he was in too deep with Tina.

Again.

CHAPTER 12

It was only 8 a.m. when Dave and Sally quit their jobs with Tina's Dive Shop. They'd decided to move back to the mainland. "Thanks for giving me one day's notice, Diver Dave." He'd come into the shop only to collect dive gear. They were leaving in thirty hours.

"I'm sorry, but Sally is sick, Tina." Dave hung his head. "I didn't want you to worry, but ...she has a lump in her breast and needs treatment. We're going to California to be near her family."

Tina grabbed Dave's arm and pulled him into a hug. "Oh, God, I'm so sorry." And she'd been ready to yell about his lack of consideration. "Is there anything I can do?"

Dave shook his head. "Just pray."

Tina wasn't much for religion, but it was worth a try. Her problems seemed small compared to a malignant lump. At least she wasn't fighting for physical health. Sally and Dave's bad news made her feel selfish, too self-absorbed. She should be more grateful. At least she was alive and healthy. Somehow Tina needed to find that version of herself who arrived on Maui eleven years earlier, after a horrendous fight with her parents about needing to find her own place in the world. The pain of defying her heartbroken mother and father was left in Seattle, along with the fear of disappointing them.

Driven by the need to prove them wrong, she'd eventually opened a dive shop, against all odds, and shown a profit. She had to get the shop back to that point. Focus on the business. Her pressing problem besides Sally's health was finding a new dive instructor. Or two.

Staring at the phone wondering who to call, she thought about how the Maui dive community must be talking about her. And now, she owned a dive shop with no instructors. Her friend Pepper had a captain's license and was a dive master, able to lead certified divers. Although she might be able to fill in for emergencies in the next two weeks, rising early was difficult for Pepper. She had a night job and needed to sleep in. And she was getting ready to go on tour with the world's most beloved rock icon. She'd try not to call on Pepper. Tina had the instructor's certification and captain's license. She needed someone like her, but who could be trusted with divers.

Her ninth call was fruitful. "Let me know if anyone over there on Kauai wants to come over to Maui to work, will you?" Tina's voice squeaked in desperation and she silently reminded herself to sound more casual.

"Aren't you selling the business?"

"No, I'm not selling." How to dispel the rumors? *Start diving again.* "Is that what people think?"

"I'd just heard something. Well, if you're serious, I have someone right here who's interested in moving to Maui. She just got here from Honolulu and Kauai is too ka-quiet for her."

"Put her on. Thanks."

After promising the instructor that Maui would be a great place, and securing a promise from her to fly over the next day, Tina stepped into the back alley to check the weather. A man in business casual clothes hammered a 'For Sale' sign on Mr. Takeshimi's tiny manicured lawn and Tina swallowed a lump in her throat. He was finally selling the house. He'd fought long and hard, hanging on to his Maui life. Mr. T shuffled across the laneway towards her wearing his house slippers. "Going to live with my daughter in Honolulu," he said.

Tina attempted a smile. "It's better to travel hopefully than to arrive disenchanted." She'd looked that one up for him, just in case. "Thank you, Tina." His smile was genuine.

***

The traffic was backed up on Papalaua and Tina abstained from honking only because the truck had her name on the side. And phone number. But she could have walked faster than driven. Should have.

When she first arrived on Maui, years before, she'd bought an old bike and rode it everywhere. Maybe she'd resurrect that old thing from the garage. Only trouble was Obi, but with summer coming up, he was better off left at the shop in air conditioning than going around Lahaina with her in a hot truck. She was five minutes late for the appointment and arrived frustrated. She really needed every second with the doctor if she was going to survive the day. Plunking down in the chair, she recounted to Dr. Chan how Jamey was a dream expert. He'd told her not to mention he was also a soldier. Apparently, there was some secret there. The psychiatrist was intrigued by the offer to read Tina's dreams and advised her to be careful with this process. "Putting your trust in someone else is risky, especially if you don't know them well," the doctor said. "I've known Jamey for ten years and I trust him," Tina fibbed, knowing the trust issue was up for debate.

"Just keep in mind that his interpretations might not be accurate, Tina." Emily Chan's brows knit together.

"What if this moment, right now, right here, is a dream, Doc? Maybe I'll wake up to discover Sally isn't sick."

"Let's try some of the triggers to wake up, then." Doc Chan patiently watched as Tina jolted and pinched and blinked. Nothing shot her into another dimension. When the appointment ended, she promised to take Jamey's interpretations with a grain of salt.

Back in the sunshine, Tina whistled for Obi to come

out from the shade of the clinic's bushes and then let him into the truck. It would be a sad day when the island became so populated that rules about dogs dictated Obi's freedom. Already with the new Kahului airport, you couldn't walk your dog through the building to greet an incoming passenger. No one trusted that you knew your dog wouldn't pee inappropriately or jump up on people. When Tina had first arrived on Maui, the airport was small and homey. Not now with international flights coming in on the hour. She called Jamey's number.

"What's up?" He sounded winded.

"You okay?"

"I'm on a run in the pineapple fields," he explained.

"Can you meet me when you're done? I need to talk to you."

"Is five o'clock okay?"

"Perfect."

The memory of what he looked like all sweaty caused a shot of electricity to ignite inside her and she quickly hung up. Her cheeks heated and she chided herself for thinking of Jamey in this way. It had been so long and a lot had happened since he'd been hers. Or, she'd thought he was hers at the time. He was still handsome. Still very sexy.

The day before, she'd been sitting at her desk when a friend called to ask the name of the guy in the passenger seat of her truck earlier. "Which guy was it?" she'd asked. "The one with ratty white blonde hair or the short-haired hunk?" She'd surprised herself describing Jamey this way. When her friend verified it had been Jamey, Tina found herself saying, "You don't want to get messed up with him."

"Getting messed up is exactly what I was thinking about."

Tina laughed, but after saying he was leaving Maui soon, she hung up, annoyed.

After picking up a prescription and some mouse traps

at the drug store, Tina drove into the McDonald's drive-through and got herself a burger and fries. The sauce dripped on to her shorts and she reached for a napkin.

Pulling into her parking space at the shop, she shut off the car, and then turned to look at Obi. The ribbon was still tied to his collar. She'd forgotten to remove it that morning. Or had she removed it and this was the dream? Oh God. Doc Chan mentioned trying to stick her hand through her body as a test for dreaming. If the hand sank into her form, it was not reality. When she tried, her efforts were met with a solid abdomen. "Great." She heaved a frustrated sigh that her life had come to these reality checks.

At her desk, the bills were piling up and Tina threw a towel on top so she wouldn't have to look at them. At least, not until she finished her fries.

"Hey Obi, get away from that thing!" Jamey's voice floated in through the back door.

It was five o'clock on the button and Tina smiled to remember how punctual he had always been.

Looking freshly showered, Jamey walked into the back room and sat down by Tina's desk. "Your pet was eating something unidentifiable by the dumpster." He looked reproachfully at the brindle-striped dog.

"Obi. Lie down." Tina made a face and pointed to a dog bed near her desk. "Thanks for meeting with me." Her smile didn't feel real but she hoped it looked convincing. "I want to talk to you about my dreams and some other stuff." After talking to Doc Chan, Tina knew she had to get some answers from Jamey, address the elephant in the room. Jamey nodded. "Okay." He lowered to the chair near hers.

"Dreams are very personal, I'm sure you know this." She took a deep breath. "It's hard for me to trust you enough to tell you what I dream about. I'd like to get past that."

"Trust is difficult." He sat forward in the chair, a crease between his eyebrows.

How would she say he'd used her to cheat on Carrie when she was pregnant? "When I met you and we had what I thought was a real connection, I gave you my heart." It hurt to admit this to his face.

He waited.

"But now I know that you had twins at the time you were with me." Jamey's eyes widened slightly.

"This is where the trust issue comes in." She looked him hard in the eyes. "You were having this fling with me while your wife, or girlfriend, it doesn't matter which, was back in Seattle with newborn twins."

An expression of relief crawled across Jamey's face that horrified Tina. He sat back in the chair. "You think I was married when we met?"

"Maybe not married, but I know Carrie was very pregnant. I did the math, Jamey. Your girls are ten." Tina sat back in her chair, matching his pose, feeling slightly smug.

"You're almost right." Jamey nodded. "They'll be ten in a few weeks. And they were premature, like most twins. Firstly, I wasn't married when I met you, Tina. I'd broken up with Carrie. Remember I told you we split up about a month before I came to Maui." His eyes searched Tina's face. "What I didn't know, and what Carrie didn't know at that time, was that she was pregnant. When I came home from Maui, all crazy in love with a dive instructor in Lahaina, Carrie told me that we were having a baby." He nodded. "We had a history of splitting up and reconciling. Our relationship was never solid. She wanted us to get married. When we found out it was twins, there was no way we could face the challenge of parenting if we weren't together. I knew I had to give you up and face my responsibility. Two babies are a hell of a lot of work." He nodded at the thought. "We formed a solidified front. 'Course now, we see the mistakes we made, but we still pat ourselves on the backs for our motives."

He looked at her, his eyes soft. "I wanted those babies

with all my heart. I'd always wanted to be a dad. I was mid-thirties. So, we got married." He shrugged. "I didn't want to give up what I had with you but I had to. I'd made two babies and I had to step up to the plate for them and for Carrie. We got married. I had to think of it as a happy day, given what was in store."

Jamey took a deep breath and changed tacks. "We stuck it out until the girls were five, then Carrie asked for a divorce."

Tina swallowed. "I thought you were cheating on Carrie with me."

He shook his head. "No. Do you trust me now?"

"I don't know. Maybe."

"Did your shrink think I was wacky, asking you to tell me your dreams?"

"She wants to hear what you say." She wouldn't tell him that Dr. Chan had advised her to tread carefully.

Jamey wheeled his chair across the small expanse between them, took Tina's hand in his two and looked into her eyes. "So, thinking I was married or at least had a pregnant girlfriend when I met you…that's what I've been feeling from you—this dislike?"

"Pretty much." Tina winced.

He laughed, the smile lines at his mouth and eyes looking sexy as hell. "You mean there's more?"

She withdrew her hand from his. "Isn't that enough? Katie said your girls were ten and that made them either born or on their way when I met you. When I remember our last day together, something was different about you."

"I was upset to leave you. I loved you."

She gulped. "You didn't answer my calls."

"Carrie picked me up at the airport and told me about being pregnant. I had to think about what to do, Tina. I thought it was the best way to make you hate me and move on."

"You should have told me the truth. All these years."

Jamey let out a sigh. "I'm sorry for the way I handled

it. You have no idea how much I regret doing that."

"Me too. I regret it."

He let go of her hands, pushed his rolling chair away. "Can we move on?"

She nodded.

"Let's hear about your dream then."

"It was different this time. I followed Hank from the other side of the wall and we approached the cave from the back. But a wave carried us out to the sand before we could go inside the cavern. Then Hank dispersed into a million particles and disappeared."

She might have said that as she reached for Hank's hand, he held out the only solid thing left—a tiger cowry shell. It fell from what had been his hand. Tina lunged for the shell and woke. The cowry had disappeared and that was how she knew she was truly awake. Thank God. Along with a precise arrangement of M&M's on her bedside table, Tina knew she was not still asleep. She'd formed the letter H with the candies just before turning out the light, and then admonished herself for eating candy in bed without brushing her teeth.

Jamey stroked his chin's stubble with one hand while conversation drifted in from the next room. Katie's friend Megan was training to be the second shop girl and the two talked about great snorkel spots. "Honolua...Mile Thirteen...Slaughterhouse Beach."

Finally, Jamey spoke. "Here's what I think." He held his arms out, like he was wide open. "What I'm going to tell you is strange and falls in that area of weirdness that most people don't subscribe to because there's not enough tangible evidence."

Tina sat forward, their knees almost touching, her eyes narrowing.

"Keep in mind that I'm not guessing on some of this stuff and making extremely educated guesses on the rest. This is my talent and I know a lot about this shit." He squinted at her. "And it would help if you believed, either in the fact that there are things we don't know about in this world, or in me." He smiled. "I hope it's me. Actually, I hope it's both, for your sake."

Tina wasn't sure what she believed in, but she nodded because she wanted to hear his explanation.

"Okay, here's what I am very sure to be true." He took a deep breath. "Hank definitely is not alive in this world. I know you're still hoping, but I feel the closure of his human life. Hank no longer exists here." He waited.

She covered her mouth to keep a sob from escaping. "I'm sorry, honey. I am. It's my guess he's lingering between worlds, unable to cross over. Maybe your hope is keeping him here.

I'm not sure."

She waited for him to tell her how he knew this for a fact.

"Or, because his body hasn't been recovered. I don't know. A lot of what I get is just a feeling, but it's pretty concrete."

Tina's eyes filled with tears.

Jamey pulled her chair closer.

"I think I always knew he was gone," she said.

He nodded. "We need to find his body, in case that's how we can help him, Tina. I think that's what he wants." He pulled her to stand with him, took her in his arms and whispered into her hair. "We have to keep looking."

Tears dripped onto the shoulder of his T-shirt. "But the cave isn't familiar. Or the coastline, or anything about the dream."

"Let's not give up yet. That's all I'm saying. We need another clue to find this place."

She didn't want to give up. They'd continue. Jamey hugged her tightly and she had to admit, it felt good to be touched. By him. Even at such a lonely moment in her life with Hank, she wanted to turn to Jamey. He was right. Hank was gone. They had to find that cave. "If it even exists," she said into his shoulder.

"It's got to." Jamey's tone gave her hope, for the first time in months, and she buried her face in him, not worrying about how he'd interpret her need for closeness.

CHAPTER 13

When the Armed Forces found James Dunn, and he completed weeks of testing to determine his exact abilities, they were impressed. Very. His country "needed him." The offer to join the top-secret division, Sixth Force, was laid out before Jamey like a contract with the New York Giants. The United States Army made it very hard to refuse. He didn't.

By this time, Carrie had remarried and the twins were almost seven years old, playing outside with other neighborhood kids, gaining their independence. Jamey convinced himself it might be a good thing if he left for a while. Going to war for his country would be one way to use his gift for the good guys. Big time.

In Sixth Force, he never met the other members who used paranormal abilities to aid the military, only heard that there was a team. "Like X-Men," he'd joked, "but no interaction." The officers didn't laugh.

Jamey had his own posse of support people who surrounded his talent like it was the Hope Diamond, people who were also sworn to secrecy. He'd been told that he was the only dream jumper in the force. Maybe in the world. "Start growing your hair, Freud, and a full face of hair," they said, giving him fake glasses. "Your identity has to be kept under lock and key."

For the first time in Jamey's life, he was surrounded by people who knew more about the paranormal than he did. They'd all been recruited because of some talent, even if it was only knowledge about the sixth sense. Other suspicious characters came and went around the base but they never interacted, as ordered. The only thorn under his saddle was the plan to use his ability to extract information from prisoners of war, men whose fear and bravery he could feel when he entered their dreams.

He'd plowed on, juggling the knowledge that the dreamers were the enemy, with the fact they had families who loved them, and that these men would ultimately betray their cause through their dreams. As Freud, Jamey was a human weapon for the American military in Afghanistan.

The upside was that his ability to enter their dreams for information was an alternative to torture techniques. During his tour, Freud helped locate American prisoners, mine fields, caches of weapons, an enemy general's hideout, and innocent children who were being used in the trade for weapons. True, the dreaming prisoners had to be drugged, but it was safe, and still better than water boarding as a technique for extracting information. Sixth Force used a secretive compound of truth serum that was similar to sodium pentothal but with much better results. The drugs ensured a much clearer picture of what the dreamer stored in his mind. Even Jamey didn't know the exact combination of drugs administered. The trick was to get to the targeted information, and then get out quickly to relay the information without the prisoner's knowledge. And so far, they'd been 100 percent successful. "A phenomenal track record," his team always said.

But jumping took a lot out of him. One dream, every few days, was all he could manage. The kind of dream he encountered with war prisoners was totally different from the friendly ones and left him drained. Four bodyguards took care of his security needs, with two constantly in his company. Those burly men rarely left his side, including when he'd fly to Germany to decompress for a few days after a traumatic jump.

The trauma and subterfuge wore thin after a while, though, and Jamey began to question how much longer he could prostitute his abilities, even for the good old USA.

On his last jump in Afghanistan, he'd been led to the prisoner's cell—a stark twelve-by-nine space with a cot on the left side and a toilet on the right. He'd seen worse. In cells, and in prisoners. The drugged young man lying on his cot held the lives of thousands in his thoughts, they'd said. If Jamey could find the location of the weapons, children would grow to see adulthood and families would be reunited. This was the payoff for what he experienced in Afghanistan—months of living the soldier's life, waiting for their compound in Kandahar to be bombed, existing on the other side of the world from his children while they reached milestones.

Jamey had named his guards No. 1, No. 2, No. 3 and No. 4. On this particular day, No. 4 accompanied Jamey into the cell and stood watch. No. 2 waited outside the cell. Once the doctor checked the prisoner's heart rate, he nodded to Jamey, who flashed a look at his commanding officer. "Ready."

Nods were exchanged and a chair was set beside the Taliban youth's head. Jamey had the best results with touching the back of the neck. He laid his hand under the prisoner's thick black hair. Jamey closed his eyes and matched the breathing rhythm. In…hold slightly…and out, out, out, pause. Slumber breathing was much slower, and it took a moment for Jamey to match the pace. He was aware of being watched by his support team, but after almost forty jumps, he wasn't bothered by the audience anymore. It was understandable to be curious.

The process took a count of ten, from the time he started to fall, to arriving in the dream. He didn't play along the way anymore. Not in the army. With friends and girlfriends, he used to somersault and then try to stand, only to arrive on his butt. But now, he focused on the task and prepared for whatever might come. It'd be stupid to risk arriving unprepared. Especially with a young member of Al Qaeda who was trained to kill first and never ask questions.

On this particular mission, Jamey dropped into the dream quickly. The soldier was maybe late teens, and in the dream, he was kneeling on the floor beside a bed, struggling to help his mother. A mother was a good start to ensure Jamey's success. The boy feared for his mother's life. More good news. Soldiers pounded on the hut's locked door.

Jamey kneeled beside him and spoke in Pashto. "It's okay. I'm your friend, here to help you."

The boy looked immediately relieved to hear that help had arrived. He lifted the covers to show his mother's life-threatening wound. Blood pumped from her abdomen.

Mother, wound, desperation. The opportunity seemed too good to be true. Jamey put his hand on the wound and spoke again. "You are healthy and strong."

The blood-soaked dress became clean, whole, and the wound closed. The mother opened her eyes and smiled at her son. Jamey nodded to the boy, whose name he knew to be Atash, and glanced at the wooden door that was vibrating with the soldiers' force. "Go away!" he said. Immediately the pounding stopped. Jamey's ability to turn the dream to his advantage was something he didn't take lightly. After a year of being in war-torn dreams, he had to use what he had to get in, get out, and expend as little emotion as possible. Atash spoke. 'Who are you?"

"A friend." Jamey watched the mother sit up, then fade away. "And now I need you to take me somewhere."

"Thank you for saving my mother." It didn't seem to matter that she'd disappeared. "Where are we going?"

"You tell me. We need to get to the ammunition." Jamey knew this next part was tricky and crucial. The prisoner could wake suddenly. Or, the dream might take a turn and they'd be on a picnic with zoo animals. Keep the dreamer focused. "Atash, take me to the hidden weapons." The boy froze. "But…"

"We need to go now." Jamey drew upon his psychological training to choose his words with great care.

Talking people off ledges was a fine art that worked only part of the time. "It's your duty. The time is now." He started for the door.

Atash followed. "But what are we doing when we get there?"

"We must fight for the cause." This phrase often worked.

They ran out the door. Bombs detonated along the street randomly and gunshots fired as they ran from doorways. Jamey knew they wouldn't be hit because this scene was of his making. Still, he pretended the threat was real. They ran at an inhuman rate, down alleys, behind buildings. It never failed to excite Jamey that in dreams his level of fitness was beyond reality. Similar to an X-Box game all the soldiers at Kandahar played in the off time, HALO, Jamey Dunn got to live the dream, literally.

They arrived at a bombed building, rubble blocking the former doorway. "Is this it?" he asked Atash. Jamey had been hoping to recognize something from his briefing on this mission.

Atash pulled him inside a gaping hole in the wall of a giant warehouse. The place was stacked to the ceiling with boxes, all similar, marked with Arabic writing.

"This is a front for the munitions storage." Atash nodded and waved him on.

Jamey followed along the rows of boxes until they reached the end of one row. Atash pushed aside a large bin, an impossible weight to tackle in waking life, and exposed a trapdoor in the cement floor. "Is this really what it looks like? When you're not dreaming?" The answer was crucial.

"Yes, it's a warehouse in the south end of Kandahar. Just like this." Atash did not seem reticent to give up the information. They never were in dreams.

"What's it called?"

Once the location was determined, and Jamey verified that Atash was leading him into the munitions storage chamber, he had one last task. It wasn't something he was ordered to do, but he could never leave these dreams without trying. He turned the young man, clutching his shoulders, and stared into his face. "You will be interrogated by some of the finest peacekeepers in the world and you must cooperate. Peace between us all is essential."

The boy in front of him closed his eyes and turned, as if to block out Jamey's words.

"Make sure that no innocent people are hurt to further this cause."

"People must die," the boy said with eyes closed. "They will be rewarded."

"No one must die for this. Your mother wants your cooperation. If you tell the interrogators what they need to know, you will be rewarded with a life, not an afterlife. Not yet. You are needed here." Atash stood frozen on the spot, hate spreading across his face. "Cooperate. They want to help you."

Slowly Atash evolved into an enormous monster with huge fangs.

What the hell? Jamey had just enough time to take off running. How did the kid just do that? The dream never backfired this way. Bursting through the building's opening and out to the street, Jamey was tackled from behind and went down face-first in the dirt. He rolled free to the side and stood quickly but before he could take off again, a swipe from a scaly arm had him flying through the air. Willing himself to land safely, he fell in a pile of concrete rubble. Unhurt. *What the hell had just happened?* The kid had conjured up a monster, but how? This was his show. He had to get out of this dream. Pronto.

Atash had somehow guessed Jamey was his enemy. Was he trained in resisting mind-bending techniques? God help him if Atash was the one in control of the dream. Jamey needed to return to the portal where he came in. He couldn't count on the dreamer waking. Atash probably wouldn't willingly wake up until he killed his enemy.

Taking off at lightning speed, Jamey zipped through alleys and streets. The beast loomed overhead and took another swipe with its tentacle-like arms just as Jamey ducked behind a car.

"You are only Atash!" Jamey shouted before he sprinted across the street to the alleyway that connected to the mother's house. The roaring behind him confirmed it didn't work. *Fuck.* He'd lost control. This was beyond anything he'd ever experienced. The young soldier no longer existed. Atash was now a killing machine. This took lucid dreaming to a whole new level.

Jamey turned and held up his hands to the approaching beast. "You are a mouse!" he shouted above the earth-shattering roar, but nothing changed. He had to make a run for the hut.

The monster followed, jumping over houses, squashing everything in its sight. "You tricked me, Dream Man," it roared. Jamey took off for the door he'd left minutes before. But the monster materialized in front of him, its slimy fangs dripping with yellow pus.

Okay, this was bad. He had to come up with something better if he was going to get out of this dream alive. Maybe he couldn't stop this monster, but what if he could still summon his own?

"Kraken!" Jamey yelled as he bolted to the safety of an alcove. *What the hell was a kraken?* It was the first thing he thought of and it turned out to be much larger than Atash's monster. Jamey willed it to attack. As the kraken towered over its prey, Jamey made a dash to the door. This was his moment. Summoning all his focus, he made the door open and ran through. Squeezing his eyes shut, he jumped into the room, imagining himself back in the prison cell. He was sucked backwards as the sounds of the monster fight faded to eventual silence. Within seconds, words from the Sixth Force doctor broke the silence. "The prisoner is awake! Cover Freud!"

Jamey woke up laying on the floor outside the cell,

with an oxygen mask on his face, a defibrillator beside him. Whose heart stopped? If he had to take a guess, he'd say it was probably his, seeing Atash was being restrained by the guards. How the hell did Atash wake up?

"The kid had control." Jamey ripped off the oxygen mask and attempted to lift his head. A lightning bolt split his head in two. His vision went black, but not before he heard Atash scream, "You were tricked, Dream Man. Not me."

Jamey had the faraway feeling of being lifted onto a stretcher as people scrambled around him. They hurried him down the hall and into an elevator. He could hear the kid still screaming in Afghani. "You will die for this."

The oxygen mask went back on Jamey's face. He must have passed out when he jumped through, flat lined, and in the commotion the prisoner woke from the drugs and nobody noticed. But dreamers never wake after the drugs. Not for at least an hour. His head threatened to burst wide open. He saw only blackness in front. The pain had robbed him of vision. The rolling gurney bounced along before he was lifted onto a bed, and then jostled and poked. Medical questions, answers and commands were tossed back and forth over his head like a game of monkey in the middle. He was the monkey. The last thing he remembered before he passed out was Sergeant Milton's voice. "The Al Qaeda knows about Freud."

***

The octopus was not in the aquarium. It was there an hour ago, but now it was gone. Dave had forgotten to return it to the ocean before he'd left for the mainland. Damn. Tina's immediate reaction was to search the floor to see if it was slithering towards the door in an effort to find the ocean. They could exist in air for a short while. "Katie!"

Katie and Megan ran into the shop from talking to the parrot guy outside.

"The octopus has gone AWOL. Help me look." A heaviness pressed against Tina's chest.

Searching the floor, shelves, cubby holes, boxes, behind tanks, aquariums, even the back room did not produce an octopus. The creature must've slithered through a one-square-inch hole at the top and made a run for it. After days of watching people in the store, determined to escape its prison, it finally chose a hostile environment over imprisonment. *Shit*. Everyone was trying to save itself but her. She had to take some control of her life. She needed to get back in the water. If the octopus was found alive, she'd release it herself. *I'll get my sorry ass in the ocean and watch it swim away.*

The shop's doorbell chimed. A moment later, Jamey called into the back room. "Tina, come here." He stood by the same aquarium the octopus had occupied until recently.

She knew he'd be upset they'd lost the octopus. He'd been feeding it bits of chicken for days. "What is it?"

"Here's your octopus." Jamey pointed to the tank. "Chameleons of the sea—octopi."

Tina looked in the glass enclosure. There was an extra rock in the aquarium. The new rock had eyes that watched Jamey's hand move a piece of chicken from right to left. "Oh, my God!" she said. "You've been watching us search for you, you little stinker." Tears warmed her eyes and she didn't question why. She clapped her hands and Obi wagged his tail at the commotion.

"Would you like me to take him to Mala Wharf? Let him go?" Jamey dropped the piece of chicken into the tank and watched it fall on the gravel in front of the octopus.

"Would you?" With all its hiding places, Mala Wharf would be a perfect habitat. "Thank you, Jamey." Then she remembered her promise to release him. "I'll come too."

***

As they waded into the ocean with the covered plastic bucket, Tina was holding her own. It actually felt good to be in the ocean. So far. She fastened her mask to her face and they took off for the wharf. Once in the shadow of the structure, she removed her snorkel and grinned. Let's do it."

She opened the bucket's top and they watched the octopus move into the ocean and pulse away to the closest hiding spot, spraying ink behind. "This has got to be better than the aquarium," she said before putting the snorkel back in her mouth.

They looked around the pylons for the next ten minutes, exploring the minute sea life that inhabited the smaller spaces and slim cracks in the cement. She could feel Jamey's watchful eyes on her.

When they reached the shallows and walked in to the beach, she smiled to herself. "That was actually enjoyable. I might be able to try diving soon."

Jamey smiled back. "I tell you. There's something about me that brings out the best in you."

***

They hadn't found the dream's dive site after four afternoons of searching the Maui coastline. Today's search had turned up nothing, and they both knew this was it. Jamey was frustrated. Tina's newfound enthusiasm after the octopus's release was being challenged. Her dreams were coming almost every night, and she looked like her last good sleep was months ago.

The only headway they'd made was that she was now entering the water. As long as they held hands, she was able to stay in the ocean. Jamey had no circulation in his hand after about ten minutes, but at least she was trying.

Not sure what landmark to look for, he'd had to rely on her drawing of the dream site. She could do a lot of things, but drawing was not one of them.

What he really needed was to see the dream site within the actual dream. Jamey wracked his brain trying to figure out how to jump in without giving away his ability. Assuming he still could jump. And even if he did get into her dream, he had to be prepared for the worst possible outcome afterwards.

Pulling into the Kihei dock that afternoon, Tina leapt off to get the boat trailer. With all the turmoil in her heart, it was hard to think how that woman had any spring left in her step. She jogged up the paved hill while Jamey kept an eye out for incoming boats, ready to back away if he needed to move aside. He and Tina had this docking routine down to an art, even though the afternoons of searching were now over. Every inch of the coastline had been covered—even areas that held no possibility. "Maybe it isn't a real place," Tina had said earlier.

"It's possible it doesn't exist in this world. If dimensions exist alongside ours, like Einstein suggested, anything is possible," Jamey said.

Goddammit. He needed to sleep beside her, which might be tricky because he had a feeling that Tina might have a boyfriend— probably a big, muscled boyfriend who hung out at her house. Jamey couldn't pretend the idea didn't irk him.

With the boat out of the water, he hooked up a hose to flush the engine with fresh water. Tina just watched him, silent, distracted. What the hell was going on with Hank? If he didn't get a grasp on things soon, she'd give up all hope. He was too far into it now to consider that. Not just the investment of his time, but the effort and emotion was adding up. And he was about to invest a hell of a lot more if Hank's body didn't turn up soon. Dead or alive.

CHAPTER 14

Tina was at the compressor changing tanks for refills when Jamey rounded the corner. Why was it he never came in through the shop's front door? Was it because Katie was excited about all the time her uncle and boss seemed to be spending together? She'd overheard Katie the day before, telling Jamey to "make a move, old man," but couldn't hear what he'd said back.

"Did you dream last night?" he asked. He tried to face her but she turned away, tired of having people witness these moments. "I hope you're keeping a dream journal," he said.

"It's on my desk." She nodded in the direction of the shop's back door. Too many dreams and too few hours of actual sleep had left her feeling only partly in this world. Every night after she woke from dreaming, she'd pace the floor and pore over maps of the coastline, wondering what had happened to Hank's body. She appreciated Jamey's concern but it was looking like soon she'd have to let all this hope go.

Jamey returned, studying the calendar. "There might be a pattern to when you have the cavern dream." He rubbed his chin. "If there is…" He showed her the paper. "Tonight, is a possibility." He smiled apologetically.

A momentary tug pulled at her heart. His slightly askew smile was something she'd always found endearing, as well as distracting. He was a handsome man, no doubt about that.

"I'd like to observe you dreaming tonight," he continued. "What I'm looking for is a sign that you're in REM. I want to see if you talk in your sleep, move your

---

Kim Hornsby

legs and arms, that sort of thing. I'll need to be in the same room as you."

"I don't think I sleep-talk, or even sleepwalk."

"I have a theory, but let's eliminate the talking and walking and make sure you're in REM."

Somehow, his request made her uneasy. "It's not like you haven't seen me sleeping before," she whispered to herself, not making eye contact with him. But this was so intensely personal, letting Jamey into her bedroom while she slept. "I don't know if I can fall asleep with you in the same room."

"You've slept with me in the same bed before." He shrugged.

Tina's cheeks warmed.

"Let's try." He seemed indifferent. "And if tonight is another dream night, wouldn't you want to make the effort?"

She desperately wanted to put a name to what was happening. "Yes." She did. "I'll call when I close the shop and you can come over then." She gulped at the thought that she'd just asked James Dunn to visit her at bedtime.

***

As she shuffled papers around her desk, the phone rang. Tina's parents were calling from the first class section of an American Airlines flight on the way to Kahului Airport. "We are getting ready to touch down on Maui in an hour."

"What? You're kidding!" Her heart rate jumped through the roof.

"Your father and I are coming to Maui to check on you." Her mother sounded peeved.

"In an hour?" Tina was not ready to see her parents. It had been over a year since she'd last been to Seattle.

"We'll see you at the airport."

150

Tina's truck sped across the isthmus that joined the two lumps that made up Maui. Pulling into the newly renovated Maui International Airport, she took a deep breath and looked at Obi in the passenger seat. "Wish me luck, boy."

Thirty minutes later her parents were driving her nuts and they'd barely been on Maui long enough to sweat. For one thing, her mother failed to mention her father had hired a car. Of course, they would prefer the luxury of a chauffeur-driven Lincoln to her pickup truck. Her parents had ridden in her truck only once, and her father had lectured the whole way on why she should've bought a Chevrolet instead of a Ford.

"Do you still have that dog?" her mother asked shortly after saying hello.

Tina's defensive bristles stood at attention. "Yes, I do. He's my constant companion, Mother, and his name is Obi."

"I'm not saying he isn't and don't get all huffy with me, young lady. I just asked."

It was going to be a long two weeks.

At baggage claim, Tina searched for their luggage on the carousel then handed the suitcases to their driver, a man who had no idea what kind of verbal abuse he'd have to endure over the next weeks.

"You can join us for dinner at eight. Father made reservations at The Bay Club for three." Elizabeth Greene looked sideways at her daughter. "Unless you want to bring the dog to dinner and we'll change the reservation to four."

She and her mother finally shared a smile, but even so, Tina didn't know if she was mentally ready for the two oddballs she called Mother and Father. She attributed the alienation to their inapproachability. Part of it was that Elizabeth was not born into money and had always been terrified of showing her meager upbringing. Or her real self. Even emotion was taboo, once she'd reinvented herself.

Raised by her drunken grandmother, Elizabeth Alton needed her life to be orderly, clean, and proper. That's why she'd set her sights on Philip and his money. After having twins, and then losing one to an accidental drowning, Elizabeth ruled the family like a crazed dictator. Kristina was kept on a short leash. Like a pet. The closest Tina ever got to a childhood pet was a bush in the garden that attracted butterflies. She'd sit and watch them circle the blooms, but when her mother noticed, she had the gardeners remove the bush.

"Bugs are dirty," she told her daughter. It took years for Tina to realize that pets weren't germ-ridden, disease-carrying dirt balls, but sources of unconditional love.

When the air-conditioned Town Car was packed with the luggage, Elizabeth turned to her daughter. "You are holding up better than I thought." From her distance of six feet away, Elizabeth Greene was exhibiting her unusual method of mothering. "I'm glad to see that, Kristina."

The absence of a hug was painfully noticeable to Tina. Her mother broke away from the moment to enter the limo, Tina hugged her father.

"She's tense from the flight," he explained.

What little affection Elizabeth had for children had died along with Tina's twin, Kristoffer.

Tina nodded and waved them off before heading to her parked truck. She loved her parents, knew they meant well, but it would be fourteen days of steely patience if they were planning on spending much time around her. Maybe they'd leave early if their curiosity was satisfied about her state of well-being. Over the next few days, she'd have to hide the fact that she was holding onto a thin ledge of sanity with the tips of her fingers.

Cruising along the coastal road, Tina sang along to a Janet Jackson song on the radio. Things were going well at the shop, and she dared to feel confident that the new instructors would work out. Finally, the shop's problems seemed under control. Pepper and Jamey had done an afternoon charter with the new dive instructor, Shelley. When Tina reached Lahaina and found Pepper unloading tanks from the shop truck, she rubbed her friend's shoulders. "How'd it go?"

"Shelley and Jamey got on like a house on fire, if you know what I mean." Pepper smirked. "Heavy flirting," she said, with a hint of envy in her eyes.

"Don't look like that, Pep. You're leaving soon anyhow." Tina couldn't help the jab.

In the alley, Shelley asked Jamey if he'd mind showing her the beach dive locations that afternoon and Tina's brows knit together as she eavesdropped. Pepper put a finger to her shushed lips.

"I'm not the best resource," he said, "seeing as I don't live here. Pepper's the expert." Jamey peeked around the corner "Want to show her, Peppie?" he called, fully aware they were eavesdropping. Pepper detested the nickname and Jamey knew it. Tina stifled a laugh. Jamey's humor was something she'd missed in the last ten years.

***

Pulling his jeep alongside Tina's truck, Jamey noted that it had been left at an angle, as though she'd been in a hurry. The house was lit up like a Christmas tree in the dark Maui night and music floated outside from the upstairs windows.

Obi barked from the deck above. Dogs who announced visitors were helpful. Jamey climbed the stairs to the second-floor balcony and met the brindled dog at the top. "Hello, boy. It's me," he said, extending his hand for a sniff.

"Come on in." Tina called from the kitchen, where she stood holding up a Corona. "Want one?"

"No, thanks." Jamey slipped out of his flip flops and opened the screen door. "Whose red truck?"

"Noble's. He must've gotten a ride to work." Seeing Jamey's expression, she explained. "Noble lives in the cottage in the backyard. Hank's best friend. Didn't I mention Noble?"

Jamey watched her search the drawers in the kitchen. "This drink will be my insurance to sleep." She held up the beer. Reggae music boomed from the living-room speakers, and Tina danced around the kitchen after finding the bottle opener. "Beer, my downfall, I'm afraid. But you already know that." She flashed a big smile his way, the first one of that intensity and honesty he'd seen since returning to Maui. This version of Tina reminded him of the nights they'd spent at the Hyatt, an empty bottle of wine and a pack of condoms on the nightstand.

He leaned on the countertop. "How much have you had to drink?"

"Not a lot." She stopped. "This is my first beer." Her voice dropped to an exaggerated whisper. "But I had wine with dinner. It's just that my parents surprised me by arriving on Maui today and it's very stressful and horrible and blah blah blah…" She stroked Obi's back with her foot, balancing precariously and taking a swig of her beer at the same time. "But I'm on medication that makes the effects of alcohol intensify."

He reached to grab her arm just before she toppled over.

"And my parents took me to dinner and all that."

"Ah, your parents." He nodded like he knew the need to escape from parents though his mother died when he was four and he loved his father with a vengeance. "I take it you're not ready for bed." Tina laughed. "Ha! In any other situation, I would've said something really funny about you needing to buy me dinner first, but…" She grabbed his hand and led him to the couch, where he was told to sit.

She fell over, practically on top of him. "Whoops." Sliding off, she scooted down the length of the couch.

"Sorry." The colorful throw pillows made a cozy nest and she patted the seat beside her for Obi. "I'm glad you're here. I appreciate your help." Her words sounded clipped, like she was making a supreme effort to speak clearly. She laughed at her own drunkenness. "I hate it when I slur. Do I sound slurrish to you?" She looked at Jamey as if she just realized something. "Oh no, did I drink too much? I don't usually do this but oh, my, God, does it ever feel good to feel this GOOOOD!" She dropped back into the cushions. "Hey, I deserve to have a fun time. I'm a widow, my business is barely surviving, I'm having strange dreams and hallucinations, and my parents are in town trying to convince me to sell the dive shop and move home to Seattle.

What the hell? I'm going to have a drink…or six." Tina took a long chug of her beer.

"They want you to sell the dive business?" Jamey was shocked they didn't know this was where she belonged.

She looked at Obi. "I'm a big girl and don't have to do what they say. Dr. Chan says that I don't have to spend my life trying to be the perfect child for them just because my brother died." Tina looked up and shook her head as if to clear it, and then leaned over to kiss her dog. "Oh, Obi. You'd hate Seattle." This was getting interesting. Tina sighed, her expression turning sad. "It wasn't my fault— Kristoffer drowning." She looked off to a corner of the ceiling. "She'd stay in the house when we played in the backyard and in those days, pools weren't fenced or anything. I didn't even see him fall in, I was so busy playing with my dolls." Tears filled her eyes. "After Kristoffer's death, I did everything they wanted. For years. Decades. Not now. I can't. This is where Doc Chan and I draw the line. I'm not going to move to Seattle and marry that boring ex-boyfriend and have 2.5 children. Heck, my eggs are drying up and I'll be lucky if I have 1.0 children, even if I got married tomorrow." She sat up straight and looked at him.

155

Jamey spoke. "Let's make sure that you don't have to move to Seattle if you don't want to." He watched her lovingly stroke Obi and remembered when he'd been the recipient of all that attention. Tina had soft hands. Once she'd said "I'm very tactile" as she lightly tickled his lower abdomen with her fingers.

"Leaving Maui won't solve anything." He couldn't help saying the obvious.

She didn't hear him, lost in her own thoughts. "I wanted a baby so badly." Tina glanced in the bedroom's direction. "Hank too."

Footsteps sounded outside and Tina eyes widened. "Shit. Here comes Noble. I don't want him to know you're here, watching me dream and talking and everything." She stood and seemed to be looking for somewhere to hide. "He's so fussy about me and I didn't tell him everything. I'm really trying to avoid him right now."

"Tina, it's okay, we're old friends." He motioned for her to sit on the couch and she plunked down.

Noble's emotions were evident even before he appeared. Jamey readied himself and watched him appear at the top of the stairs outside. When Noble saw Jamey he froze and took stock of the sight in front of him. He opened the screen door and walked in. This was the person he'd seen on the deck when he drove away with Hank's wallet. A strange aura surrounded Noble that Jamey interpreted as anger. "What's up?" He looked collected, but Jamey knew he was mad as hell.

"Nothing," Tina said. "Noble, this is my friend Jamey Dunn. And this," she waved her hand towards the Hawaiian dude in the doorway, "is my beloved rock, Noble." He was big, up close. "Hi, Noble." Jamey stood to shake hands but Noble stayed halfway across the room, oozing hatred.

"Jamey." His gaze never left Tina.

She smiled in her tipsy fog, looking between both men. "Are you guys just hanging out, or what?" Noble walked in a few steps.

Obi sniffed at him, his tail not wagging.

"Hangin' and talkin'," Tina said in a singsongy voice that revealed her level of inebriation. "Come join us." She sat on the couch and Jamey followed.

Noble sat on the armrest of the couch beside Tina, his leg brushing hers, and Jamey almost let a laugh escape. He didn't have to be psychic to understand what Noble was trying to convey. If body language didn't already say it all, he could almost hear Noble's territorial growl.

In a few sentences, Jamey learned that Noble had just finished work at the Hyatt show, *Drums of the Pacific*. He was a hula dancer.

"Tina's favorite show in the islands," Noble said.

"How'd it go tonight?" Tina slurred.

"Good."

"Were you a dancer growing up?" Jamey needed to get to the heart of this guy.

"No."

Tina and Noble smiled at each other, and Jamey nodded at them like this was really interesting information. So this was the man in Tina's life. The one she was excited and confused about. Jamey hoped Noble couldn't read his thoughts.

"Jamey is helping out on dives." Tina grinned. "He's Katie's uncle."

Noble looked down his nose at Jamey.

"He's supposed to be on vacation, but we've put him to work." She gestured to Noble. "Noble was Hank's best friend."

This whole situation was uncomfortable, but it was more than that. It was downright strange. Jamey would have to back off. Noble was probably waiting for her to put Hank to rest before he moved in emotionally. But she'd said she was avoiding him. Looked like he already had moved in physically. How the hell was he going to watch her dream with this guy hanging around?

The conversation was stilted for far too long before Tina took the last sip of her beer. "Well guys, I'm tired now, so I'm going to bed." She stood and looked between both men. "Party is over." She clapped her hands once. "Chop chop. Time to go. Everybody up and out." She made a swishing motion with her hands, as if to sweep them from her house. Noble seemed to be waiting to see what Jamey was doing, but Jamey wasn't sure if Tina remembered he was staying.

Jamey took the lead. "I'll walk you to your room and see that you actually find your bed."

Noble stepped between them. "That's okay, newcomer. She knows where her bed is."

Jamey wasn't sure how to diffuse this situation, but before he could, Tina stepped in, giggling. "Newcomer! Oh, Noble. You are too funny." She play-slapped his chest. "Good night, sweet, noble Noble. Don't worry about me." Her words slurred together as she turned to Jamey. "I've known Jamey a long, long time—longer than I've known either you or Hank. Isn't that funny new information?" Tina grabbed Jamey. "See?" She stretched up and kissed him full on the lips. Jamey broke off the kiss, gently easing her away.

Tina didn't seem to notice. "Jamey is no newcomer. He's an oldcomer." She laughed at her joke. "Sweet dreams, Noble." Tina grabbed Jamey's hand to lead him to the bedroom. "Noble's house is out back," she called over her shoulder.

He turned to Noble. "We're old friends. That's all." He considered leaving, but he still needed to see her dream if he was going to help her. It was too good an opportunity to waste. "I'm a yell away, Tina." Noble's scowl would've brought lesser men to their knees.

"She's safe with me, man." Jamey felt like an intruder. Why was Tina avoiding Noble?

"Goodnight, Noble." Tina jumped in. "Jamey's just going to tell me a bedtime story." She walked to the bedroom and Jamey followed, prepared for the possibility of Noble jumping him from behind.

Once inside the room, Tina slammed the door shut. "Oops!" she called. "Sorry, Noble!" She fell onto her bed. Face first. And didn't move. "G'night," she whispered into the bed.

Jamey eventually opened the door, but Noble was gone.

Tina looked like she was out for the night. The nicer side of him wanted to move his car and pretend to drive away, just to set Noble's mind at rest, but he didn't want to miss the dream, especially because a long dream could be over in less than a minute.

Then again, she might take a while to get into a dream state from passing out drunk. He closed the door and locked it, and then quietly lay down on the far side of the bed, facing Tina. He needed to be close, touching. At least, he told himself that as he lay staring at her, drinking in her scent.

CHAPTER 15

At 1:36 a.m., Jamey was still awake in Tina's bed thanks to the coffee he'd had at nine. Thinking about Jade and Jasmine's approaching birthday, he was pulled out of his thoughts when Tina started falling into a dream. He reached over and touched her balled up hand, and then matched her breathing, concentrating on the journey.

He melted into her sleep pattern and fell. It was like sinking below the surface of reality when he entered a dream. Like being slowly sucked backwards. Uncle Don had named it jumping because leaving the dream required a jump. Sinking in, jumping out, unless the dreamer woke and that was a sucking sensation. Don had joked that 'dream sucking' didn't sound quite right.

And now it appeared that after several months of stagnation, he was able to jump again. Like rediscovering a favorite childhood toy, he was thankful, relieved almost. His body sank slowly into a sunlit ocean and the dream materialized as though a fan had cleared smoke to reveal a scene before him.

Tina stood on the ocean's bottom, below him, oblivious to his arrival. Her flimsy gown swirled around her body like a jellyfish membrane. He landed behind her, out of sight. She seemed distracted by something further along the rock wall. Next thing he realized was that they were breathing underwater.

Jamey stayed close when she took off, swimming with purpose. How long could he keep his presence a secret? If he remained undetected, Tina never needed to know he'd been in her dream. He'd simply follow her until the dream ended, taking note of anything that might be a clue to the body's location. But he'd have to hang around to exit the dream with her. Leaving before the dreamer woke would involve returning to the portal—the exact spot where he'd landed. This time it had been the surface of the ocean. Finding that portal would be impossible. When Tina popped out of the dream, he'd leave too. It had been years since he waited until the dreamer woke up.

Tina navigated around a jutting rock, falling out of sight, and Jamey hurried to catch up, eager to not lose her. Rounding the turn, he stopped. She was right in front of him, waiting for him. The look of question and disbelief on her face was difficult to read. Jamey shrugged, unsure what she was thinking. Then he caught sight of something ahead of them, twenty feet away. Moving. A man.

When he pointed, Tina spun around. Her hand flew to her heart. The look of sadness on her face told him it was Hank. Even if he hadn't seen the pain in her eyes, he knew. It was embarrassing to invade Tina's dream like this. Embarrassing and awkward. But this might be the dream that showed the location of the body. He had to persevere.

As they approached Hank nodded at Jamey and the three of them continued along the wall until it curved into the shallows. Massive boulders lay strewn across an expanse of sand, like a giant's board game. Closer to shore, the rocky outcrops were connected. In the middle of one large rock face, blackness indicated an entrance. Hank and Tina kicked towards it, Tina always fifteen feet behind him.

The opening was black as tar, as big as a garage door, and revealed nothing of the interior. Jamey glanced towards the surface. Twenty-five feet deep, he'd guess. This was where the dream usually ended. If the pattern continued, he might have less than a minute to get a handle on where they were. Soon Tina would wake and it would all be over.

One last look confirmed Hank had entered the cave and Tina was trying to follow him. As the swell then pulled her away from the mouth, its opposite force then pushed her closer. He saw her strategy in trying to use the movement to take her inside. She kicked when the force propelled her towards the cave.

With time almost up, Jamey exhaled his way to the surface to reduce the possibility of an air embolism. Just as his head popped through to the air, the familiar pull of being drawn backwards took him. He opened his eyes wide to see more before blackness set in, but the sucking sensation won over and soon he was lying on a mattress.

He was in Tina's bedroom. In the dark. His heart was still beating and the pills he'd brought with him remained in his palm. No CPR necessary. Four months, two weeks and six days after the fiasco in Afghanistan, he was able to dream jump again.

When he looked over at Tina, his happiness clouded. The dreamer was still dreaming in REM. What the hell? He could feel her dreaming. How did he manage to wake up? He hadn't returned to the portal.

First, he had to remember what he'd seen in the last few seconds of the dream. Then he'd question this new turn of events.

When he got sucked out, he'd barely had time to break the surface, but he did see the expanse of ocean in front of him. He'd also noticed a tall shadow looming to his right. The sun was at his left, which could be important, or not. He hadn't had time to see if Lanai or Molokai was behind him. That would've helped. Damn.

Tina startled. Jamey jumped off the bed and her eyes fluttered open. She looked disoriented, and then focused on him sitting in the chair, staring at her. "I had the dream again, and you were in it."

***

Tina looked over at Jamey and felt the front of her

body. She was soaking wet. "I had the diving dream. I'm soaked." Tina licked her hand. "Salt. Did I sleepwalk to the ocean? Did you see?"

"No. You didn't leave the room." He looked as scared as her.

"I didn't go anywhere? Were you watching me?"

Jamey nodded.

The good news was that someone else had been in the room to set things straight. The bad news was that Jamey verified she hadn't left the room. But she was drenched. Last time she'd woken wet it hadn't been real. This time, Jamey Dunn was sitting on the edge of her bedroom chair, staring at her like he couldn't figure out what happened.

He stood, searched the floor for water and walked into the hall. "Nothing unusual out here," he said. He sounded puzzled. That was good. Someone else had been let into the horror of what was happening.

Tina got off the bed. The flimsy dress she'd worn to dinner with her parents was clinging to her shape, revealing more than she wanted to. She peeled off the dress and her underwear, letting it fall to the floor. As she reached for her robe she felt a presence and turned to see Jamey standing in the doorway, staring at her. At her naked body.

He took a deep breath and crossed to her as though he expected something.

She wrapped the robe around her shivering body. "You said I didn't leave the bed, right?"

The hunger in his eyes was disconcerting. "You got wet, just as you woke."

"This might still be the dream." Tina lowered herself to sit on the edge of the bed. She looked up. "Where's Obi?" She hadn't seen her dog.

Jamey sat down on the bed beside her, their legs touching, and spoke softly. "Not here. Let's just lie back in the bed and wait…" He pushed her backwards, gently, but the look on his face was frightening. Predatory.

Tina's eyes flew open. She stared at the ceiling of her

bedroom. It now looked different from seconds before. The fan whirred above her. She wasn't wet. Obi lay at the bottom of the bed with the blue ribbon on his collar. What had just happened? She and Jamey had been sitting on the bed. And now she was waking again? Jamey stood beside the bed, looking at her expectantly.

"I had the dream again and you were in it," she said.

***

Jamey moved towards her and Tina scooted back to avoid contact. She looked scared of him. Obi jumped off the bed and, when she called him over, she fingered the ribbon on his collar.

"Tell me about the dream." He wanted to hear her version. Her eyes were wild, her breathing erratic. "You okay?" He wasn't sure. He sat on the side of the bed.

"Yeah, I just dreamed that I woke up, and we were having this conversation, but Obi wasn't here and you weren't like this...you were strange. But this seems like reality now." She held the ribbon on Obi's collar.

Tina methodically recounted the diving dream to Jamey, as if he'd had no knowledge of it. Good. They'd been underwater. Hank led them to a cave. Jamey surfaced while she followed Hank. Once inside the cave, she couldn't find Hank or see anything. No matter how far she swam, in any direction, she touched nothing. That was when she woke up. Or thought she did. "I was drenched in salt water. You were here. Obi was gone. You went into the hall to see if there was water on the floor. I got into a robe. We sat on the bed together. Then, I guess, I really did wake up. Obi was at the end of the bed."

That would account for the extra seconds Tina stayed in the dream. Jamey turned on the closet light and looked inside, not sure what he'd find.

She pinched her arm so hard it would definitely leave

a bruise. "This is reality, Tina. I assure you."

She didn't seem convinced, and her haunted eyes frightened him. She scooted back in the bed, against the wall, hugging her knees. He was unsure which door to open in his explanation of what had just happened. "Lucid dreaming is when the dreamer recognizes they are in a dream. You are having lucid dreams, which is not unusual. As well as knowing you're dreaming you're also having a precognitive dream. Like when a person gets a weird feeling about boarding a plane and then it crashes. But your dreams are different."

Tina nodded for him to continue even though the expression on her face told him to stop.

"Some theorists, Einstein included, introduced the idea that the past, present and future all exist together and that time is not linear." Jamey shook his head. "It's hard to conceive, but that was Einstein's theory. Here's what I think." Tina's eyes were wide.

"I think you're getting what I call a glimpse." He'd present this carefully. "I still think maybe Hank hasn't crossed over completely. He's between." Jamey took one of her hands, feeling her tension. He had to tell her. Had to. "I'm going to share a secret with you. And it's a strange one."

She looked into his face, all innocence for another few seconds.

"I hope you don't think I'm crazy." He said this more to himself. "I know you dreamed about the cave with Hank." Jamey met her eyes. "I was there. I could see you in the dream and you saw me, right?"

"You had the same dream? What? How did you do that?"

"I'm not sure how I do it, exactly, but I can enter people's dreams if I try, and sometimes I do it even if I don't try. It's beyond lucid dreaming. Way beyond."

"Oh, my God, Jamey. Is this part of your ESP thing?"

"Yeah, you could say that. And lately, I haven't been

able to do it. That's why I'm on leave. I'm no good to the army without this ability. But just now it worked and I was in your dream. That's what I was trying to do tonight, to help you find the site. And it finally worked again."

Tina looked like he'd told her the moon was actually made of cheese. She took a deep breath. "Let's say that's all true. Aside from the obvious questions about how in hell you visit people's dreams, did you see anything?" She squinted at him. "I didn't surface this time."

"No, I did, but I didn't see much. Just a shadow from the corner of my eye."

"Did you see Hank?" Her voice reminded him of the mistrust you feel on a foggy day for what you can't see.

He nodded. "I did."

"Tell me."

"Long black hair, dark shorts, short wetsuit. You looked concerned that I was in your dream. Hank looked like he'd been expecting me." Jamey considered how much to reveal to a widow still grieving for her husband. "He looked like he knows I'm trying to help."

"Oh, Hank…" The words had the fragility of tissue paper.

The closet light extinguished and Jamey looked over. "Hank?" His whisper hung in the air, waiting. The streetlight outside was the only illumination in the room. Jamey's hand motioned for Tina to wait. "Hank? Are you here?"

"Jamey, you're scaring me!" The sound of Tina's voice had Jamey beside her in one second.

He put his arm around her shoulders and whispered, "The light went out just as you said his name, and I'm just wondering something. Don't be scared."

Tina shivered. "Hank?" Her voice held such hope. "Honey?"

Nothing perceptible happened. "If it's him, I'm sure he *wants* to communicate, Tina, but from what I know about this, it's very difficult to cross spectrums."

They waited. Finally, Tina broke the silence. "His body is in that cave."

Jamey nodded and took her hand in both of his. "I think so too. And Hank is trying to show you where to look."

***

As outlandish as it sounded to enter someone else's dream, it was comforting for Tina to think that Jamey had been there. But now it looked like he was paying the price.

He sank his forehead into his hands and moaned. "Have you got any ibuprofen?" His body tensed with a spasm.

"I'll get two."

"Get six and some water." He fell back on the bed.

When she returned, Jamey had two small pills in his palm. He grabbed the water and downed the tablets. "What was that? Should you mix these?" She dropped six ibuprofen into Jamey's hand.

"Yup."

What was happening?

"You know CPR, right?" It looked painful for him to talk.

"Yes, but…"

"Good. The painkillers should kick in soon," he grunted.

"Jamey, should I call the doctor? Take you to emergency?"

"Not unless I stop breathing. Until then, there's nothing anyone can do. This is kind of off the radar for a doctor." His face was contorted in pain, and when convulsive shivering started, Tina pulled the blanket over him and ran to get an extra duvet from the guest room.

When she returned, he was so still that her heart jumped into her throat. She touched his shoulder to make sure he was alive.

"Jamey?"

He moved slightly.

"Should I call an ambulance?"

"No. It'll pass." He buried his head in the pillow and she watched helplessly from the edge of the chair. They'd switched places so quickly. His eyes were scrunched in pain and his breathing was ragged. A frighteningly thick vein throbbed at his temple, and she laid her hand gently on his forehead.

"Don't." He cringed.

If she called the paramedics, they'd arrive in less than ten minutes. Did he have that long? She slipped her silk robe over her shoulders, knotted the belt and glanced to the clock. It was after two a.m., pitch dark outside and terrifying inside. She was in control of a potentially serious situation and didn't feel competent to make decisions like whether or not to trust that Jamey would recover from this excruciating migraine without medical intervention.

Besides the fact that he was obviously in horrendous pain, she thought about the repercussions if they had to call an ambulance. Or worse—what if he died in her bed? Her first thought was the horror of Jamey dying, the second thought was that it would be her dream's fault, and the third was that her parents would find out she had a man in her bed. Dead. Should she find Noble?

She had to trust that Jamey knew what he was talking about. Didn't she? He had exceptional abilities that she knew nothing about. And she never had. She watched him shiver, his teeth making a clacking noise. Jamey. He had never been who she thought he was. Ever. "Should I get in bed to warm you?"

"Not cold. Keep the car keys handy. In case."

She mentally located what she'd need to rush him to the clinic in town. Keys, backpack. Obi, who was usually perceptive about these things, stayed at her side, either concerned that Jamey was in their bed or sensing something bigger. Tina counted the seconds, and then minutes, waiting for Jamey's pain pills to take effect. As she watched him struggling, she hoped to God that whatever it was, it would pass before it took his life.

***

The searing stab in his temple robbed Jamey of sight as he endeavored to block it. Jumping had been risky. The pain wasn't as bad as last time and came late, but it still made him feel like his head would explode; like hot blood pounding in his brain, unable to escape, violently strained against his cranium in an effort to release the pressure. At least his heart hadn't stopped. Not yet.

If the Advil and Percocet didn't do it, he'd go to the emergency room for morphine and hope that worked. Tina would drive. Good thing he'd brought Percocet.

After his last jump, he'd spent days on the morphine drip. When they told him what happened, the emotional pain of knowing a man died had him wishing he was still on morphine and seeing spiders on the ceiling. The dreamer died. And it became one of the military's dirty little secrets. Jamey hadn't bothered to ask for particulars. Details would make him feel worse.

It wasn't until weeks later that Sixth Force revealed their theory that the Al Qaeda prisoner was planted to find "the Dream Man." The weapons Jamey'd seen in the dream did not exist. Sixth Force believed that the whole incident had been a red herring to throw the Americans off the trail of a rebel cache. The idea that Atash's mission had been to kill Jamey became big news within the force. And justifiably so.

But Atash died before they could extract information needed about Al Qaeda's knowledge of a dream jumper. Why they hadn't kept him around longer was a mystery until he guessed that it had been an accidental death, not an execution.

The existence of a soldier planted to kill the Dream Man put Jamey in a shaky position, wondering if Al Qaeda had a file on him. His inability to jump was only part of the reason Jamey left Afghanistan. Although Sixth Force recommended he stay within the confines of an army base until they extracted more information, Jamey knew if the bad guys hadn't identified him he'd be safer off base. He'd gotten a good feeling that they had no idea who the Dream Man was, only that he existed. Leaving seemed like the only option.

Jamey's head was still pounding when he woke in Tina's bedroom, but his vision had returned. The clock read 5:06. Tina was asleep in the chair, curled around a pillow, her breathing barely audible. Jamey didn't even try to use his ability to see if she was dreaming. The pain had subsided to a tolerable level. Tolerable for him.

When he took a deep breath, a stabbing jolt of pain seared through his head like a soldering iron. Jamey fought against blacking out. He must have called out because Tina was there, kneeling beside him, her gentle hand on his forehead. "Jamey?"

"I'm better." It took everything he had to say that.

"I'm worried you might die." Her voice was shaky.

"I won't."

"Do you always get these headaches?"

"Lately." It hurt to talk. He closed his eyes. "Sorry I took the bed."

"I'm sorry this happened because of my dream," she whispered. Jamey tried to nod but grunted instead.

Minutes passed and finally she spoke. "Would you mind if I lie on the other side of the bed?" She waited for his answer. "I want to be closer to keep an eye on you."

"Get in." Jamey tried to shift over and Tina put her hand on his arm.

"Don't move," she said.

He barely noticed her slip in under the covers.

"The alarm is set for 6:30." Her hand hovered above his arm. He could tell she was afraid of touching him. "Will it hurt your head when it beeps?" Tina whispered into his shoulder. "No." He closed his eyes and prayed for the searing pain to subside. And to live to hear the damned thing beep.

CHAPTER 16

When Jamey woke, sunshine oozed from behind the drapes and spilled into the room. The bedside clock read 11:24. Sleeping had erased most of the pain. It was just a dull migraine now. He was alone in the bed, the door closed, Obi and Tina gone.

Carefully, he eased out of bed and looked out the window. Tina's truck was gone. Noble's red truck was there. Shit. He wasn't up for a confrontation with Noble this morning.

Any other time he'd be happy to be in Tina's bedroom on a sunny Hawaiian morning—under much different circumstances. But Jamey had urgent questions that needed answering, especially because Tina's sanity was at stake, with the lines of reality smudging. A note was taped to the inside of the bedroom door.

J: I hope you feel better. Call me ASAP. I'm worried. It looked bad last night but better at 7. What happened? Kind of made me forget my dream. Please be well. Tina

Yeah, what had happened? He'd never been in a dream with a dead guy before. Was Tina simply dreaming about her husband, or was Hank giving his wife this vision to show her the location of his body? If so, he'd jumped the mind of a dead guy. Fuck. This was getting complicated. If Hank's ghost was lingering in the bedroom, then Jamey needed to think long and hard about what to do next. Probably sleeping in Tina's bed wasn't a good idea if Hank was the jealous type. Noble sure was.

He poured a cup of coffee from the pot in the kitchen and took a careful sip. Caffeine was good for migraines, but Jamey wasn't so sure he had a textbook migraine. The warmth of the liquid felt good going down. With the mug in hand, he went back in the bedroom to get his watch from the nightstand. Wearing metal on a jump was dangerous. It was one of the best pieces of useful advice Uncle Don had given him about jumping. For that reason, Jamey had never worn a wedding ring to bed, or his watch. In the testing he'd done with Sixth Force, he had helped determine that wearing metal ran the risk of losing control of the dream; strange things happened, he stayed too long, lost the portal. And that was deadly when he jumped with the enemy.

With the watch in hand, he noticed a presence in the room. The temperature dropped. Quickly. Someone was with him; someone who was not a living person. "Hank?" He spun around slowly, stopping to stare at the closet. If he flicked on the light, maybe Hank could turn it off again. "I'm trying to help her find you." His words were soft. "Can you help us?"

A piece of paper on the nightstand moved. Jamey watched until it shifted again. It moved to the edge in jerky motions, then fell to the floor. This was not his area of expertise, but he was pretty damn sure someone was trying to communicate. "I saw that." The air in the room was still cool. "Where is your body, Hank?" A whisper of a breeze moved through the bedroom, leaving an icy wake and then, just like a switch had been thrown, it was over and the room was warm again.

As Jamey bent to pick up the paper from the floor, his mind was racing with possibilities. The paper was cold. Frozen almost. What just happened? Dammit, he was a dream jumper, not a ghost expert.

Exiting the bedroom, Jamey felt another presence, but this time it wasn't a spirit. On the deck outside Tina's patio door stood two older people, perfectly alive and staring at him from the other side of the screen.

The man was about seventy, gray cropped hair and slightly paunchy, and the woman was country club-ready with steel gray hair and an overly formal dress for Hawaii.

Feigning innocence, he slid open the screen door. "Hello."

"Is Kristina here?" The older man's suspicious eyes grazed Jamey's form. These were the dreaded parents from Seattle, and they'd just watched him come out of their daughter's bedroom, fastening a watch around his wrist like he'd spent the night. Which he had.

"No, she's at the dive shop." He stepped through the doorway. "You must be her parents?" Jamey flashed them his best policeman smile.

The mother looked down her nose at him. "And you are…?"

Jamey extended his hand to the mother. "James Dunn. I'm an old friend of Kristina's, on vacation from Carnation, Washington." Maybe they'd think he knew her growing up. When a hand did not meet his, Jamey turned to the father. "Nice to meet you, sir." He gripped the father's hand with strength, hoping he'd appreciate a good handshake.

The parents blocked the stairwell.

"I'll be on my way now, but I hope to see you again. I'm diving off Tina's boat this week." When Jamey nodded towards the stairs, he hoped they'd move. Instead, they stood firm.

"Why are you in our daughter's house?" The woman looked ready to pounce.

Jamey knew the question was coming and had prepared an answer. "Tina forgot something here and asked me to swing by to get it."

The mother took a lingering look at Jamey's cup of coffee and neglected to hide a scowl. "I see you helped yourself to Kristina's coffee."

Geez, these two were a tough audience. "Yes, your daughter makes a good cuppa joe. Are you two sightseeing today?"

The father answered this time. "We've done all the sightseeing on Maui that anyone ever needs." He stepped closer, as though his next words were a secret between men. A cold steel wall had shot up around him. "We're here to make sure our daughter is not doing something that will ultimately bring her more heartache."

The message was clear and Jamey nodded as though that was his mission too. "I served in Afghanistan and can appreciate protecting someone." Mentioning the army didn't seem to help. They continued to stare at him like he was vermin. He said a quick goodbye and snuck behind them, to get as far away from the Greenes as possible. How had Tina turned out so sweet?

***

At least now Jamey was in on her secret, and for that, Tina was grateful. The burden had been lessened and broadened with the involvement of a second person, like diluting a stain.

After signing the invoice for gear she couldn't pay for and unpacking delivered boxes, Tina grabbed her coffee and found her way to the back room of the dive shop. Caffeine could not, in any way, be responsible for the bizarre dreams that haunted her. Could it?

"Anyone home?" Jamey's head peeked in through the back door. "How are you feeling?" Tina jumped up and almost hugged him, stopping just in time. She noted the difference between the Jamey who lay shivering and moaning in her bed the night before, and the vibrant, healthy man standing at the door.

"Better. Sorry to scare you."

"What was that last night?" she asked.

"Like a migraine, but before we talk about that, your parents are right behind me, looking for you." He glanced towards the store like they might be hot on his trail. "They saw me coming out of your bedroom twenty minutes ago. I told them I was picking up something for you."

Tina hid a smile with her hand. "Don't take it personally. They don't like anyone I know. Who did you say you were?"

"Your bisexual, homeless lover." He grinned. "Actually, I said I was a friend from Carnation."

"I'm looking for Kristina." Tina's father's voice boomed through the store. Jamey was right. They *were* hot on his trail. "Who?" Katie's voice was small in comparison.

"Speak of the devil," Tina whispered to Jamey, and disappeared into the shop. "Good morning, Father." She kissed his cheek, introduced him to Katie, and when Jamey didn't emerge from the back room, knew he was gone. She didn't blame him.

"Your mother and I are going to the golf course for breakfast and want you to join us."

"I ate already and have some work to do here, but I'll join you for lunch, or dinner later."

Her father looked around the shop like it was one of her childhood forts messing up his perfectly landscaped yard. "Fine. At least come outside to say good morning to your mother." This wasn't a suggestion. Even though she didn't live under their roof anymore, or take money from them, her father's requests still had the same effect as when she was little. She'd always obeyed.

Elizabeth sat waiting in the back seat of the Lincoln Town Car, her veined, bony hands folded across her skirted lap. "Good morning, Mother."

With a scowl, she got right to the point. "Kristina, there was a man at your house, coming out of your bedroom." She paused for effect. "Your father and I feel, regardless of your relationship to him, this is inappropriate behavior for a widow still in her grieving year." She looked over her glasses at her daughter, lips pursed.

Tina silently counted to five before sliding in beside her mother. "That man is Jamey Dunn, a former decorated police officer in Seattle and now a soldier in Afghanistan." Her parents would probably appreciate this information. She did. "But aside from that, he's not my boyfriend. He is an old friend and was only at the house this morning to get something for me." The truth was not an option.

"He was in your bedroom." It was clear Elizabeth thought this would be disturbing information, but Tina only nodded. "You must be careful. People will misinterpret."

A sigh slipped out before she could censor it. "This is Maui, Mother." She softened her voice. "There's no upper echelon here to police my improprieties, even if I was being inappropriate for a widow." Tina resisted the urge to mimic her mother's voice.

"Don't remind me that you now live in a society we don't approve of." She lowered her voice. "Now, come to breakfast with your father and me." Her voice took on a tone of finality.

Tina attempted a smile, even though Elizabeth was now busy straightening her skirt, her eyes lowered. "I have things to take care of here, but I'll join you later."

After watching the Town Car round the corner, Tina ran over to the Sunrise Cafe to get a smoothie. She hadn't eaten like she'd told her father and now needed something in her stomach. She hated to rock her parents' boat, especially after her father's heart attack two years ago, but dammit, she was an adult. Would she ever get used to disappointing the people she loved?

Poor Noble. He hadn't been amused at Tina's tipsy display the night before and she couldn't blame him. Why had she been so unnecessarily flippant to a man who'd been her rock all these months? And then, this morning in the kitchen, when she'd tried to explain Jamey's presence, he cut her off. "Aside from my own feelings about this, Ti, you can't be getting drunk and letting men into your bedroom. I know you, and that is not you," he'd said. "If you have something to say to me, then say it. Don't use…Jamey," he'd spat the name, "to tell me something."

Tina cringed at the memory of the conversation. She ordered her mango smoothie and sat on one of the cane chairs in the cafe to wait. Noble didn't know the full story.

Later she would find him and apologize without revealing everything. How could she say that Jamey was hanging around to help her because he was psychic and could jump into her dreams to help find Hank's body? That made him sound like some crazy-ass liar who just wanted in her bed.

***

Pops had a theory. "Maybe you're not the jumper, Jamey. Maybe the ghost of Hank is able to enter his wife's dream or she's jumping into his thoughts."

Jamey stretched his long legs to reach the balcony railing and slouched down in the cane chair. "That sounds crazy, doesn't it?"

Pops laughed. "More than jumping dreams?" His breathlessness told Jamey that his father was smoking again, despite his emphysema. "This would be new territory, so be careful, son."

"Maybe Tina is somehow jumping into Hank's 'glimpse' and I'm piggybacking her jump," Jamey said. "Do ghosts have glimpses or dreams? And if they do, how can Tina jump into them?" He sighed. "I wish I could talk to Uncle Don about this." It came out of Jamey's mouth before he thought that the comment might resurrect painful memories of Uncle Don's sudden death. But his uncle had been the one to explain the intricacies of being able to enter a dream.

He'd been the one to call memory dreams 'glimpses.'

"Me too, son. I'm not thrilled you got the headache." Pops' cough was back too.

"It wasn't that bad. Not like last time." Jamey watched a humpback whale breach and smack the surface with its massive weight out in the channel.

"I don't know what to say." Pops' voice was filled with concern. "Aren't you under orders to not jump?"

"It was a suggestion." No one could control Jamey's

jumping. It was his skill alone, and the military didn't own him. If he was done with jumping, they'd be done with him faster than he could say 'medical leave.' That wouldn't be so bad. Not when he thought about Jade and Jasmine. "They advised me to not jump." His voice was filled with hidden meanings.

"Be careful, James. I don't want to get a call from the hospital saying that you're in a coma…or worse."

"I don't want you to, either." But now that Jamey knew there was a ghost involved, the game had changed. Unfortunately, he knew precious little about ghosts. Sixth Force probably dealt with this kind of shit, but he wasn't privy to that information. Maybe if he presented the situation and asked what they thought, he'd get some suggestions but telling them would be costly. At the risk of letting on that he was jumping, he needed some answers, because Hank's presence added a whole new level to a game Jamey wasn't equipped to play.

***

Unless Tina's parents lightened up, it would be an excruciatingly long visit. In the past, she'd fantasized about getting them drunk and asking them all the questions that puzzled her. But that would never happen. Her mother didn't drink and Philip could hold his liquor like an elephant. Still, they seemed miserable, and they were making her equally miserable with their smothering concern for her wellbeing. Funny thing was they neglected to see what could actually make her happy.

After lunch, once again, they suggested she sell the dive shop and come back to Seattle. "Take the bar exam, Kristina. Join your father's practice," Elizabeth said. Their disappointment in her not following the life plan they'd made for her was still holding up after all these years.

"I love it here, Mother." Tina imagined herself

standing with a shield in front of her body, like Doc Chan suggested. "I'm just saying that the memories are painful." Elizabeth seemed to be searching for the best way to get her point across. "You need a change right now. Maui will always be here if you decide to return some day." The word 'if' stood out to Tina like an arrow headed for her heart. Elizabeth took a mint from her purse and handed it to Tina. "Garlic," she said.

Tina popped the mint into her mouth.

The Town Car navigated her twisty driveway. "I'll think about it. Thank you for lunch and I'll talk to you later." She kissed both parents on the cheek, always her custom.

Rounding the side of the house, she and Obi crossed the backyard to find Noble sitting on the front porch swing of his cottage, watching her.

"Are you available for an apology, or should I come back when I'm not an asshole?" Tina tilted her head and tried smiling.

"I'm available." Noble didn't smile back.

"I am the worst friend, so stupid, ungrateful. I feel badly about how I talked to you last night. And this morning. I was severely hung over." She sat on the top step and stared at the traveler palms in her yard. "Did you know that those palms are nicknamed 'Helpful Imposters'?"

Silence.

"They grow east to west, helping lost travelers. You know that, right?"

Nothing.

"But do you also know they're not palms, but are in the bird of paradise family?"

"Tina, stop."

"I'm sorry, Noble. I'm selfish." She didn't look over. More was needed. "Jamey and I are not lovers." It sounded ridiculous to say it aloud. "He slept in the chair beside my bed because I asked him to stay. I've been having bad dreams." She cleared her throat, buying more time to let

Noble speak, but he said nothing. "I didn't want to burden you anymore. I rely on you too much. I just want to get us back to normal."

A mynah bird screeched from the lemon tree beside the cottage, and the caged bird next door called back. "Jamey ended up getting such a migraine that I almost rushed him to the clinic." Still nothing. "He's an old friend. I scuba-certified him long before I knew Hank." She looked over and noticed a slight twitch in Noble's jaw.

"That explains it," Noble whispered.

She took a run at the next part. "Noble, I want to talk about what you suggested the other night." How to approach this without sounding callous? "About having a baby."

His silence was making this more difficult. He usually finished her sentences, if she needed it. Not today.

"It would be easy to give in to the feeling that the loss of Hank was also the loss of my opportunity to have a baby."

"Ti, if you're worried about what Hank would think..."

"No. I'm not." Hank might approve of Noble taking over the honor. More like the task. "But I can't think of having a child right now. It's the worst time for me to make a huge decision. I have to figure out how to let Hank go. I just can't seem to be able to do that."

"I can help." Noble looked softly at her.

"You have helped. I think until Hank's body is found..."

"Ti…" Noble was one sentence away from a lecture.

She held up her hand to stop him and just then her cell phone rang. "Might be the shop. Just a sec." She glanced at the screen to see it was Jamey, let it go to message, and then asked Noble to forgive her for being insensitive. "I'm doing the best I can."

"I know." Noble's forehead was lined in worry. They hugged, holding on to each other tightly.

"I'll get us a movie to watch tonight." It was a question.

Noble pulled back and smiled. "Something with robots."

Back upstairs, she fixed Obi's food and set the dish on the floor. Her phone rang again. "Hi, Jamey."

"Hey there." He sounded happy to hear her voice.

Standing at the dining-room window, she stared out at the wide open channel to the south. "What's up?"

"I've been talking to my father, and my counselor in Afghanistan, who both know something about jumping dreams." He paused. "I have some ideas. Assuming that the dive in the dream is a real site, we need to find that beach."

She knew that already. Hadn't they tried?

"I'm not sure I should jump your dream again because it was risky for me."

She imagined him pacing the floor as he talked. "I agree."

"I think the next step is to look from the air."

It was a good idea. They didn't have any other fresh options. "Okay."

"I reserved a plane for eight a.m. tomorrow. I'll pick you up before seven."

She hung up the phone and went into the kitchen to get a Coke. For the first time in months, the heaviness on her chest had been lifted. She was lighter. Jamey had gone ahead and taken the initiative to rent a plane. He genuinely wanted to help her find Hank's body. This was what she needed. Not the hugging kind of help, or someone telling her to move on, but the kind of assistance that might bring her closer to moving on. Jamey actually cared about the one thing that was keeping closure at bay.

Noble had given up months ago, when he persuaded her to have Hank declared dead at the two-month mark. That was his closure.

He'd pushed her to sign the papers and Tina had given in, thinking he might be right. When her parents concurred, she'd signed on the dotted line. She'd expected closure for both her and Noble, but he seemed more miserable once his friend was declared dead. Something told her that if Hank had deserted her, he wouldn't have left Noble, like this. He loved his best friend fiercely. For twenty years. He wouldn't have left Noble in this state of misery.

Still, closure hadn't come for Tina. Even with the surfboard, the wallet and Jamey's verification of Hank's death, she needed something more, something to prove to her that Hank was not in Europe or South America living a new life. Better evidence was needed to prove her husband's death. Something that verified he hadn't intended to leave her.

* * *

Hank had seemed overly sophisticated for Maui when Tina first met him. Here was a man who'd lived all over the world, had a degree in art history, and was semi-retired at the age of forty. She'd heard through the gossip circles that he was independently wealthy. He'd followed his Grace Kelly–lookalike girlfriend to Maui. Her father owned art galleries on Front Street and she managed them.

The night Tina met Hank at the party in Kapalua, she had just signed the papers to buy the dive shop and was feeling incredibly full of herself. With every intention of making a success of her life on Maui, she celebrated her bravery by enjoying too many glasses of wine. Pepper told her to remain seated, drink some water, and eat the plate of appetizers placed in front of her, while she got herself some food.

But from her poolside seat, Tina noticed an intriguing man across the expanse of the deep end. His lanky comfortableness drew her in and she stared as she ate. Later, when her head cleared a bit, she found herself in conversation with him.

"What do you do, Tina?" He took a sip from his highball glass. "I bought a dive shop today. I teach scuba and have a degree in business." For the first time in her life, she wanted to tell someone that she had an education beyond the knowledge of Maui's sea life. Talk of the ocean led to recipes for seafood dishes. "By any chance, do you have a good recipe for seafood bisque?" he asked.

She laughed to think how useless she was in the kitchen and told him so.

"Really? I love to cook." He rattled off his favorite recipes.

"You are frighteningly in touch with your feminine side," she teased.

"Cooking isn't feminine. Besides, I love to eat." He said it in a way that made Tina think there was an underlying meaning to that statement.

He then introduced her to his friend Noble, a large Hawaiian man. They'd been friends for many years, and when Hank excused himself, Noble moved in, letting it be known that he was available, where Hank was not. Noble was handsome, probably more so than Hank, but there was something about Hank that reached out and grabbed Tina by the throat. Noble's presence barely made contact. Months later, Hank would tell her that he tried to ignore her that night, "but you were just so damn cute."

At an art gallery opening days later, Tina was sipping a glass of merlot when she saw Hank, his arm around his girlfriend's ivory shoulders. Again Noble tried to engage Tina in conversation. They pondered which paintings were more marketable. But she couldn't keep her eyes off Hank. Noble was a player, and she had no time for the uncertainty of him when her desperation to have a baby was gnawing at her thirty-two-year-old body. She wanted a life partner and a family, not a hula-dancing playboy.

Two months later, Tina found herself invited to the "New Year's Eve Party of the Year" at a Hollywood producer's house in Wailea. She'd recently broken up with a boyfriend from Honolulu and needed something to brush away her feelings of inadequacy. This was her social debut, not only after the breakup, but after her recent accident with an exploding tank. The chin wound that resulted from the explosion was healing nicely and could now be covered with makeup.

Earlier in the day, Pepper had insisted she get out of her wetsuit and make an effort. "Come on, Tina. We're thirty and single. Let's do the party. We're on the guest list," she'd pleaded. Without really trying, Tina looked smashing in a sequined mini dress and stilettos. And from the moment they walked past the bouncer at the door, the two women attracted male attention from every direction.

Hank stood by an outdoor fountain, talking to a group of rock stars. He did a double take when he noticed her. This time he excused himself and approached her. "I remember you. Tina, right?" His twinkling eyes made her heart flip, and she secretly hoped the absence of the girlfriend was significant. After an initial conversation about the paintings in the house, Tina professed she knew nothing about art. "I am a total Crayola girl."

Hank took her by the arm. "Let me give you the twenty-minute art history crash course," he said as they strolled towards the hallway's collection. At some point, she revealed that she owned paintings. "Inherited," she said. "They were my grandmother's. I'm not sure if they're worth anything. It doesn't matter because I'll never sell them. Some painter named Hebert. Maybe Jacques, or Francois. Francois, I think."

"Never heard of him, but perhaps you'd like an appraisal?"

Tina stared at the sexy man in front of her, sizing up what he'd said and how he said it. "They're at my house." She smiled coyly, unsure of what direction they were taking and how far they'd go with this.

"Airtight containers?"

She shook her head.

"The salt air will ruin them." His voice was all business now. There was a pause, and then Hank's attitude changed, like someone hit him in the chest. "I'm engaged."

Tina thought he was kidding. "Did you mean to say, 'I'm engaging'?"

He paused. "I'm getting married next month." He knew this conversation was on the wrong track. Flashing a sweet conciliatory smile at her, Tina's face reddened.

"I know you're engaged," she lied. "Congratulations, by the way." Flirting came to a grinding halt.

"Thanks. Although I'm not entirely sure we'll make it to the wedding."

"I'm not surprised with you making," she made air quotes, "'appraisal appointments' with single women." Tina turned on her sexy stilettos and avoided him for the rest of the evening.

Weeks after, she heard that Hank and his fiancée had split up.

Later, he'd say that his conversation with Tina had been a turning point for him. "As Ingrid and I fought our way closer to the wedding date I had doubts and she did too. It was a mutual split."

Tina wondered. Then one bright Maui morning, Hank found Tina painting the interior of her new dive shop, just off Front Street on Dickenson.

"And you told me you weren't artistic." He stood in the doorway with a huge grin on his face.

"I remember you," she laughed, holding her paint roller over the tarp. "Hank, the art appraiser." She'd actually been using him in her sexual fantasies for months.

"You're painting alone?"

She nodded and adjusted her painter's cap.

"If I jump in here to help you, I can't guarantee you'll end up with a run-of-the-mill store." He smirked like there were twenty other meanings to what he said.

"I'd love the help, but no fancy stuff on the walls, just bluc."

He came back the next day and the next, finally taking over the remodeling of her dive shop. Weeks later, Hank had turned it into one of Hawaii's coolest-looking stores, with aquariums covering two walls and a giant model of a humpback whale hanging from the ceiling.

"It looks more like a trendy nightclub," she said admiringly.

"Then it shall function both as a dive shop and as a work of art." He'd taken her in his arms and kissed her passionately. They'd all but set the date, at that point.

They were married in a little ceremony on the beach in Wailea. After that, Hank took his job as the shop manager seriously—as serious as Hank Perez could be about anything. He set up a juice bar in a corner of the shop, played current pop music, and hired the Parrot Guy to take Polaroids to draw people around the corner from the main street. The sign, "Tina's Dive Shop," came down soon after and a grand party followed to celebrate the raising of the new sign designating "Tina & Hank's Dive Shop." Everything had never been more perfect in Tina's life.

CHAPTER 17

Tina sat on a poolside lounger at a lush tropical resort, an umbrella'ed drink on the table beside her. A man walked from the bar towards her and stopped. She glanced from beneath her wide-brimmed straw hat, but the sun was in her eyes.

"Excuse me, do I know you?" she said.

"Yes, you do." He moved closer and blocked the sun.

It was Jamey. His expression held such love that she blushed. She hadn't seen him in a very long time, but he still loved her. Something stopped her from jumping up to wrap her arms around him.

He knelt and took her hand in his. "It's good to see you." He kissed her palm, never taking his eyes from her face.

The feeling of warmth and safety that enveloped her was like nothing she'd ever known. Without a doubt, this man was hers. Jamey would never do anything to hurt her and had always put her first, even though he'd been gone a long time. In contrast, Hank's head turned with every young girl who passed by, every bikini, cocktail waitress, female dive instructor, the heiress from Atlanta whose interest in Hank almost had Tina cancel the wedding. But not Jamey. Tina sank into his arms. "Yes." She breathed in the musky scent of him.

Then they were in a room barely big enough for the brass bed covered in snowy white linens and fluffy pillows. Open windows framed three sides of the small room and a light breeze rustled the poplin curtains. Hovered over a turquoise ocean, the bedroom was like a balcony jutting over a Tahitian sea—the perfect fantasy.

Jamey lay back on the pillows, smiling lazily at her. His tanned skin contrasted with the stark white sheets. She went to him and, taking his angular face in her hands, kissed him long and deep, her tongue tasting the sweetness of this man. He responded, almost hesitantly. When his kiss deepened, he flipped her over to her back and pressed himself into her thighs. His face, inches from hers, was almost pained. "Tina, you have always been my reason."

His words left her breathless. She sank into his blue eyes and imagined taking him into her soul.

"I don't know if I can stop this," he said. "I've waited so long to be with you."

"Don't." She drew him to her, and their need escalated. She wiggled out from under and pulled her shirt over her head. Pushing him down, she then mounted him. Clothes were tossed aside in a rush to get naked. Skin on skin, hot breath, legs wrapped around each other. "I love this." She kissed his hard stomach and slid lower.

"And this."

"No." He reached down, his whisper gravelly.

Inching up, she kissed his neck, burrowing into his salty scent.

"Slower?"

She could feel his hardness against her legs.

"I don't want to do anything you'll regret."

"I won't regret this." She smiled at him.

"If you knew..." He drew back and studied her face. "I trust you, Jamey." She'd melted into him with bottomless emotion. God, she loved this man. Rocking her hips on him, she whispered, "I want this."

He chuckled, pulling her into a hug, as if to stop her movement.

He smelled of the ocean. Like possibilities. "Give in." She kissed just below his jaw line and he moaned. "Jamey, let go," she coaxed.

His facial muscles slackened and he heaved a long sigh. "Come with me…" Tina slid her way from his throat to his belly, making a trail of kisses down the front of his muscled body. All the way to the birthmark. "I remember this." She'd waited so long for him to come back to her.

When she slid her breasts across his erect penis his moan was something she'd anticipated. She knew he liked this. She remembered every little thing that drove him wild with longing.

Sweet man that he was. He'd defended her, sheltered her. She couldn't remember how he'd done all these things but it didn't matter. Only the complete love she felt for him mattered. More than anything, she wanted to be a part of him. She wanted to bring him to climax, give him something he'd waited for. She'd waited for. Tina slithered up his body, ready to receive him inside her warmth. "My love."

Firm hands grabbed her shoulders and stopped the momentum. "No. I can't do it." He looked panicked.

"We're doing it." She smiled like there was still a chance to finish what was started.

"I'm not here with your permission."

"Oh, you have my permission."

"Not really. I'm not sure how this happened, but I don't have your *waking* permission." He looked at her hard, and suddenly, she knew what he meant. She was dreaming.

She sat up in bed. Her bed. Alone. In her house. Her bedroom. Obi slept in his usual spot on a cotton blanket at the bottom of the bed with the ribbon on his collar. Looking around, she verified Jamey was not with her. Silence filled the house. Obi looked over.

"I'm going crazy." She dropped her head in her hands. "Oh, God. It was just a dream." She took two deep breaths. Then she walked to the window. Sexy feelings for Jamey lingered. They'd been making love and he'd stopped because he jumped into her dream. Or had he? Jamey had told her for jumping he needed to be touching the dreamer.

She got back into the bed and closed her eyes, but she

couldn't stop the memory of making love with James Dunn. It had been wildly exciting—his scent, the look of bliss on his face when she stroked him, his soldier body. Oh God, she had to stop thinking of him this way. She was a widow, for Christ's sake. And he'd taken advantage of her in the dream, knowing she wasn't herself.

***

Jamey woke up horrified. He knew what happened, but how had he jumped Tina's dream from miles away? Again? How in bloody hell was he able to get into Tina's dreams without touching her?

He jumped out of bed, his first instinct to look around the room for Tina. As a precaution, he turned on the light and searched the condo. The bolt on the front door assured him that Tina couldn't be inside. Physically.

Regardless, he peeked in an empty bathroom and, turning to look in the mirror, Jamey noticed his erection was still healthy. *Down boy.* At least he didn't have a headache. That was good news.

Had it been anything but a sexual dream, he'd have called Tina for information. But he couldn't call her in the middle of the night to ask if she'd dreamed about making love in a bedroom overlooking the ocean. Dammit. She was probably awake this very minute. Thank God, she wouldn't realize that it was actually him lying with her on that bed, letting her ravage him until his conscience wouldn't allow him to take advantage of the situation any longer. She'd think she simply had a sexy dream about him. He almost smiled, but not quite.

Settling back in bed, his penis stayed at attention with the memory of Tina. After finishing what she had started, Jamey drifted off to sleep knowing he needn't worry. She wouldn't realize he'd jumped.

When he pulled into her driveway the next morning,

Tina had a look on her face that said it all. The absence of her smile spoke volumes. Her eyes avoided his, and she looked like she was strung tighter than a tennis racket when she jumped into the passenger seat. "You ready?" he asked, turning the jeep around in the driveway.

"Ready for what? You fucking me in my sleep, or the plane ride?"

Jamey put his foot on the brake. So, it *was* a dream jump. "I didn't mean to jump in." One of the driveway's palm trees dropped a coconut and it rolled in front of the jeep. "I have no idea how I got in that dream."

"I don't believe you. Just drive." She waved her arm for him to go. "I still want to search the coastline."

He pulled onto the street. "I need to be touching the dreamer when I jump. I can't figure out how..."

"You are such a rat, James Dunn. I am horrified at what you did last night." She exhaled like she'd been holding her breath all night. "It was an invasion of privacy, in the worst form." Tears pooled in her eyes.

Jamey steered the car to the side of the road. "Tina?" His voice was grave. "I'm sorry it went so far. At first, I assumed I was just dreaming about you. Then I thought I might be jumping and was just about to leave. But all of a sudden, I...I just went from hugging you to...to...having sex with you. I tried to stop and couldn't, which told me it was your dream."

"I wasn't dreaming about you until you jumped in." Her voice rose.

"I hate to ask this, Tina, but are you sure?"

"You let me do things to you."

"I did."

"I wasn't myself in that dream."

"I understand, and I hope you realize I wasn't myself either." Her look burned through him.

"You were exactly yourself."

"I thought it was just my horny dream about you."

They paused.

"At first I did. Honestly." He took a deep breath. "It's not unheard of for me to dream about us. I've had lots of dreams about us over the years. I thought it was another one of those."

She looked horrified. Jamey touched her shoulder gently. She moved closer to the door.

"Tina, I would never do anything to hurt you. You are a widow, grieving for your husband. I'm sorry. I can't direct my subconscious thoughts."

She turned and looked at him full-on. "I feel weird having a dream about you like that."

"It wasn't real. And it isn't like we actually had sex. Or, like we haven't had sex before." He was grasping at anything now.

"I don't know who I hate more right now—you, or me for letting it go so far. Just drive, will you?"

The fact that he'd made it through a jump without feeling like he was going to die was interesting. Twice now. Maybe it had something to do with jumping from miles away?

When they arrived at the private airstrip just south of the Kahului International Airport, Jamey parked and they got out of the jeep, still silent. Hopefully, they'd be lucky today and this would be over soon. Tina could bury her husband and get on with her life and Jamey would return to Seattle. He couldn't think beyond that right now. This morning, he and Tina had the Maui coastline to search. He'd be looking specifically for the dream's rocky outcrops to find the exact shadow he'd seen in his peripheral vision.

Tina squeezed the armrest so tightly that her fingers were bony white. "When did you get a pilot license?" she asked Jamey.

"After the divorce."

When they were airborne, she relaxed her grip only slightly and looked over at him. Yup, he was flying the plane, alright.

"Are you scared to fly in small planes?" Jamey asked. She didn't want him to know anything more about her than he already did, but he could read her well enough to feel her terror. "Yes, and with our past trust issues..."

Jamey laughed out loud. "Try to trust that I know what I'm doing. I fly a lot." He looked over at her and patted Obi, who sat between them on a folded blanket, shivering from his own fright.

"And try to pull it together, for Obi's sake."

He was right. She took a deep breath and wrapped her arm around her dog's neck. "S'okay, boy."

The morning light streamed in through the windshield. In the buttery glow Jamey looked handsome. The way his hair curled slightly behind his ear, his strong jaw line, the faint trace of whiskers, even his tanned hands on the wheel were all reminders that she'd once known every inch of this man. Last night's dream had left memories. She had to stop thinking of him in this way. For one thing, he was intuitive and might read her thoughts. She tried filling her mind with thoughts of her parents, but that just made her more anxious.

They flew north to Waihee, along the coastline at about four hundred feet. Maui's northern edge was jagged like a torn hem. The ocean's waves pounded against the walls of rock that stretched up to meet high grassy meadows. The rocky beach from the dream did not grace this stretch of the Valley Isle.

As they flew over the village of Kahakuloa, Tina hoped her queasiness wouldn't ruin the search. Vomiting would be embarrassing. A pocket of air made the small plane dip and swerve. Her tummy clenched and she gripped the sick bag she'd found under the seat. On their left were pineapple fields; on the right was the coast. Jamey steered towards the area where Hank's truck was found that morning, an area that surfers called Hobbit Land.

Tina set the binoculars on her lap when they reached

Cliff House. Jamey gazed at her, questioningly. She shook her head. He turned the plane to cross over the West Maui Mountains to the airport side. "Nothing at all?"

"Nope." Tina barely got the word out of her mouth.

He made a beeline for the famous wave break on the other side of Paia, where surfers were injured on a regular basis. "There's no way he was surfing Jaws that morning?"

Tina shook her head. "His truck was at Honolua. Part of his board washed up near Kahakuloa." The heaviness threatened to take her down again. They followed the coastline to Paia and turned around, back to the airport. "Maybe it's just a dream, plain and simple, not Hank telling me where his body is." The headset crackled with Tina's hopeless words.

"Don't give up, sweetie." Jamey didn't sound so sure himself.

The morning had held such promise. She hadn't realized how much, until it was taken away.

***

On the drive back to Lahaina, Jamey offered to buy Tina breakfast, but she wasn't hungry. He tried to engage her in conversation by suggesting they try dream jumping again.

"Are you crazy?" She muttered something about risking his life and she "sure as hell wasn't going to have another person die on me."

At least she wasn't worried about last night's sexy dream anymore. He drove her home to get her truck, and followed her up the stairs to the second-story deck. She plunked down on a deck chair, her head in her hands.

Jamey perched on the edge of a chair opposite her. He had to think of something. Why couldn't he get a feel for the location of the body? "Don't give up yet."

She looked up, her expression stony, cold.

How in hell would they find the body without more help from Hank? Jamey glanced at the patio door that led to Tina's bedroom. The night they'd purposely dream jumped, she'd been freaked out when he whispered Hank's name. He was pretty sure that Hank was still around but he didn't want to give her hope, just in case he was wrong.

"Tell me about Hank." He handed Obi a dog cookie from the treat jar on the table.

Tina hugged her knees to her chest. "Not today."

"Humor me. This might help." She couldn't be worse than she already was. "He was fun." It seemed like that was all she was going to say. She sighed. "Everyone loved him." Tina laid her cheek on her knee and looked out at the ocean. "He loved me. And in the last two months before he died, he wanted us to have a baby. I did too, of course. I had all along, but now Hank was on board, like something stung him, like he needed me to have his baby. Almost like he knew he was going to die." Her eyebrows wrinkled and tears came to her eyes.

"He wasn't sick?"

"No. I thought of that. I even talked to his doctor. He was healthy, positive, excited to become a father. Hank was kind. Very sweet. He loved Noble. He was a good friend to Noble. He wasn't sure if Noble would stay with us on Maui forever. We hoped."

Jamey watched tears roll down the leg where her cheek rested. "He loved art. When I met him, he was engaged to an art dealer and they'd come over here to manage galleries. When they broke up, she left Maui." Obi whined and Jamey gave him another cookie. "Hank had a degree in art history." She smiled. "He appreciated the beautiful things in life. I was one of them, he said. He appreciated women."

"Where'd he go to college?" Jamey wanted to keep her talking.

Tina looked at the sky. "Some art school in California." She sounded surprised that she didn't know. "I forget."

***

Later, Jamey drove north to the lookout near the Ritz Kapalua and parked in the little lot by the church. There were only eight parking spots and his was the only car there. It was not yet noon. He walked towards the sign for the Hawaiian burial ground, a two-acre patch to one side of a multimillion dollar golf course. Buried bones had been found only a few years earlier, by someone walking their dog, and a giant excavation was ordered to determine the exact nature of the ancient cemetery. Building the Ritz-Carlton on the site was postponed until they decided what to do. First they planned to gather the bones for relocation, but then the Ritz came to an agreement with the Hawaiian people that the dead bodies could stay, and hotel guests would be asked to avoid the site.

Jamey felt the power of the remaining spirits swirling around the wooded patch of hillside. Like all cemeteries, the energy recharged him. Standing by the sign that warned people to stay outside the sacred ground, Jamey closed his eyes and tried to draw from the power of the spirits. Like plugging in to a charger, he was surprised at the intensity of the site.

He continued to the point of land between Ironwood Beach and Fleming—a peninsula of jagged lava rock known as Dragon's Teeth. The surf crashed against the wall of volcanic teeth as Jamey stepped around inside the dragon's mouth, thinking about Hank. His military counselor had cautioned him in an earlier conversation to be careful with ghosts. "This is not your area, Freud. You know very little about this side of things and might end up worse off than you are now."

He'd had to tell Milton that he suspected he was getting glimpses from a dead man. "Believe me, I know

I'm no expert, but I'm all she's got." *Not to mention the ghost.*

CHAPTER 18

When Katie picked up the shop's phone, Jamey decided to throw her the million-dollar question. "What does M.O. stand for?"

"I don't know. Wait. Is this a joke, or what?" Katie asked.

"No joke, I just saw it on a sign. I think it's a place." He needed to get to a computer. "Maui something?"

"No idea. Let me ask Tina. She's right here."

Jamey turned the jeep north to his father's condo. M.O. might be initials.

"Jamey?" Tina took the phone.

He was excited to hear her voice. More excited than he wanted to admit. Being hurt twice by the same woman in one lifetime seemed stupid for a hardened soldier. He had to stop letting her get to him when he'd tried so hard to forget this woman.

"What is M.O.? Modus Operandi?" she asked.

"I'm wondering if it stands for something here on Maui."

"Like?"

"No idea. It was just a question I had for Katie. How are you now? Still air sick, or better?"

"Define better. I'm busy. And pissed off. Apparently, there's a surprise party for my birthday tomorrow night and the thought of having to smile, and appreciate being a year older, makes me feel like vomiting."

"I'm not invited." He waited.

"Consider yourself lucky. You won't have to watch me pretend to make nice with everyone, when all I really want to do is curl up in the fetal position with a straw in a beer." She didn't laugh.

When they hung up, Jamey thought of the wedding photo in a silver frame in Tina's bedroom. She and Hank looked deliriously happy, gazing into each other's eyes. It twisted his heart every time he saw it, and lately he'd avoided looking at it.

The time he'd spent on Maui with Kristina, many years ago, had been like a fantasy. Had one month in his whole forty-two years been that incredible? It was only a month. Having just broken up with Carrie, he'd been at a low point. Meeting Kristina was a nice distraction. At first. Jumping had been making him feel crazier than usual, and he'd vowed to avoid dream jumps on vacation. Since leaving Seattle, Jamey had steered clear of any triggers. But when he and Tina had started sleeping together, it was difficult to stay out of her dreams. He found himself jumping when he didn't want to, and he had to turn around to get out before he saw anything. Tina was a big dreamer.

On the last night of his vacation, he was in her dream before he realized what was happening. The scene was fuzzy at the edges, like he needed glasses. It had paler colors than his usual dreams, but Jamey could see everything. Lost in a crowd of onlookers, he watched a couple on a dance floor. A tall, dark man held Kristina lovingly, gazing into her eyes with such emotion, Jamey's heart twisted. When someone moved in front of his line of vision, he stepped to the side and noticed the wedding cake. The bride wore a long off-white dress and everyone smiled at the happy couple. A photographer took pictures. The mood was festive. Wearing only his jeans and a scruffy T-shirt was the least of Jamey's worries as he watched couples move in to fill up the dance floor. A ringing, like a fire alarm sounded way off in the distance.

This was Kristina's wedding. Who the hell was the groom? Not him. Why was she dreaming about another guy when she was sleeping beside him and had been for weeks?

Beyond the deck, the pink glow of a Hawaiian sunset completed the wedding scene. Jamey backed up to the portal where he'd jumped in and leaned against the wall. Like watching an accident happen, he couldn't look away. Emptiness moved in and he felt cheated, after having spent the previous weeks falling in love with the bride.

Only hours before, they'd made love, satisfying each other's every need. Tina confessed she was falling in love with him. He hadn't said the words, but he planned to, before he got on that plane.

Before he jumped through the portal, Jamey looked back to see the horror that would haunt him for years, the scene that would cause him to wake in a cold sweat that morning. The man holding Kristina in his arms had become a grotesque, skeletal body in a tuxedo, his head cracked wide open, his long black hair hanging in strings.

When Jamey jumped out of the dream and woke, he silently rose from the bed he shared with Kristina and phoned Uncle Don from the kitchen. The hushed conversation with his mentor squashed all hopes for a life with Kristina.

"Remember we talked about this when you were nine? Precognitive, it's called." Don sounded excited and scared. "I only had two in my life, but they both came true. Blurry edges." He paused. "Jamey, remember your promise about not changing the future?"

"What if I'm totally wrong and it's just a dream?"

"It's not. The ringing sound you mentioned, the colors, the lack of clarity. You have to let this girl go, just in case. Remember your promise. Messing with the future could bring consequences, not just for her, but for anyone involved. You made the promise. You have to keep it."

He had promised his uncle, way back when he was a young boy. It had been a day in Uncle Don's backyard, when he was helping him mend a fence. They'd been talking for an hour about dream jumping when Don stopped what he was doing and turned to his young nephew. "Because we don't know what could happen, how one little change in the past might trigger many changes and alter the course of the world, you need to make me a promise."

He'd have done anything for the uncle he adored.

"Hold up your right hand, like this." Uncle Don demonstrated.

The man's face was so serious, it scared the eleven-year-old boy.

"Repeat after me. I promise to never use dream jumping..." He repeated his uncle's words.

"...for doing bad...and if I ever have a dream about the future..." Jamey continued.

"...I will not try to change what I see."

He promised. They sealed the deal when Don took out his pen knife and drew a speck of blood from their thumbs. They pressed their thumbs together. That day, an eleven-year-old child knew his gift was something too serious for jokes. Although there were frivolous jumps in the coming years, Jamey stuck to his promise and never questioned its wisdom. Until he dreamed of Tina's wedding. After the hushed phone conversation with Don, Jamey was crushed. Kristina would marry this man, and as if that wasn't bad enough, it looked like tragedy was headed her way. Leaving Kristina that day was difficult. Their kiss goodbye had been longer than intended, his hug too tight. She commented on how they'd see each other in a month, maybe sooner.

But when the plane landed in Seattle, news awaited that would take him out of Kristina's life, regardless of his dream. Carrie was pregnant. The lifeline to Kristina had been cut from his end, leaving the woman he loved to drift until the dark stranger arrived.

***

On the day of her thirty-fifth birthday, Tina woke reminding herself of her long-term plan to find her soul mate and have a baby. She was back at the beginning with neither. Today was Pepper's surprise party, where she'd have to pretend her world wasn't in shambles. The familiar heaviness pressed against her chest and she tried to take a deep breath.

Katie had let the details of the party slip the day before. Everyone would arrive while Tina was out to dinner with her parents. She would have to feign ignorance for Pepper's sake. For everyone's sake.

Jamey was not on the guest list, but he promised to show up afterwards. She was relieved he'd be spared the ordeal. She wasn't even supposed to know about the party, so inviting him was out of the question. He'd sweep up the after-mess. Figuratively. If the pattern that Jamey suspected was correct, tonight was another dream. He had a new theory about avoiding the headache and said he'd try to jump from Pops' condo. If that didn't work, he was getting in the car and "coming over to your bedroom to try the good old-fashioned way." When Tina imagined him joining her in the bed, a thrilling shiver shot through her. "Whatever's necessary," she'd said, trying to sound disinterested. But denying her interest in Jamey was becoming more difficult.

An hour into paperwork and phone calls at her desk, Jamey walked through the back door. "Come on, birthday girl, I'm taking you for breakfast."

He must've known she was hungry. "I'm going to let you, only because I'm ravenous, but you have to stop reading my mind."

He grinned. "I swear I didn't. I just want to take you to breakfast." He held out his arms, palms up.

She hadn't strolled along the picturesque main street of Lahaina in years. Several hundred feet of pastel-painted shops sat on prime Hawaiian real estate. The store fronts were fairytale pretty. At that hour, shopkeepers were just rolling out awnings to shield T-shirts and clothing from the sun, and to keep the boutiques at tolerable temperatures, workers hosed down the sidewalks, put out 'open' signs, and readied for a day of selling souvenirs to tourists. Longhi's Restaurant, located in a house left over from the whaling days of the 1800s, dominated the north end of Front Street. The sky-blue, historic building overlooked the Lahaina coastline to the north and the craziness of Front Street to the south. Jamey held up two fingers to the hostess and looked around, almost suspiciously.

Following the woman upstairs, they were led to one of the best tables overlooking the seawall. Jamey pulled out the chair for Tina, his finesse and manners still impressive. Hank hadn't done this sort of thing and she chided herself for comparing.

After ordering eggs and toast, they talked about the plan for that night. "Call me when you get into bed, whatever time that is. I'll get an idea of when you're going to dream. Don't drink much at the party." He added sugar to his steaming coffee and stirred. "I'm not sure if that contributed to my headache."

She looked across the breakfast table at Jamey, aghast. "Oh God, I'm sorry."

"Don't worry. I'm just grasping at anything here. My last dreamer in Kandahar was heavily drugged with something new and my heart stopped, so I'm trying to figure it out." Jamey took a swig of coffee and stared her down with his steel blue eyes.

"I've been thinking a lot about the jump into your sexy dream the other night. For technical reasons." He waited for the waitress to set their plates of food on the table before he continued. "Being able to enter that dream and not wake up with a headache gave me hope. For jumping," he added for clarification.

"Let's set the record straight," Tina said, digging into her scrambled eggs. "It only became sexy when you arrived and made it that way. So, maybe it's the type of dream that gives you the headache."

Jamey passed the salt before she asked for it. "If so, I should offer myself up as a dream gigolo."

The sound of her own laugh took Tina by surprise. It had been a while since she'd laughed out loud and it felt good to release an emotion with a laugh, end it with a smile. And here she was in Longhi's eating a meal, not just grabbing something to quell her hunger pangs. Maybe she'd turned a corner in her grief and was headed towards anger, or one of the last stages. Around Jamey, she'd become more like herself again.

They ate in comfortable silence, passing each other the jam, commenting on the beauty of the day, talking about her past birthdays. The year before, Hank had taken her for dinner at Swan Court in the Hyatt Hotel.

Jamey's eyebrows lifted to hear mention of the Hyatt.

Tina fell silent. The Hyatt had special memories for Tina and Jamey. It had been their love nest ten years earlier. She'd thought of Jamey during that dinner, and hated herself for betraying Hank that way. "I don't usually make a big deal out of my birthday, but this year Pepper got a bug in her bonnet and is having this big shindig." Sitting back in the white rattan chair, she folded her hands over her full tummy. "I haven't eaten here in ages. And I haven't eaten like that in a long time. Thanks."

"Happy birthday." Jamey didn't look up, popping the last bit of toast in his mouth. "You're looking a little scrawny."

She smiled. "I'll get back up to my fighting weight with this meal. I'm kind of relieved you're not invited to the party tonight."

"Sounds like it'll be a bunch of people drooling over how wonderful you are and making me feel terrible all over again for leaving you." Jamey's gaze made her laugh nervously.

"S'okay," he said. "I don't know the words to Happy Birthday anyhow, and even if I did, you might remember that I sing like a moose in mating season."

The freedom of laughing was like something had been stuck all these months, not allowing anything to emerge. "I don't recall your singing voice being that bad."

"Trust me."

They'd laughed the day before about something, but she couldn't remember what. "Did you ever figure out what M.O. is?"

"Nope."

"It has to do with me, doesn't it?"

"Now who thinks they're psychic?"

"Does it?"

"Sorry." Jamey shook his head.

"Where did you hear it?"

"Someone used it."

"Ask them."

"Yeah, I guess I better, if I can get in touch with them again." Jamey handed his credit card to the passing waitress.

***

With Tina fed and relatively happy on her birthday, Jamey was pleased he'd done something, however small, to make her happy. He pulled into her driveway and parked. Noble's truck was there, but when he entered the house, he saw no sign of the man and didn't feel his presence.

As he opened the bedroom door, a wave of heat hit him. The curtains were closed and, judging from their lack of movement, so were all the windows. Even the closet door was closed. Sweat beaded on his forehead immediately. The framed photo of Tina and Hank was missing. Only a dust-free rectangular spot remained on her dresser.

"Hank?" He had no idea if this would work, but he held the paper in his hands along with a light marker. "Are you there? Hank, I don't know what M.O. means." He listened and closed his eyes to feel something. Did Hank mean 'M.O.' to be mountains and a bay? Today he had to get to the questions sooner since automatic writing seemed difficult to sustain.

Seconds passed, then a minute. Jamey stood and paced the room, wondering what tactic might get results. He didn't feel a presence. Had the ghost left? His need to communicate didn't guarantee contact.

Feeling nothing but the stifling heat of the room, Jamey left and pulled out of Tina's driveway. What in hell was M.O.? Maybe he was going about this wrong. Then he passed a real estate sign with the name of the listing agent, 'Monty Okawa,' and it hit him. Maybe M.O. was a 'who.'

CHAPTER 19

The Grill and Bar had been Tina's choice for her birthday dinner. Philip Greene was not pleased.

"I like it here," Tina said, having thought her father would appreciate the ambiance of the restaurant associated with the Kapalua Golf Course. "Sorry."

"It's more of a lunch place, isn't it, Kristina?" her mother asked.

Tina held firm. "The food is fabulous. Wait."

She ordered the artichoke appetizer while her father perused the wine list, knowing he'd find something absurdly expensive. She kept her mouth shut to allow the evening to go smoothly. Her mother had already started in about the lack of fine dining on Maui.

Tina had been grinding her teeth for twenty minutes. When a bottle of four-hundred-dollar wine arrived, Philip Greene poured three glasses. "To our daughter." He smiled. "Who means so much to us."

"Thank you, Father." She sipped sparingly, remembering Jamey's headache. She did not want a repeat of last time's brush with death.

Dinner went well. They actually shared a few laughs together and when Philip paid the bill and Tina thanked him for a wonderful dinner, she meant it. Exiting the restaurant, Tina recalled that Jamey's condo was just across the street in The Ridge complex. She remembered torturous nights, years ago, driving along this road, wondering why he'd given up on them so easily. Her heart twinged and she had to remind herself that it happened for the best.

According to Katie, Jamey was staying at the condo

this time too. "Not far from your house," she'd said. Katie had been dropping hints of her uncle's availability for weeks. Her obvious attempts to get them together were amusing. "I think he really likes you. You should see Pops' condo, it's so beautiful, and you'll love the view. You should ask Jamey if you can see the view." Little did she know? The Greenes' car twisted along the lower road towards Tina's house. Elizabeth talked the whole way about her daughter returning to Seattle. "Even just for a few weeks. You need a break from here." Her mother only had one thing on her mind. "Maybe at the end of the summer."

"You need a break now. Your health is suffering. You haven't even had a good haircut in years."

Tina bit her lips together before saying something she'd regret, like, "Blah, blah, blah." She'd learned the hard way never to cross her mother. There was no winning that battle. Instead, she avoided these conversations. Usually. But when she stole a glance, her mother looked far too smug to give Tina reason to think she'd given up completely.

The house was dark when they pulled into her driveway. No extra cars. "That's strange," Tina said. "I thought I left a light on." She stepped out of the car and Obi barked from above, his head poking between the railings of the deck. Pepper would be hunkered down inside, telling people to "shhhh."

"Hi, Obi." Turning to her parents, she asked, "Would you like to come in for a nightcap?" There'd better be a party about to happen, because she had nothing to back up that offer of a drink.

"That would be nice." Philip helped his wife out of the car and they mounted the stairs.

With the flip of a light switch, the house came alive with people, like a group of happy burglars. "Surprise," they yelled at different intervals. Tina staggered backwards in fake shock. "Oh, my God! What's going on?!" Her

hands flew to her mouth. This was the move she'd
rehearsed in the mirror earlier. "Where did you come
from?" She scanned the group of friends smiling in her
living room. These were people she hadn't talked to in
months. Some, not since the memorial service at Honolua
Bay. Pepper hugged her, and Tina smiled beyond the
embrace to Katie, who clutched her boyfriend Ned with
one arm and waved with the other. Noble grinned from his
place near the stairs.

"Where did you all park?" Tina laughed.

Drinks flowed, music blared and Tina schmoozed, all
the time wishing that she had insisted Jamey come. He
would've been a welcome addition, after all. His smile and
jokes would've been a beam of light in a room full of
worried faces trying to avoid talk of Hank. At least Jamey
hadn't known Hank.

Although she drank only one glass of wine during the
course of the night, and it was mostly filled with ice cubes,
inebriation took over her body and by the time the limbo
sticks were pulled out for Hank's favorite party game, Tina
was flying high. "Where's Jamey? He'd love this. Where
the heck is James Dunn?" Elizabeth grabbed her daughter's
upper arm and led her through the crowd of people to the
bedroom.

"Kristina, you are drunk." The look on her mother's
face said it all.

Tina swayed. "Strange thing is I've hardly had
anything to drink, because Jamey said not to!"

Noble filled the doorway and glanced at them
sympathetically. "Are you alright, Ti?"

Elizabeth shut the door in his face, and Tina tried not
to laugh. "Sorry," she called above the party music. Then
she whispered, "I've only had two or three glasses of wine
the whole night, Mom." Tina crossed the bedroom floor,
opened the door and threw her arms out to Noble, who was
still standing there. "Sorry. Oh. Suddenly I don't feel
very..." She rushed past him to the bathroom.

"I'll help her, Elizabeth." Noble's voice broke through the din of conversation and music from the party room.

Hugging the toilet to empty her stomach of the evening's expensive wine and food, Tina wondered why she was sick. A cold sweat invaded her body.

A wet cloth felt bracingly good on her face. "Thanks, Noble." She was hardly able to see her swervey self in the mirror. She had to go back out to join her guests. "You're okay now, Ti." Noble's voice was comforting.

When they opened the door, her mother's stern face greeted her. God forbid Elizabeth Greene should ever come into a bathroom where her daughter was puking. She did look a bit worried. "Say good night to everyone, Tina. You're going to bed." It wasn't a question, or even a suggestion. She handed her daughter a glass of water.

"Good idea. I feel better, by the way. But first..." Tina broke free of her mother to weave a path into the great room. Holding her glass above her head, she attempted a whistle, but her lips didn't work. Pepper quieted the room full of revelers and then motioned for Tina to continue.

"Friends, thank you so very, very much for coming to the first birthday party I've had since Hank disappeared." She swayed a bit, and someone put an arm out to catch her. "I say 'disappeared,' because we still haven't found the body." Uncomfortable expressions blanketed the room. "Oh, it's okay, because if we never find Hank's body, I can pretend he just left me…" Her voice trailed off and she tried to walk among her guests, her glass still raised above her head.

"Anyway…" She sighed. "Long story short, I know I've been a mess, but thanks to my mother and father who just flew in, and to my dear friend Noble, I'm surviving." She winked at him. "Oh, and Pepper too. Thanks, sweetie, for this grand soirée. And, thanks for coming, everyone." Tina took a drink of her water and Pepper rushed in before she fell over. She helped Tina into her bedroom.

Tina flopped on the bed. Obi barked, thinking it was

playtime, while Pepper spoke to her mother in the doorway, the only recognizable word being "Noble." Her mother's brows were wrinkled, her lips pursed. Lately, Tina got the impression that Pepper disliked Noble.

"This party is over. Thank you for coming." Her father's voice was firm in the other room, where he was probably herding people to the door. His stern words made her feel like the party was some teenager's attempt at being naughty. No one would linger. People obeyed Philip Greene.

"Thanks for coming!" Tina yelled. "Thanks for the party, Pep!" she called as Pepper left the bedroom on her mother's orders. Obi licked Tina's face, and she giggled. "Oh, Obi. Thanks for coming!"

From her vantage point on the bed, she could see through her patio door to the deck. People shuffled down the outside stairs, like an orderly crowd at the end of a concert.

Noble entered the room and she kicked off her shoes. "Sleep well, sweetie. Happy birthday." She smiled at him. "Thanks."

Philip and Elizabeth stood in the bedroom doorway, talking in whispers. She didn't want to imagine what they were saying about Noble. Or her.

Noble joined the conversation in the hall, nodding at her parents like all three were in cahoots on something. Elizabeth ignored him, as usual. As Tina's eyes got heavier and she drifted off into oblivion, the last thing she remembered was her mother rudely turning her back on her dear friend Noble.

***

Jamey still hadn't heard from Tina by 11:30 p.m. and after an unsuccessful attempt to connect to her from miles away he drove to her house. If the party was still going strong, he'd wait in his car for everyone to leave.

But when he pulled up to the house, it was dark, and the only vehicles were the usual two trucks. It looked like the festivities had been over for a while. Had she forgotten about jumping?

Standing under her bedroom window, he closed his eyes, took a deep breath, and exhaled slowly. He sensed that Tina was up there, but someone else was in the bedroom with her. Noble. He'd know that feeling anywhere—it was like a cement wall of hostility. Noble's presence might explain why she hadn't called him. Tina had once mentioned that in the early days of her grieving, they slept together for comfort. "Just sleep," she'd pointed out, like it mattered to him. Turned out it did matter. The idea prickled him, but Jamey reminded himself that Tina's love life was none of his business. In the darkness of the front yard, he stared at the window. Should he risk a jump? She'd promised to have only one glass of wine with dinner, but when Katie called him at ten o'clock to invite him over, the party sounded like a big bash. Laughing, shouting, music. Must've ended quickly. Focusing, he sensed that something happened to end it. Something to do with her father. And now, she was sleeping with Noble. She must've been upset.

Jamey lowered himself to sit on the grass. His back rested against a papaya tree, and the warmth of the tree leaked through his T-shirt to his back. He couldn't very well sneak upstairs to see what was going on. So far, his presence in her yard had gone undetected, but there was no breeze to carry his scent through the screen windows to Obi.

What did Hank think of Noble sleeping in his bed? Fingering the Percocet bottle in his pocket, Jamey considered his recent jumps. His two theories about the headache involved distance from the dreamer and drinking. He wasn't touching Tina this time. If he jumped, and he detected she'd been drinking, he could always leave the dream. *If* she appeared inebriated in the dream. Prisoners in Afghanistan weren't under the influence of alcohol, but they were drugged and never appeared loopy in the dream so that idea might be unreliable.

An hour passed as he waited in the peaceful silence of the yard. He changed positions several times, and at one point a rat ran by, unaware of his presence.

Finally, Jamey felt what he'd been waiting for. Tina was falling into a dream. He imagined himself alongside her in the journey, breathing in and out. With the backward pull, he let go and fell in.

Not touching. *God dammit, it worked!*

He landed in an empty room. Muffled voices drifted in from outside the door. He was in a small room—white walls, twin bed, no sheets, and no other furniture. A faint light from the door made it possible to see that the mattress had a striped pattern.

He snuck up to the doorway and peeked into the dark hall. Candlelight flickered on the wall up ahead, indicating an open door. Soft voices drifted from the room. Tina's was one of them. Curiosity took him down the hall.

"No," Tina said, first playfully, and then more emphatically. "I said no." During the conversational moments Jamey moved closer, until he could hear better. The other voice was a man's whisper.

"I can't," Tina said.

"Yes, you can, Ti."

"I know you want this, Noble, but you need to understand something."

At the sound of Noble's name, Jamey leaned closer.

"It's hard to explain, but I'm in your dream."

Jamey held his breath.

"I'm not sure how this is happening," she said.

What the fuck? Tina jumped? Jamey listened.

"Ti, I don't care if it's a dream." Noble chuckled. "You look pretty dreamy in that little…"

"Noble, wait."

Sheets rustled in the room.

"Okay, Noble," she chuckled. "I'll be right back." Her voice was husky and seductive. Footsteps padded across the floor. As she exited the room and rounded the corner, Jamey gently covered her mouth and signaled for her to be quiet. She recognized him and followed him down the hall. Once inside the other bedroom, Jamey whispered, "Did you jump into this dream?"

"Is that possible?" Tina looked horrified.

"Are you trying to get out?" He needed to be succinct.

Noble called from deep inside the next room. "Ti, I'm waiting." His voice was filled with suggestion.

"I want to wake up," she whispered.

"Where were you when you arrived?"

"In bed with Noble."

He frowned. "I have an idea." He'd never jumped with another jumper before, but he was hoping this would work.

"Ti?" Noble sounded impatient.

"If I can't pull you out with me," Jamey said, "just go back to where you arrived and do what we're going to try here." Jamey held fast to Tina's hand. "This is where I came in. I'm going to count to three. Bend your knees and jump on three. Imagine yourself back in your own bed."

Tina looked worried. "Don't leave me."

"I'll try not to, but remember, if it doesn't work, go back to Noble and do this. Regardless of what Noble says, okay? I can try to help from the other end by waking you." Tina nodded.

"Ready?"

Tina looked scared.

"One, two, three." They took a leap into the air. There was a sucking sensation into blackness. He could feel Tina's desperate grip on his hand. Then the feeling was gone, and he woke on Tina's front lawn. A headache loomed. Already. He had to get something into his bloodstream as soon as possible, just in case.

"Jamey." Tina stood above him on the deck.

Jamey popped the Percocet dry and raced upstairs. Noble was still asleep in Tina's bed. They continued to the bathroom.

"What the hell?" she whispered, two feet from Jamey's face.

He wasn't sure if she was asking about dream jumping, his presence, or his interference. "You jumped." He mumbled through the pills in his mouth.

"How?"

"Beats me. I'm as shocked as you." Jamey stuck his mouth under the faucet and gulped several times.

"Why is Noble in my bed?"

"I don't know. You invited him?"

"I don't even remember going to bed last night."

This was bad.

She looked at Jamey, her eyebrows knitted together. "I dream jumped?"

"Seems so."

"Oh. my God. My life just keeps getting weirder." Tina glanced in the mirror and then quickly crossed her arms over her scantily clad chest. "And what am I wearing?" She gestured with her chin to the lingerie barely covering her body. "Who put this on me?"

"It's not yours?" In one second, Jamey had Noble tried and sentenced for rape.

"Do you think I wore it back from the dream?"

Jamey had never heard of half this shit before. "In all my years of jumping, I've never worn clothes back from a dream. But just to be safe, you should take it off." Then he noticed her wedding ring. Shit. The dreamer could wear metal, but jumpers could not. If she was the jumper... The headache was threatening the edge of his consciousness. *Did the ring have anything to do with his pain?*

Tina ran back to her bedroom and returned in a blue robe, holding the lacy lingerie in her hand. She pointed to a price tag still clinging to the garment. "I think this was a birthday present. There's wrapping paper on my bedroom floor." She pinched her arm, punched her stomach and blinked rapidly.

"You okay?"

"When I think I've woken but haven't, I'm usually wearing something I didn't wear to bed. I'm checking to see if I am awake."

"You're awake, Tina. Trust me on that. But you can't dream jump with metal." Jamey pointed to her wedding band. "And now that we know you're the one who is jumping, this makes a lot more sense."

Tina stared at the ring on her finger.

"You gotta take it off before you go to sleep from now on." Jamey squinted against the pain in his head. His mind raced with possibilities of what had been happening if, in fact, Tina was the one who was jumping dreams. If Jamey was only piggybacking her jumps and she'd been wearing a gold wedding band, he had a lot to think about. But not now. They had to get Noble out of Tina's bed, if that was what she wanted. If Noble was still dreaming about having sex with her, it would be a rude awakening. Literally.

CHAPTER 20

"Noble! Wake up." Tina said.

"What is it?"

"Why are you in my bed?"

His voice was groggy. "You asked me to stay. Are you okay now? Did you throw up again?"

"No, I'm fine, but I want to sleep alone." Her nice tone irked Jamey in the other room.

"Are you sure?"

Jamey strained to hear. "I was having the strangest dream about us," Noble mumbled.

"Here are your pants." Tina's voice was too low to decipher all her words, but "negligee" was clear enough.

"You got that for your birthday and wore it to bed."

Okay, Tina hadn't brought back clothing. That was good news.

Then, Noble said something Jamey couldn't hear.

"No, Noble."

Jamey stood, ready to run in.

"I feel ill," she argued. "I want to sleep alone. But thanks for offering." She was patronizing him. Jamey had to think that if he'd been the one in the sexy dream with Tina, he might be begging to stay in her bed too. He ducked back into the guest room and waited.

Noble's steps thudded down the back stairs. From the window, Jamey watched him cross the lawn and enter his cottage. Tina's bedroom was illuminated by a shell nightlight on the wall, just enough for Jamey to see her sobbing into a pile of tissues. He paused at the door. "Are you sad he left, or…?"

Her nose blowing was abnormally loud for such a

little person.

"No, I'm not sad he left."

He sat beside her, kissed her shoulder and waited.

She blew again. "I don't want to jump into dreams." She sniffed and wiped her eyes. "I'm having a hard enough time with everything. I don't want a creepy ability, too. And why was Noble sleeping with me tonight? I have no memory of going to bed with him." She sniffed and blew again. "Maybe we had sex." She said the last part in a very tiny whisper. "Probably consensual, but I'll never know if I can't remember." She looked at Jamey. "I don't know which is worse, having sex with Noble and not remembering, or discovering I jumped into his horny dream."

Jamey bristled. "Tina, this is serious if you can't remember if you had sex with Noble, consensual or not."

"As serious as dream jumping?" She looked pitiful. "That seems pretty horrible, if you ask me. Oh God, I feel like I'm losing my mind and there's no way back."

"Think about how we jumped out together. There's always a way back, Tina." He took her face in his hands and nodded. Jamey didn't trust himself to say more about Noble.

"Why were you here, anyways? I thought you weren't invited to the party?" Their faces were inches away.

Had she forgotten? "I was going to jump your dream tonight."

"Oh, yea." She seemed disoriented.

"When I arrived, Noble was here, so I sat under the window." He gestured to the front yard below. "And I jumped when you entered a dream."

Tina wiped her nose. "Wow. You're good." She threw her pile of tissues into a wastebasket.

"I wasn't sure it would work, but I seem to be able to piggyback your dream jumps." He squinted at her. "Have you ever jumped someone's dream before tonight?"

"I don't think so, unless I jumped into that sexy dream

with you? Or was that my dream and you jumping?"

Aha. There was a new possibility. "No idea. You were the jumper tonight, because you arrived in Noble's dream before me." She groaned.

He knew how it felt to discover you had a scary talent you didn't want. He smiled, apologetically. "I really don't know that much about it, except how it works for me." Putting his arm around her shoulders, he pulled her in. "You entered Noble's dream. Probably you two were touching in the bed."

Tina looked exasperated. "I don't remember a lot. There was a surprise party. I drank too much, which was weird, because at dinner I only had two drinks with a lot of food, and when I got back here I only had one, or maybe none."

"What were you drinking?" Jamey squinted.

"Wine at dinner, water here." She pointed to the glass on the bedside table.

He picked it up and swirled the last few drops in the dim light. "Do you mind?" Jamey reached for the switch on the bedside lamp and turned it on.

"What is it?" Tina inched closer to Jamey, their shoulders touching.

"Sediment. Maybe a sleeping pill."

"I didn't take one, I know that."

Jamey frowned. "It's never good to mix alcohol with that stuff. I'll have it analyzed tomorrow." In the light, he noticed how drawn her face looked. "You've got to be exhausted. Should I leave, or stay, in case Noble comes back?" He preferred staying, but given what Tina had gone through already, she might not agree.

She sat down on the bed's edge and put her head in her hands. "I hope I took my pills." She looked up. "Do you have that headache again?"

"Not nearly as bad."

"Do you think you should stay in case you get worse? I can watch you. Or what about if I fall asleep and have the diving dream?"

His heart melted and pooled at his feet. She was still trying to help him first, and then herself. A good sign. "Maybe." Jamey looked at her. "I'll stay." He knelt and took her hands in his. "I can also drive you to the clinic, if you want to do a rape test."

The corners of her mouth twisted. "No. I couldn't do that." She looked away. "I just couldn't, especially seeing Noble and I…maybe

I led him on, in my drunkenness."

"Taking advantage of a drunken woman..." Jamey cut off the words that would impose his opinion on her. "Your choice, but if you want to go back to sleep, I'll take the chair."

She bit her bottom lip and glanced towards the door. "Noble and I almost had sex one night when I wasn't drinking anything at all, so..."

"That isn't the same thing. Sex without consent, or even mumbled consent when one partner is drunk, is a serious offense." She shook her head and he didn't know if that meant they hadn't had sex or she didn't consider sex with Noble a crime. Regardless, Tina had plenty to be scared about. Noble taking advantage, dream jumping, a ghost in her bedroom, and getting drugged—all on her birthday.

"You can sleep in the bed, Jamey. There's lots of room." She said it so casually.

He agreed. A few days earlier, they'd shared the bed. "Okay, but I'll take the side closest to the door." If Noble was slipping drugs into her drink and raping her, this game just leapt to a whole new level.

***

Tina and Jamey woke to the sound of the doorknob jiggling, and then Noble's voice.

"Tina, open the door." He knocked against the barrier as his voice rose to a frantic pitch. "Tina, open it."

She lifted her head off the pillow. 7:04. "Noble, what is it?"

Jamey lay awake on top of the covers, fully clothed, watching her, his jaw clenched.

"I just saw Jamey's jeep parked on the road." Noble sounded upset.

She sat up in bed. "Noble, relax. You are waking me because you saw a jeep?"

"I don't trust him."

"Oh, my God, Noble. There are loads of yellow jeeps on this island." She was glad that she'd locked the door. Noble was becoming more of a problem every hour. "Start coffee. I'll be out in a few minutes—now that you woke me."

Jamey lay still while she shot him an apologetic look. "Headache?" she mouthed.

He shook his head slightly and sprang silently off the bed.

By the time she pulled on a pair of patterned board shorts and a T-shirt, Jamey was inside the closet. Maybe he didn't have a headache, but she had a whopper. Ibuprofen would have to come before coffee. Her mouth was parched and her head felt stuffed with cement. She hated this feeling.

She popped some pain relief, poured her coffee and confronted Noble in the kitchen. "I'm hung over and feeling nasty, so just tell me you didn't drug me to get into my pants last night."

He looked at her incredulously. "Tina, I'm really worried about you. Things are getting weird. It's like you don't know what's true anymore." He looked genuinely concerned. She sipped her coffee until Noble spoke. "It might be a good idea to get off Maui. Get some perspective. I mean, look at us. Now you're thinking these terrible things about me." His forehead wrinkled.

He could be right. She wasn't sure anymore. Had she gotten too obsessed with finding Hank's body? What if she never found it? "Maybe." She took her coffee and headed for the bedroom. "I'm going to work."

When she returned to her room, Jamey was gone. Had he jumped out the window with his soldier moves? No sign of him remained. Then the room dropped in temperature. Strange. The windows were open but the curtains were absolutely still. This coolness came from inside the room. And it was not pleasantly cool, like an early morning Maui breeze. More like swimming into a cold patch of water. Acutely alert, Obi whined and sniffed the air. It wasn't her imagination. Tina looked around the room. She waited. Did this have something to do with Jamey? Or Hank?

A tingling sensation crept up her spine like a centipede headed for her neck. Then the temperature returned to normal and Obi trotted out the bedroom door and raced for the deck. He wagged his tail, looking down the long driveway.

Maybe dream jumps robbed the room of heat. She knew nothing about it, but if she was going crazy on top of this new skill, then she seemed to be taking Jamey with her. Thank goodness for friends. Finally, she had someone to witness her bits of insanity.

***

Jamey didn't want another confrontation with Noble. What was tedious a few days ago had now turned to something else. But as long as Tina coddled the friendship, Jamey had to tread carefully. Before he'd leapt to the garden below Tina's window, he'd swabbed the drinking glass sediment with a tissue, in hopes of having it analyzed. If there weren't traces of a sleeping pill, Jamey would be surprised. He suspected Rufinol, the date rape drug, but it could be anything.

Driving away from Tina's house, he phoned Katie. "What are your thoughts about this Noble situation?"

She sounded slightly panicked. "I don't really know what to think. I'm not an expert. It's weird, but I try to stay out of it."

She thinks Noble's weird, too. His mind overflowed with questions and concerns. Katie had to go and he hung up. Was *he* an expert? Tina had jumped Noble's dream. She'd come back through Jamey's portal. After a lifetime of dream jumping, Jamey's learning curve was taking a drastic climb. This was all new territory.

Settling onto Pops' couch with a cup of coffee, he called his Sixth Force superior, the man he most trusted in Afghanistan,

Sergeant Pete Milton. He'd already spoken to him recently about jumping but this time Jamey needed to get the sediment analyzed and couldn't just ask the Maui Police.

"I have reason to think a friend was drugged, and I need to have something analyzed."

Milton paused to think. "I'll see if I can arrange for that. But Freud, you gotta avoid trouble, y'hear?" He took a drag on his cigarette. "You're supposed to be lying low."

"It's my niece. She might've gotten roofied," he explained. Now wasn't the time to reveal that he was piggybacking jumps and that he might never be able to initiate his own jump again. That bit of information was his secret for the time being. He'd never tell Milton about shaking Tina's hand, her fainting, and the possibility of something passing between them. Never reveal that now she was taking him along on her dream jumps, or that he might've passed something off to her. Maybe his ability had been lying dormant since the last jump in Afghanistan, waiting to transfer. And if so, why hadn't Katie been the one? Or his daughters, or Carrie, or Pops?

If he told Milton about all this, they'd want Tina. And

they couldn't have her. Ever.

Next, Jamey called Pops to run everything by him. "I tried automatic writing with a friend's deceased husband, and I got a drawing that looked like the letters M.O."

"I don't know anything about automatic writing, kid. Was it M as in Molokai or N as in Niihau?" Pops asked.

Jamey spilled the cup of coffee on the table in front of him. "Molokai. Wait! You might've just solved the mystery." Staring at the paper with 'M.O.,' Jamey phoned the dive shop to verify that Tina was ten miles down the road.

"She just left the shop with her parents. They said something about postponing their flight until tomorrow," Katie said. "Her truck is still here. Obi too. Tina's mother was angry with her, but with a really quiet voice. You know. One of those. And Tina seemed really tired and almost like she has the flu. Her dad was trying to lead her around and she let him take her elbow and walk her out to the car, like she was some sort of zombie. I think she's sick."

Yup, Jamey thought. She's hung over from being roofied. He'd send off the tissue, but it would be a few days before they had an answer on what was in Tina's glass. He hoped Tina had a few days. In the meantime, finding Hank's body and keeping Tina away from Noble were his top priorities. "Katie, if someone lost a boogie board, say at Honolua Bay or Fleming, could it potentially drift all the way to Molokai? Or is the channel too wide between Maui and

Molokai?"

Katie had no idea, but said she'd ask around.

Jamey flew up the stairs with the writing tablet clutched in his hand. The main room of the house was in a messy state from the night before—bowls of half-eaten snacks, beer cans, plastic glasses on every flat surface and decorations doing the second-day droop. He hadn't noticed any of this when he'd rushed upstairs the night before.

He entered the bedroom. "Hank? I think I understand. It's Molokai, isn't it?" He sat in the bedroom chair and drew a 'Yes' and a 'No' on the page, all the while talking, expecting an answer about Molokai. "I need to talk to you. Tina's trying to help you." Jamey sensed someone in the house. It wasn't the spirit of Hank.

The presence was coming from outside the bedroom. Not Noble.

Someone was frightened, and moving down the hall towards him. He stood ready. Tina's mother peeked in the room, fear fixed on her face. "Mrs. Greene. It's just me, Jamey Dunn. Sorry if I scared you."

She'd just heard him calling to Tina's dead husband. "I can explain." Her facial expression changed to anger in a flash. "You again. Back to get more coffee?" She straightened and looked at his pad of paper. "Get out of here."

Jamey's mind searched through all possible explanations, but there were no rational reasons for him to be in Tina's bedroom calling out her dead husband's name.

"Leave my daughter's house, Mr...."

"Dunn." He was caught. Damn. What the hell was Tina's mother doing in her house? Weren't they just at the dive shop? "Were you looking for Tina, or...?"

"That is none of your business." She shot him a look. "Don't think I won't be telling Kristina you were in her bedroom, calling out to her dead husband. You are as unbalanced as..." Elizabeth caught herself and closed her mouth. She took a quick look around the room and then faced Jamey, like a brick wall.

"Leave." She arched her eyebrows as if to express her strength of character.

Wow. Tina didn't have a chance with this mother. Jamey planted his feet, a tactic he'd learned in army training—Body Language 101. "Let's call a truce. We both have Tina's best interests at heart." He covered his heart with his right hand. "You don't have to like me, but I am a former police officer, a decorated soldier, on leave from Afghanistan."

"I think the important words are 'former' and 'on leave,' Mr. Dunn." She pointed to the patio door. "Out, or I shall be forced to call the real policemen."

He was done for now. Jamey pretty much knew that if it was possible for something to float all the way to Molokai, he would be on his way to the airport before sunset. Tina had told him the night before that the only good thing about tomorrow was that her parents were leaving for Seattle. He wished they hadn't postponed.

Jamey left the house. Although he didn't look back, he felt the mother's contempt but something else accompanied her dislike of him that he couldn't place. Worry, of course, but a feeling more like subterfuge. Something was very wrong, and Jamey was sure that Tina's safety was not the only thing in jeopardy.

CHAPTER 21

Tina had thought so much about Noble that her head hurt. Was it rape if the aggressor was someone you'd once led on to the point of almost having sex? And you were drunk? Someone you trusted, and briefly considered to be the father of a future baby? Noble was one of her most trusted friends. It was possible that she'd agreed to or initiated it. He'd never do anything to her she didn't agree. If they'd had sex, she must've encouraged him.

The one thing Tina was sure about was that she felt like shit. Her head was pounding like a sidewalk under a jackhammer. If she'd been as drunk as her hangover indicated, the likelihood of letting anyone have their way was pretty good.

Earlier that morning, her father had recounted what a fool she'd made of herself at the birthday party. "Acting like a Goddamned bar girl," he'd said. "Dancing around and hugging everyone." He'd never appreciated her choice in friends, or understood Kristina's closeness to any of them. No one was good enough, especially if they lived in Hawaii. Her parents hadn't warmed to Hank when they met him at the wedding, and they had avoided Maui afterwards, choosing phone calls instead. Especially after Philip had the heart attack and couldn't travel. Then 9/11. The last time she'd seen her parents was just before Hank disappeared. She'd gone to Seattle for a few days when her mother begged or her to come home for a while.

After parking in the back alley of the shop, Tina followed the noise of a hammer rhythmically pounding. A man in dress shorts and a pressed Hawaiian shirt hung a 'Sold' sign at Mr. Takeshimi's place. Her heart squeezed into a tight, hard ball. Mr. T was leaving. Seeing her neighbor at the front window, she smiled, but his gaze was on the sign that told the world he'd be leaving his life in Lahaina.

She waved at him sympathetically, wanting to call out her own proverb to console him, but he turned and walked away without seeing or waving back. Her hopes sank. If he couldn't stick it out, how could she hope to? He'd been fighting for freedom in America, and then for acceptance in Hawaii, and then for the right to keep his home. She'd only just begun her fight against the elements of her life.

***

Tina and her father sat silently in the waiting room at the Kaiser clinic. The emergency appointment she'd made to appease him about her 'current state of mind' would hopefully get her parents off her back and help them get on that plane tomorrow. According to her father, he had enough evidence against her stability to gain a power of attorney over her. "I should know," he'd said on the drive over.

Tina was tired of fighting with her parents. And tired of feeling hung over. She'd chased some more Advil with a big glass of orange juice, but the symptoms wouldn't go away. Slumped in the waiting room's leatherette chair, she thought of how easily the little girl whose judgment was always questioned by her father, had risen to the surface to allow him to call the shots.

Her cell phone rang. Seeing Jamey's number, she let it go to message. She'd return the call after Doc Chan told her father that she was healing at an admirable rate. Jamey was probably still disappointed she'd gotten drunk when he needed to dream jump. If he found the remains of a sedative in her glass, she'd add that to the growing list of unknowns. Had she drunkenly added a Xanax to the water to ensure sleep? She'd been woozy, that much she remembered. The memory of everyone yelling "surprise!" was her last clear one. Her father handed her a glass of wine after that...or was that Noble? When she called Pepper that morning, she was told she'd been 'wasted,' and that "everyone agrees it's perfectly fine to get drunk at your own birthday party, especially after all you've been through this year."

Finally seated in the doctor's office, Emily Chan explained that when two people shared a session, she let each person take a turn to speak, uninterrupted.

Philip Greene went first and got straight to the point. "Kristina's mother and I feel a change might work well for her right now. Quite frankly, Doctor, we were shocked to see how much worse she is." Her father had a way of nodding while he spoke, to pull the listener into his perspective. "She's not better, and she is surrounding herself with strange characters." He held up his hand to count off her problems. "She's unable to dive, her supposed livelihood; she's drinking heavily, taking pills, mismanaging her business, and now she tells me she's having nightmares so she's not sleeping." He exhaled. "Frankly, we're worried sick about her." He looked at his daughter, who was itching to defend herself. "I'm sure you would agree, Dr. Chan, our daughter would benefit from a change of scenery right now, as well as being around her parents. All we're asking is for Kristina to come to Seattle for a rest. To get away from all the memories this island holds. Just until she feels stronger."

Philip Greene was finished for now, but he sat on the edge of his chair, ready to jump to his own defense. Tina knew the underlying threat he hadn't voiced. *And if she doesn't agree, I will declare power of attorney and take over anyhow.*

Doc Chan nodded at him. "Well, I think having people who are looking out for your best interests is valuable, and I'm sure Tina would agree with that. But I have to say that

I disagree with you on several accounts, Mr. Greene." Oh, thank God!

"I think Tina's progress is admirable. Considering what she's been through."

"We know it's a process," he countered. "And that's why we feel that Kristina's healing would best be served by a change of location. Namely, home."

"This is my home, Father." Tina looked at Dr. Chan as if to say *don't sell me out now*.

"And you've had a good time in Hawaii, Kristina, but we feel…" He looked like words were fighting to leave his mouth. He leaned forward to take his daughter's hand. "Mother and I are worried about you, and we feel it's best if you are where we can offer you our support in the coming months. You are not getting better since Hank's death. You are getting worse."

His eyes were misty and she wondered if it was real. Of course it was. "Can I talk now?" She had to defend herself.

The doctor nodded. "Yes, let's have Tina talk."

"Father, I know you mean well but Maui is my home. I'm not just having a good time, as you said. This is my life, and this is where I want to live and recuperate."

"It's not working, Kristina. Look at you." He caught himself and backtracked. "All we ask for is a month. Come to Seattle, sleep in your bedroom, see old friends, think about something else for a while." Philip shot a steely look to the doctor.

"I can't leave here, Father." What about Obi and the shop? A month was a long time. "I know it's hard for you and Mother." She turned to the doctor and reminded her how the death of her twin brother had made her parents protective of their remaining child. "My whole life, they've worried about my safety." While she talked, her father's lips trembled and suddenly he looked like a sad old man to her. "I appreciate that you love me, Father, but I won't uproot my life for you."

He looked over at the doctor. "I'm sure you would agree that our daughter has been severely traumatized in the last year." The doctor leaned in and nodded. This quiet sensibility was the very thing her father was known for in court.

Within minutes, Philip's words had Dr. Chan agreeing. "It wouldn't hurt for you to have a change of scenery, even just for a few weeks," Emily Chan said to her. "But it's ultimately Tina's decision."

Tina was shocked. How could the doctor be steamrolled like this? Tina fleetingly thought about phoning Jamey for support, envisioning herself holding onto the doctor's leg to wait for Jamey while her father tried to pull her off. Two weeks was on the table now, but Tina knew better. They would try to convince her to stay longer. She thought about the day she picked up the phone to hear that her father had a heart attack and was on his way by ambulance to the hospital. That flight to Seattle had been six of the longest hours of her life. "I don't want to take more than a week. I have a business to rebuild and can't afford to be away."

"Fine, Kristina. A week is better than nothing." Philip looked pleased, satisfied.

But Tina knew better than anyone that seven days could turn into a month, which might turn into a year, and then Maui would be a memory. Given the hold they had over her, she worried that she'd never get back to her beloved island.

***

The Beaver 251 plane dipped and rocked through gusty pockets of air as Jamey followed the Maui coastline at eighteen hundred feet. Coming up to the northern tip of the Valley Isle, he noticed cumulonimbus clouds hovering over Molokai in the distance. "Uncle Jamey? Right over there must be that current, the Molokai Express." Katie sat on the edge of her seat beside him, her face almost pressed against the windshield.

"Yup, between the two islands. They said it was strong?"

"Extremely." Katie squealed in the headphones. "This is totally radical! Ned is going to be so jealous I got to come with you in a plane," She was a good distraction, filling the small cabin with her enthusiasm, even if she had no idea they were looking for a dead body. The sound of the engine roared outside the headphones while Katie's voice chatted on the microphone.

Looming in front was Hawaii's second largest island, Molokai. This time of year, it was green and lush, waterfalls striping the northern end, like movie scenery. The owner of the rental plane had warned Jamey to watch for sudden wind gusts. "I flew a few days ago from Maui to Molokai," Jamey said. "I'll take care of your beauty." With hands on the steering wheel, he aimed for Molokai's uninhabited northern coast.

"I didn't think it would be so noisy in a little plane," Katie said.

"Not like a commercial flight, is it, kiddo?"

"Better."

Jamey flipped a switch to contact the air traffic controller.

"This is Little Beaver, at the north of Maui. Request permission to drop to fifteen hundred feet."

"Little Beaver, this is West Maui Airport. You have a small plane at fourteen hundred feet heading your way, rounding Kahakuloa. Please wait."

Jamey looked below to verify, waited for the aircraft to pass, and when given the go-ahead, he dropped lower to cross the channel. Closing in on his destination, Jamey next reported in to Kalaupapa Airport on Molokai. "Little Beaver at fourteen hundred feet, heading west towards you."

Seconds later, they verified a clear route along the Molokai sea cliffs and got clearance to drop lower.

Jamey scanned the coast for the dream's beach as he approached the cliffs. From the recent rains, the waterfalls were majestically active, dropping tons of fresh water to the sea from hundreds of feet, all along the cliff face. As Katie oohed and ahhed and clapped her hands at the stunning view, Jamey searched the ocean, wondering if Hank's body waited below this postcard scene. No sign of the beach from the dream yet, but this had to be the stretch. He'd asked the guys at the private airport about the Molokai Express and was told that things washed up on the north shore from West Maui on a regular basis. When he mentioned a body, he'd been told again that a body would never get that far because of the sharks. One of the pilots even laughed at the thought.

A headache crept to the edge of his skull. Maybe residual feelings from last night's jump. The hum of the plane's engine was irritating. He'd bring Tina here tomorrow. Hopefully he'd know what was in the drink residue at Tina's house. If it was a roofie, then Noble didn't cover his tracks very well, leaving the glass on the table like that. It irked him that she wouldn't do a rape test, but he'd reminded himself many times that it wasn't his decision. Possessiveness over Tina was probably clouding his opinion of Noble.

Circling back towards the long Molokai coastline, Jamey took inventory—tall cliffs, rocky shoreline, waves, but nothing familiar. Nothing that jumped out at him as the brief vision he'd had from the dream. Maybe he'd been too optimistic about recognizing anything. Would Tina see something familiar if she came with him? He hoped so, because he had to get back. He'd been flying for a while and the plane was getting low on gas.

***

Defending herself at the doctor's office left Tina feeling exhausted and empty, like she'd been awake for days. She was tired of the grief, the frustration, and not only the possibilities, but the lack of possibilities. And now she was weary of everyone's interference. "I'll call you later, Father." Tina drove to the shop to collect Obi. "I'm going home for a while, Megan. When Katie gets back, tell her I'm off today."

Her feet dragged on the stairs up to her deck and she tripped, catching herself by grabbing the banister. The heaviness was back, like a brick pressing against her chest, her head still fuzzy and weighted. Taking a deep breath was a chore. Dropping to the floor for a nap was tempting. It was a struggle just to get to the bedroom and flop onto the bed. Her mother had just called her cell phone to suggest she take a nap. They'd fly tomorrow to Seattle.

When she woke up, Tina would make a veterinary appointment for Obi. If she was running out of steam, she had to get one last thing done before she gave up, and gave in.

"Ti, I want to talk to you." Noble appeared at the bedroom door just before she dropped off to sleep. He looked like he meant business. "I'm concerned about you." He moved to sit on the bed beside her. "Did Dr. Chan recommend you take a break?"

"Did my parents talk to you? They want me to go to Seattle tomorrow." She looked at Obi. "I don't know if I can leave Maui. Not even for a week." Noble stared at her. "I'll watch Obi, and the house. You have people to run the shop."

She nodded, feeling layers of defensiveness drop away. "I know but...maybe you're right. I'm tired of trying so hard. Blacking out last night was freaky. I can't remember most of the evening, which isn't like me. The doctor says I might have blocked it out because things are getting too painful. She says that sometimes people do that to protect themselves from emotions they can't deal with. She gave me some new pills."

Noble stroked her arm lovingly. "Blocking out the bad stuff can be good sometimes."

Tina wanted to know that Noble was still her rock, her safety net, when things got beyond the realm of tolerability. "Noble?" She searched his face. "I'm not sure you answered this question, but we didn't have sex last night, right?" She waited.

His expression was unreadable. "Why would you ask that?"

"Because I don't remember most of the night, and I woke up in a sexy outfit…and you were naked." She frowned and waited for his reply.

Noble took a deep breath. "I didn't want to add to your troubles."

She waited, her heart sinking. That wasn't an answer. "Did we?"

"You wanted to but no, we didn't."

She'd wanted to. "Sorry, I was so drunk." At least Noble had done the right thing, not that it was any great gift to have sex with her right now. This current version of herself would be considered clearance material, especially when she was so fragile. "Noble…" Searching for words allowed him time to move in.

"It's alright." He hugged her to him once more. "Just know I'm here for you."

Maybe he was right. She was being paranoid. It wouldn't hurt to leave Maui and clear her head. It would get her parents off her back, and she might just return feeling recharged. Tina hadn't been away from Maui since before Hank's death. Afterwards, she hadn't been able to leave the island, in case he showed up. Tina pulled away from the hug. "Maybe everyone's right. I need to get off this rock."

When Noble left, she leaned back against the pillows, remembering another time in her life when she needed to get away. Run away.

At five-years-old, she'd been invited by her beloved grandmother for a week at her estate. Kristina desperately wanted to go. Her twin brother, Kristoffer, had only been dead a year, and she missed him. Her parents had more rules since her brother went to heaven. Going anywhere without them was not allowed. But soon she'd start kindergarten and they'd have to let her go there. Visiting her grandmother might never come again. Gramma was getting old, and after she finished kindergarten she'd heard her mother say she was leaving for sleepover school.

"Please?" little Kristina asked her mother, with fingers crossed behind her back.

"No, not this year," Elizabeth answered. "Maybe when you're older."

When she told her Gramma the bad news, the woman said, "I'll try to think of something, Kristina. Don't worry. We'll have our time together somehow."

"How?" Kristina asked.

"I'll use my special powers," Gramma said, patting her granddaughter's head.

But Elizabeth would not let her daughter visit overnight. Not even when Gramma asked her son to intervene.

"Mother, my wife has the final word where Kristina is concerned," he'd insisted.

Gramma's special powers had not worked. She asked about them the next time her grandmother came to visit. "I'm sad I can't sleepover, Gram."

"I'm still hoping to change your mother's mind," her grandmother said, picking a daisy and handing it to the little girl.

"But what do your special powers do?" She needed to know.

"They help me have nice dreams with friends."

"Can you dream with me?"

"Only if you come to my house, I'm afraid."

She had to find a way. Gramma promised to try again for a visit at Easter break, but Kristina couldn't wait and woke up the next day with a plan.

When her mother left for a luncheon, Kristina went to their backyard playground with her nanny. The pool had been taken out the year before and replaced with a garden. As usual, Nanny Helen fell asleep in the sunshine. Seeing her opportunity, Kristina snuck through the bushes and out the front gate. She had to get to town a different way so her mother wouldn't catch her. Kristina took unfamiliar streets, sure that all roads led to where Gramma lived. If she could find the library, she knew how to get to Gramma's house from there.

Four hours later, the authorities found a scared little girl sitting at the side of a road, crying, with her tiny jeweled purse full of snacks. When the policeman radioed that he'd found the Greene girl, someone on the other end yelled, "Thank God!" Kristina did not recognize the voice.

Her father was out of town on business and her mother was too distraught to talk to the policeman back at her house. Left with the housekeeper, she was scooted inside and slapped on the bottom. "Bad girl," the housekeeper admonished in broken English. "Mama thought she lost the other twin."

Nanny Helen was gone forever. Her mother was upstairs, sleeping. After speaking to her father on the phone about what a bad girl she'd been, she was sent upstairs to bed without dinner. The next day her mother carried on as usual, as if nothing had happened and it was never spoken of again.

Gramma went to heaven before the summer was over and Kristina grieved, not only for her wonderful grandmother, but for the magic sleepover that never was.

CHAPTER 22

After a brief nap, Tina found herself back at the shop. "Oh God!" She held the *Lahaina News* in her hands, staring at the front-page story.

"What?" Katie looked over.

"A shark attacked a tourist swimming off Olowalu." No one would dive for at least a week. Probably two. Activities would suffer until a new wave of tourists who'd never heard of the unfortunate accident arrived. It might be a month before the story cooled off. This would be a good time to escape to Seattle after all.

Tina read aloud to Katie: "*The victim snorkeled into an area filled with sharks feeding on a dead whale carcass. The dorsal fins and thrashing were mistaken by the two women for dolphins at play, according to the survivor.*" Tina cringed and continued. "*By the time they realized it was feeding sharks, it was too late for one of the women.*"

Nausea rose in Tina's throat. Another death in the ocean. Another life claimed. The tragedy made her wonder about the friend who'd escaped death. Survivor guilt was a bitch.

After instructing Katie to tell potential customers that the victim swam directly into feeding sharks, and that boat diving was perfectly safe, Tina loaded Obi into the truck and drove to the vet. She needed to have Obi's lump examined before she could think about leaving Maui in twenty hours.

Putting one foot in front of the other, Tina marched up to the clinic's counter and said in a clear, steady voice, "My dog has a lump on his underside." She'd rehearsed the words on the drive, but every time Obi looked over and wagged his tail, she wanted to turn around and take him home.

Fortunately, the wait was short at the Lahaina Veterinary Clinic. By the time the receptionist showed her to an examination room, Tina was perilously close to tears. But the vet was a dog lover, and he stroked her dog's head while they talked. Obi was clearly not happy to stand on the cold, metal table and submit to the examination of his underside. When the needle poked him to extract a sample, Tina buried her face in Obi's neck and cooed words of comfort. "You're a good boy, Obi Wan," she told him. "Mommy's gonna give you a treat at the house."

On the ride home, Obi hung his head out the truck window. "It's all for the greater good, my sweet dog," Tina said, reaching over to pat his haunches. That expression seemed to be invading her thoughts on a regular basis. "You are really going to be upset if you have to get that thing removed." She didn't dare think about cancer. Not yet.

Once back at her house, Tina headed for the bedroom, exhausted. She had to lie down for a nap; just an hour or two, and then she'd go back to the shop. Lately, she had no energy. This was more than exhaustion. She was probably fighting the flu or a virus. The last twenty-four hours had been too much—her father and Doc Chan ganging up, Noble agreeing, then the emotion of taking Obi to the vet. Everything had taken a chunk out of her. And now her parents were planning to fly out tomorrow. With her.

Jamey hadn't returned her call, but she needed to give him a heads-up about Seattle. Jamey. If she left for a week or two, would he still be here when she returned? The thought of not seeing him again made her feel panicky.

While Tina and her father had been at Kaiser with Dr. Chan, her mother had packed a bag and left it by the bed with a plane ticket on top. Elizabeth had been confident of her husband's influence. "Our plan is for you to come with us," she'd said earlier on the phone.

"I don't know if I can be ready to go tomorrow, Mother. Maybe the day after," she balked. Little did her mother know that there'd been a shark attack and Tina was becoming more available by the hour.

The small suitcase lay open by the bed, everything folded and orderly in the various compartments. Her mother had included lingerie, jeans, and shirts, several pairs of socks, a sweater and a pair of shoes. Anything else Tina needed, like coats and boots, could be found in the closet of her old room in Seattle. Tina almost smiled to think how out of date her clothes would be. She and Hank had never visited Seattle together. "Too rainy, maybe someday," he'd said.

In the bathroom, the medicine cupboard was open. Before closing it, she noticed that her pills were out of place. Although mayhem ruled her life in many areas, Tina was fastidious about her medications, especially lately. With three pills to take at bedtime, it was imperative to have a system. She kept the birth control pill dispenser on the right and the others on the left. Always. When Hank died, and her hope of having a baby was obliterated, Tina began taking birth control pills again to keep her painful periods under control. But something was askew with the dispenser. For one thing, it was on top of the Lexapro bottle. Had she drunkenly moved it the night before? Tina checked the dates on the dispenser. Tuesday's pill was gone. Yesterday. That was good. But tonight's pill looked different. She popped it out a little too easily. Thursday's too. And Friday's. She was at the end of the foil packet and had no others to use for comparison. It was possible that in her drunken stupor she'd taken out too many pills and then put them back in. She didn't remember. Trouble was, she didn't remember. From now on, she had to pay closer attention at bedtime. Maybe buy one of those day-of-the-week pill dispensers.

"I'm a mess, Obi." The dog followed her into the bedroom. Her eyelids felt like lead weights and she had to lie down before she fell down. Exhaustion was winning the battle.

Obi snuggled into the bend in her body, his blocky head on her arm. Until she got the pathology report that told her Obi's lump was benign, her heart would be heavy with worry. She couldn't leave Maui until she heard, could she?

Tina would talk to Jamey later, maybe even divulge that her father was threatening to get power of attorney over her. Even if he had proof she wasn't making sound decisions, he'd only said that to scare her. But first she needed a quick nap and then she could think clearly. Her last thought before she succumbed to sleep was that she hoped when she woke, things would look brighter. This mood resembled a rainy November day in Seattle, when the sky turned dark at four p.m. and months of rain were imminent.

***

Jamey hadn't found the beach by the time he delivered the plane back to the airport. Damn. What did it look like, anyway? He needed more information. As he drove across the island from the airport, he had one mission in mind: to get the location more clearly defined by communicating with Hank. He needed Tina to be at the shop so he could get into her bedroom undetected.

His call to Tina's cell phone went right to message. "I need to talk to you, Tina, so call me at this number." She hadn't been answering her phone all day.

The turnoffs for Lahaina sped by as he continued north to her house. He'd sit in her bedroom until he felt a presence, until Tina's husband elaborated on where his body was. Man, this was getting weirder every day.

After parking two blocks down the street, Jamey ducked into the driveway and caught sight of Tina and

Noble's trucks. Would she be home this early? For her, four p.m. was midday. He dreaded seeing Noble today. Jamey was two beats away from turning Noble in to the police for using a roofie on Tina, but until he had confirmation from the toxicology lab, he'd have to wait. The patio door was locked, for some reason. He ran downstairs and let himself in through the back door.

Tina lay on her bed, asleep. Obi merely raised his head. "Good boy," he whispered. *Smart dog knows when to bark and when not to.*

Jamey reached over to pat Obi's head and thought about sitting in Tina's bedroom chair to try to summon Hank. Instincts told him that she was not dreaming. Not yet. He eased himself quietly into the green chair, Obi's eyes tracking him.

With the pad of paper on his lap and a slim pencil in his hand, Jamey closed his eyes and attempted to summon Hank. Breathe, in and out. Focus. Breathe, breathe… Let it all go. He fell slowly into a familiar oblivion…into Tina's dream. No. He had to get out. For one thing, he didn't have permission. But what if it was the diving dream? He was close to solving the mystery of the cave and the rocky beach. Ignoring his plan to jump out, he continued just until he could see that beach again.

The fall quickened until Jamey felt water around him. The darkness cleared, and he found himself in water, thirty feet under. The rock wall was on his left this time. He turned in a circle to see that no one was with him. Where was Tina? Wasn't this her dream?

He swam to the safety of the wall and then noticed something in the shadows. The shark. It moved lazily up ahead. Without natural floatation, sharks sank if they stopped moving. Remembering this was the form Hank had taken, Jamey continued. The shark might be a clue to this whole story. Without Tina in the dream, the possibility still existed that the dream was Hank's, as strange as that sounded.

The shark swerved along the wall and he followed. Crashing waves rolled above him in the direction of the wall. When they reached the cave's opening, the shark stopped and cut back. Jamey nodded, and then motioned above. He had to surface. Otherwise, what good was this dream?

Kicking himself up, Jamey exhaled, pulling hard with his hands. He broke through just in time to see the topography of the land in front. He was on the sea cliffs of Molokai; the area he'd just flown over. The rocky beach was to the left. In the previous dream, he must have ascended facing the other way and thought the cave was directly in front of the beach.

Jumping out of the dream, he took longer than usual to return to his body. But when his eyes flew open, his breath was ragged and shallow. Had Hank orchestrated the dream? If so, both he and Tina might have been jumping into Hank's dreams all along. This was brand-new territory. Goddammit.

Tina was still asleep. Not dreaming. He could tell. He clutched the pencil in his hand. He hadn't expected to jump, only summon Hank. Although it was a lead pencil, he hadn't lost control of the dream. Exactly the opposite. He'd been able to stay long enough to see the cliffs and jump out without the portal.

He hadn't piggybacked Tina's dream jump. She hadn't been there. She'd slept through it all. The dream wasn't meant for her. It was meant for him. Hank must be in the bedroom. "I got it, man. Molokai Sea Cliffs," Jamey whispered.

In the bathroom, Jamey grabbed the ibuprofen bottle, just in case, and noticed a plastic pill dispenser on the counter—the kind with the days of the week on each separate compartment. Birth control pills. His first thought was that Tina shouldn't leave her pills out like this, especially in a house that was easy to wander into. A pile of pills lay beside the container with holes in the slots for the next few days. What was she doing? He contemplated waking her just as footsteps sounded on the outside stairs.

It was probably her parents. He slipped back into the bedroom. Only a few hours earlier, Tina's mother had warned him to get out of the house. If she caught him again, the situation would be uncomfortable, at the very least.

The closet door was open and he ducked in finding a perfect hiding spot behind a grouping of long skirts. The sliding door in the main room opened and closed. He imagined the parents crossing the carpeted floor and peeking at their sleeping child, curled on the bed. He'd forgotten to close the closet door. Jamey watched Obi lift his head. The dog stood up, hair raised on his back, and growled at whoever was in Tina's bedroom.

***

Tina was dreaming that she and Hank were making love. He was bringing her to a frenzied climax, something they'd never actually achieved to this degree in reality. Then she woke to Obi growling at the foot of her bed.

Noble stood in the doorway, his expression one of concern. "Are you sleeping this early?" He advanced and sat on the bed, beside her knees.

Could he tell she'd been woken from an erotic dream? Did she appear to be on the verge of something that had just been taken away? "What time is it?" she asked.

He brushed the hair out of her eyes. "Almost five."

Tina sat up, sliding away from him, pressing her back against the wall. "The show?"

"I'm going soon. But I need to talk to you." His expression was too serious. "Why is Jamey's jeep out on the street?"

Not the jeep again. "I don't know, Noble. Give it up, please. Did you ever think there might be more than one yellow jeep on this island?" She really didn't want to have a discussion with Noble when she was this groggy.

Noble stroked her exposed arm. "I don't trust that guy." He softened. "I probably know you better than anyone right now." Tina wasn't sure. He had no idea about the dreams, or her history with Jamey, but she nodded.

"You've been under so much stress this year. And things aren't getting better." He looked apologetic. "Not really, Ti." Tears came to Tina's eyes. He was right.

"No one could have gone through what you did and still feel fine." He rubbed her back as she sank into his shoulder. "I'm here for you." His hand made circles between her shoulder blades. Slowly, lightly.

"Sometimes I don't know if I can continue," she said through tears.

"I know." He stopped rubbing. "Sometimes I wonder about Hank being dead. If he has a life somewhere else. Not in this world.

A better life than we're having here without him." He took a deep breath. "Sometimes I think about being with him."

Tina pushed away, horrified. "Don't say such a thing."

His eyes were filled with pain. "I think about it."

"No, you don't. Shut up. Don't talk like that."

Noble's face changed. "I just wonder. That's all." He pulled back from her and stood. "If you want to go to Seattle, I'll look after everything here."

He would be the only one who could. "Obi has a lump. The vet took a sample today."

Noble nodded knowingly. "Ah, that was the message. They called to say all is clear."

What? Didn't they have to send the biopsy to the mainland?

"Really?"

He shook his head. "Apparently not."

"Oh, my God." Tina heaved a huge sigh and hugged Obi to her chest.

"I'll handle everything here while you're in Seattle." Noble was the only person who could take over her life while she was gone. He lived on the property, knew Obi, was even able to dive if need be, which was more than Tina could do. She'd return in a week or two and start diving again. A group was coming in four and a half weeks and counting on her. She had to be ready to dive with them. She was the expert in Hawaii on paraplegic diving and this week had been booked for a year. Maybe time in Seattle would help get her back on track, she'd be able to fulfill her obligations. "It'll be a good change of scenery," she agreed. Then the room got unusually cool, like earlier. "Do you feel that?"

Noble frowned. "No. What?"

Tina looked over to the window. "It feels like air conditioning." Obi whined.

Tina continued, "Don't worry about me. I'm fine. Go do your show." She hugged Obi again. "Oh, my God. I'm so glad you're okay, Obi."

"Will you go to Seattle tomorrow with your parents?" Noble asked.

"Or the next day." She closed her eyes and leaned back against the pillows.

Noble was generous. Always had been. Of course, he could run everything on her behalf. She trusted him, even if she'd been clouded by his romantic feelings for her recently. But he'd loved Hank too, and had suffered so much in the last ten months. Each day that they didn't find the body, Noble had come home with his head hung and his heart screaming for absolution. The guilt had taken him under—guilt that he hadn't surfed that day with his best friend. He hadn't tried to talk Hank out of attempting the monstrous waves, and by the time Noble got to Honolua Bay, Hank was gone.

Afterwards, he and Tina comforted each other, mixing their tears, hoping to find Hank's body against all odds. Then he gave up, because he had to or it was going to kill him.

Yes, she trusted him, no matter what Jamey said.

* * *

When Noble left, Jamey emerged from the closet. "Tina, it's me." She had gone back to sleep so quickly. He touched her arm.

She startled. "What are you doing here?"

"I came to talk to you. I hid in the closet when I saw Noble."

Her droopy eyes searched his face. "Why?"

"Tina, you can't go to Seattle." He had to tell her about Molokai.

"It's just for a week." Her eyes closed.

"I think Noble's pulling a fast one on you." He had to convince her to put it off. At least until she was thinking clearly. "Honey, you have to believe me."

"Stop Jamey, I'm tired."

He had to engage her. "I found the dream site." Her eyes fluttered open.

"It's Molokai. I'm ninety-nine percent sure that's the place."

Tina squinted at him. "Did you see the beach?"

"Yes, but I want you to come with me to look before I dive it." Jamey's senses were on what he called 'spidey alert' and he could tell Noble was approaching again. "Say you'll come to Molokai with me." Jamey needed to lock eyes with Tina before all hell broke loose and Noble saw his 'girlfriend' with another man. Jamey wasn't ready to face Noble with accusations. Not just yet.

But, Noble's hatred preceded him and oozed through the house.

"I thought I could smell a rat," Noble stood planted in the bedroom's doorway.

"Tina and I were just leaving, so if you will step aside,

248

Noble…" Jamey wanted to get Tina out of this house. He gently pulled her to sit up. They'd grab a coffee for her, rent a plane and verify the Molokai location before it got dark.

Noble softened his look for Tina. "Don't worry, Ti. I won't let him take you anywhere."

"Oh, God. Please don't have a pissing match over me." Her face looked drained, her eyes at half-mast. She sat on the side of the bed.

Jamey shot her a meaningful look that she did not catch. He turned to his opponent. "Look, Noble," he said, his voice dripping with dislike. "Tina and I have somewhere to be, so if you'll just go to work, this has nothing to do with you, pal."

Noble took two steps closer to Jamey. "I'm not your pal. And it doesn't look like Tina wants to go anywhere, Jameeeeey." He poked Jamey in the chest. Not hard. Even though Noble had sixty pounds on him, Jamey knew who would win if it came to combat. He felt the conclusion as if it already happened. Jamey wouldn't be the first to swing, but he'd be the last.

Jamey kept his eyes on the big guy in front of him. Peripherally, he could see that Tina was prone on the bed again. "Tina, you gotta come with me now. Tell him, or I'm afraid something is going to happen and it won't be pleasant for your friend here." The sizzle in the air was thick with hatred. Jamey tried to ignore Noble. Why wasn't Tina getting up? He had to look over.

A second before Noble lifted his arm to punch him Jamey knew it was coming. He was able to block the left hook, and then take Noble in a twist and headlock. "Don't do it, Noble."

Noble flipped him, as he knew he would, but Jamey was ready and landed on his feet.

"STOP!" Tina yelled. "Both of you. Stop it! I will not have you fighting in my house!" Her words filled the room, probably the whole neighborhood. Her face was splotched with red. "Get out!" she yelled.

Reading her thoughts was difficult. Beyond the anger. She was exhausted, and only partially cognizant.

"Now!" Although her eyes were glazed, there was fire behind her words, and Jamey knew what he had to do.

"Tina, I'm pretty sure Noble's drugging you. That's why you're so tired." He shot a look at his opponent.

"I am not, you slimy…" Noble stepped forward.

"Oh, this is too much!" she said. Jamey braced himself for what would come next out of her mouth. "Leave this house, both of you." Her whisper was full of venom.

Jamey backed up against the patio door, and Noble glanced at the bedroom door.

"Jamey, get off my property." She looked at him, and then turned. "And Noble, get out of my house, or I'll call the police on both of you."

CHAPTER 23

The wind had come up at Airport Beach. Any year now they would take out the sugar cane and put up hotels. They'd already removed the former airport's leftover shack that once hosted the tiny Windsock Lounge. As Maui became more developed, some of the quaintness had died.

Tina walked on the path through the kiawe bushes to the deserted beach. Obi flushed out two Franklin birds, who squeaked their way to another corner of the cane field. Nausea had set in and she had to remind herself that this feeling of being weighted down was due to her hangover, not a sedative. Or depression. Drinking a Coke on the car ride had helped a bit.

Although it seemed almost impossible, focus was needed. There were things to do before she left for Seattle tomorrow. She'd decided to get on that plane, let Noble take over, and get some perspective on everything. Eighteen hours separated her from going to Seattle. She dug her toes in the sand at the edge of the water. A turtle's head poked through the surface, just off the beach, and Obi barked. He loved the surprise of their leathery heads materializing from what seemed like nothing. The south side of Molokai was visible from this beach, but not the north side. The Molokai Sea Cliffs. The wind blew Tina's hair around her face, and she took deep breaths to try to shake this foggy feeling. What if Jamey was right, and her pills had been switched out for sedatives? Hadn't they popped out of the foil easier than usual?

After that pissing match between Jamey and Noble, her house didn't seem safe anymore. Jamey was paranoid, and Noble was acting weird. As unthinkable as it was, Tina had to wonder if Noble had drugged her. Jamey had no reason to lie to her, but then, neither did Noble.

Obi dodged waves as they rolled into shore. Watching him play, she was profoundly thankful that the pathology report was clear. There'd been a misunderstanding, obviously, about waiting for days. Knowing Obi was healthy was one more check mark on the side of being available to leave Maui tomorrow for a week. Or two. But Molokai. Her parents' flight to Seattle left in the afternoon. They'd reserved a seat for Tina in first class with them. She already had Seattle plans to look up a college friend, lunch at her favorite restaurant in Capital Hill, ride at her old stable. But before she did anything, details loomed. If she could identify the Molokai location, she might have to give up that seat, at least long enough to exhaust this theory. The what-ifs made her dizzy. As much as she needed to do something to piece her life back together, Tina had to explore this one last possibility before she left for Seattle.

She called Jamey's cell phone, a number she'd committed to memory by now.

"I'm in the parking lot of the West Maui Airport with a plane on stand-by," Jamey told her. The sun was low, and night would advance in another hour. "It's late but I'll check to see if we can still go."

As she sped north, he called back. "You gotta get here in five minutes."

"On my way." Turning right, she sped up the hill and parked beside Jamey's jeep. He was on the tarmac, inspecting the polar white Cessna. The look on his face when he saw her was not familiar. Guarded, mistrustful. She'd distanced him and he'd retreated. The drama she brought to the table had taken a toll on him.

She put her hand on his arm in apology. "I'm operating on one cylinder here. Sorry." Her shoulders slumped.

Jamey pointed to the stepstool at the plane's open doorway. "We only have forty minutes to get the plane back." His cool demeanor was unsettling.

At the cliffs, he took the plane down to three hundred feet so she could get a better look. Clutching Obi, Tina honed in on the area ahead and squinted through the binoculars.

In her dreams, she'd only glanced briefly at the beach, and she couldn't be entirely sure. It was a beautiful scene, the Molokai Sea Cliffs at sunset. "Looks promising." Her voice in the headset sounded like an astronaut broadcasting from the moon.

"Right over here." Jamey steered for the beach, alongside a big slab of rock, and then glanced at Tina.

"That's it!" She shot him a look. "Oh, my God, this is the site." She grabbed his free hand and squeezed. Her heart rate sped up. "We'll dive here tomorrow. Launch the boat at dawn." His voice was calm.

Between the hangover, the fatigue, and the shock of finding the dive site, Tina was completely spent by the time the plane landed on the short landing strip back at the West Maui Airport. The last flight of the day was boarding the prop plane to Honolulu. When she saw Mr. Takeshimi and his daughter, Tina ran over.

"Are you leaving now, Mr. T?"

A smile spread across his face. "Life without endeavor is like coming out of a jewel mine with empty hands, Tina."

"I'm endeavoring, Mr. T" She hugged him to her, even though she felt his resistance. "I'm better for having known you." Pulling back, she looked into his hopeful face. "We learn little from victory, much from defeat." He'd said this to her once. They nodded, and then Mr. T and his daughter disappeared inside the plane's cabin.

"You okay?" Jamey touched her arm.

"Yes. I have to call my parents to tell them I won't be leaving with them tomorrow." The overwhelming urge to curl into a ball and go to sleep would have to wait. "The shit will hit the fan with that call."

"I want you to stay at my place tonight. For safety."
Jamey looked perfectly serious. "Oh, Jamey…"

"Humor me, even though you trust Noble." He looked
hard into her face. "Remember, I found the site, and I
haven't steered you wrong, not so far."

"I'm okay at my own house. I told Noble…"

"Tina, please. There's more I want to say about Hank,
but not here." This got her attention.

She looked down the hill in the direction of her house,
and thought of what she might need for the night. Not
much besides pills and a toothbrush. "Okay, I'll meet you
at Pops' condo."

"Ten minutes, no more, or I'm coming to get you."

Tina thought of saying that she could take care of
herself, but she wasn't so sure anymore.

***

No one takes that long to grab a toothbrush. How had
he ever agreed to let Tina go back to her house alone?
Especially if Noble knew that they'd taken a flight over
Molokai to look for Hank's body. Had Tina told Noble?
After seeing them on the bed earlier and feeling the bond
between them, he didn't want to bet against Tina's
relationship with Noble. It wasn't just their mutual
connection to Hank that he felt. Their friendship was
something more. Tina wasn't telling him everything about
Noble, and maybe it was none of his business.

All he knew, as he drove to Tina's house at the
twenty-minute mark, was that she was not safe with Noble.
Until he could prove something, it would be hard to get her
to believe him.

The drive to her house took less than a minute, seeing
he waited at the end of the street. He ran up the stairs, two
at a time but didn't feel Noble's presence. "Tina?" Obi ran
out of the bedroom. Something was wrong.

When he saw her sprawled across the bed, his first thought was to look for blood. His senses quickly reassured him she was asleep. Or unconscious. He knelt at the side of the bed and pulled her to a sitting position. "Tina? Wake up." This was not exhaustion. This was pharmaceutical. She was out cold. Jamey laid her back down and went to the bathroom to find her pill dispenser. She'd only come back for a toothbrush and pills. He grabbed both, and then returned to lift her into his arms. "Come on, Obi. We're sleeping at my house tonight."

Tina woke long enough to mumble something that sounded like *thanks.*

The last time he'd carried Tina, many years before, he'd jokingly picked her up to throw her on his bed. He'd stood over her, beating his chest like a caveman and she giggled. "Show me your club, Gronk." Drastically different circumstances.

Jamey unlocked the condo door and kicked it open with his foot. Remembering that Tina was only asleep, not sick or hurt, he allowed himself the blissful feeling of having her in his arms again. He hadn't been intimate with anyone in so long he could barely remember what it felt like to have his hands on a woman's body. Unless you counted the dream with Tina in the cottage, the last time he'd actually made love had been at least eight months ago.

Living and working in Afghanistan had hugely curtailed his love life, if that's what you called sex when you met someone who was shipping out from Ramstein the next day, and was willing to indulge in one night of frenzied passion. There weren't many women in Afghanistan, and those who were in service were off limits. Jamey laid Tina's small body on his bed and covered her with a woven blanket Pops had bought at an upcountry craft market. She wasn't wearing her wedding ring. Good. For several minutes he stood admiring her sleeping form. She was so goddamned cute. Obi jumped up and snuggled into her side. The dog's head lowered on Tina's arm and he heaved a woeful sigh.

"You're a good boy, Obi." Jamey patted him and, as he drew his hand away, Tina made a little noise, like a squeak. Her chest rose and fell with each breath. Taking the pill dispenser out of his pocket, Jamey noticed that tonight's pill had been taken. If the dispenser held a different kind of pill than she thought, she'd be out for the night, drugged again. He contemplated taking her to the hospital to have her stomach pumped but thought better. She'd probably been taking these pills for days. Maybe on purpose. Before he sent one of the last two pills for analysis, he'd ask her if she'd taken a sedative when she woke.

Watching Tina sleep on the very bed he'd vacated twelve hours before led to memories of them together in bed. After all, they'd slept in this bed before. And more than slept. He took a deep breath to rein in his sexy thoughts of Tina who, he reminded himself, was in emotional crisis, drugged and defenseless. But how could he not remember her this way, when she was lying only a few feet away, on his bed, looking like an angel with her head on his pillow? And wearing short shorts and a T-shirt. These days, she was much slimmer than the shapely little dive instructor he'd fallen for, but still very cute. Jamey assumed that pounds had been lost in the months since Hank died. Poor thing. Hell, they had to find the body soon. She didn't have many more pounds to lose.

The bedroom chair sagged as he sank into it with a beer in one hand and the remote in the other. He'd keep an eye on Tina while she slept. Scrolling through the channels, Jamey found nothing more interesting than his thoughts of Tina, but he settled on a rerun of a cop show, the volume low. When they found Hank's body, Tina would move on with her life. When that happened, what was he going to do with his life? Go back to Afghanistan to dream jump? He wasn't even sure he was jumping with his own ability these days.

What had Milton said when he left, months earlier? "I hope to see you back here but, in light of what's happened, we might not meet again."

After the last jump, the medical tests turned up nothing unusual to account for his near-death experience. CT scans and MRIs eventually registered normal brain activity, even after Milton said he almost blew up the brain scanner during the jump. The medic on duty had been sure brain damage would result, but, weeks later, all the tests were normal.

"How you lived through that is a miracle." The medic had shaken his head.

Jamey had no idea what went on in his brain during a dream jump, but many times since the last one, he'd wondered about the repercussions of doing this long-term. Especially after the tortured dreams he entered in Kandahar. There were so many unanswered questions about this psychic shit.

Taking a swig of Corona, he stared at the TV and thought about his recent jumps. The first strange dream had been Tina's. First, he was Hank, and then the shark. Somehow, she jumped into Hank's thoughts and he'd been a part of that.

The second dream, without a headache, had been with Hank and Tina diving to the cave. Jamey leaned forward and grabbed the pad of paper on the nightstand to write all this down.

In the next dream he and Tina were making love. He now guessed that was his own dream and she'd jumped into it unintentionally. It seemed like there was no headache as long as Tina was the jumper.

He'd never known another jumper besides Uncle Don, and they'd never tried to jump together.

The strange thing was that, in Afghanistan, the worst headache came with a straight jump on the prisoner, Atash. Sixth Force was pretty sure that the Al Qaeda knew the Americans had someone who visited dreams. And that

Atash was planted to draw out the man who could jump. He'd summoned a monster in the dream before Jamey knew what was happening. But how? That was the million-dollar question that neither he nor Sixth Force had been able to answer. He and Milton had talked about it again the other day on the phone. Sure he could've been trained to kill the jumper if they found themselves in a dream together but how did he create that fanged monster?

Then it hit him. What if the kid was a jumper, too? The idea sent chills up his spine. Could that be possible? The thought that the other side had someone like him made Jamey's blood run cold. Now that the prisoner was dead, there was no way to confirm this. He made the call to Sergeant Milton.

It took several tries to reach the Kandahar base, but he eventually connected. "Atash might have been a dream jumper." While talking, Jamey scribbled question marks all over the page. Milton questioned how Jamey came up with this theory.

"I'm not sure." Jamey couldn't tell anyone about Tina jumping, or she'd be courted by Sixth Force to join the military. And, as long as he had breath, he would never let that happen. "I have this idea, that's all." Milton was probably accustomed to psychics having bull's-eye hunches.

"Right now, we've only assumed he was trained to kill in a dream but this new idea could be the answer we've been looking for." He took a drag on his cigarette. "We'll need to contact you for more information. Stay available." The dread in Milton's voice verified it would be very bad news for the American military if the bad guys had jumpers. And Atash had died before they could study him.

When Jamey hung up, he sat back and took the last pull on his beer. If the Al Qaeda knew about the Sixth Force jumper, he was glad he'd left the Mid-East. If they knew it was him, he'd be dead by now. Or captured. He was sure of this. And beyond that, Jamey had other things to think about. Tina's jumping and her W.I.L.D. dreams, thinking she was awake when she wasn't. Probably the diving dreams were Hank's glimpses and when they were over, she simply kept dreaming on her own.

Jamey was sure this experience was unsettling for Tina, having lifelike dreams that got confused with reality. But, she had other problems right now. For one, she was probably being drugged by Noble. Shit. If she'd taken a roofie when she meant to take a different pill, she might be sick for days. Rufinol not only made you groggy, but nauseated.

Goddamn Noble. Luckily, Tina hadn't had any alcohol tonight, which intensified the drug. Jamey put a water dish down for Obi, watched another mindless TV show, and grabbed a blanket from the hall closet. He'd find out tomorrow what the pill sediment was, and if it was Rufinol, Jamey would gladly blow the whistle on Tina's trusted friend Noble.

CHAPTER 24

The water was surprisingly calm in the channel between islands as Tina steered *Maui Dream* along the West Maui coastline towards Molokai. Jamey positioned himself beside her, probably waiting for her to crumble. But she wouldn't. Now that she had hope of putting all this to rest, she felt better than she had in months. She was terrified to find Hank's body but determined. Turned out, she did want to move on. If Hank was dead, she wanted to know. She'd woken at Jamey's place with this new attitude.

Passing Kapalua Bay, Jamey pointed to a turtle breathing on the surface. Sea turtles had to breathe every few minutes. Couldn't stay down forever. Everything was a fricking metaphor for her life even if sinking below the surface was not a possibility now.

Jamey attempted to keep her distracted on the boat ride, pointing out sights, asking questions, keeping it light. Never had it been more important to find closure. He'd know what was at stake for her. What she'd known of Jamey, years before, didn't equal how much she'd learned about him in the last weeks. He was a complicated man but still small-town nice.

"How did you ever figure out that you were jumping dreams?" she asked as they motored along.

"My childhood friend, Mark, told me about a dream on a sleepover at my house. We'd been fighting some bad guys in the dream, and I remembered the fight. When I told him I was there, he said I was crazy. I shut up after that, whenever I found myself in friends' dreams. I told my dad, and he told his brother, who was a jumper. Uncle Don sat me down to swear me to secrecy." He grinned at her like it was a simple boyhood inconvenience, when it probably had frightened him to death.

"My grandmother had strange dreams. Did I ever tell you that? I wonder if this is related in any way. 'Magic dreams,' she called them."

Jamey's eyes widened. "What are magic dreams?"

"I never knew. She said we needed to have a sleepover for me to have a magic dream with her."

"You have got to be kidding." Jamey's face went white.

"You think my grandmother was a jumper?"

"Don't you think it's strange?"

"I do, now that you say that. I just remembered this yesterday." But she'd never entered dreams before Jamey came back into her life. Not that she knew of, anyways.

"Maybe you got this ability from your grandmother, and it lay dormant until my ability passed to you, or Hank's ghost did something. I don't know." Everything was up for grabs.

As they passed Honolua Bay, the site of Hank's supposed death, Jamey stepped behind her and wrapped his arms around her shoulders, his chin resting on the top of her head. He'd always been a touchy-feely guy. She remembered years ago telling him jokingly to keep his hands to himself, and he'd said, "When you're within touching distance, no can do."

The wind picked up as they headed across the channel towards the garden island of Molokai. Obi found his usual place on the rubber mat between Tina's feet. She recalled Obi's lump, something she hadn't thought about since the day before. The biopsy report seemed suspect now that her head was clearer, and now that Noble's integrity was in question. The vet said it would be at least four days before they knew anything. She'd call the clinic when they opened today.

See if they'd actually found it benign.

Molokai was not getting larger fast enough for Tina, and she struggled to lower her expectations with every mile. She needed closure but was still frightened. If they found Hank's body, she'd be an emotional junk pile. And if they didn't find him, she'd be a different kind of mess.

***

When the boat broke down two miles from the closest Molokai shore point, Jamey tried not to swear in frustration. His knowledge of marine mechanics was somewhat limited. If it was something serious, they'd have to paddle to the nearest shore.

"We're about six miles from Maui, and maybe two from Molokai." Tina said, opening the engine compartment like she knew what she was doing.

"You any good with motors?" Jamey was hoping.

She propped open the cover and stared at the engine. "I know my own motor a bit."

Jamey watched her bend over the engine compartment. "Go for it." The boat rocked with the push of the wind and waves in the exposed channel.

Obi jumped up on the bow to get a better view of what was out there. The boat was drifting, but not towards Maui, or even Molokai, just straight down the widest part of the channel, towards the open water between Lanai and Maui. They'd eventually hit a deserted side of Lanai sometime around midnight, he figured. If they didn't want to spend the day waiting for that to happen, they'd have to start the engine soon.

Glancing at the compartment over Tina's shoulder, Jamey squinted. Clean motor. "I'm impressed you know about this stuff," he said. Tina was checking fluids, half her body upended, like a duck diving for food. He tried not to stare at her butt, just in case she could see his reflection in a shiny engine part. He knew a bit about motors but wouldn't intervene until she exhausted her knowledge.

From his vantage point, he could see something lying on the floor of the compartment. He reached down and grabbed the culprit. "It's the S belt."

"I just replaced that thing." She straightened up sounding peeved.

The serpentine belt was a pretty necessary piece of the motor, but they might be able to jury-rig the thing to get them up and running long enough to reach land. Not the sea cliffs. Risking a trip to the back side of Molokai with a broken S belt wouldn't be smart. "Have you got duct tape?" They were drifting farther from their target of Kanaha Rock, and were now headed out into the vast channel.

Tina looked hopeful. "Yes. Think we can rig it?"

Jamey turned the belt in his hand. "Maybe." It didn't look worn. Instead, it looked cut. He filed that information under 'Noble' and took the duct tape from Tina.

She steered the boat to take advantage of the drift while Jamey taped the belt together. In the distance, they could already see the shipwreck on the uninhabited side of Lanai, the pineapple island. He hoped they wouldn't get much closer.

When the engine was running again, they set a course for Kaunakakai on Molokai. "I know the mechanic in town. He'll have an S belt." Tina sounded optimistic.

Jamey fixed the belt one more time on the way and they eventually motored in at the Kaunakakai Wharf just after two o'clock. Three other boats were tied to the wharf, and a small marlin hung alongside a set of fish scales. Jamey jumped to the concrete and tied up *Maui Dream*. As he stopped to admire the catch, Tina asked some men standing around drinking beer about the whereabouts of the mechanic. No one knew where he was.

"Can't we just go to the marine supply store to buy a new serpentine belt," Jamey offered.

"Very funny. This is Molokai. There is no marine

supply store." Tina jumped back on the boat. "There aren't even any traffic lights on this island."

"Then what are we doing here instead of Maui?" He watched her extract the belt from the engine compartment to ensure the boat wouldn't start.

"Molokai was closest. This guy, Kalani, should have some stuff. If not, we'll have it flown in."

Tina was in her element. He watched her move around the boat, securing it, locking up the dive gear. She pulled a T-shirt over her head and slipped on her board shorts. "Let's see if we can find him," she said. They strolled down the wharf like two friends on vacation. This was the closest to the real Tina that he'd seen in weeks. "And let's grab some food."

The thought of teriyaki or a hamburger sounded better than the drinks and snacks they'd packed for the day trip. "We don't worry about leaving the boat?" Jamey asked.

Tina held up the S belt as Obi ran in and out of the bushes, sniffing at mongoose trails.

One charmingly short street accommodated most of the shops in the town of Kaunakakai, making the downtown area resemble the main drag in a Western movie. Where Dodge would have had the saloon, the mercantile, and the blacksmith, Kaunakakai's shops had names like Mango Mart and Kanemitsu Bakery.

The first stop on their walking tour was Molokai Fish and Dive Shop, where it was determined that Kalani, the mechanic, was off island. Gone to Honolulu and not expected back until the morning. When Tina introduced herself as the owner of Tina's Dive Shop the man behind the counter squinted. *Probably remembering Hank's mysterious death.*

"My boat broke an S belt in the channel. We're tied up on the wharf until we get a new one." She stared out the window in the direction of the ocean.

"I'd say fly one over."

Tina nodded. "I agree. Thanks." She looked at Jamey

and they walked out the door.

While eating lunch at a picnic table in front of the burger joint, Tina made calls to arrange to have the belt flown in from Maui to the Molokai airport. They'd either ask someone out there to bring it from the plane when it arrived, or they'd hitch a ride to pick up the package themselves.

"Nothing to do now but eat." She smiled at her burger. "What?" she asked, when Jamey chuckled.

"It's good to see you happy."

She took a bite and spoke with a full mouth. "Getting off Maui feels really good."

He picked the wilted lettuce from his burger and set the droopy leaf aside. Sitting at a picnic table on Molokai, watching Tina, the warm sun on his back, mynah birds calling from the trees, Jamey felt almost carefree. For the first time in a long time.

"I haven't gone off island for a while," she said.

When Tina's nose crinkled, Jamey had an overwhelming urge to kiss her. At least her nose.

"It's nice here. Slow." He doused his fries in ketchup and picked out a clump. "And even though," he paused, searching for words that wouldn't break the spell, "the boat broke down, I'm enjoying myself." He chewed and swallowed. "Eating lunch on Molokai, like this." He gestured to the town and then his plate. "Want fries?"

She declined just as Jamey's phone rang. Noting the number, he covered the mouthpiece and whispered "Kandahar" to Tina. He moved to the farthest empty picnic table for privacy.

It was Pete Milton. "We believe that the new mix of sedatives had more to do with your headache than anything." The connection with Afghanistan was not good but the message was clear. The autopsy report indicated that the dreamer had an allergic reaction from the sedatives hours before his demise. "We think what made your heart stop was the dreamer's violent reaction to the drugs. We're sending you to Honolulu for some tests related to this information. We'd like to know more."

Back at the picnic table, he polished off his fries and Root beer, watching Tina from the corner of his eye. The more he thought about her strange dreams, the more he believed that Hank was stuck between life and death, not necessarily because the body was still out there, but because Tina hadn't completely given up the hope of his being alive. Maybe her tenacious nature was holding him to this world until she was absolutely sure he was dead.

Obi stared at Tina's burger with the same intensity Jamey stared at Tina. He hoped he wasn't drooling like the dog. "Because you're jumping on your own, I need to tell you everything I know about the logistics of it, but you have to swear to keep this a secret."

"Are you kidding me?" Tina gave Obi a piece of burger and popped the last bite into her mouth. "Why would I tell anyone something as crazy as this?"

"Someday you might want to. Believe me. And it seems crazy to you now, but remember, magic is only science we don't understand yet."

Tina made a face. "I'm extremely opposed to having this ability."

"Your new talent might not stay," Jamey said, trying to reassure her. "It probably has something to do with me, and when I leave, it may leave with me." For her sake, he hoped he was right.

"When are you leaving?" Tina's face fell.

"Soon."

***

When the serpentine belt finally came in on the 5:30 flight, Tina was sure they'd have to find a place to stay on Molokai overnight. Even if they got the boat fixed and got out of the harbor, sunset would be upon them and there wouldn't be enough light to dive at the cliffs.

"Don't you need the boat on Maui for tomorrow?" Jamey asked.

"I'll tell Katie to reschedule." The customers would just have to wait.

Jamey found them a room at one of the only hotels on the island—Hotel Molokai. In all her twelve years in Hawaii, Tina had never stayed overnight on this island. When they arrived at the circular drive in a taxi, she was surprised she'd never made the effort. The hotel was much smaller than the Maui monstrosities she was used to, built in the old Polynesian style with all rooms facing the ocean to catch the trade winds. The only available room had a king-size bed and couch, which made Tina first laugh, and then worry. As they walked to the room, Jamey put his arm around her shoulders and reassured her that he'd take the couch.

"Stop reading my mind, Jamey." She added just the right amount of anger to her voice, but he laughed and professed it didn't take a psychic to figure out she was worried about sleeping arrangements.

The room was lovely, reminiscent of old Hawaii. With wooden beams running across a high ceiling, palm tree–printed fabrics, and pineapple lamps, the charm was not lost on Jamey. He threw his backpack on the couch and whistled. "Hawaiiana."

Tina was suddenly appreciative of everything—the distance from Maui, and being here with a friend. Tears came to her eyes. She'd been so consumed with her problems in the last few months, she'd lost sight of the fact that the world existed outside of her worries. The relief that resulted from this respite was suddenly overwhelming. Leaving Maui felt great. Seattle might be a good idea except for the fact that Jamey wouldn't be on Maui when she returned. He'd taken a call from Kandahar at lunch and then mentioned he was going soon.

Opening the door to the lanai, she then walked out on

the deck and stared at the beach. The sun had set, only a peachy glow remaining in the sky, and soon the light would fade. An urge to bolt down that beach, tire herself out, and then jump into the ocean and swim was barely suppressed. She could hear Jamey running the water in the bathroom and listened to the soft noise mixed with the rolling surf below.

"Thirsty, boy?" Jamey said to Obi.

She smiled at his thoughtfulness. The least she could do was offer to take the couch tonight.

After a long walk with Obi on the beach, they ambled over to the poolside restaurant, drawn in by the Hawaiian music. They agreed it would be nice to listen and order a beer or cocktail. What else did they have to do?

When the waiter arrived, they ordered a papaya salad to share and a plate of fresh opakapaka, baked in a lime-cilantro sauce.

"I haven't eaten fish in so long," Tina said. Jamey looked at her strangely.

"What? You think because I live near the ocean, I should eat fish?" Truth was she'd had no interest in eating anything from the ocean since Hank died.

They ordered more cocktails and talk came easily, even if they were only approaching safe subjects like diving, how she found Obi, Jamey's retirement from the police force, and his daughters.

When the waiter brought the food, he set it between them. "Just let me know if there's anything else you need," he said. For some reason, that struck Tina as funny, and she had to suppress her laughter. She needed so much these days.

Jamey ordered a bottle of Sauvignon Blanc and handed the wine list to the waiter. "One bottle, two glasses."

With miles between them and Maui, the lingering sadness that shadowed her was now easily shed. She smiled at Jamey and picked up her fork. "This looks appetizing."

The wine arrived and Jamey poured them each a glass. Tina recalled that only two days earlier, she'd ended up in a drunken blackout. Or she was drugged against her knowledge?

Jamey raised his glass for a toast. "To Molokai."

They clicked wine glasses gently and, as thoughts and worries abandoned them, Tina vowed that the next few hours would not be filled with heavy thoughts.

By the time Tina reached the bottom of her glass, she could almost believe that she was on a charming vacation. Obi sat dutifully under the table as Jamey talked about his life in Carnation.

"It's a little town with a lot of heart and a great place to raise kids." Jamey didn't ask her to talk, maybe sensing she couldn't. Tina was thankful to simply be in the moment.

Staring at Jamey was a good distraction, the softness in his eyes, his smile, sweetly familiar. She rubbed Obi with her bare toes and listened to Jamey brag about his daughters, Jade and Jasmine. "I know every parent says this but, honest to God, those two are brilliant in everything they do. And they do a lot. Soccer, art classes, dance classes, basketball, swimming." Over the last few weeks, Tina hadn't heard him talk about himself or his life, probably because she hadn't asked. Her own problems had occupied her constant thoughts, but now Jamey was talking. Hearing him say he knew when to step aside and let another man help raise his children on a daily basis tugged at Tina's heart. "Doesn't having a step parent intervene hurt your feelings?"

"The stability that Carrie and her husband provide is golden," he said explaining that a large family had been formed in Carnation, where the twins had two dads, one mother and a mixture of grandparents, cousins, and uncles. One dad was present on a daily basis, while their real father flew in and out of their lives but loved them as much as anyone.

"Jade and Jasmine are what keeps me going, when things get tough. They're the reason I want to make the world a better place." His eyes were soft, loving. "To keep the Al Qaeda from crossing that ocean."

"I bet." The familiar pang of longing for a child, the need to feel the weight in her empty arms, took over Tina's thoughts. When Jamey turned around to applaud the musical duo, she noticed small lines fanning from his blue eyes, an indicator that not only was he now in his forties, but that he smiled regularly. Then it hit her. Jamey was back in her life and she had barely noticed. Even though their new relationship was more of a friendship, he'd returned nonetheless. Something she'd wanted so badly for years. "How old are you, Jamey?" She felt buzzy from the wine, enough to make her bold.

"I'll be forty-two next month." He took a sip of the scotch he'd ordered when the wine ran out and crunched an ice cube in his mouth. "You're what? Thirty-four?"

"Just turned thirty-five."

They smiled at each other, remembering their age difference. The twinkling reflection off the pool danced on a divider screen behind Jamey. The scent of the gardenias in the center of their table was heady. Tina took a deep breath.

Jamey tilted his head, his eyes mysterious. "You look pretty tonight."

Absently, her hand flew to her cheek. She hadn't looked in a mirror for days and had hardly slept one good hour in the last few nights. "I can't imagine." A heated blush had returned to her cheeks. "Thanks for saying that, though." She paused. "Can I ask you something?"

Jamey nodded.

"Before you discovered that Carrie was pregnant, did you hope to ever see me again?" She fished for reassurance that he'd intended to return to her.

Jamey rubbed the stubble on his chin. "You and I had a pretty good thing."

She lowered her voice so that the next table couldn't hear. "But it wasn't just…you know…the physical thing for me. I really, really liked you. As a person."

"Me too." He took a sip. Crunched another ice cube. Stared at her.

"When you were with me, did you think you might reconcile with Carrie?" The answer mattered more than she wanted it to.

"No. Carrie and I were done. We both wanted that. At least I thought so, but I found out later that Carrie didn't. Ultimately, what she wanted was for me to marry her and give up my life in the police force. And, it's hard to love me with all the psychic shit." He hesitated, shifted in his chair, and continued. "There's something I never told you." His hands fidgeted with the unused cutlery on the table. "But now that you're dream jumping, you deserve this information."

Tina tensed.

He looked almost unsure whether to continue, and then took a deep breath. "The morning I left you ten years ago, I'd had a precognitive dream. I jumped into your wedding."

She set her wine glass on the table and stared at him. "You knew I'd marry Hank?"

Jamey nodded. "I knew another man would end up with you. I left Maui knowing I couldn't change it. I wanted to. Believe me." He looked out at the beach. "Remember I told you that my Uncle Don was my dream mentor. When I was a kid, he taught me everything about jumping, including how to stay safe." He chuckled. "One day, after my dad figured out I was jumping, my uncle sat me down at the picnic table in his backyard. I thought he was going to chew me out about teasing my cousin who had grown boobs, but he wanted to talk about jumping. He said he'd been jumping all his life. He suspected his

271

grandmother was a jumper too. I was so surprised. You can't imagine what a relief it was to hear that someone else had weird dreams."

Tina nodded and smiled. She could imagine.

"We talked about the responsibility that came with this. 'Like Spiderman,' Don said. It was a serious talk. I was just glad to know I wasn't a freak. Well, that I wasn't the only freak." Jamey smiled at her. "That day he got me to promise him two things." He held up one finger. "One, never intentionally jump for my own personal gain. After that, I really tried not to. I never jumped to influence anyone to give me anything, even though I wanted to plenty of times." He held up his second finger. "And the second promise was the one that I had to keep because the consequences might be horrific. And that was not to mess with the future. If I had one of the dreams with fuzzy edges, faint colors, I couldn't try to change things."

Tina hadn't heard him talk this much in a long time. She nodded, hoping he'd continue.

"That day, I vowed to never willingly change anything from one of those dreams." Jamey looked at her, and the impact that promise made on a boy's life was evident in his expression.

"Don died during a jump many years later. Technically, he died the day after the jump, but his brain never recovered. We weren't sure what he was doing in the dream. We suspected he was in the mind of a serial killer. I developed my own theory about what killed him."

Tina reached across the table and took his hand. "I'm sorry."

"When I dreamed of your wedding day with another man, Uncle Don was still alive and told me to walk away from you. I went home to Seattle knowing you weren't mine to have. When Carrie told me she was pregnant, I asked her to marry me, but she wasn't sure. Then we found out it was twins and knew we had to do it. What else was I going to do? You'd marry someone else."

The wedding dream was faintly familiar to Tina. It was only a wisp of recognition, like a scent in the air, and then gone in a second. Why would she remember it? It hadn't been hers. "You left me knowing we were done." She took a deep breath and thought about how Jamey had to give her up. He hadn't wanted to, but he did the right thing for her sake.

The musicians took the stage for the next set and played one of her favorite Hawaiian songs. Tina gulped what was left in her wine glass. "I appreciate your honesty." She stood. "Come on, Mr. Dunn, let's test out the dance floor." She wanted to be held. By Jamey. By the man who surrendered her to the man in her future, and then went home and married the pregnant girlfriend he didn't love.

The small floor filled with couples. Fitting into Jamey's arms, she breathed in his musky scent which brought back memories of their sexy dream in the bed over the ocean. Now she knew that dream hadn't been hers. She'd only been the jumper into Jamey's fantasy. His hand was warm on the small of her back. Firm.

"No fancy twirls or dips please, Tina," he warned. "I'm not a great dancer."

"I'll try to keep my moves simple, but you accepted the invitation, Twinkle Toes." She grinned.

"I just wanted to hold you, not dance." He pulled her closer and sighed into her hair. "Ah, Tina."

They'd never make it to morning without something happening between them. Even without any psychic abilities, Jamey had to know that too.

CHAPTER 25

Entering the hotel room had its own special form of nervousness after the implications and innuendos at the restaurant. Dawn was still eight hours away. Time to either get a good night's sleep, or not.

Tina pulled the drapes shut and opened the sliding door a crack, letting the sound of the surf drift into the room. Even if Jamey wasn't looking sexy and smelling so good, this moment was pure romance. His skin had taken on a golden bronze recently that made his blue eyes twinkle.

Obi was stretched out on the couch, his body taking up most of the space. "Looks like that spot is taken." She nodded to her dog.

"Oh, oh." Jamey glanced at her, and then at the bed. "It's a big bed."

"Think we could sleep together without any funny business?" There was something wildly familiar in flirting with Jamey Dunn.

"Doubtful." He crossed the room and cupped her face in his hands. "Shall we?"

She closed her eyes. "We shall." His soft lips met hers and she melted like molten lava beneath his kiss. The effect he had on her was still there. His kisses moved to her neck, and she felt her knees almost give out. "Jamey?" Her breathy whisper barely had volume.

"Hmmm?" He scooped her up in his arms and carried her to the bed.

"I'm safe with you, right?"

"Yes. You are safest with me." He kissed her lips tenderly and set her on the turned-down bed, unzipping her hooded jacket. Her hands ran up under his T-shirt, his abdomen tightening under her touch. First he pulled off her shirt, then his own. His hands encircled her small breasts. "I remember these." Jamey eased his body half over her, half stretched out beside her. They looked into each other's eyes as he fingered her nipples. Fondling, pinching lightly.

"I remember you," she said.

"Hmmm. Good." His voice was raspy.

They knew how to do this. She and Jamey had their own way together, familiarities reserved only for them— subtle but important tricks of how to bring the other to the highest point before letting go. Things escalated quickly.

Breaking away, she pushed him flat, removed his shorts and moved down along his length to take him in her mouth. He moaned and she drew back slightly. "Do you still like this?" She took his growl for affirmation and slid her teeth gently along his length. "Stop, just a second, Tina." His hands threaded through her hair. "We have to slow down, make this last." He pulled her up to him, taking her into an embrace, burying his face in her hair. "You are still the sexiest thing I've ever had on top of me," he whispered. "Or beside me. Or anywhere near me." He nibbled at her earlobe. "Do you have any idea?"

She didn't want to compare, but not even in their first few months together did Hank seem desperate like Jamey, who was crazy with desire for her. He kissed like he had to have her, all of her, or else. She remembered that about him.

Her kisses traced his jaw line to his mouth. She brushed her lips with his. "Do you like this?"

He chuckled. "You could sing the national anthem and I'd get rock hard."

"You've never heard me sing." She deepened the kiss, and Jamey ran his hands down her back to grab her buttocks.

He pressed his erection into the V of her thighs. "We have all night."

"Or not." She smiled. Reaching down, she guided him into her warmth. As he went deeper, he licked his lips and moaned. With hands splayed across his chest, she gently rocked back and forth on him, never taking her eyes from his.

"Tina." He said her name with such tenderness.

She leaned over to kiss him deep, deeper, and he pushed himself in, as far as he could. Once, twice. Again.

Then he stopped. "Me on top." It wasn't a question. She remembered. They flipped over and he mounted her, their hands woven together.

Taking him deep into her, to the most guarded parts of her, there was no holding back now. This was it. Everything they'd been thinking, dreaming, was about to come true. Hungry, they devoured each other in kisses, licks, bites. Their breaths mingled and the intensity increased. The run to the top was fast and when she exploded into pieces of shattered light, Jamey gave one last push and soon collapsed on her, stifling his cry in the pillow. Their heartbeats pounded against each other's chests, a testimonial that they'd become one, even if just for a brief moment.

Wrapping her arms around his broad back, she lay listening to their tattered breaths. Tears filled her eyes and she pressed her lips together, wondering if he could read her. Then, without warning, a sob escaped her lips.

Jamey lifted his head. "What's wrong?"

She sobbed again and squeezed her eyes shut.

"Why are you crying?" He stroked her hair. "Tell me I didn't hurt you."

"You didn't." He hadn't read her feelings. Her bundle of mixed emotions, like a ball of string she didn't want to unravel, was almost too lovely to reveal. "I'm happy."

He kissed her mouth tenderly.

Smiling through tears, she tried giving him the message that couldn't be put into words.

"I understand," he whispered. "And not because of

intuition. Just because."

His expression told her that he did. She was grateful. All she had to offer him was this small moment on Molokai that touched something in her she'd buried. This stolen time. She had no idea who she'd be when morning came.

"I'm sorry," she whispered.

He kissed her forehead. "Don't be." When he withdrew, and pulled her into the warmth of his embrace, he whispered into her hair. "This is enough, Tina."

***

She was falling; falling into another dream, one she had no control over. This dream was different than the others. She was not in the water, not wet, not diving, not sinking into the salt water of the Pacific Ocean.

When she came through to the dream side, she stood beside Hank's black truck on a pullout road used by surfers, just north of Honolua Bay. Hobbit Land. The sky was barely light, thick with the kind of clouds that threaten to ruin everyone's vacation. "Fucking eh, I'll do what I want." Hank's voice invaded the silence.

She froze. "We make all decisions together, Henry." Noble's voice was quiet but stern.

Who was Henry? Tina was blocked from view by the truck. She held her breath and waited, not daring to peek.

"Get your board, dumb fuck. We'll surf." Hank sounded amused.

"I'm not surfing until I get a promise from you that we leave this morning. That was our plan. I have a buyer for the paintings."

She flattened herself against the truck and very slowly inched up to look over the truck's edge. To her right, Noble's old red truck looked empty, the driver door still open. Thirty feet away, at the head of the path leading to the well-known surfing spot, stood Noble and Hank. Only one man was prepared to surf.

Hank sighed. "I'm not leaving today." He rested his board on the ground.

"You have a ticket to New Orleans, Henry. Just like our plan. I'm going to Reno."

"I'm not going to fucking New Orleans, Nolan. I'm staying until I know for sure that Tina's pregnant. Don't oppose me on this, man. It's the only thing I asked for on this one." His hand went to his back pocket and pulled out his wallet. "Take this back to the house for me." Hank tossed it.

Noble caught the flying wallet. "Lizzie'll get us, Henry. You know that. The only other time you went soft was Miami, and I had to drag you out then too, remember?"

Hank nodded. "This is different." He turned and chuckled. "You know this is different. This is Tina."

Her name was spoken with such reverence, Tina's breath caught in her throat.

Hank continued, "If I wasn't being forced, I'd stay. This was where I wanted to get off the bus. You know that. I'm not giving in to Lizzie's bribery. And I'm not selling Tina's grandmother's paintings. Neither are you." He looked at Noble pleadingly. "Come on, man."

Was this a dream born of her imagination, or did this actually happen? A glimpse, Jamey called it. Tina had never witnessed a conversation like this, between these two men who called each other 'Nolan' and 'Henry.' Tina's breathing was shallow as she listened to catch every word.

"I don't like this any more than you do, Bro," Hank said, "but I don't think Lizzie's going to do anything immediately. I asked her for a few weeks, and I think she'll give it to me." Hank put his hand on Noble's arm, and it was shrugged off.

"I don't agree. Tina's mother is dangerous and we can't risk it. And you know that. Deep down." They stood staring at each other.

"I think it's better for Tina if we just disappear now. We shoulda been gone a year ago, when you figured out where the paintings were."

"I can't." Hank's tone changed, like the closing of a door. "You can." Noble sounded like he was used to making all final decisions.

"I'm not going. That's that."

"If I have to drag you, you are. Our buyer's ready. The timing is perfect." The tone in Noble's voice made the skin on Tina's arms crawl.

Hank picked up his board and started down the steep path to the put-in point. "You go," he called over his shoulder. As Noble lunged to grab the board, the wallet fell unnoticed into a mound of thick scrub grass. Hank whipped around, his face full of fury. "You will not tell me what to do this time. She is *my* wife. And now, I'm going surfing." He continued down the path.

Tina's overwhelming desire to hear the conversation to the end spurred her to follow them as closely as she dared.

"Hey, Hot Shot!" Noble sped after Hank.

Hank stopped. Tina ducked back in the kiawe bushes, the prickly thorns nothing compared to the conversation.

Tina only saw the tops of their heads, but she desperately needed to see Hank's face. A large boulder was only a few feet away. If she could duck behind that, the position would afford her a better view. If she didn't make a sound and kept her head low, they might not see her. She took off.

"Is that what you think? That you love her?" Noble laughed, and threw his arms out. "You think that you can actually feel love? Tell me you're not just trying to knock up Tina to get back at her mother."

"I'm not, you goddamned motherfucker. She wants a baby. And I want to be the father of that baby." Hank glared at Noble and poked him in the chest. "If I'm going to break her heart, thanks to her fucking mother, at least I want to give Tina what she's wanted her whole life." Hank's voice was frantic with emotion.

Noble laughed at him.

"Shut the fuck up, Nolan!" Hank grabbed his board with both hands and swung it, knocking Noble into the side of the cliff to rebound off the rock. "That's just it. She wants a baby, not you." Noble advanced. "Who the hell do you think you are now? You'll only ever be Henry Santiago, one of the pitiful Santiago kids. Stealing food, getting in trouble—just one more sob story from Compton. We're just two kids whose junkie mother ran off." Noble backed Hank to the edge of the path.

"Goddammit. I'm not like you in a lot of ways, and you know that. At least my father wasn't a user." Hank said something else that was undetectable and swung the board around to head back up the path to the truck. Tina crouched lower. "And you know what Nolan? I'm going to tell Tina the whole thing. Then no one will have anything to hold over my head." Hank's march uphill was interrupted when Noble grabbed the board and spun him around with it. "Like hell." Noble's face twisted into a mask of rage.

They were thirty feet away from Tina.

"This gig is over, Brother. No paintings. We're not leaving Maui. At least I'm not."

"Then you give me no choice." With both hands, Noble wrestled the board free from Hank, drew it back, and whacked Hank across the chest.

The shock on Hank's face displayed not only his surprise, but something like disappointment as he stumbled backward, clutching his chest. He tried to get his footing under him, but failed. Noble didn't have time to drop the board and get to him. "Henry!"

Hank flung out his arms to grab something, anything, as he disappeared over the edge of the cliff. She sprang from her crouch. "NO!" Her scream mingled with two other cries in the morning air.

Still unaware of Tina, Noble raced down the path and disappeared from sight. "Henry!"

The quiet Maui morning was deafening.

From her vantage point, Tina couldn't see below. She held her breath, listening, waiting, and reminding herself this was a dream. Even so, she stifled the urge to vomit. Then, Noble's cry of anguish made her heart jump.

Oh, God. Tina wanted out of this nightmare. Blinking violently, she tried to wake herself. Then she attempted kicking the rock in front of her. Pinching. Pushing against her stomach, her hand sank through her torso.

But then her need to leave the nightmare was overshadowed by her need to see if Hank was dead. Even if it was a dream. Hearing nothing more than the surf below, Tina ran down the path. Flattening herself on the scratchy grass, she inched farther to the edge. Ninety feet down, Noble crouched over Hank's form, which was sprawled across the lava rocks. The surf board lay off to one side. Every time the surf crashed against the rocks, salt water sprayed the scene.

The sound of sobbing came from below. When Noble shifted, she had a view of the body. Hank lay in a grotesque twist of arms, legs and torso, sprawled across the rocks. Tina swallowed the bile that rose in her mouth and buried her scream with her fist. Of course, he hadn't survived the fall.

Noble looked around and she ducked, flattening her face on the scruffy grass. When she dared to look again, he had Hank's lifeless body in his arms.

She had to get out of this dream before Noble walked up the path but she couldn't look away. Instead of choosing the trail, Noble stumbled to the farthest point of rock with Hank. The surf crashed only a few feet away. He took a wide stance, braced, and lifted

Hank's body above his head to heave him into the retreating wave.

Tina swallowed a scream and took off running up the hill. She didn't know where she was going once she got out of the dream. Police maybe. But something made her look back. She wanted to see that she'd been wrong. That it had only been an illusion in the early morning sunlight. Down below, Noble picked up the board, and flung it out to sea, as far as it would go. She had to get to the truck, try to jump out of this dream. She turned again, and raced up the steep path.

"Tina!" Noble's voice echoed off the cliff beside her. He'd seen her. "Stay there!"

She turned to see if he was running. If he was, she'd never make it to the truck before he caught her.

Noble took off at full speed as she darted up the path. "Tina, wait." His legs were longer than hers, and he was in better shape, but still she ran like she had a chance, her legs burning with every step.

Noble's feet crunched the lava pebbles just behind her, the sound gaining volume as he gained ground. At the top, with her lungs bursting, she knew he was just behind her. Thirty feet separated her from the portal where she'd jumped in. If she could make it to Hank's truck, she'd be safe. And that was assuming she could jump out of this nightmare.

"Ti, wait!" His voice was close, not winded. "Hank drowned."

Steps from the portal, she lunged forward, but when Noble grabbed the back of her shirt she screamed and went down on the red dirt, her face scraping against the hardness of the ground.

***

Jamey woke to Tina's scream. Something was terrorizing her as she lay beside him in the Molokai bed. Should he jump? He'd find out what was happening and jump out if what he saw was none of his business. Obi had leapt off the bed and was now staring up from the floor.

"S'okay, boy." Jamey grabbed Tina's hand, and in less than five seconds he was in the dream, behind a black truck, only feet away from Noble and Tina. They were struggling on the ground, but Noble easily overpowered her by more than a hundred pounds. She was trying to slither out from under him, but he held her wrists.

Jamey took note of the portal and rounded the truck, sure he could take out the big man if he had to. "Noble. What's going on?" Noble grabbed Tina's shirt front and pulled her to a standing position, like she was a rag doll. He swept his arm around her neck in a chokehold. "Stay out of this, soldier-boy. Tina's and my business is none of yours." One firm twist and he'd break her neck.

"He killed Hank." Tina's voice was strained.

Jamey threw out his hands to show Noble he was weaponless. "Noble, what are you doing?" He could read that Noble didn't want to kill Tina but would, if he had to. Jamey had to turn things around, and get Tina out of there. Dying in a dream was serious. His uncle's mysterious demise came to mind. Jamey backed off several steps. "Dude, why are you treating Tina like this?"

Noble's voice overflowed with panic. "I'll snap her neck if you come closer."

"Okay, I'm not moving. Don't hurt her, man. You love her. I'll do anything you ask. I'll just go over here and sit down on this rock." Jamey put his empty hands behind his head and sidestepped in a wide circle to put Tina halfway between him and the portal. If Noble backed up, Tina would be closer to the portal—a moot point if she didn't know enough to jump out.

What else could Jamey try? She had no idea about summoning monsters to help with fights. But Jamey did. Care was needed if he was going to bring in a dangerous animal. He didn't want some monster hurting Tina instead of Noble.

"Noble, please." Tina's voice was calm. She didn't know what was at risk. "This is just a dream, and nothing is real. Don't panic. Everything's okay."

"She's right, Noble. It's just a dream. Watch this." Jamey called for a tiger to appear close enough so it would make Noble back up to the truck. "Tiger." He waited for the animal, but nothing happened.

"I wish it wasn't real." Noble's face crumpled in misery. "Believe me."

"Snake," Jamey said. He happened to know that Tina was not afraid of them, but a lot of people were. Nothing happened. What the hell? Then he realized it was Tina's jump. Maybe she was the only one who could summon. Jamey didn't know the rules for piggybacking jumps. "Tina, picture a tiger over there." Jamey pointed and Noble turned just as a tiger appeared twenty feet away. "What the fuck?" The tiger paced as Noble backed up closer to the portal.

"Noble, it's a dream. See?" Jamey watched the tiger. "Tina, take it away now." The thing looked ready to leap, and then disappeared. "Only a dream."

"Please, Noble, let go, you're hurting me, honey," she said.

He didn't. They were still too far away for Jamey's plan to work. "The portal is marked, Tina." He'd left a rut with his foot when he landed—a little trick he'd developed over the years. "It's your dream, Noble. You can do anything you want. We aren't real, you just made us up, so if you let go of Tina, we can disappear." Noble shook his head. "But Hank died just like this."

"You're remembering it in a dream, then," Jamey whispered, almost to himself.

"If I'm remembering, why are you here? And her? You weren't there." He took several steps back, Tina stumbling with him. Her glance behind the truck told Jamey she was thinking of the portal. "You tell me." He shrugged.

"I don't want you here." Noble looked doubtful, and in that moment Jamey knew he would win this.

"Consciously, you don't. I can disappear if you like." He advanced again, forcing Noble to back up more. "But I need to take her. These are the rules, man. She wasn't there either."

Tina struggled with Noble's hold on her. "Noble, you're choking me. Please let me just stand on my own, beside you." She tried to look up at her captor.

"It's just a dream," Noble whispered. He released Tina from the choke hold, but grabbed her arm.

Tina stumbled to gain a few feet, putting her in line with the back of the truck.

Smart girl. Jamey had to get Noble to release her arm, and then he'd lunge forward to push her into the portal. Noble needed a distraction. "Tina, find Noble someone to share this dream, someone more interesting than us." He took a step towards the portal. "Stop! Don't come closer." Noble pulled Tina to his side at the same moment Hank appeared in front of them. Noble gasped. "Henry!"

Tina's voice turned to sobs. "Oh God, Hank."

Jamey could see she was torn between leaving the dream and staying with Hank.

"Henry, I'm sorry." Noble let go of Tina and walked towards the man.

Jamey sprinted, grabbing Tina on his way, and in four steps was over the rut in the dirt and jumping into the air. She was ready.

CHAPTER 26

As they were sucked back to reality, Jamey watched
the form of Noble embracing a disintegrating Hank. In less
than two seconds, he was sitting up in the Molokai hotel
bed, with Obi staring at him from the bedside.

Tina woke up gasping. "Oh, my God!" she cried.
Jamey was still holding her hand.

"You okay?"

She didn't answer.

"You jumped Noble's dream." He wrapped his arms
around her shaking body. "It's okay."

"Noble killed Hank!" She wrenched herself free to
face Jamey. "Noble pushed Hank, and he fell off that cliff.
They were fighting."

She wasn't crying and he worried that she was beyond
that point. He nodded. "It's true, then."

"You suspected Noble?"

"I had a hunch."

"Oh, my God, Jamey. I watched Noble kill my
husband in this dream." Tina's eyes were frantic. "And
then you arrived."

"You screamed." He took her hand. "Remember, we
don't know if it was a true remembrance, or only your
dream, or Noble's dream, or what."

"It happened. I know it." Her voice was tiny and far
away. "They were brothers, criminals, and this was all
some sort of scam. My mother figured it out, somehow. I
bet she had an investigator on Hank from the very
beginning. She did that to another one of my boyfriend's
years ago, and he broke up with me. When I told my
parents that Hank and I were marrying, she probably hired

an investigator. She would've spared no expense digging up dirt on my fiancé." A sob escaped from her throat.

Jamey whispered into her hair. "It might have been nothing, Tina. It might have been just a dream. Nothing more." He needed to soften the blow if he could. She'd just had her first dream about the past and it was a whopper. Like holding a pillow against her stomach to absorb a punch in the gut, he offered what he could. "It might have been just your subconscious telling you what it suspects. Not real."

"They were after my paintings. Hank and Noble were con men and wanted my grandmother's paintings." She looked at him. "Those things must be more valuable than Hank told me."

Jamey kissed her hair and she slumped against his chest.

"And if it was real, everything I knew about Hank would be a lie." Her voice was pitifully small.

"No. Hank loved you. I know that for a fact." He had to tell her about being inside Hank's psyche, feeling Hank's emotions for that short time. He rubbed her back. "Remember the dream where I became Hank? We were in the same body, and I felt his love for you. It was a profound love like nothing he'd ever known. And I knew he had a secret." He pulled back and looked directly into her face. "I know he would want me to tell you this. He thought you were too good for him and that he didn't deserve you. Hank adored you, Tina. I know that because I was inside his head and a part of his heart in that dream. You were the one thing in his life that was good and honest."

Tina pushed away and disappeared into the bathroom to cry by herself.

When Jamey returned from the continental breakfast buffet with coffee and muffins, the shower was running. He'd call Katie at the shop to check in, while Tina was showering.

"Everything is fine," Katie said breathlessly. "Shelley is taking the scheduled boat divers on a free beach dive up north, like Tina offered. I'm in the shop all day with Megan."

"Have you seen Noble?"

Katie paused. "What?"

"You know, Tina's big Hawaiian friend, Noble. He lives in her cottage in the backyard?" If Noble knew the sediment was being analyzed and that they were out searching for Hank's body, he'd probably be on his way to the mainland.

"You mean he *lived* in her cottage."

"What? Is he gone?"

"Well, if you call dead, gone. Can you hold on just a sec?"

"Katie, wait!" *What the hell?* Jamey sat on the hotel bed, the sound of the shower still strong on the other side of the wall. *Noble was dead?*

"Okay, I'm back," Katie said. "Oh yeah, Noble. You know he shot himself in Tina's cottage."

He paused, knowingly. "Not recently."

"No. Like six months ago."

A chill spread up Jamey's back to his head.

"Don't talk to Tina about him, Uncle Jamey. We're not supposed to say his name around her because she went ballistic and had to go in the hospital for a week, and Dave said she still thinks he's alive sometimes. She only talks about him with her shrink."

When Jamey hung up the phone, he remembered all the times he'd spoken to Noble at Tina's house—the man with the strange aura around him that he'd mistaken for hatred.

***

Walking along the Molokai wharf towards the boat, Tina reached for Jamey's hand but not out of affection. Her attachment to him was an anchor to reality in turbulent water. Sadness and fear emanated from her. He would not let her out of his sight all day. He might not be dream jumping, but there was nothing wrong with his intuition, unless you considered he hadn't guessed that Noble was a dead man. Goddammit. How did he miss that one? No wonder Tina believed Noble was still alive. He walked around her house all day. This was the weirdest thing he'd ever experienced, and he'd been through a lot of shit.

Nothing that resembled romance lingered from the night before, and he knew that today would be all business. Tina only had so much to give. Treading carefully had never been so important, now that he knew Noble was dead and Tina didn't remember.

The boat ran smoothly as they rounded the south side of Molokai on their way to the sea cliffs. Jamey fingered the old S belt in his jacket pocket. His theory that Noble cut the belt had flown out the window with the knowledge that the man was dead. The belt must have snapped clean after all. Probably was a faulty belt. If Noble didn't put a sedative in Tina's glass, who did? And why? Her parents were next in line for the nasty role of possible suspects, but why would they sedate their own daughter? Questions fought for immediate answers in his mind, and Jamey had to set them aside until later. The task at hand was big enough.

The current on the north shore was predictably flowing west to east as they pushed along at seventeen knots. The local dive shop said that no one had been out diving on the north shore in the last few months. When Tina asked about a cavern, the man just snorted and told her she'd never get close in spring conditions.

"Probably not even summer. The swell is too strong to get inside that cavern," he'd warned. "It'll smash you on the rocks before you can get close enough to the opening.

It's more of a blowhole in the winter."

"He's probably trying to get a dive charter out of it," Tina commented dryly, once she and Jamey were outside. But Jamey wasn't so sure it would be the ocean's conditions that stopped her that day. She looked terrified. Although they'd brought gear for two, he was prepared to dive solo. If things turned out the way they hoped, they'd find a body today. And a body that had been in salt water for ten months would be gruesome. Especially someone you loved.

When they passed the Halawa Valley, Tina made Jamey take the wheel. Her hands shook. Seated at the bow, she pulled her knees up to her chest and looked out from under her hood.

With every mile, Jamey felt they were closing in on Hank. When they reached what they thought was the site, Tina dropped anchor according to the swell, the current, and what she knew about the underwater topography. "I'm going to make sure we're stuck in the sand," Tina said. After donning her fins and fixing a mask to her face, she jumped into the water.

"I'll be damned," Jamey said to Obi. "Just like that." Obi wagged his tail and looked over the side of the boat for Tina.

Back to the boat, she grabbed her gear. "That's it."

He'd hooked up two tanks, just in case. "Are you diving?"

"Yes." She didn't meet his eyes.

"I can do the first or second alone." The first dive would confirm the presence of the cave and case out the conditions. Jamey envisioned the second dive would be too much for her.

"No need."

She slipped into her gear, and then sat on the boat's edge and rolled backwards. "Stay, Obi," was the last thing said before slipping below the surface. Jamey followed.

Sediment from the west had stirred the water to where

they could only see thirty feet in front of them. The amazing clarity from the dream was nowhere to be found. The wall wasn't visible yet. Cutting the sand ripple lines at a right angle, the two divers headed in the direction of the cliff. When Jamey put his hand out for Tina, she shook her head and proceeded.

The swell made the going slow, but they finally reached the wall. Tina looked in the direction of the cave and took off.

Jamey felt two things as he swam through her trailing bubbles. One was that Tina was not going to make it much further. Her terror was too intense. If she did something foolish, their safety would be jeopardized. And two, the presence of Hank was as strong as if he was the third diver. If they didn't find a body today, it wouldn't be because Hank had never been here.

When Jamey caught up with Tina, he placed his hand on her arm. She jumped. A mass of bubbles flew out of her regulator. She was sucking back the air too fast, and an eighty cubic inch tank wouldn't last long if she didn't calm down.

Gripping her elbows with his hands, he stared into her eyes and attempted to give her strength. He'd done it before, and she'd said it worked. They pushed off and continued, hand in hand, until a familiar cavern doorway loomed.

The ominous black hole looked like a screaming mouth. Jamey gave Tina an "okay?" sign, and she nodded. Bubbles raced frantically out of her regulator and up to the surface. She was using more air than usual but, he had to admit, they were now evenly matched. Being small, she used very little air. Usually. Jamey signaled for her to stay and hang onto the rock, but she shook her head and proceeded.

The ocean's movement carried them further. He had to believe Tina was a much better diver than him and knew the risks. But what if she panicked at the sight of the body?

He wasn't trained in underwater rescues. Not like Tina. Water funneled into the black cave opening. A few seconds later, bubbles poured out the door as the water shot towards them.

Tina must know that aerated bubbles indicated a blow hole, a connection to the surface. What if the force inside was too strong for them? The dive master had warned against the dive. If Hank's body was in there, it had to be stuck, or it would have come out the top. Jamey had no idea what to do. He wasn't the underwater expert. As Tina drifted by, he wondered if she was at risk of killing herself. A flash of panic exploded inside him. Maybe Tina's intention was to die here. She'd said they only had last night. No more.

She'd been depressed, lonely for Hank. Had her behavior last night been only a smokescreen, or a final goodbye to him? And why was she diving with this terror? His heart pounded in his chest as the what-ifs added up to include Tina's possible suicide.

When she turned and gave him the signal to wait, his first instinct was to ignore her order and follow. But he could be wrong. Probably was. There's only one boss on any dive, and Tina was it. Jamey asked her again if she was okay, and she nodded. He had to believe her. What could he do? Grabbing onto a boulder near the sandy bottom, he waited.

As she drifted to the mouth of the cave, Tina reached inside her pocket and pulled out something. In the murky visibility, Jamey couldn't see what the lump was. In their haste to jump in the water, he'd forgotten to defog his mask, and the condensation inside the lens clouded his vision. Whatever was in her hand, she held it tightly, and then kicked hard to the side of the cave mouth. He could see she was aiming for the doorway edge, not the hole. She made it and grabbed on, but the force of the surge pulled all but her hands off the rock, like a flag on a windy day, anchored only by her grip.

When the wave switched directions, she jabbed something into the rock. She'd brought a thin yellow rope, now attached to a wedge in the rock.

She tied the other end of the rope to her dive jacket, and then pulled out a pair of gloves. Was she going to inch her way in by letting the water's force pull her through the mouth? If it had been him doing this, Jamey would've just powered into the cave and assumed his strength would get him out eventually. But Tina was not taking any chances. When had this plan been hatched? He had to think that if her intention was suicide, she wouldn't go to all this trouble.

He kicked his way over to the wall and watched her round the mouth into the cave. Tina looked back, nodded once, and disappeared through the black opening. As he watched, the rope remained taut. That was a good sign she was still attached. He thought about easing himself into the cave on the rope, hopefully without ripping open his hands, letting go, or killing himself. Weighing chivalry with his inexperience, everything pointed to letting Tina do her job. He had to trust she wasn't trying to kill herself. If she had let go and shot out the top of the blowhole, the rope would've gone slack by now.

A flashlight beam illuminated the cave's mouth from inside and flashed twice. Was this a sign for him to come in? He cursed the fact that they hadn't made a dive plan. She'd had a plan, and it didn't involve him. Tina's gloved fingers appeared, then her arm, shoulder and head. She inched herself along the rope with the ascender. Jesus Christ, she was smart. And tenacious. She must be exhausted. Sliding along the yellow rope carefully, he reached to grab her hand. Soon she would be within reach.

Then the rope snapped and in a split second, she disappeared.

***

The last thing Tina saw was Jamey's arm reaching for her, a wild look in his eyes, like he knew before it happened. The force threw her against the cave wall, and she rolled off the jagged rock, hitting her head. Luckily, she'd worn a full wetsuit to cushion the bumps and scrapes, but would she live to appreciate her choice? Her heart pounded, remembering what she'd seen in the cave before the rope broke.

Hank's body was up there. Or someone's body. Her flashlight had illuminated something that resembled a foot dangling ten feet up near the blowhole. Before she panicked and suffered a self-induced heart attack, she had to remind herself that it was probably Hank's foot. Something she was familiar with. They'd given each other foot massages. She had to think of that to keep calm.

Tina grabbed at anything to keep from being thrust upwards to the blowhole, wedged in with Hank's body. Her strength had been tapped already, and her arms felt like jelly. The only light in the cavern was coming from the mouth above her, where she'd seen the foot. Her flashlight had dropped to the floor of the cave when the rope broke, along with her chances of getting out.

Fighting the rush of water that was taking her up to the blowhole, she found nothing to grab onto. Just before she entered the hole, the water slowed and began its retreat. She aimed for the cave door and prepared to kick towards the doorway. Jamey. Her arms were numb, but her legs still felt strong. Kicking as hard as she could, she made it ten feet from the opening. She hoped to kick over and grab the wall. But the next force was stronger than the last, and it deposited her farther inside and ten feet up. Her shoulder brushed against Hank's foot and she glanced over her shoulder to see the extent of his white leg, whole and terrifying. Oh God! She fought nausea, and concentrated on Jamey waiting for her at the cave mouth. No good. She vomited into her regulator and quickly pushed the purge button to clear it for breathing. More air wasted.

The next pull of water was stronger, and Tina kicked hard enough to make it half way to the opening. Her gauges swung in front. Her tank might be getting low on air. Heavy breathing did that. She did not want to go too far back into the cave with the next wave, so she used her last bit of energy to face the force. Kicking herself downwards to the floor to avoid losing ground, she was hopeful. The bubbles rose around her, like she was in a Jacuzzi. Her air supply wouldn't last long with this exertion. Digging her hands into the sandy floor of the cave, she waited for the next wave to leave the cavern, planning to ride it out.

There was nothing Jamey could do from outside the cave. If he risked coming in, they would be even worse off, with two bodies tumbling around inside this washing machine. As long as her air held out and the waves didn't get worse, she had a chance of surviving.

When the next pull gradually built to take her near the mouth, she let go of the sandy bottom. The familiar slow suck of a dwindling air supply kept her from getting a full breath. Shit! One more breath and she'd be out.

She was going to suffocate in this cavern, die with Hank. *Oh, my God!* Jamey would never know what really happened. She didn't inhale, knowing she had maybe a breath left, then nothing. Getting to the opening was now absolutely imperative before she blacked out. She needed a breath. Pulling hard on her regulator, she got very little back—a crumb to a starving person. No use sucking anymore. A quick ascent might get her a tiny bit more expanding air as she surfaced, but this was a cave with a roof. Her only hope was to try to get out the blowhole. Somehow, she had to get past Hank's body to the surface, even if it meant getting thrown out the top at an explosive force to be dropped on the rocks below. Suffocation was the only other option.

But then, Jamey rounded the corner against the force, and her plan changed. No blowhole. Getting to Jamey was the plan. Jamey's tank. She was going to pass out. Reaching his air supply to buddy breathe was the only way to save her life now.

When the wave tornadoed into the cavern, Jamey let something trail in front of him like a filament, a lifeline. As blackness threatened the edges of her vision, she could see Jamey was too far away to grab the rope. She made the sign for out of air. Now she'd be taken up to the blowhole. With Hank. At least, Jamey would know how she died.

CHAPTER 27

Tina was out of air. And the 300 psi left in his tank meant about another minute or two of breathing. That might be enough to save her, and maybe even get them out of this dark hole if he could reach her. His return to the boat to get a line of rope had taken a lot of air. At least he'd snorkeled on the surface. He could have changed tanks at the boat, but he was desperate to get back to her. Now time was even more crucial.

His heart flipped as he watched her go limp and float upwards.

Jamey pulled against the force, and as the movement of the water switched directions, he aimed for Tina's body, now headed for the roof of the cave. When he shot forward, he grabbed her hair with his fingertips and pulled her to him. They crashed into the cave wall. His second regulator was already in his hand. Jamey shoved the mouthpiece through Tina's lips and purged it to force air into her mouth.

She jerked and her eyes flew open. She sputtered in the regulator and took a breath. He put out his free hand to try to prevent them from being knocked against the rocks, and then watched her take another few breaths, coughing into the mouthpiece. He'd have to hold his breath as long as he could.

Hooking Tina's jacket to Obi's leash, which he'd brought back from the boat, Jamey looked directly into her mask to see if her eyes showed that she understood what was happening. She looked terrified but conscious. He motioned for her to hang onto him and crawled along the side of the wall, towards the mouth. Tina's bubbles made a gurgling sound behind him, and he risked a shallow breath for himself. It wouldn't suit anyone if he passed out.

Inching along the wall, Jamey figured it would take another minute to reach the opening, if they could resist the force trying to pick them off the wall. If.

Then he noticed the shark. It was tucked in under a ledge in front of them, directly in the doorway's path. The beast was big for a white-tipped reef shark. Weighing the risks, he continued to pull them to the light, towards the shark. He had to take another breath. When he did, it was like sucking through a narrow straw.

They were running out of air. Tina must've felt it, too.

Jamey hoped to hell they could make it before both of them blacked out. If not, they would die in this blowhole, together with

Hank's body. How appropriate. Maybe that was always their fate.

The shark swam past them, and then Jamey felt himself being pulled back. No! Away from the opening. He looked to see why and noticed that Tina had grabbed the shark's dorsal fin! Attached to Tina by jackets, he had no choice but to go with her. The shark rounded, and Jamey was eye to eye with the beast for one long second as it headed to the cave opening. His lungs were going to burst.

The shark swerved against the flow of water coming through the cave doorway, and within seconds they'd rounded the mouth of the cave and were outside in the sand and light. Freedom.

Tina let go and the shark continued out to deeper water as they kicked towards the surface, dropping weight belts to ascend faster.

Jamey exhaled his way to the surface to prevent an air embolism.

Breaking through to the air, they ripped off masks and gasped. Jamey held tightly to Tina's jacket. They were too close to the rocks for safety.

"Let's go!" He exhaled. The force threatened to smash

them against the jutting lava points if they didn't get out of there fast. With everything he had, Jamey kicked against the force, pulling Tina with him until they were forty feet out, where the swell wasn't dangerous. "You okay?" One of her eyes had burst a vessel and was blood red. "Your eye."

"Is it red? It's okay." The boat was about three hundred feet away. "I don't know how you had the strength just now." She lay on her back and heaved a sigh.

"Kandahar obstacle course," he said. "I'll pull you." He grabbed the neck of her jacket and, as she lay on her back, kicking slightly, he took off. When the surface swells rose too high and obscured the boat, Obi's barks kept them on course.

Jamey reached for Tina's hand to pull her to the swim step and felt a jolt of horrific sadness. She must have found the body in that cave.

Once on board, they laid the gear on the floor. "Oh, my God!" she said. They embraced. Tina's small body was wracked with sobs.

"He's in the cave, stuck in the blowhole," she cried.

All Jamey could do was hold her until she'd calmed. He stroked her head with one hand, held her tight with the other, and absorbed her misery. When she finally pulled away and fell into the captain's chair, Jamey wrapped a towel around Tina's shoulders. "That shark saved our lives." He shuddered to think how close they'd come to dying.

"I had a hunch that if I grabbed the fin, it would leave the cavern," she said.

"Is that normal shark behavior?" Jamey asked.

"I doubt it." Her face was drawn, pale, her eyes empty. She sat down. "Noble's dead. He killed himself." Her monotone voice struck fear in Jamey. She looked up at him. "Did you know?" Jamey shook his head. "He fooled me too."

"I remembered, down there. I was the one who found

his body. In the cottage."

The look of confusion on her face made his heart hurt. He laid a hand on her shoulder. "I'll call the police," he said. "Then we can talk about Noble, if you want."

"Wait. I remembered something else I need to tell you."

***

The night before James left Maui, ten years ago, Kristina had dreamed of a wedding. She was the bride, but she didn't recognize her dance partner. Unlike her new boyfriend, James, this tuxedoed groom was lanky, with long, dark hair. He had had a slightly rakish look to him, like a pirate. Whoever he was, he was not the fastidiously neat James. And the strange thing was that she'd observed the scene from the sidelines, as a second Tina.

The couple danced to a favorite love song. The bride looked radiant. Blissful even. And her groom looked smitten as well. From the far side of the room, her parents did not look nearly as happy. Her mother wore her fake smile, the one she used when pretending to agree with something she vehemently opposed, and her father's expression was one of neutrality. No smile, but no grimace either, which Tina knew to be his attorney face, usually saved for courtrooms. Why were they not happy for her?

Knowing it was just a dream, her attention returned to the dance floor, and to the couple dancing. When the dancers twirled, Tina jumped back. Her partner now had a skeleton's head. The groom's tuxedo was hanging off the bones of his frame, and the only remnant of the former man was his long, black hair. The guests didn't seem to notice, nor the bride, who continued to dance with the skeleton. Tina wanted out of this dream and instinctively turned to run. Bumping into a man, she woke up and realized she was in James' condo. She let out the breath she'd been holding and snuggled in closer to James. It had only been a bad dream, rooted in her own insecurities about her beloved James' departure to Seattle in the morning. Soon it was a forgotten memory. Until now. In the cave, she'd had a flash of memory that showed the skeletal body on the dance floor, and then the dream appeared, like a movie in front of her.

"I saw it too, but I'd forgotten," she told Jamey. "Last night when you told me about having that dream, there was something familiar about it, like déjà vu."

He nodded. "I must've jumped into your dream that night. Even back then..." He looked into her eyes. "This means it was your precognitive dream and we were able to dream jump together ten years ago. Has this been happening all your life?"

"No. I don't think so. Maybe it's just when I'm around you."

They contemplated the possibilities until a pinprick in the sky became a helicopter. It got bigger until the chopper flew over them, its noise adding both dread and hope to the moment. The chopper landed a mile away at the Kalaupapa airport. Soon after, Jamey's cell phone rang to say the police were on their way.

Tina sat perfectly still, clutching Obi, until a Coast Guard vessel approached from the other direction. "Here comes the cavalry," she said quietly, knowing this was the beginning of the official ending.

When the vessel pulled up alongside *Maui Dream*, one of the men jumped on board. "I'm Officer Hensley." He shook both Tina and Jamey's hands. "I'm sorry, Mrs. Perez." Tina nodded.

When the police arrived from Kalaupapa, the boat filled with people. Questions about the body's position were tossed around like dinner party plans, but there was nothing festive on Tina's end and she looked pleadingly to Jamey. Handling most of it, Jamey switched to cop talk while Tina cringed to hear her husband spoken of as a corpse. The boat rose and fell with the swells as they waited for the dive rescue team. Tina, who sat in the bow hugging Obi, was unneeded for now.

The blue sky had clouded over, and wind moved in to stir the surface. The rescue divers arrived by boat, and Tina gave them her best idea on how to get into the cave safely with a rope system, keeping in mind there might be a tiger shark waiting. "Wait! What?" Jamey said. "A deep-water shark?"

"Yes." Tina was surprised he hadn't noticed. "That was a small tiger."

The shark was Hank's manna, his totem, wasn't it? This was all too strange to comprehend.

After the rescue team suited up and launched into the water armed with a sack of ropes, pulleys, and motorized scooters, Jamey made a request. "Can someone take this woman back to Maui? There's no need for her to witness this."

"I don't want to leave him." She meant Hank, and Jamey knew.

"I'll be here." He encircled her with his arms and the silver space blanket crackled between them. "It's only a matter of another hour or two. I'll stay." He looked at Officer Hensley. "Where will you take him?"

"Wailuku. To the coroner." The man looked from Jamey to Tina.

"Go back to the Hotel Molokai and wait for me there." He rubbed her back. "We can drive the boat back tonight or tomorrow."

"I want to see if my paintings are gone."

"Don't go back to your house tonight." Jamey didn't know what to think about Noble. If Hank was lingering in Tina's bedroom and the ghost of Noble had run of the property, Jamey was afraid for Tina. Especially now that she remembered he was dead. Jamey needed to keep her close. "Go to the hotel. We'll drive the boat back tonight."

***

"Take me to the West Maui Airport," Tina said. She had no intention of waiting at the hotel on Molokai, not knowing if the paintings were gone. She could hardly breathe until she found out. Noble might have sold them and stashed the money somewhere, and if that was the case, how would she recover from that betrayal?

Running from the helicopter, she flagged a taxi and settled into the back seat with Obi for the short ride down the hill to her home. Her cell phone still had enough juice for one call to her mother. She would've only just arrived in Seattle.

"Hello, Kristina?"

"Did you switch out my pills?"

The pause was all Tina needed to hear to confirm that her mother had a part in this. "How could you drug your own daughter?"

"I'd prefer to talk about this in person." Her mother's voice was shaky. "Philip, she knows about the pills."

"Damned right I know. I know everything, and if you are hoping to ever hear from me again after this phone call, you'd better come up with some pretty good answers about why you sabotaged my marriage, bribed my husband, and drugged me." The taxi driver looked in the rear-view mirror, but Tina didn't care. Hot blood raged through her body.

Her mother sounded panicked on the other end of the line. "I understand you're upset, Kristina. You have every right to be. We love you and didn't want you to suffer alone on Maui."

Her father came on the line. "Krissy?" He used his pet name for her.

"Just a minute, Father." Tina paid the cab driver and got out.

"I had no idea that your mother gave you a sedative. All this talk about Noble being in your house had her worried you were going over the edge. The night of your birthday, you kept talking to Noble like he was standing beside us, and she put half a valium in your water. She is very sorry. Naturally, I am extremely upset."

"Not as upset as I am, Father." She watched Obi sniff around the yard.

"We'll turn around now and get on the next plane, come back to

Maui to talk to you. Don't cut us off. Your mother has been frantic.

She was worried you might try..." He caught himself.

"To kill myself, like Noble?" She could hear her mother crying in the background, a sound all too familiar. Elizabeth Greene had two emotions: cold as ice and despondent. "No, Father." Obi disappeared around the side of the house, and she waited for him in the driveway. "I am beyond livid with that woman who calls herself my mother. She blackmailed my husband. Did you know that?"

"I do now." His voice was tense.

"I don't want to see her. But I do want you to get her a psychiatrist as soon as possible. She is sick."

"Sweetheart, your mother has had a weekly appointment for thirty years with one of the top psychiatrists in America, but this new turn will need to be addressed. And now that I know she interfered in your marriage, we are going to need to see a counselor together." Elizabeth said something in the background. "Shut up, Elizabeth. For once, just shut up and let me handle this."

The silence on the other end was what Tina needed to end the conversation. "Daddy, it's been a long day." She stared at her house, wondering if Noble would be gone now that she knew he was dead. "I'll call you tomorrow."

She ran upstairs and flung open her bedroom closet's door, silently praying everything was still there. Moving everything aside, she pulled out the black container and, with the small key on her ring, opened the lock. A whoosh of air rushed in, and she pulled aside the covering. Her paintings were there. She still owned the landscapes she'd cherished on the walls of her grandmother's house—the home she'd been forbidden to visit except in her mother's company. Tears pooled in her eyes for many different reasons.

Pulling them out one by one, she was grateful. *Thank God Hank didn't follow through*. For the first time in a while, she felt close to Hank. Relieved, yes, but it was much more than that. He was close by. She knew it. "Hank?" She waited, but nothing presented itself. There was something different about Noble's cottage. She knew it even before she opened the door. Like a knife through her gut, the moment she found Noble's body flashed in her mind—his head blown to bits, parts of him all over the wall behind the couch, the gun lying beside him on the couch. The goodbye note on the kitchen counter even had splatters of blood. She'd mistakenly assumed he'd been unable to get past the loneliness without Hank. Now she understood it was the guilt that did him in.

The cottage was stiflingly hot. Who had cleaned up all the blood? The couch was gone, the wall painted. No sign of Noble or his life inside these walls. He was gone, now that she knew.

Pulling the door closed, she returned to the house, her heart heavy. The men who'd made up her happy life were now dead. Obi ran up the back stairs to his water dish. At least she still had her dog. A quick phone call to the vet confirmed that the test results were not back yet.

"Probably tomorrow," the perky receptionist said, like it wasn't the end of the world.

"You are not sick, Obi." She beckoned him onto the bed and got under the covers. The image of what was left of Hank's body wouldn't be pushed to the back of her mind. A box of tissues sat within reach on the bedside table, but tears wouldn't come. Instead, she felt shell-shocked and dry. Her breathing was shallow, barely sustainable.

Thoughts of Jamey were reassuring until she remembered he would return to Afghanistan soon. She'd fallen for James again. It hadn't been difficult but dammit, he would desert her for the second time, and she should've known better.

When Jamey suggested Noble was switching out her pills, Tina wondered what her friend could possibly gain by doing that. "Only the opportunity to have sex with me and that's no great privilege these days," she'd said.

"Don't be so sure," he'd said.

Now she knew it had been impossible to make a baby with a ghost.

Jamey had seen Noble too. The two men had fought. Some psychic he was. Hadn't Jamey realized? Or her parents? Noble had been at her birthday party. Hadn't everyone seen him that night? Then she remembered Noble hadn't talked to anyone at the party. He'd been on the periphery, watching her. Even her parents, who were rudely ignoring him, didn't look at him. Only she and Jamey saw Noble. And if they could see Noble, why couldn't she see Hank?

"Hank?" Her own pitiful voice scared her. "Are you here?" Obi jumped off the bed and ran to the next room. He'd be waiting at the door. Her dog's innocent expectation made her heart hurt. If only it was that easy.

Her cell phone broke through the stillness. Jamey's number. "Jamey?"

"Are you at the hotel? Where are you? I'm pulling into the wharf at Kaunakakai and it feels like you're gone." His voice had an urgency she'd never heard before.

"I came home."

"Tina, you're supposed to be on Molokai."

"I needed to see the paintings. They're here."

"Is Noble with you?"

"No. No one is here, alive or dead." She understood his concern. "I'm just lying in my bed."

"Stay there. Don't go anywhere or do anything, please. I'll be there soon. If Noble shows up, don't go anywhere with him."

What did he mean by that?

***

Jamey bounded onto the Molokai-to-Maui prop plane, and the flight crew closed the door behind him. He took his seat and fastened his belt, hoping he wasn't too late. He had to get to Maui, just in case Hank and Noble were still at the house. Jamey wasn't entirely sure that at least one of them didn't want to take her with him.

He'd secured the boat at the wharf under the watchful eye of a fisherman who was happy to make a hundred bucks. Luckily the next flight off Molokai to the West Maui Airport had empty seats.

The day's ordeal was finally coming to a close, but until he knew Tina was safe, he wouldn't let down his guard. The day was adding up to full physical and mental exhaustion. Like a dream jump in Afghanistan. And Tina would probably be feeling it tenfold.

She'd seen her husband's dead body, and now she knew that Noble was dead, too. How had Noble's ghost managed to remain all these months, walking around the house, while Hank's hadn't? He hoped to hell that her shrink believed in ghosts.

***

Noble's footsteps sounded on the outside stairs, and his body filled the doorway.

"Hi," Tina said, scooting to a sitting position. He

looked remarkably real, although a look of surrender shrouded his face.

"Scale of one to ten?" he asked.

"Zero."

Obi growled at the man who'd moved to the end of her bed. Now she understood why Obi did this. Her dog mistrusted this ghostly form of Noble.

"Did you know that I'm not here anymore?" Noble looked on the verge of tears.

She nodded. "You died." Had he not known before? "We found Hank's body." Her voice was like a scratch on rough pavement.

Noble nodded. "I killed him."

"It was an accident." She wanted to believe that or she'd never get past this tragedy.

He didn't question how she knew. "Still…"

She folded her arms across her chest and slid back against the wall. "Hank loved me." It was more of a question than she wanted it to be.

Noble looked up. "Hank loved you. Yes. He really loved you." His eyes were clouded with pain. "You know about the plan to leave?"

"I dreamed of your argument at Honolua."

He nodded. "Your mother said she'd turn me in and then found out Hank had priors. She was trying to force us out of your life."

Tina's feelings for her mother plummeted to a new low. "She blackmailed you."

Noble nodded, his own feelings for Elizabeth Greene apparent. "When she heard that you were trying to get pregnant, she told Hank she'd turn us in if we didn't leave and never come back."

Tina had no other emotion than hatred for her mother, a woman who sabotaged her daughter's happiness. The light behind Noble was now visible through his body. "Noble, you're disappearing."

He continued like he hadn't heard. "Hank wanted a

baby. Mostly for you, and then in case it changed your mother's mind. With you pregnant, he thought she'd back off. Taking the paintings was always my idea. When you first met him, you said you had these paintings, worth a lot of money. I thought it would be a quick job. We'd retire on it."

She was pained by the words coming out of Noble's mouth.

"We didn't know you then, Ti. We came from nothing. It was how we survived. Me and Henry had been cheating people out of money since we were kids." Noble sighed. "That's who we were. I don't expect you to understand that, growing up rich. But it was our way to survive, until things changed. You changed Hank. Then me."

The verification of Hank's love had to be enough. Later she'd process the rest, but she'd never question their love. She stared at his fading form.

"Come with me, Ti." Noble walked to her and took her hand. His was fluttery, like a feather. "You, me, and Hank. We'll all be together again. He's waiting for you."

CHAPTER 28

As the plane descended on the west coast of Maui, Jamey searched for Tina's house below, not sure what he was looking for. Ambulances? Fire trucks? Nothing unusual stood out, but when he located the clay roof, he noted Noble's truck in the driveway. Funny, but it had always been there, even when the man was supposedly at work. Which he never was, because he was confined to the house. Why hadn't Tina noticed that? That, and the fact that Noble only ever appeared at her house. Never at the shop. He didn't know how clinical denial worked; maybe she rationalized all that too.

Jamey prayed the whole taxi ride that Tina would be safe, both physically and mentally. If she wasn't, he didn't have a clue what to do next. If they'd taken her, or killed her, he imagined himself entering a dream and finding some way to make them pay. He hoped if it came to that, something was possible, because he didn't want to live his life without her now that he'd found her again.

The day he'd met Hank, Jamey's first thought was that this was a guy he could hang out with, look up when he came to Maui. They'd been standing in line at the bank, struck up a conversation, and realized they had something in common—diving. Hank was an avid surfer but his new girlfriend was a dive instructor and had just certified him all the way to Dive Master. "So now, I'm a hot shit diver." He was doing a dive that night with his friend Noble for octopus if Jamey wanted to come along.

"Sure!" Jamey loved to night dive.

"We'll meet you at the Honolua Store at seven. Get in the water at dusk. Bring a light though, man. Those things are stuck way in the cracks." Hank grinned at Jamey like the fun would never end.

When Jamey jumped in Hank's truck at the rendezvous, he was puzzled. "Your friend meeting us there?"

"Nah. He couldn't come. Just you and me, buddy." They sped up the road to Slaughterhouse Beach, parked and trekked down the steep hill to the water.

That night they got two octopi, and Hank said he'd give them to his friend to make ceviche for them. If Jamey wanted to come over to the house, they could "have a few beers, shoot the shit. My girlfriend might be there, but she's cool. I just moved in with her, so we haven't gotten to the nagging stage yet," he'd said. They'd laughed.

But when Jamey drove his rental car up to the house, he'd known.

Kristina was the girlfriend.

This man was the skeleton from the dream. He'd stopped the car at the top of the lane and thought about what to do. He couldn't go in there, see Kristina. For one thing, it would be too painful, and for another thing, he'd promised to walk away from her. Them.

Hank saw him in the driveway and beckoned him down the lane. "Hey, my buddy is on his way with the beer and limes. The girlfriend is on a night dive." Hank's smile was infectious, and Jamey found himself nodding.

"Nice house." Jamey couldn't help himself.

"The old lady is loaded." Hank shrugged. "What can I say?"

At that moment, Jamey knew the man standing in front of him was up to something, maybe after the money, or at the very least motivated by the money. Jamey had to fight to look casual. "A rich scuba instructor?" He tried to grin.

"Rich family." Hank moved in and whispered

311

conspiratorially. "And she's really cute, which is a bonus."

Jamey had an idea of what was going on here, and his lip almost curled in disgust. "Nice. Hey, man. I actually came over to tell you that a woman I met this morning wants to meet me for a drink."

After what Hank just said, Jamey knew Hank would understand choosing a date over a beer with some guys. "So, I can't stay, but thanks again." They shook hands and Jamey retreated from Kristina's life for the second time in eight years.

Thoughts of her being taken advantage of wouldn't die, and over the next two days he fought hard to leave Hank and Kristina alone. He'd promised to walk away from precognitive dreams. Leave the scene as it was. And that promise meant a lot to him, especially because Uncle Don wasn't alive anymore. He needed to keep the promise he'd made to his uncle. Jamey flew away from the Hawaiian Islands the next day, his heart twisted into a hard ball.

The following year, Jamey was back on Maui before leaving for his tour in Afghanistan, and saw Hank in Safeway grabbing some steaks. Jamey watched Hank flirt with a woman who was contemplating the best cut of meat. He was definitely charming the pants off the blonde in the tight shorts.

Hank headed to the checkout and the woman moved on. But not before Jamey's eye went to the paper with her phone number on it and the wedding ring on the hand that had been pocketed. Jamey's heart sank at the prospect of Hank and Kristina married.

When Jamey found Hank's same truck parked outside near his rental car, he walked over and hidden from view, grabbed the door handle briefly. The sense of trickery was still there, mixed with something else he couldn't place. Maybe fondness. But one thing was clear. Hank was not who he said he was and Kristina was destined for heartbreak. He could almost taste the tragedy that awaited her.

Writing her parents the anonymous letter had been a difficult decision, but in the end Jamey had mailed the warning from the Maui post office and hoped to God that he was doing the right thing. He'd broken his promise to Uncle Don. He'd interfered. He told himself that no one knew what might happen if he messed with the future. It could be good. And this was Kristina. If there was something he could do to help, he had to try before he left for Afghanistan. Knowing he'd done what he could, he walked away, the promise broken. The future up for grabs.

***

Tina, Hank, and Noble. It had been a good combination for a short time. "I can't come with you, Noble." Tina slid back against the wall. "I have a life to put back together." She didn't consider the possibility of leaving even if there was a guarantee that an afterlife existed and she could be with Hank again. "Why can't Hank appear, like you?"

Noble shrugged. "Maybe I had to set things right because I killed him and then killed myself. That's a pretty horrible sin for a Catholic." He almost smiled. "At first, I thought I stayed because I had to give you the baby you wanted. I ruined your chance with Hank. Penance. But then I wondered if killing myself was only a nightmare. That I was still alive. You could see me, and that was good enough."

Knowing she was about to lose him, too, Tina finally let her emotion rise to the surface. "I forgive you, Noble. And I forgive Hank. I loved both of you." She stood to hug him, but he wasn't solid enough to grasp, and he faded from her like a snowball melting frighteningly fast. Nothing remained of the man named Nolan Santiago, known to her as Noble. She spoke aloud

313

the one word that she could.

"Hank?" This time Obi merely cocked his head. Nothing. Was that it? "Hank?" If she was able to see Noble again, why couldn't she talk to Hank? Jamey had said Hank's spirit had given her the Molokai clue. "Please." The desperation in her voice was frightening.

The house phone rang, but she didn't answer. Jamey would call her cell phone. It sure as hell wouldn't be Noble. Come to think of it, she hadn't spoken to Noble on the phone for months.

Doc Chan would have some work to do getting her back to functionally normal. Tina hoped her shrink was up for the challenge and that she wouldn't guess the parts of the story that had to be withheld--like Noble was actually walking around her house in solid form. And that Hank's body was found through dreams. Funny thing was, Tina felt better now than she had in a long time.

Distracting herself with thoughts of Jamey, she lay back in the bed and pulled the covers up over herself and Obi. God, she hoped Jamey wasn't another figment of her imagination. He felt real, too. Could you have sex with a ghost? They'd had fantastic sex last night. Several times. She could still feel him inside her.

Sleeping with Jamey again had been wildly exciting but also familiar, like remembering you had a gorgeous singing voice that made beautiful music. Finding Jamey was the reawakening of something that had been dormant. Only twenty-four hours ago, before she had the dream about Henry and Nolan, before they'd found Hank's body, and before she realized Noble was dead, she'd felt free enough to imagine herself happy with Jamey when his tour in Afghanistan was over. It was hard to believe that was only yesterday.

In the past weeks since Jamey arrived on Maui, she'd been totally preoccupied with finding Hank's body. Now, free from that, she knew James Dunn was the love of her life. She was crazy about him and always had been. Life without him was unthinkable now.

She turned on the TV and flipped channels, finally settling on the Visitor's Channel. A show about the best snorkeling beaches touted familiar sites. "Tourists enjoy Black Rock off the Sheraton Hotel…"

Hank's original plan was to get the paintings and run. Then her mother ruined everything by blackmailing him and his brother.

The television volume was soft. "Snorkeling Maui can be done from an arranged boat tour or simply off one of Maui's countless beaches."

After Hank died, it seemed like he lingered in their bedroom, maybe unable to move on like Noble. Somehow Hank had been giving her his body's location through her dreams these past weeks. 'Glimpses,' Jamey called them. And it all started when Jamey walked back into her life. Their hands had touched, and she'd passed out. It was almost like Jamey unintentionally passed her something that would enable her to communicate with Hank. Had Hank's ghost been lingering all along, unable to reach her?

Jamey would be back on Maui sometime around ten. It was only seven now. She had hours to wait. Opening the covers, she left the bed and crossed the room to the picture window, she looked out to Molokai. Was Jamey following the coast in *Maui Dream* on his way home already? She tried his cell phone, but it went to message. Probably out of range.

"Call me when you get this," she said. What else was there to say?

The narrator on TV listed the virtues of a visit to Haleakala Crater. "Renew your spirit amid stark volcanic landscapes and subtropical rainforest with an unforgettable hike through the backcountry."

Jamey would arrive and she'd still be wearing the shorts and T-shirt from the last few days. In a burst of anticipation, Tina jumped in the shower to wash her hair and lathered her body with gardenia-scented soap.

315

Once dry, she grabbed a yellow rayon sundress from her closet. Stepping into the shift, she smiled to think she was getting pretty for Jamey. But was Hank still here?

Just as she thought this, a burst of cool air swept past her from the closet and rustled the curtains. Obi barked and sniffed, tracking something in the room. She realized now that this cool air always came from the direction of the closet.

Her eyes skirted the bedroom. If it was Hank and she only had a few minutes before he was gone forever, what did she want to tell him? "I love you. I still love you, regardless of your past. I know about you and Noble, and the paintings, and my mother." She waited. "And I know you loved me."

Had the curtains moved again? Obi jumped on to the bed, barking at the window. Warm tears trickled down Tina's cheeks to fall from her jaw line. "I'm so sorry it ended this way." She searched every inch of the room for abnormalities. Obi stared at the closet. Her breath caught in her throat. "I know you love me, Hank."

The narrator on TV was now talking about the twisty road to Hana. "Just miles past the charming town, you'll find a state park that offers…"

"Tina?" A voice behind the announcer called her name. It was a tinny sound, layered below the narrative. *"Tina?"* Again. It was a question.

"Hank? Is that you?!" She tried to block out the announcer's voice, listen beyond the Hana descriptive.

Static blocked the audio for two seconds. There were no discernable words to the noise, but the static had a definite cadence—four syllables that sounded like they could have been *"I love you, too."* She wanted to believe that was what she heard. The room's temperature warmed quickly, returning to normal. Tina stood in the center of the room, holding her breath.

Minutes passed, and she sank to sit on the edge of the bed. Had she just heard Hank on the TV? That sounded too strange to be true.

He'd never meant to leave her. Not now, not then.
Without summoning it, closure engulfed her. Hank
didn't want to leave her. He'd loved her. What would
Jamey say when she told him that she'd heard Hank?

All these months with his spirit in the house, inside
their bedroom, Hank had finally been able to
communicate—to say he loved her. She stared at the TV,
realizing that it hadn't been switched on in months.

After checking her computer, she found that
according to paranormal experts, communication was
possible through the TV. She could hardly wait to tell
Jamey. Outside, the channel looked calm enough for her
to hope that Jamey was making good time on the boat.
He'd call when he got back into cell range. Off the coast
of Molokai, hours before, she'd said, "Just make sure
they treat his body with respect." She'd cringed to say
'his body,' and Jamey had hugged her.

"I'll stay with him until the helicopter takes off."

But, Hank's spirit had been in the house when Tina
arrived home. Noble's too. Both had waited to say
goodbye.

***

The taxi turned onto Tina's street, and a flash
appeared in Jamey's mind--a vision of Tina standing in
front of Noble, the two facing each other silently. Then
the scene was gone. Jamey tried to concentrate but
couldn't get anything except for a steely look on Tina's
face. The yellow cab navigated the long driveway to the
house. Noble's truck was parked in its usual spot. The
house was dark. It was well after eight. He handed a bill
to the driver and raced up the front stairs, fully prepared
to confront Noble.

Obi barked once from the deck and he looked
ahead.

317

Tina stood at the railing, looking guilty. "Don't be mad I came home instead of staying on Molokai."

Was she kidding? He dashed up the last few stairs to her. "Are you okay, baby?" He pulled her into his chest and encircled her with his arms.

"I have so much to tell you," she said. "I was sitting here thinking about how to tell you how much I love you."

He kissed the top of her head. "You just did." He let out a long sigh and drew back to search her face. "You know I love you too, right? My goofy obsession with you has probably been obvious since the day we met."

She raised up on her tiptoes and kissed him, long and deep. Jamey didn't want this to end, but when she pulled back, he had to ask. "Hank?"

"He's gone." She took his hand and pressed it to her cheek. "Noble too." She locked eyes with him. "But, I heard Hank speak in the TV. Is that possible?"

Wow. "The experts say so. It's called Electronic Voice Phenomena." Jamey nodded. "What did he say?"

"That he loved me. And I told him I forgave him." She gestured to the bedroom.

He wouldn't have been so forgiving but it wasn't his place to say. "What about the sedative in your drink?"

"My mother's way to make me compliant. My father didn't know any of it."

Her mother was a piece of work, alright. He nodded sympathetically and looked around the room. This was the first time he felt nothing from the spirit who'd lingered in the bedroom. No sense from Noble, either. "I don't feel them."

"Noble disappeared in front of me when I forgave him."

Jamey shook his head slowly. "That must've been what he needed." He took her face in his hands and kissed her. "You are an amazing person, Tina. All you've been through, and you can still find it in your heart to forgive."

"I'm not sure about my mother."

"Wait 'til the smoke clears." Guilt stabbed at him. He'd been the one to alert her parents to Hank's motive for marrying Tina. Would he ever tell Tina that he'd sent her parents the letter about Hank's integrity, reveal how he'd broken his promise to never interfere with precognitive dreams? And admit that he might've jinxed her marriage? Not tonight, he wouldn't.

For the past twenty-four hours, he'd wondered if Hank's death could've been avoided if Elizabeth Greene had never gotten involved. Maybe Hank would've stayed with Tina, lived happily ever after. But then, what about the skeleton in the dream he had ten years earlier? Was Hank destined to die young? Had everything been predestined, even his letter to her parents? He'd think about that another day. Right now, Tina had a look on her face that made his heart stop.

"Tell me you're not going to leave me next week," she said, "or next month. Please don't go back to Afghanistan, Jamey. I can't do this without you."

"I'm not going anywhere. You're stuck with me." He wanted this to be the truth. Did that count? "If I start jumping on my own, I'm still done with Afghanistan, done with the army." He looked deep into her big brown eyes. Even if he didn't desperately want a future with Tina, which he did, jumping with soldiers was probably a death sentence for him. "I plan to stick around Maui, see if I can get a job with a dive shop or something." He grinned at her and said what he'd wanted to say ten years earlier. "I love you, Tina. With everything I have. I love you so much, it hurts. Do you think you can ever love me that much?"

"Just watch me." They kissed and walked into the bedroom. Tina turned off the TV. When she turned to face him she looked different. Peaceful. Almost radiant.

His gaze raked her from head to toe. "You look so pretty. It's a shame to take off that dress, but I'm thinking it's got to go." He deftly undid the shoulder strap bows and the dress fell to the floor.

"And you're overdressed for this occasion, Mr. Dunn." Tina pulled off his T-shirt and with her thumb hooked in his shorts, pulled him down to the soft bed.

***

In the dream, Jamey saw another version of himself walking on Fleming Beach, the sun dropping towards the horizon to leave a lavender pink sky it its wake. He sank to the sand and watched. The other Jamey held Tina's hand as Obi ran circles around them, flirting with the surf, running back to the dry sand. A small child rode on his shoulders, a hand buried in Jamey's hair. When a turtle's head popped through the water's surface, Obi ran into the ocean to investigate.

"Obi Wan Kenobi," Tina shouted. "Get back here, you old turtle hunter." Tina's hair was longer, halfway down her back.

The toddler tapped on Jamey's head in glee. "Obi, Obi."

Tina turned and walked backwards, smiling at the little boy.

"You love Obi, don't you, Kai?"

"Mama!" The boy reached for her and she lifted him off Jamey's shoulders to set him on the sand.

The child was the spitting image of Jamey. He even had the slightly lopsided smile. The two watched their boy carefully navigate the uneven terrain, his arms flung out from his sides for balance. He squatted to pick up a stick, and then continued. "Da Da." It was a present for his father.

"Thank you, Kai," Jamey said, the collection of sticks in his hand growing.

Tina took Jamey's hand and she twirled under his arm, into his hug. "My father would've loved Kai. I wish he'd lived to meet him."

"Me too."

"Lucky for Mother, I finally understand how fiercely a mother will fight for her child's wellbeing. Without that, forgiving her would've been difficult. I can't imagine what she went through when Kristoffer died." Obi dug for something in the wet sand at the edge of the surf. "What if Kai is a jumper? What'll we do, Jamey?"

"He'll use it for the greater good, like us." Jamey stopped and looked into her eyes. "No war."

"Maybe he'll help you look for missing kids." They watched Kai follow Obi along the sandy shore. "Do you miss it?" she asked.

"Jumping? Not when you bring me along." Jamey ran to catch the boy, playfully sweeping him into his arms, and then set the child on his shoulders.

When Tina caught up, she linked her arm in his. "I love helping you find kids, even if it means putting them to rest."

"You use your gift well."

"You do too. And as the guts of our dive business now. You know I love your guts, James." He laughed, and as they moved in to kiss, Kai grabbed a fistful of both parents' hair and yanked hard.

Jamey woke in the darkness of Tina's bedroom, timbered ceiling above him, the fan spinning. Tina lay beside him, and he was thankful that part hadn't been a dream.

He listened to her even breathing and thought about the fuzzy edges and muted colors in the dream. He'd had a sense that he and Tina had come through difficult times. Their lead up to this walk on the beach hadn't all been hearts and roses. The feeling that their lives would be threatened in the days ahead, hung over the dream like a storm cloud caught in the mountains. But, it looked like they came through it. He hoped he could count on this premonition being accurate.

The future *could* be changed, and no one knew that better than him right now.

THE END

The story continues…

The Dream Jumper's Secret

Prologue

Tina Greene felt herself being sucked backwards in the darkness, at high speed. Airborne and blind. Jamey's hand was still in hers. That's all she knew.

The jump out of the dream had been too fast to catch a look before the darkness took them. Suddenly, her hand was empty, and her eyes flew open. She was still in the hotel bed of the AMTEX Hotel, the only place in town that catered to foreign visitors. The only refuge in a dangerous country besides the American Military's Kandahar Airbase just across the street. She glanced around the room quickly and noted that she was alone and exactly where she'd been when she tried to jump into Jamey's dream.

It fricking worked.

She smiled. Finally, she'd entered Jamey's dream. And he'd jumped out with her. Thank God. This made the trip to Afghanistan worth all the worry.

The bedside clock said 6:23 a.m. Tina took a deep breath and let it out slowly. Jamey was finally out of the nightmare he'd been stuck in for a week. Would someone from Sixth Force still come for her at seven o'clock even though they didn't need her now? She desperately wanted to see Jamey, make sure he was alive, tell him she was sorry for everything.

In anticipation of the best-case scenario, she slipped in to the small bathroom's shower stall and turned on the water. The hot water pelted against her stiff shoulders, easing some of the tension of the day before. The flight yesterday had been rough. Flights. Twenty-six hours of traveling had made her feel like she was stuck inside an old woman's body. With a crazy woman's mind. Flying to Afghanistan had been the bravest thing she'd ever done. But it worked. That's all that mattered at this point. Jamey was out.

She'd phone her mother later, reassure her that all went according to the plan she'd lied about to keep her mom from the crazy truth. Tina would be on her way home today. She'd never tell her mother exactly why she'd come and what she did.

After pulling on the only outfit she brought on this rescue mission-- jeans and a T-shirt, Tina lay back on the twin-sized bed to wait. At 6:45, a knock sounded on her hotel door. Sargent Milton or one of his cronies was fifteen minutes early to pick her up. The military wasn't as punctual as they boasted. Swinging her legs over the side of the bed, Tina wondered if Jamey outside her hotel room door, and with that thought, raced across the small room to fling open the door.

But it wasn't Jamey, Milton, or even an American soldier. One of the men kicked in the door causing her to stumble backwards and fall onto the floor. Her worst nightmare about coming to Afghanistan was coming true. The men rushing at her were dark-haired, with black beards, dressed in foreign fatigues with gauzy scarves around their necks like they'd cover their faces if anonymity was needed. They both held large guns. She tried to stumble to her feet and then remembered to scream. Too late. The bigger one clutched her throat and dragged her to her feet. She tried to scream but couldn't make any noise with his iron grip on her windpipe. This wasn't Sixth Force or anyone associated with the American military in Afghanistan. Her heart went into full panic mode pounding wildly against her ribs, and Tina thought she might lose control of her bowels in fear. As she was dragged along the floor to the door, the bedside alarm went off, beeping loudly. The two men looked over at the clock. With the brief distraction, Tina twisted around and kicked her captor in the balls as hard as she could in bare feet. He went over and the other man grabbed her by the arm from behind and with his other hand got a firm grip on her throat, calling commands to his partner on the floor. His moves were quick and rough. She thrashed out, kicking with her right leg and swinging her arms. They knew exactly where to squeeze to keep her from using her vocal chords. One of them pulled her hands behind her back and the other held her still enough to stuff a dirty rag in her mouth. Kicking, she aimed for his crotch again but too late. The bigger man with the blue scarf pushed her on the bed and grabbed her legs to duct tape them together. Her muffled screams didn't go farther than the room's closed door. Maybe someone would hear the alarm clock that was still beeping. She managed to kick Blue Scarf in the gut with the combined efforts of her legs but he barely stumbled.

They covered her head with one of the pillowcases, taped it at the neck and then she was picked up by the shoulders and feet. She couldn't kick them. Once out the door, she heard them close it quietly, then they moved through the hall. This wasn't anyone associated with the American military.

This was very bad. It felt like a nightmare and Tina hoped she was right. She'd had dreams where she thought she woke up but didn't and the dream continued into chaos. Her trick was to try to stick her hand through her abdomen to check reality, but she couldn't. Tina struggled and squirmed and tried to scream, but it was useless. One had her feet and the other around the chest. Were they Taliban or at least insurgents disguised as Afghani soldiers? If so, these maniacs were the worst kind of terrorists there was. Crazy. Ruthless. Desperate. Very little to lose. Willing to die. They'd rape her and torture her, maybe cut off her head if their ransom demands weren't met. She had to keep her cool, concentrate on the fact that Jamey just woke up on the base only miles away. Once he realized she'd been abducted from AMTEX, he'd come for her. Or send someone. That was *if* the jump out had been successful, which still wasn't a certainty. And if Sixth Force told him his fiancé was in Afghanistan.

Outside the hotel, words were exchanged in a language Tina didn't understand and suddenly she was thrown in the air. Landing hard, her shoulder took the worst of it while her head bounced off a metal surface. The shooting pain confirmed it was reality. Fuck! She imagined they'd thrown her onto the floor of an idling truck. Smelling rust and exhaust fumes, she guessed it was an old truck. Maybe during the transport, she could wiggle to the side of the bed and throw herself out of the truck if it wasn't going too fast. Only if she heard other cars on the far side of the truck. Not somewhere out in the desert. She needed someone to see her. Preferably an American soldier.

But then, something very heavy was put on top of her. It felt like a roll of carpet. Then another and now the heaviness made it hard to breathe. Darkness through the blindfold, a moldy smell, and muffled voices told her she was now well hidden under something. Out of view.

The vehicle took off and Tina knew she was screwed.

CHAPTER 1

Two Months Earlier

The day of Hank's second funeral it rained on Maui.

Tina tipped the open urn and watched the heavier pieces of ash fall directly below the cliff into the thorny kiawe bushes. Then the wind swirled, carrying the lightest ashes back towards her, covering her hair and face. She made a strangling noise, swiping at her mouth and batting at her hair like she was fighting a swarm of spiders. She spat into the dirt at her feet and frantically backed up.

Jamey rushed in, pulled off his damp T-shirt and brushed her face and hair, holding her still with his other arm. "All gone, Baby."

She hurried to the truck to drench his shirt on the rain-splattered hood, and wiped her face, careful to get the ash away from her mouth. The three friends who'd joined them that evening to memorialize her dead husband spoke with Jamey at the cliff, nodding and glancing back at her.

Obi, the pit mix, hopped into the truck, moving to the middle of the seat. When Jamey jumped in the driver's seat and stuck the key in the ignition, the truck wouldn't start.

"I'll wait a bit."

Between the two of them, he had all the patience. Tina looked out the window, hugging Obi, her eyes dry. Her fingers made circles in his chest fur. On Jamey's second try, the engine roared to life and they silently drove back to her house, the windshield wipers beating out a slow rhythm. *It's all over, it's all over, it's all over.*

Tina walked straight to the bathroom, stepped in to the shower--clothes on--and let the water wash away the last physical remnants of Hank. Piece by soggy piece, she removed her clothes, leaving them in a pile on the shower floor. The water's temperature was hot enough to sting and redden her skin. After washing her hair twice, she turned off the water. The room was thick with steam. Balancing on the tub's edge she opened the window wider and saw Jamey in the side yard. He stood in the rain, his cell phone to his ear. His firmly set mouth and tense stature might have told her something was wrong but another thing told her first. A feeling of secrecy and deception had slipped in through the window like a burglar's invasion.

"Hang on," he said in a conspiratorial whisper, and then disappeared around to the front of the house.

The fine hair on the back of Tina's neck stood on end. Having been lied to and kept in the dark by both her dead husband and her scheming mother, Tina had good reason to be suspicious. Even with Jamey. And good reason to know these hunches weren't to be ignored.

She wrapped a bath towel around her and snuck down the back stairs.

The laundry room was empty, the garage too, and with the door open to the driveway and front yard she confirmed that Jamey was not there. Obi sniffed around the base of a papaya tree in the lush yard, his tail wagging like he'd found a mongoose's scent. She crept through the garage.

Then, she heard a noise from the storage room to her right--a room where she kept an airtight case for her valuable paintings—her most expensive possessions, including this house on prime Maui real estate. She moved closer to hear the words coming from beyond the hollow core door.

"Well here's the coincidence," Jamey said. "I keep seeing the same dude everywhere I go. So, if you haven't got someone following me, then I'm in deep shit."

There was a pause long enough for Tina to think Jamey was talking on the phone.

"Give me a fucking yes or no." The words were clipped, Jamey's anger, unfamiliar. He was probably talking to Milton, his superior officer in Afghanistan. "Cut the crap," he said in a hoarse whisper. "I'm going to beat the daylights out of this guy, if you don't tell me. I saw him again just now. He drove by me at a remote pull out."

She hadn't noticed anyone suspicious.

"Is this guy ours, or not?" Jamey asked. Was Milton back-peddling? Something he did well according to Jamey. A fat centipede the size of her longest finger scuttled across the garage floor near her bare feet and disappeared under a pile of boogie boards. She'd get the bug spray later. You couldn't just let those things run around, even if it was the garage. Obi might find it.

"I can save you the trouble. I'm not." Jamey's voice was filled with surrender. "Pretty sure you lost the cash cow on that last jump in Kandahar."

Milton was probably trying to get Jamey back to the war to continue his work with Taliban prisoners, or at least get tested to make sure their psychic phenom had lost the ability to jump into their dreams.

"I'm headed back to Seattle in a week for my kids' birthday. Tell your man to pack his bag."

The call was wrapping up, and Tina thought about sneaking upstairs to pretend she wasn't eavesdropping. But she didn't. In the last year, she'd earned the right to ask questions, and Jamey knew that better than anyone else in the world.

Finally, the door opened, and Jamey stepped out, a look of surrender on his face. He knew she was on the other side of the door, waiting.

"Are you going back to Afghanistan?" She sounded pitiful, even to her own ears.

Jamey stepped forward and took her in his arms, folding her into the warmth of his chest. "The less you know, the better, Tina."

She thought about succumbing to the comfort of his embrace. Instead she took a step back. "You owe me this, Jamey. Are you going?"

He bit his bottom lip, looked beyond the driveway to the ocean, and then back at her. "I'm hoping it doesn't get to that."

"If it does?'

"I'm useless to them, remember? I'm as useless as Mikey is to your business."

He was trying to make her smile, knowing her latest part-time employee, Mikey, spent most of his time on his phone, and avoiding his duties at the dive shop. "Yes, or no."

"Yes. If Milton insists, I'll have to go back for tests. No, if Milton is convinced I can't jump, or comes to Seattle to oversee my testing." He took her hands in his, closing the distance between them. "I don't know yet. He wants me to go back to Afghanistan, or Germany, but I don't see the point. I'll try to convince him to come to me." He kissed her forehead.

This conversation made Tina want to curl in a ball and sleep for a month. "No secrets from me, Jamey. No lying or secret phone calls, okay?"

He stroked the side of her face with the back of his hand, something that made her feel like a lovesick teenager. "Only the ones that keep you safe, Darlin'."

Continue the story…

THE DREAM JUMPER'S SECRET

Acknowledgements

This novel was born from years of leaning on friends, using people, and ignoring others. Hi Honey!

A big shout out goes to my critique partners, and my girlfriends who listened to me plot and unplot (ad nauseum) and kept the enthusiasm up for years.

A special thank you goes to Lynn who lives in Tina's house on Maui and let me write on her deck, Kate Folkers, who was the first to read the book and offered brilliant advice, Cherry Adair and Carol Cassella who gave their time and expertise, the Maui Police Force and a generous park service worker on Molokai who answered my many questions. To two authors—Alicia Dean, who knows what she did, and Pat White who pointed my pen in the right direction many years ago.

To my early readers, Eliza, Lauriann, Tricia, Kendal, Lynn, Susan Hornsby, Suzi, Kristi, Susan Smart and Ila Hornsby. Thank you for your support. It's only encouraged me. I hope I didn't forget anyone. I'm sure I did.

To Top Ten Press who helped launch this project and believed in this story. And to Cajun Flair Publishing's Lori Leger, who rides in on her horse whenever I send smoke signals.

Mahalo Maui, for being my rock and giving me these memories.

Lastly, to my family, Roland, Jack and Ila who live in a messy, disorganized house and never tell me to stop writing. I love that you let me chase this dream.

RECIPE

Teriyaki Chicken with Mango/Pineapple Chutney

Chicken

1 (3 pound) whole chicken, cut in half
3/4 cup granulated sugar
3/4 cup soy sauce
1 tablespoon grated fresh ginger
2 cloves garlic, minced

Directions
Rinse chicken halves, and pat dry with paper towels.
Place chicken cut side down in a 9x13 inch baking dish.

In a medium mixing bowl, combine sugar, soy
sauce, grated ginger and garlic. Mix well, and pour
mixture over chicken. Cover and refrigerate for at least 3
hours.

Preheat oven to 350 degrees F (175 degrees C).

Bake chicken uncovered in the preheated oven for 1
hour, basting frequently. Test for doneness, making sure
there is no pink left in the meat. Let cool slightly, then
cut into smaller pieces to serve.

Mango/Pineapple Chutney
2 tablespoons vegetable oil

1 large sweet onion, minced
4-inch piece fresh ginger root, peeled and minced
1 large yellow bell pepper, diced
3 large ripe mangoes, peeled, pitted, and diced
1 small pineapple, peeled and diced
1/2 cup brown sugar

½ cup apple cider vinegar

½ tsp curry (optional)

Directions

Heat the vegetable oil in a large saucepan over medium heat. Stir in the minced onion. Reduce the heat to low, cover, and cook, stirring occasionally until the onions have softened, about 20 minutes. Remove the lid, increase the heat to medium, and stir in the ginger and yellow bell pepper. Cook and stir until the ginger is fragrant, 2 to 3 minutes. Stir in the mangoes, pineapple, brown sugar, and vinegar. Bring to a simmer, and cook for 30 minutes, stirring occasionally. Cool the chutney completely when done and store in airtight containers in the refrigerator.

Reading Group Guide

1. The Dream Jumper's Promise was classified by the author as Commercial Women's Fiction with elements of romance, paranormal and suspense. Discuss how you would classify the book if you were asked to put it into only one category and how much of each element is part of this novel.

2. The story takes place at the worst point in Tina's life. Did you sympathize with her struggle and appreciate how difficult it was for her to move on when Hank's body was unrecovered and forces lived within her house to keep him alive?

3. Tina and Hank had their ups and downs as a married couple.
Discuss how her life might have played out if Hank hadn't left to surf that morning.

4. Did you find Noble a sympathetic character in this story? Did your feelings unfold and change for him as more information came to light? Were you correct in how you perceived him originally?
Why do you think Tina could see him and not Hank?

5. Was Jamey destined to be with Tina or did his actions alter the future to get what he wanted? How ethical do you feel Jamey is and did this change how you feel about Tina loving him?

6. Did Tina's mother ultimately cause Hank's accident? Did you sympathize with her, as a mother who lost one child and desperately needed to keep the other safe?

7. Do you think the military employs psychics? If so, what do you think a psychic would be able to offer the military in the field?

8. The author is fond of metaphors. When Tina says "everything is a god-damned metaphor for my life" the turtle is surfacing for a breath. List some other metaphors used in the book to depict with Tina's situation.

9. Did you think that Hank might be alive? If so, at what point did you give up on this theory? What was your early idea of what actually happened the day he supposedly went surfing?

10. Did Jamey plan to see Tina the day he walked in to the dive shop and she fainted? If so, was he there selfishly or was his motivation to help her? If he'd regained his ability to jump dreams in the end, do you think he would've returned to Afghanistan?

CPSIA information can be obtained
at www.ICGtesting.com
Printed in the USA
FSHW020459300819
61574FS